Dear Reader,

Have you had your vacation yet? Even if you can't get away for a while, why not take the phone off the hook, banish your family and/or friends for an hour or two, and relax with a long cool drink and one (or all!) of this month's *Scarlet* novels?

Would you like a trip to London and the English countryside? Then let *The Marriage Contract* by Alexandra Jones be your guide. Maybe you want to visit the USA, so why not try Tina Leonard's *Secret Sins* and *A Gambling Man* from Jean Saunders? Or perhaps you'd like a trip back in time? Well, Stacy Brown's *The Errant Bride* can be your time machine. Of course, I enjoyed *all four* books and I hope you'll want to read them all too. So why not stretch that hour or two into three or four?

One of the aspects of my job which is both a joy and a challenge is getting the balance of books right on our schedules. So far, I've been lucky because each of our talented authors has produced a unique *Scarlet* novel for you. Do tell me, though, won't you, if you'd like to see more romantic suspense on our list, or some more sequels, or maybe more books with a sprinkling of humour?

Till next month,

Sally Cooper

SALLY COOPER,
Editor-in-Chief – *Scarlet*

TINA LEONARD

SECRET SINS

Enquiries to:
Robinson Publishing Ltd
7 Kensington Church Court
London W8 4SP

First published in the UK by Scarlet, 1997

A copy of the British Library Cataloguing in
Publication data is available from the British Library

ISBN 1-85487-955-3

Printed and bound in the EC

10 9 8 7 6 5 4 3 2 1

Admiration for the sport of racing made it easy to write this book. I moved some dates and a track to fit my story, but otherwise tried to stick to the spirit of NASCAR. Any mistakes in this book are my own.

To Lisa, 7½, and Dean Michael, 3½, both growing up on me too fast – thank you for believing in my dream.

And to my husband, Tim, for letting my dream be his.

Many thanks to my critique group: Karen Leabo, Judy Christenberry, Karen Morrell, Barbara Harrison, and Anne Franklin, for all your support in writing and many other matters.

Also heartfelt thanks to my extended family scattered throughout the United States who read my work with such anticipation. Most particularly I must thank my two grandmothers, Isabel Cather Sites and Irish Kalberer, who brag on me so proudly to their friends.

A final word of unending gratitude to Georgia Haynes and Kay Weedn, whose enthusiastic joy in my writing makes me believe I can get to 'The End' every time.

PROLOGUE

'If I owned Texas and Hell, I'd rent out Texas and live in Hell.' GENERAL SHERMAN

Though twilight was waning, it was still a hundred degrees on the weathered porch. Caleb Dorn closed his eyes against the Texas heat and settled wearily on the wooden step. If he kept his eyes closed the parched wheat fields surrounding his small house didn't seem so accusing. The stunted wheat only reached his knees, when in a better season it would touch his shoulders. Caleb hung his head in defeat. A crop nearly useless, as he was himself.

If time could be measured in grains of sand, then he was on the last sparse sprinkles. He acknowledged the fact without pity and tucked the whiskey bottle more firmly between his legs. He was nearing seventy, and he'd lived the last thirty-seven of those years without his wife, Sakina. For him, she'd been the sun and sky and passionate darkness . . . woman. The darkness he knew now was the absence of passion, the absence of his woman. Thirty-seven years without her had made him feel as old as the scriptures in the Bible.

1

Tonight was the last night he would sit on this porch. There was no need to linger to harvest this crop. There was no need to deny the withdrawal from this life his spirit craved.

Opening his eyes, Caleb swept his gaze over the pathetic wheat one last time. He picked up the whiskey bottle, carrying it with him as he rounded the house. The rose garden Sakina had forced from the dry land was his only passion, the only thing he lavished with adoring attention. Besides his niece, Kiran, and his nephew, Steven, there wasn't any family he cared to bother with. He hoped they would keep the land he himself had not wanted to sell, because what was left of his heart was still here. As long as Sakina was here, he could not leave. She was all around, all the time, with the generous love she'd always given him.

Caleb picked two perfect roses from the well-tended bed at the back of the house, the only shaded spot. He clasped them in the hand that held the whiskey bottle as he lurched toward a stand of straggly oak trees. The wind whipped up, bringing a taste of the storm that had been threatening all afternoon. It was too late – much too late – for rain to soothe the land – or him. It was too late for anything. He reached the grave he'd dug long ago, his breath locking in his chest.

'Sakina,' he murmured.

The wind blew harder as he placed the whiskey bottle on the ground. He pulled the petals from the roses, letting them drift on the wind across the

2

grave. Though he hated to remember it, Sakina had gone away. He'd never known why. Five years later, when she'd died of an early cancer, her family had come to him, admitting that they had helped hide her from him. It had been her wish, they'd said, though she'd never stopped loving him. She simply had been unable to live in his world.

His beautiful Sakina . . . and their baby – stillborn. That was a further savage twist in his heart. He and Sakina had dreamed of a daughter; though it was more true to say that he'd dreamed of a daughter in Sakina's likeness.

He lowered his head, then opened the whiskey bottle to lift it to his lips. The shame of Sakina's death was on him for not recognizing the danger sooner. Ugly words spray-painted on the side of the house should have been warning enough in the frothing racial hatred of the late fifties. Words damning Sakina for her African heritage, watered down though it was. Caleb hadn't even thought twice about the light-complexioned loveliness of Sakina's skin, of its warm tint that boasted of an African great-grandmother. For her sake, he should have.

The fire of whiskey cleared from his throat as tears gathered in his eyes. 'I'm sorry, Sakina,' he whispered.

The trees whipped the silent answer of the nearing rain. He dropped to his knees, tearing at the soil covering her grave with his fingers. To be close to his wife once again was all he asked. Sudden rain slung angry lashes against him, but Caleb didn't notice. The whiskey bottle tipped over, pouring the liquid into the ground even as Caleb could feel his own time running out, yet he didn't stop his frantic burrowing into the dry-beneath-the-surface dirt. He wouldn't need the whiskey to keep him warm anymore.

Tonight he would be with Sakina.

CHAPTER 1

'Caleb, it's me!' Father John Lannigan shifted a full, unopened whiskey bottle to his other arm as he held one hand against his forehead to peer in the window. 'Somewhere in the world it's cocktail hour. Open up!'

No curse-words were flung back at him. John waited for a moment. Caleb rarely went anywhere, but if he'd had a sudden itch to drive out his truck would be gone. The priest walked to the side of the house, seeing at once that the truck was in its customary spot. It being noon, he didn't think Caleb would be sleeping or taking a shower . . . but he might be ill. The June heat was a killer, dangerous in a house that didn't have air conditioning, and today was chokingly humid after last night's thunderstorm.

The thought flashed through John's mind before he could stop it. It would be best if he somehow checked – and hang Caleb Dorn's temper.

At the front door, John pounded hard enough to break the wood. When no response came, he set the whiskey bottle on the splintered wood of the porch. He was getting more worried by the moment. 'I'll probably get shot for my efforts,' he muttered, turning the doorknob out of curiosity's sake. To his surprise, it moved easily. With a slight push, the door creaked open. 'Caleb! Don't shoot!'

Fully expecting a blast of Dorn wrath, he felt instead the eerie silence make the hair on the back of his neck tingle. John stepped into the house, the musty smell of rickety belongings assaulting him. His eyes finally focused in the dimness, and the three white squares lying on the dusty Revere-style dining table jumped out so startlingly bright that John's antennae immediately quivered.

Stepping closer to the table, he leaned over so he wouldn't have to pick them up to read them. ' "Kiran",' he read out loud, ' "Steven". "Father John Lannigan".' Shock jumped inside of him at seeing his own name. He checked again. 'First time you ever used my full name, Caleb, you old hound,' he murmured.

The envelope bearing his name was quite thick, while the other two were slim. He broke the envelope seal and pulled out a yellowed piece of paper. Caleb wouldn't have spent a dime on anything so trivial as paper. The crooked handwriting set John's heartbeat racing.

Dear John Lannigan,
    You are my friend, and the only person I've ever trusted in this godforsaken back-

6

water. Maybe it's because you're the only person I know who can drink more than me at one sitting. Truth is, I've always felt you were coming around for some reason besides waiting on me to croak. You've been more than just a cloth-wrapped Bible-thumper to me.

All right, enough jabbering. If you're reading this, you're about to be swinging one of those damn incense pots over my pine box. You'll find in the accompanying paper that I've willed forty acres of my farm to you. Don't get all starry-eyed over this small token, 'cause forty acres is hardly enough to grow hops on. But you could build you a little shack, or maybe start making your own wine. If nothing else, you can sit out on your own porch at night after you've finished visiting useless types like me. On your own porch, you can sit and burp to yourself and nobody gives a damn.

Caleb Dorn

P.S. I've left the rest of the land and the house jointly to Kiran Whitley, my niece, and Steven Dorn, my nephew. I'm asking you as a favor – actually, I'm telling you, as the other enclosed paper will inform you – to be the executioner of my will. If Kiran or Steven want to hang onto this old place, fine. It has to be a decision they agree upon, and one that you think is right. No rassling over a dead man's stuff. I hope you will guide them.

Whatever happens, I don't want my sister, Agnes, or my brother, Butch, to get their filthy paws on what's mine. Sakina and I want to rest in peace, now, on our land – and God knows, if Agnes or Butch decide to live here, we'll end up in the county landfill.

John shook his head, undecided as to whether he was amazed or unhappy. He'd have to explain the situation to Monsignor at once. 'Executioner,' he said aloud, frowning at the word that should have been 'executor.' The priest read over the postscript of the letter again, praying he hadn't been thrust right into the middle of a firestorm.

That thought sent another blazing through his mind. *Where was Caleb?* He checked the back rooms, instantly worried that he should have looked for the old man first. They were empty. He ran out onto the back porch and hurried to the truck. It was empty as well. Frustration spread through him, until he saw the lone, large bird circling over a grouping of oak trees. Terrible premonition galvanized him. He ran until he reached Caleb Dorn's final resting place. Shock kept him motionless as he stared down at his friend.

Though wet from the night's summer storm, the craggy, unhappy man appeared peaceful, for once. A few flies made meandering paths across his skin, and there was dirt under his fingernails. Yet it

8

seemed the man had reached the end of a long journey and found what he had been seeking at last. John knelt and gently brushed a chunk of mud from Caleb's ear.

Saying a quick prayer under his breath, he took off his jacket and covered the corpse with it. Without further hesitation, he hurried back to the small shack to call the local police. To his immense relief, the phone had a dial tone – though he couldn't have said why the thought hit him that the old man might have discontinued his phone service.

John relayed the information quickly to the dispatcher, then hung up. Through the dirty windowpane, he spied the unopened whiskey bottle sitting on the porch where he'd left it. Retrieving the bottle, he murmured, 'Guess I won't need this anymore,' before pushing it into a dark recess of a kitchen cabinet.

The wind blew hard and contrary against Kiran Whitley's long skirt as she stood at the side of Caleb Dorn's grave. Father Lannigan was intoning words that were supposed to be comforting, but Steve Dorn wasn't listening. He focused on what nice ankles Kiran had, since that was all he could see of her legs. Steve was a leg man by nature, preferring them long and salon-waxed, but that long skirt would have concealed gorilla thighs. Still, it appeared she was tallish and trim, so there was hope that in the years since he'd seen her last she might have grown a nice pair of stems.

9

Her breast situation was a bit more obvious to his discerning eye. He studied the area where her breasts pushed against a white lace blouse suitable for a vestal virgin but not Texas heat, as he tried to keep his expression meek and sorrowful. Well, sorrowful was something he was. His uncle had saved him from a miserable childhood.

Meek he wasn't. He had a reputation for being a hot-shot race-car driver who had made it to the top by being brash and unafraid. It had been inconvenient as hell to come out from California to Texas right now; he'd had to cancel out of one of the biggest races of the year and let his replacement driver take over. Respect and love had dictated he attend this funeral, but he planned to fly back tomorrow. Losing out on the race had meant jeopardizing revenue, as well as letting down the fans who adored him, made him feel as if he was worth something when he was behind the wheel and blowing it out down a speedway. He couldn't afford to miss another race.

He watched Kiran brush away a tear and felt a momentary tightening around his heart. This was a bad place to be, he decided. Ugly, flat land, and a shack fit basically for white trash disguised a situation he could feel had tentacles that might pull his mind away from its one-track direction and onto matters more painful to the heart.

The priest finished the service and Steve dutifully passed him a hundred-dollar bill. The good father gave him a stern eyeing before slapping it back into

Steve's palm. He shrugged, returning the money to his pocket. If John Lannigan wanted to give his services away for free, that was fine by him. No one could say he hadn't tried to observe the formalities.

'Good service, Father,' he murmured, offering his hand, feeling odd addressing the man that way when they were probably close in age. The priest took his hand after a moment, before giving him a brief pat on the back. The pat was more out of rote than true condolence, Steve realized.

'It was a lovely service, Father,' Kiran said, coming to stand beside the two men.

Light blue eyes locked with Steve's for just a moment, long enough for him to realize that they had changed along with the rest of Kiran. Though her hair was shoulder-length and smooth, with no pretensions, it framed her incredible eyes. He had the feeling that she saw a lot with those eyes. He had the feeling that she would see a lot inside *him*, if he let her. Breaking eye contact, Steve left the chosen resting place of his uncle and walked toward the shack.

It had been too long since he'd seen Kiran Whitley. She was not the same person he had chased through wheat fields and watched hours of *I Love Lucy* with on Uncle Caleb's black and white TV.

He wasn't the same person either. They couldn't be light-hearted friends anymore, he knew. He wasn't a light-hearted person and she didn't seem that way herself, though at a funeral it was difficult to tell. There was no flirtation in her eyes, no blink of something that might signal easy rapport between them. His uncle was gone, and so was the Kiran he had known. There simply wasn't a reason for him to feel any ties to this remote place on County Road 147 in Cottonwood, Texas.

Kiran watched her cousin leave, though she pretended to listen to what John Lannigan had to say. Well, Steve wasn't really her cousin, she reminded herself. She wasn't of true Dorn blood – not that it had ever mattered when they'd been kids. In fact, it had strengthened the bond between them, leveling the playing field, so to speak. They neither one came from whole, functioning families.

She and Steve had been sent to visit Uncle Caleb like cast-away children every summer. As soon as school was out, she was on a train to Texas, 'visiting family'. The truth was that she had been sent away to be 'out of her mother's hair' while Agnes Richardson made the social rounds with men she met at the diner.

Kiran didn't remember her father. The one part of her life she was certain of was that Uncle Caleb had watched after her like a hawk, had believed in her like an avenging saint. To this day, everything she had ever done had been to pay him back for his faith. She would protect what he had loved with the same ferocity.

Steve's broad back disappeared inside the old house and Kiran realized the person she had thought most likely to feel the way she did seemed quite detached from the situation. If she hadn't spent years as a teacher and then as principal, watching students act tough to cover soft shells, she might have been fooled by this macho act. Surely underneath that hard exterior was the boy who had cried down by the pond from the criticism his father had blasted constantly at him.

Kiran pursed her lips, glancing up to find the priest staring at her. Since she was the only mourner left at the gravesite – Steve having left without saying a word to her – and the men from the funeral home were standing by to lower the casket into its grave, she decided it was time to give John Lannigan a break and leave. 'Shall we go up to the house?' she asked.

'Are you ready?' he inquired. 'We can stay as long as you like.'

She was touched by his sincerity. It was no surprise that Uncle Caleb had trusted this man. Kiran decided she did, too, though she'd been taken aback at first by his astonishing eye appeal. Steve was handsome, too, but so brusque that it was hard to feel anything but coldness from him. John, on the other hand, was a priest, Kiran reassured herself, and therefore someone she could allow herself to feel comfortable with. With a final kiss toward the grave, Kiran turned to the priest.

'I'm ready to go back,' she said. Besides, there was an awful lot she and Steve had to get sorted out, and the faster they started, the faster it would be over.

From behind the trunks of native oak trees, two women watched the priest and the girl leave. 'It's over, then, Lakina,' the elderly woman murmured. 'Caleb's gone home.'

'I guess so.' Lakina watched the woman walk away from the gravesite. Without being able to help it, she felt envy that she couldn't have been there, too, as the blonde woman was. 'I wish he was still alive.'

Maybe that feeling didn't make sense. She had never spoken to Caleb Dorn. An occasional spying into his life was all she'd ever been able to do. It had been hard to watch those two kids visit in the summers, receiving the affection she, too, should have shared. But it hadn't been meant to be, and there was nothing she could do about that. Well, maybe there had been. 'I shouldn't have waited so long,' she said sadly.

Her aunt looked distressed. 'Who would have thought he would die like that, without warning? It's like he made up his mind to go and he did.'

'I never fitted into his life anyway.' But they had, those people who had stood beside the grave. The tall man, with his cold, stiff posture. The prim-looking woman, with her cultured clothes. And the priest, who was better-looking than any man she had ever seen. Why such a man chose not to marry, she couldn't understand. If man had ever been made to draw sighs from a woman's body, it was that one. It was enough to make a sinner go to confession.

Only she wasn't interested in confessing. Her heart hurt too much and her life felt empty. Tugging on Aunt Grace's hand, she hurried away from the place she had never been able to call home.

'Caleb Dorn's finally kicked the bucket, damn his hide.'

Maypat Andrews jumped at the harsh sound of her husband's voice as he walked into the formal living room. What he'd just said appeared to please him for some reason, so Maypat put a nervous smile on her face and worked to find the right thing to say. 'Oh?'

Jarvis slid her an impatient look. 'Is that the best you can do? "Oh"?' he mimicked.

She pushed back a gray lock of hair before trying to meet his eyes. 'Well, I hardly know what to say, Jarvis.' Privately, she hoped Caleb Dorn's passing had been peaceful. God only knew her husband had made his life hell on earth.

'Well, you could be glad, damn it. That son-of-a-bitch isn't in our way any longer.'

He slumped into a chair and Maypat winced for the lovely chintz covering on the delicate seat. How she wished Jarvis would be more careful with her fragile belongings!

'Remember, Jarvis, I'm not as quick as you are. If you'll tell me what you're thinking, then I'm sure

15

I'll understand,' Maypat said soothingly. 'The truth is, I'm not sure what Caleb Dorn was in our way about.'

Jarvis sighed in long-suffering torment. 'For cryin' out loud, Maypat. That's a hell of a lot of acreage the old coot was sitting on. If you haven't noticed, it's only about ten miles from where the rich folks who don't want to live in the city built their homes. In three to five years someone's going to figure out what a goldmine that land is. Why can't it be me they buy it from?'

She felt her fingers start twitching suddenly, though she desperately wanted to be still. A tic jumped in her eye. 'Surely he left that land to someone?'

'Naw. Caleb Dorn didn't care about anybody, and nobody cared about him.' His thick fingers drummed the deeply varnished top of an antique table.

It wasn't true. Jarvis knew it as well as she did. But it was a secret, the darkest sin between them, and it would never be mentioned out loud. Caleb Dorn had worshipped the black woman he'd married like some men worshipped money.

Maypat had often wished that Jarvis would love her just a little bit more, the way he had said he did when he lured her away from Atlanta. Oh, the words he had whispered to her – and the promises of the wonderful house he would build for her to show his love. Well, he'd built the house, but it had been to showcase the southern belle he had wanted for himself.

16

Remembering the way Caleb had watched Sakina walk through the market made Maypat's heart clench. Jarvis and his friends had run Sakina off. Maypat had known that they were tormenting that woman. By her compliance, Maypat's hands were stained, too. But what Jarvis was talking about now wasn't right. They'd taken from the old man once before, by harassing his wife. Taking from him again by getting at his land would only compound the sin. She could never feel good about it.

'Let's leave it alone, Jarvis,' she murmured. 'Please?'

He frowned at her. 'Maypat, I don't know what's eating you. You don't understand the simplest things, but for once I'll try to get something through your dense head. We're in big time financial trouble.'

Her heart jumped, and she must have, too, because Jarvis smirked at her.

'Did that get your attention, Maypat? Does the thought of losing your house bother you? Will losing these fancy little knick-knacks that remind you of the way you used to live upset you?'

Hands clenched, Maypat tried to stay calm. Jarvis was trying to upset her. Her gaze darted around the formal room, her favorite room in the house. Dresden figurines, Chinese porcelain and expensive crystal all sat in their proper places. They wouldn't look so right anywhere else. She'd hidden from Jarvis's rough, bullish personality in this room for more years than she could remember. If they lost their home, if they had to start over, she'd certainly not have anything like this again.

Sneaking a glance at Jarvis, Maypat noticed his grim expression as he stared down at his boots. The sudden thought struck her that this time Jarvis wasn't just manipulating her. They honestly were in trouble.

'Where did our money go, Jarvis?' she dared to ask.

'Maypat, don't start asking questions now.'

She stiffened, realizing at once she wasn't going to get an answer. She wouldn't want to know the answer, and he knew it. Maypat stood, walking past her husband's slouched figure on her way into the kitchen to get a cup of soothing tea for her nerves. His booted foot shot across her path, halting her.

'I'm going to figure out a way to buy that land cheap, Maypat, and I expect you to keep your mouth shut – if you know what's good for you.'

She avoided her husband's cold eyes as she swept past. 'I wish I'd known what was good for me many years ago, Jarvis.'

In the Dorn house, Father Lannigan got to his feet. 'I'd better be going. The two of you are probably tired and want some time to yourselves. I'll be out tomorrow to discuss the will, but feel free to call if you need anything in the meantime, Kiran, Steve.'

Kiran smiled as best she could as she saw the priest out. The last thing she needed was to be alone with Steve. It was going to be a long, awkward night, but one that had to be gotten through if they were going to settle the estate, such as it was. Closing the front door, she walked back into the shabbily furnished den and forced herself to meet Steve's gaze.

'What?' he demanded.

As if he weren't staring at her.

'Nothing,' she shot back, instantly irritated by his attitude. He acted as if this den was his kingdom, and she'd just trespassed. Her neck stiff with pride, Kiran turned to head to the sanctuary of her bedroom.

'Are you hungry?'

She halted. 'Not really.'

'Me neither.'

He scratched at his face and Kiran realized Steve had just run out of his available conversation. 'I could go for a soft drink, though,' she said. 'It's hotter here than I'm used to, or maybe it's the humidity.'

His gaze traveled the full length of her skirt. Kiran held her head up higher. So she hadn't dressed for stifling heat. He was obviously used to women from the dunes of California who wore less. He wasn't exactly dressed for beach volleyball himself.

With a flash of disquieting awareness, Kiran realized Steve looked mouthwatering in the blue jeans he'd changed into. He lounged in Uncle Caleb's old easy chair, his sandy hair tousled and his sea-green eyes tired, yet looking like a man comfortable inside his skin.

19

She suddenly felt a lot hotter.

'Let's go check the fridge,' he said.

Steve got up and crossed the room. Kiran's eyes followed him, noticing with some resentment that his backside looked as great as the front side. She closed her eyes, amazed by the decidedly un-school-teacher-like longings melting over her. More men than she'd ever wanted to see had passed through Agnes's house to date her ever-flirting, ever-on-the-hunt stepmother, and Kiran bore the scars to prove it. She had worked hard to earn a college degree and a secure job, but the last thing she'd ever penciled into her dream diary was a man. They caused pain and misery.

It was just her luck that bristly Steve Dorn was jolting her with feelings she didn't want.

'No soft drinks,' he called. 'I can't even find instant coffee. Wonder what Uncle Caleb drank?'

She walked into the kitchen and peered over Steve's shoulder to look in the nearly empty refrigerator. 'Well, I guess we won't need a lot, but we'll certainly need a bit more than he's got in there.'

'Hey, I'm not going to be around long enough to buy groceries.' He slammed the door and turned to face her. 'I've done the funeral. There's no reason to hang around when a realtor can sell the place.'

'Sell?' Kiran's mouth pinched with dismay. 'Why?'

'Why not?' Crossing his arms, he leaned against an age-flecked kitchen counter. 'You don't want this dilapidated joint, do you? I sure as hell don't.'

'Well, no.' Kiran shook her head. 'But wouldn't it be a little disrespectful to sell it so fast?'

'Disrespectful to who? Uncle Caleb's dead; he doesn't care.'

'I think he does,' Kiran insisted.

'Oh, spare me the sentiment.' Steve's expression was stubborn. 'I realize you're on summer break, but I've got a race next weekend I need to get in gear for. I don't have time to be sentimental.'

'Obviously.' Kiran took a step away from Steve. 'Have you read your letter?'

'What letter?'

'The one on the dining room table addressed to you.'

'I didn't see it.'

She stared him down. 'You're in too much of a hurry to see much of anything.'

'Listen, Kiran, I'm not trying to be mean.' Steve ran a hand tiredly through his hair. 'I missed a race to be at Uncle Caleb's funeral. But I don't make money hanging around in holes like this.'

He stomped out of the room, leaving Kiran to ponder the empty refrigerator.

Steve knew what was burning his butt. Kiran had turned into a model of responsibility, and she was also too damned attractive. She was right about his attitude and that bugged him. Women were made to be looked at, and most anything they had to say was unimportant. She, however, concealed her body with long sleeves and skirts, forcing him to focus on her incredible eyes and what lurked behind them, and that was bothering the hell out of him as well. It would be so much easier to relate to her on a sexual level – as he did every other attractive woman.

He snatched the letter from the dining room table and read it quickly. It was standard fare for a man's last words, typical 'I love you and I'm proud of you' stuff. Skimming the bottom half, he crammed it back into the envelope. There. He'd read it. After a moment, Steve shot a guilty look toward the kitchen, where he knew Kiran was still standing. Slowly he pulled the letter back out and made himself read the bottom half.

You've got my eyes. Kiran does, too.

Steve puzzled over that, wondering if the old man had been a little senile. Kiran did not have Uncle Caleb's moss-colored eyes. Whoever Kiran's father had been, he had brought her with him when he'd married Agnes. When he'd pulled his fast exit, he'd left his little girl behind for Agnes to raise. Steve shook his head, making himself continue reading.

I hope my eyes help you see my world the way I did. I may not have done the best I could, but I loved only three people in my entire life, you, Kiran and Sakina. I'm counting on you to look out for all of us now, Steve. I have a feeling it's going to be a difficult thing I'm asking of you, but if ever there was a man up to the challenge, it's you. I'm going to enjoy the fight.

Uncle Caleb.

CHAPTER 2

'Damn,' Steve muttered under his breath.

'Oh?' Kiran said, too brightly. She stood framed in the kitchen doorway. 'Got to the part about the only three people he ever loved, did you? Or was it the part about keeping us all safe?'

The tears in her eyes made a liar out of her mocking voice. Steve stuffed the letter in his back jeans pocket. 'What'd he do? Throw a guilt trip on you, too?'

'He didn't have to.' She hesitated for a moment. 'When was the last time you came to see him?'

Steve went stiff. 'I think the summer I was fifteen. You couldn't come, and it was damn lonely.' He hated admitting that.

'I wanted to, but my mother thought I'd be better off at an all-girls camp.' She smiled a heartbreakingly beautiful smile. 'I think she was afraid you and I might get too close. I'd developed, much to her discomfort and –' She looked down. 'I don't know.'

He snorted. 'She thought Uncle Caleb might slip in the babysitting role our parents had thrust on him all those years and give us a chance to do it in the dirt? What a summer that would have been.'

It would have been a lot more interesting than the summer he'd spent without Kiran. He remembered the hurt he'd felt that she hadn't come, remembered believing he hadn't been the friend in her heart that she'd been in his. Uncle Caleb and he had spent maximum time fishing and camping, but it hadn't been the same. Kiran was the only girl he had ever considered a friend.

'I doubt my mother's fears would have come to fruition,' she said primly. 'Still, I feel guilty that I never came back to see Uncle. I wrote, but I got busy with graduating, and then college, and then . . . well, I guess I didn't expect him to die so soon.'

He hadn't either. Kiran was no more guilty of putting the old man on the sidelines than he was. 'What are you suggesting we do with this old place, then? I can't imagine he meant for us to live here. I wouldn't know the flat end of a shovel.'

'I'm not suited for living in Texas myself.' Kiran suddenly looked tired, and for the first time Steve felt his heart soften a little. 'I'm still in shock, I think. Let's sleep on it tonight, and maybe it will all look clearer in the morning.'

She met his gaze and he nodded a stiff agreement to her suggestion. Kiran started down the hall to the room where she would sleep before she turned. 'Should I ask why Uncle Butch couldn't make his brother's funeral?'

Steve snorted. It had been a shared joke between

them that neither Steve's father, Butch, nor Kiran's stepmother, Agnes, would be bothered to visit their brother, even if he was on his deathbed. Steve smiled grimly. 'If you don't ask where my father is, I won't ask where Agnes is.'

She smiled in return. 'It's much better this way. I wouldn't be comfortable with them around.'

'I wouldn't either.'

For a moment, they shared silence, looking at each other in the dim room. He missed the good old days, the easy relationship they'd had. But Aunt Agnes had been right. Kiran had developed, and the two of them getting cozy with each other wouldn't be any better a thing now than before.

'Steve?'

Kiran's soft voice jerked his attention back to the present. 'Yes?'

'Did it ever get any better for you?'

He hesitated, knowing full well what she was asking. Then he shook his head. 'No. You?'

'No.'

She seemed to be looking into the past. Steve held his breath, instinctively recognizing where she was.

'I kept waiting for a fairy godmother to come and whisk me away from it all,' she said quietly.

They had both known at an early age there was no such thing. It had to have been pretty bad for her if she'd pretended that there was.

'Uncle was a pretty close second, though.'

Her voice had grown warm with affection and Steve nodded reluctantly. 'Yeah. He was for me, too.'

'Well, enough of that.' Her discomfort was obvious. 'Goodnight.' A sad, forced smile hovered on her lips as she turned.

'Goodnight, Kiran,' he said softly.

He watched her walk down the hall. If Kiran thought she was keeping herself covered in that matronly skirt, she had misjudged how the longer length pulled the black cloth nice and tight around her rear. In his opinion, the view was fine.

Thinking about her body kept his mind away from what she'd said about Uncle Caleb. It was an emotional escape hatch, one he'd used many times. It always worked.

He needed it to work this time.

Steven dozed in the ratty easy chair for a couple of hours. Something awakened him, but as he let his eyes adjust to the darkness that had settled over the house he couldn't figure out what had disturbed him. Of course, he hadn't expected to sleep like a baby on this trip, since his mind was elsewhere anyway.

He wondered how the race had gone today. His mind wandered to Ginger, and what she was doing.

Or who she was doing it with. The logical person was his arch racing rival, Dan Crane. Ginger had dumped Steve for the man she thought was going to earn more fame this year. What she'd based her conclusion on, Steve wasn't quite sure. Women's intuition, she'd told him with a catty smile. It was a shame, because Ginger had been a very convenient woman. She hadn't minded his frequent traveling, and had often wanted to accompany him. The situation had been so much better than having to choose from the usual women hanging around hoping to sleep with a famous racer that Steve had kind of gotten used to her.

His ego rumbled at the fact he couldn't have been at the race today to kick Dan's butt around the speedway. He didn't want Ginger back, but he sure hated giving up a piece of the thing he loved most.

Speed. That was what he loved. The screaming noise, the hyper fans, but most of all the focus. Alone in his car, testing centrifugal force to its limit, he could focus on not thinking about a thing except winning.

Now that his mind was whirring about what had happened today, he wasn't going to be able to sleep until he knew, so he searched out the only phone in the house. It sat on a little round table in the den, its black rotary dial without numbers. Steve cursed, realizing that his calling card wasn't going to do him any good because he couldn't punch in the number, and that he was going to have to turn on the overhead light because there were no lamps.

He flicked the wall switch, flooding the room with yellow light. Overhead, he could hear the sound of bugs scurrying around in the old glass light fixture. Sighing, Steve glanced at his watch. Midnight here, so ten o'clock in California. If he hurried, he might be able to catch Mitch, his best friend and crew chief, on the carphone before he hit the social circuit.

The phone was answered instantly. 'Hello?'

'Mitch. It's Steve.'

'Steve! How's it going?'

He grimaced. 'Fine. Give me an update.'

Mitch laughed. 'Don't you have a newspaper out there you can read in the morning?'

'No, damn it. Tell me.'

'I'm just giving you hell. I was going to call you as soon as we got to the restaurant. Dan cracked up his car today. He couldn't finish the race.'

'You're putting me on.' As much as he disliked the guy, it was a man thing. He hated to see a good piece of machinery bite the dust. 'He's all right, though?'

'Of course.' Mitch laughed again. 'He'll still be chasing your tail.'

'Just what I need.'

'Keeps you on the edge. There's something else I think you'll want to hear.'

Instinctively Steve knew he was about to get updated on Ginger. 'So tell me.'

'Your ex-girlfriend blew him off today.'

'Unsympathetic bitch.'

He heard a loud bark of laughter. 'Yeah. Apparently she was expecting him to win. Had visions of herself in the papers, I guess, because she was so mad she told him off in the hospital, where they were putting a couple of stitches in his forehead.'

'What made her so certain he'd win? She's been around the track long enough to know there's no sure thing.'

'I don't know. Her comment to him was that he'd never be the driver you are.'

Steve's eyebrows shot up. 'How the hell do you know all this?'

'I went to see Dan at the hospital. He's pretty sore about the whole mess. By the way, you might expect a call from Ginger.'

'I doubt it. I didn't give her the number.' Actually, he hadn't told her where he was going. There had been no need.

'I did.'

'You did what?' Steve's mind had been elsewhere.

'Gave her your number.'

'What the hell for?'

'Thought you might want to hear from her.'

'I don't.'

There was silence for a moment before a loud crackling came over the line. 'I guess I've hit a bad cell, Steve. I'll call you tomorrow and check on you.' There was more rasping and then silence.

Steve swore as he hung up. The last thing he wanted to do was to talk to Ginger and Mitch knew it. When he was finished with a woman, it was sayonara and no regrets. In this case the old male pride had been wounded, and that was the bolt in the door. Ginger wasn't going to dump him and then wiggle her painted nails for him to run right back.

Steve went outside, closing the door softly so he wouldn't wake Kiran. She had to be exhausted, and hopefully she was managing to sleep. Sitting on the porch, he stared at the moon and then at his bare feet, wishing his best friend hadn't taken sudden leave of his senses. The problem was, Mitch was a softie. He was nice to everyone. Ginger wouldn't have had to ask him more than once to tell her how she could get in touch with Steve.

Such softness did not exist in Steve's nature.

Dan Crane had lost the race today, and lost Ginger. Steve had lost plenty of races without Ginger hightailing it. For some reason, Ginger's behavior bothered him. One of the reasons he had liked her was that she knew the score in racing, knew that every day was a different day and there were no sure bets. Nor had she ever been hot or cold in her support of him. It had always been enough for her to be seen in the spotlight. When she'd started going out with Dan, Steve had known that she'd merely changed tracks, going over to the side she thought would benefit her the most.

While it had infuriated him he had also understood. Men did that kind of thing all the time. Trying to move up in life wasn't based on matters of the heart, nor did it have much to do with great sex. Moving up sometimes meant moving on. But dumping old Dan so fast kind of made Steve feel sorry for him. What a hell of thing to happen to a guy in one day. But he had enough here to deal with, and the last thing he needed was Ginger calling with some feminine tale of Steve being the only man for her.

Kiran and her long skirt suddenly flashed into his

mind. He scratched at his shoulder, realizing uncomfortably that she probably wouldn't have sex with more than one man in her whole life, and she wouldn't leave someone just to get on a winning track. He thought about the prissy white blouse that reached to her wrists, and frowned at the next thoughts that came into his mind.

If he were to try to describe his life to Kiran, she would never understand. Fitting her into it would be impossible.

Kiran hadn't slept well, so when she heard rattling in the kitchen in the morning, she threw on a peach chenille robe and poked her head around the door. 'Hungry?'

Steve shook his head. 'Not really. But since it's going to take us today to wrap up our business, I thought I'd run out and get a few snacks. Maybe some pretzels. And some soda pop for you.'

'That would be wonderful. Just some cola, please. I don't drink coffee.' Her entire body had jolted alive faster than a shot of caffeine from looking at Steve. He wore the same jeans he'd had on last night, but no shirt. She had never imagined his chest could be so broad . . . and muscular. His skin was more tanned than she would have guessed too, though being in California probably gave him lots of opportunities to lie around on a variety of beaches.

He turned to peer inside the refrigerator and Kiran's eyes widened at the smooth expanse of his back. Either God or hormones had blessed

31

Steve with a wonderful physique, because he'd been a pathetically whip-thin child.

'I'm not planning on being here long enough to use up a can of coffee, and I hate instant,' he told her, glancing over his shoulder.

Those thickly-lashed summer-green eyes sent a shock through her. Willing the sensation away, Kiran merely shrugged to indicate his plans were fine with her and turned to go.

'Kiran,' he said, just as he had last night. The soft huskiness of his voice warned her that he had something on his mind.

'Yes?' she asked, facing him.

'I was going to take a look at some headstones when I go into town. If you think that's a good idea.'

She raised her brows. 'Headstones?'

'Yeah.' He nodded and leaned against the wall, crossing his arms so that she couldn't help but notice the way his muscles tightened. 'Something nice for Uncle Caleb and Sakina.'

Sakina's grave had a headstone, but it had gotten pretty crummy-looking over the years. Kiran was amazed that such a thing mattered to Steve. The way he talked, he couldn't wait to blaze a trail out of Cottonwood, much less slow down to do something thoughtful for someone. His behavior had made her think he was hot to get his share of the inheritance – and the faster the better.

'I think it's a good idea,' she murmured. 'Headstones are kind of permanent, though.'

'Well, they are permanently dead.' His expression

told her he wasn't sure what her point was.

'I meant that you said yesterday you wanted to sell Uncle Caleb's land. Whoever buys it isn't going to want our relatives lying in their backyard,' she pointed out.

'Oh.' He scratched at his five o'clock shadow. 'Maybe we should sell most of the land and keep this house and only a couple of acres surrounding it.'

'What would we do with that? I'm not trying to shoot down your idea, Steve, but I –'

'Do you have a better idea?'

'No.' She didn't have a better idea. She didn't want to sell, but hadn't come up with a reasonable alternative. 'Um, just check on the headstones and see how much they run and how soon they can be made up. Or engraved, or whatever it is that they do. We can take it from there.'

'Okay.' He looked relieved as he pushed away from the wall. 'Just cola?'

'Maybe some fruit, too,' she called, heading out of the kitchen before he could walk past her. The last thing she needed was to have those fabulous biceps of his brush against her. She and Steve had business they needed to work out, and her mind needed to stay on that. 'I'll take a shower while you're gone. Then the bathroom will be free when you get back.'

There was no answer, but a few seconds later she heard the front door slam on its hinge. She peered from behind a faded curtain to see Steve stride into the front yard, pulling on a shirt as he went. Definitely a man of action. He got into the rental car, obviously not realizing he could drive Uncle Caleb's old truck – or perhaps he knew the car was probably in better shape.

The telephone rang, pulling Kiran away from her spying. She found the phone after about six rings and answered it.

'Dorn residence.'

'Dorn residence? Who are you?' a female voice demanded.

'I – who are you?' Kiran was proficient with the question- and-answer games her students liked to play and was quick to turn the query around.

'My name is Ginger Foxworth. I'm calling to speak to Steve Dorn.'

Kiran felt a series of odd little twinges run through her heart. 'I'm sorry. Steve isn't here.'

'Are you the help?'

It was obvious the woman on the other end wanted badly to know if Steve was visiting with a ladyfriend. Kiran saw no need to enlighten her. 'No, I'm not the help. However, I will tell Steve you called.'

She hung up with more force than necessary, telling herself it was none of her business if Steve had a girlfriend who called from California.

At six o'clock in the morning, West Coast time.

CHAPTER 3

Steve put the groceries he'd selected on the counter at Andrews Grocery Mart and waited for them to be rung up. The gray-haired cashier peered at him with interest. He stared back, unwilling to strike up a conversation.

It wasn't until he pulled out cash to pay with that her curiosity spilled out.

'Are you from around here?'

He shook his head.

'I know just about everyone in these parts,' she said, her voice friendly. 'Are you visiting relatives or just passing through?'

There was no harm in talking to this lonely old woman, Steve decided. She was probably used to her customers stopping to gab with her. 'I'm sort of doing both,' he said. 'I don't plan on being here long as I'm in town for a funeral.'

'Oh?'

She'd been putting the cola cans, red grapes and apples into a sack, but her hand stilled as she glanced up at him. Steve noticed her friendly demeanor change to something he couldn't define.

'Friend or relative?'

'An uncle. Caleb Dorn. Did you know him?'

The old lady seemed uncertain, and any vestige of friendliness had downright disappeared now. 'Well, I'd heard of him. But I didn't *know* him.' She swallowed and looked around nervously, as if the cans on the dusty wooden shelves might provide her with something to say. 'He didn't come in often.'

Steve nodded. That much had been obvious from looking in his uncle's refrigerator. The woman studied him closely for a moment, then pulled her gaze away. He stood there, his hand outstretched so she could take his money, but she didn't see it.

'Here's my money,' he said, glad that he could pay with exact change and get out. The old lady was starting to give him the creeps. Upon being told that someone had died, the stock reply was *I'm sorry to hear that*. This poor old soul acted as if she was taking Caleb's death personally.

She finally accepted the money, but wouldn't meet his eyes. Steve shrugged, grabbed the sack and walked out. It suited him just fine if she wasn't in the mood to talk anymore. He hadn't been in the mood in the first place.

Driving home – *not home*, he reminded himself sternly – Steve couldn't help thinking that Uncle Caleb had lived a terribly isolated life. Pangs of guilt beat at his usually iron-clad conscience. It wouldn't have hurt to get away from the racing circuit once in a while and visit the man who had done so much for him. For that matter, he should have flown Uncle Caleb out to some of the races. He might have gotten a kick out of that. But Steve had gotten busy with his life and the pursuit of winning. Everything else had become secondary.

He pulled up next to Uncle Caleb's old truck and grabbed the groceries. 'Drink break!' he called as he walked into the house.

Kiran came out, wearing jeans he couldn't help but notice fit her nicely and a cheery red-and-white check blouse with short sleeves. *Well, there's a little bit of skin*, he thought, before reminding himself that it didn't matter. But her smile was big and welcoming, and somehow that did matter.

'Am I ever glad,' she replied, taking the can he handed her. 'I checked the ice tray and, believe it or not, there were some ice cubes.'

'Water must have been what Uncle liked to drink.' Steve sat down on a rickety kitchen chair with a straw back that was fairly shot. 'Headstones are expensive. They're also not much fun to shop for.'

Kiran set down a glass of ice on the table in front of him, though she hadn't asked him if he wanted it. He would have told her no, just to be contrary. The last thing he wanted was the two of them falling into an easy rhythm. She was just too sweet and innocent for a man to be around and not start thinking about getting her in the sack.

'I should have gone with you,' she said, popping

the top on her cola can and pouring the liquid into her glass of ice. 'By the way, Ginger Foxworth called just after you left.'

Kiran had known what kind of phone call it was, yet it still felt a little funny to see the strange smile on Steve's face. She looked away.

'What did she say?'

A bit of feminine righteousness reared up inside her. 'I didn't have a conversation with her. I merely told her I would tell you she called.'

Instantly she realized how snotty she sounded. Ginger could be Steve's secretary, and Kiran had jumped to a conclusion that just wasn't like her. But she couldn't apologize because then it would sound as if she cared if Steve had a girlfriend.

Which she most certainly did not.

'I'll call her later.' He stared at the glass he hadn't poured anything into for a moment. 'Did it bother you that nobody came to Uncle's funeral? Did it strike you as odd that not even a neighbor came to pay their respects?'

'Well, I . . .' She mulled that over for a second. 'It might be hard to have neighbors when you're fifteen hundred acres away from the next human.'

'The lady at the grocery store said he didn't shop there often.'

Kiran wondered why Steve seemed concerned that their uncle hadn't had anyone who cared about his passing. 'Why should he need much food, Steve? He was only feeding himself.'

'Yeah. I guess.' He still seemed troubled.

'Father Lannigan seemed to know him pretty well.'

'That's weird, for a man who didn't go to church. In fact, I think that priest is weird.'

'He's not *weird*. Why would you say that?'

'I don't know. Just a feeling I got.'

'Because he's terribly handsome and committed to –' She nearly said *not having a Ginger of his own* before she realized that was *not* going to sound good at all.

'You think he's handsome?'

She was shocked. 'Oh, yes. He's an extremely good-looking man. And very nice. And considerate.'

'Oh.'

'Didn't you think he was nice?'

'For somebody mumbling Catholic verses, yeah, he was fine.'

Kiran felt sure there was something she was missing for Steve's attitude to be so antagonistic. 'You were worried about Uncle not having any friends, weren't you? Well, he had one.'

'That's a helluva nice thing, isn't it? One friend.' Steve ruffled his hand through his hair. 'Jeez.'

She was worried. 'You're taking this awfully hard, aren't you?'

'I don't know.' He let out a sigh. 'Maybe I just need some sleep.'

'Why don't you go lie down for a while? I was going to try to do some sweeping around here, anyway.'

'I might. I didn't sleep much last night. I'm sorry, Kiran. I shouldn't bum out on you, but I do think I'll –'

'Yoo-hoo!' a voice called through the screen door. 'Are you in there, Kiran?'

The door opened and sprang back. Kiran and Steve glanced at each other in shock. 'Oh, Jeez,' he muttered. 'Your stepmother. I'd know that rabid voice anywhere.'

'Steve, son! Are you around?'

Kiran reached out to lay a consoling hand on Steve's. 'And I'd know your loving father's voice anywhere.'

She pulled her hand back just before Agnes came into the kitchen, all fake affection.

'Kiran! And Steve! I'm so sorry we couldn't make it any sooner. Such a trying time! Butch and I wanted to fly in together and we couldn't get a flight until this morning. I hope you haven't had to do too much without our help.'

'Just bury your brother,' Steve said mildly.

Kiran's gaze snapped from Agnes and stocky Butch to Steve, hearing the underlying sound of resentment in his voice. It was like listening to knives being sharpened. His eyes touched hers and she had the oddest sensation that he had just withdrawn from the whole situation. Her heart sank, and despite the small humid breeze emanating from the fan in the kitchen she suddenly felt suffocated.

* * *

Steve could hardly believe his eyes when his father walked into the kitchen. They hadn't spoken in the last ten years, except for the Christmas call Steve grudgingly put in, and which he made damn sure didn't last beyond three minutes if he could help it. The old man was a son-of-a-bitch and Steve disliked him with an intensity he could only compare to hate. If the man walked into a lake of gators tomorrow, Steve doubted he could be bothered to pull his father out.

Agnes was cut from the same cloth. Caleb had been the only worthwhile person in the family. The nerve of these people showing up now was more than Steve could swallow. They knew full well the funeral had been yesterday. He'd canceled out of a race to show his respect, yet they weren't going to change their ways enough to thank a man who had basically been summer camp service for them, free of charge. He gritted his teeth. Kiran's gaze was on him, her face white and strained.

Suddenly he couldn't take it any longer. He wasn't going to get dragged down by family garbage he hadn't wanted to be involved with in the first place.

He stood. 'Glad you could make it,' he said bitterly. 'Excuse me. I have to make a phone call.'

'The phone is out,' Kiran said, jumping to her feet.

His mouth dropped open for a split second. She'd just told him Ginger had called so he knew that wasn't true. Intuition hit him like a lightning bolt.

41

'Then I'll have to go into town. Didn't you say you had some things you needed to pick up?'

'Fruit and cola.' She hurried past him.

'We'll be back later,' he called over his shoulder.

'Must you go right away?' Agnes called. 'Can't it wait? We need to discuss what's to be done about poor Caleb.'

Kiran was already in the passenger seat of his car. 'I'm sure he's not worried,' Steve called over his shoulder. He slid in next to Kiran and turned on the ignition, crushing the accelerator with his foot.

They shot onto the main county road and cleared the small bridge. 'Where's the checkered flag?' Kiran asked.

'What checkered flag?' He glanced over at her, catching her cocked eyebrow. 'Oh,' he said sheepishly. 'I am a little over the speed limit.'

'Just a little.' She smiled, rolling her head to look out the window. 'If you slow down, we won't get back as fast.'

'You've got a point there.' He let the car cruise to a crawl. 'I had to get out of there.'

'I wasn't letting you go without me. You're not feeding me to the lions. However, the fact that you were about to abandon me strikes me as being somewhat ungentlemanly.'

He snorted. 'Obviously your survival instincts are as keen as mine. You would have thought of something.'

She looked back at him. 'We're not going toward town. I thought you had a phone call to make.'

42

'I'm not calling anyone,' he said. 'I'm driving until this car runs out of gas, and then I'm going to fill it up again and drive some more.'

'We can't do this all day,' she reminded him. 'Eventually we have to go home and face the vultures.'

'We could get a motel room.'

'Oh, be serious,' she said, laughing.

'I am. I would really like to get some sleep.' His expression was innocent, though he had only been half-kidding about the motel room. Sex would definitely keep him from thinking about his father's sudden appearance. 'Oh – did you think I was suggesting –? Kiran Whitley, get your mind out of the gutter.'

She laughed again, and Steve was glad he could put a smile back on her face. The color had returned to her cheeks. Rolling the window down, he let the wind blow around in the car, wishing he felt like smiling, too.

As long as his father was around there wasn't going to be anything for him to smile about.

At Andrews Grocery Mart, Maypat was having a terrible day. It had all started when Caleb Dorn's relative came in for groceries. She had started feeling nervous, as if her high blood pressure medicine wasn't acting right. It wasn't her medication that was making her feel jittery, though. Seeing that man had made her hair practically stand on end.

She was never going to be able to stand the strain

43

of what her husband wanted to do. Jarvis might not have a conscience, but she did, and lately it was beginning to scream at her. In fact, she was starting to scream herself – at night. Bad nightmares haunted her, spooky ghouls of condemnation that made her wake shrieking. She could never remember what she'd been dreaming about, and Jarvis was right put out with her 'antics,' as he called them. The fact was, it was all getting to her, and having to face that nephew had jangled her so badly she'd barely got his groceries rung up.

The worst part was now that Jarvis had told her that they were in trouble financially she had begun to realize things she'd ignored. Like the fact that they had a lot less customers than ever before – that big supermarket south of Cottonwood was really pulling their business away. Even the fishermen weren't coming in to buy bait as often. The farmers hadn't harvested good crops this summer, with everything being burned up in the heat, so there was less local produce to sell. Having to compete with the big grocery chains was difficult.

She sat on the stool behind the counter and forced herself to breathe deeply. Jarvis had obviously been wrong. Caleb had at least possessed a nephew who cared about him, and who had probably inherited the Dorn land. The nephew hadn't looked like a man who could be taken in easily, so her husband's plan to get at that prime acreage cheaply probably wouldn't work. She felt a perverse satisfaction in that.

It might be sneaky, but she decided she wasn't going to tell Jarvis she had met one of the Dorn clan. He would only tell her she was stupid not to have dug out more information. As it was, she hadn't even asked the nephew his name. She stood, pulling off her apron.

'Lita!' she called. 'You run the register for the rest of the day. I'm going home.'

That done, Maypat walked out into the sunshine. She usually tended the register because it gave her a chance to visit with folks in Cottonwood. Jarvis liked her to do it since he didn't trust anyone but the two of them around the money. Actually, he *had* accused her a time or two of taking out some money to put in her nest-egg, but he was apparently willing to overlook that since nobody except her would work for free. But today she was going to make herself relax and forget all about meeting Caleb's kin.

The path up to the house was gravel and Maypat tried to watch where she was stepping so she wouldn't slip on an uneven patch. It was hot, but the half-mile walk always went fast, and there was air-conditioning waiting at the end of the trek. She took a deep breath, telling herself that walking was good for her health.

Without warning, black spots swam in front of her eyes. Dizzy nausea hit her. She felt cold perspiration break out at the back of her neck. With a moan, Maypat realized she was going to faint.

* * *

45

'This is the best cheeseburger I've had in a long time,' Kiran said.

She and Steve had bought a bag of burgers and drinks from the local drive-through. They'd parked in a field underneath a spreading oak tree. It might not be the world's greatest burger, but with her hair pulled back in a rubber band she'd found under the car seat and her shoes kicked off Kiran was determined to enjoy the moment. She was glad Steve seemed more relaxed, too. He didn't even appear to be anxious to call Ginger, though she would have sat through that to avoid being with her stepmother.

Leaning against the trunk of an ancient oak, Kiran focused on the chimney swifts chasing dragonflies in the field.

'Mine has onions even though I said no onions,' Steve said. 'Do you care if I eat them?'

She eyed Steve with a cautious smile. 'You should do with them whatever you please.'

'Very funny. I'm asking you if you mind.'

'I doubt it's really going to impact my life in any way, Steve.'

'Fine,' he said crossly. 'You'll just have to put up with onion breath.'

She shrugged nonchalantly. 'I'm eating mine. Anyway, it's not like we're going to be kissing.' Kiran's eyes widened, and she immediately wished she hadn't said that.

'You said it, not me,' he grumbled, taking a big bite. 'Mmm, I needed something solid in my stomach.'

'You didn't have breakfast,' she reminded him.

'I wouldn't have been able to hold it down.'

He was referring to their parents' abrupt appearance. 'Steve, maybe we should form a battle plan. We can't sit out here for ever. They came for a reason, and I doubt they'll leave until they're satisfied.'

'Yeah.' He wiped a bit of mustard from his mouth with a napkin. 'When you think of something, let me know.'

'Oh, that was helpful.' She snapped her fingers. 'We'll tell them that Uncle Caleb owed everybody in town money.'

Steve looked up for a moment. 'That could be a fact.'

'No.' She shook her head. 'I couldn't find any bills lying around except an electricity bill, which was tiny.'

'One light bulb, a small refrigerator with no food and a kitchen fan wouldn't use up much,' he agreed.

'Uncle didn't have cable, and he didn't have a new car, so, while there may be some small city services to pay for, and what we'll spend on headstones, I think the estate is free and clear. But we don't have to tell our parents that.'

'Don't you think they'll come to the same conclusion you have? They blew money on airline tickets, and that means they believe they have something to gain.'

Kiran tossed the rest of her hamburger into the brown paper bag and took a sip of her drink. 'I wish

I could think of the right thing to do with Uncle's place.'

'We're not keeping it, Kiran. It doesn't make a damn bit of sense. I mean, we could lease the land and rent the house, but that seems more trouble than it's worth.'

'What if we agree to do that for a year, to give us enough time to figure out what we really want to do?'

Steve thought for a moment. 'That might work.'

'They're going to want to know what we're going to do with the money that's coming in.' Kiran felt a driving need to have every pin in the plan nailed down before they went back.

'Screw them.'

'Steve!' Kiran was shocked.

'Of, for the love of – We'll just tell them it's none of their damn business. Or that we have to lease everything in order to pay off the bad debts Caleb left behind.'

'Hey.' Kiran sat straight. 'The wheat field looked sickly, Steve. And the corn looked puny, too. All we have to say is that he'd taken a farm loan against this crop.'

'Of course the next question is going to be why we're not selling the land,' he said morosely.

'I guess that's where the fight will be. But Uncle didn't will anything to them. He left it to us and we'll just have to stand firm.' She heaved a sigh. 'I'm so glad we're on the same side.'

Something inside him automatically pulled back

at the idea of being a team with Kiran. She'd been right; he *had* been leaving her to deal with their parents. He hadn't put any thought into his actions, of course, but with the hammering inside his head at the sight of his father Steve hadn't been rational. He'd shot instantly into overdrive to escape. He would have abandoned her without even thinking twice.

That was the trouble with emotional demons. The same emotional demon was warning him now that they were getting too cozy, too friendly with this team spirit thing. He lived alone; he raced alone. Kiran was not going to slide into the empty slot where his emotions were supposed to reside.

'Well, we've beat that horse to death,' he said nonchalantly. 'So. You like living in Tennessee?'

Instantly the smile he found so attractive appeared on her face. 'Oh, yes. I love my house. I love living near the mountains. But I imagine that's very different from California?'

He nodded. 'Anyone special in your life?'

Kiran frowned at him. 'Lots of people.'

'I meant a boyfriend.' He hated to specify that, but for some reason he wanted to hear that she did so he could widen the distance between them.

'Is Ginger your girlfriend?' she countered.

'Not anymore.'

He felt her stare before she stretched her feet out in the yellow grass. There was red polish on her toes, which seemed completely out of character for Kiran. He would have guessed pink. Somehow he found that subtle hint at her personality intriguing.

'Are you deliberately avoiding my question?' he demanded.

'I don't have a boyfriend.'

'Ah.'

She cocked her head to look at him. 'You sound disappointed.'

'Why would I care?'

'Why did you ask?'

'To be polite.'

Kiran started laughing. Steve looked out over the open land, feeling as if he'd gotten caught prying. Since he had, he decided he might as well go ahead and satisfy his curiosity – under the guise of cousinly interest.

'Ever consider getting married?'

'To you? No, thanks.' Her tone was definite.

'What's that supposed to mean?' He sat straight up, offended somehow but not quite sure why. Usually he was the one doing the altar-avoidance dance. Kiran was starting to bug him.

'It means that you wouldn't suit me at all.' She patted his hand, which made him feel like jumping out of his skin. 'Don't take it personally, Steve. I haven't found anybody who suits me.'

'Women can be so damn picky,' he complained.

'Oh. Have I struck a nerve?' she asked, her eyes shining with innocence. 'Have you suffered a rejection lately?'

'No, you haven't 'struck a nerve', he mimicked, choosing to forget that Ginger had dumped him for his rival. A strange sensation rose inside him, clouding and overwhelming in its intensity as he stared into her laughing blue eyes.

'Kiran Whitley, you're starting to bother me,' he said, supremely wishing he hadn't eaten those onions. Otherwise he would have shown her that she need not be so picky where he was concerned. He was a great kisser; he'd been told many times. But a kiss couldn't be done properly after onions, as much as he'd like to kiss that sassy mouth of hers silent.

Instantly he realized the urge he was feeling to put her in her place was a reaction of sorts, however chauvinistic. He usually felt neither hot nor cold about a woman. The last thing he should do was have a reaction to Kiran.

He wouldn't let that happen, no matter how kissable she might be. Their lives were as different as the states they lived in – and there was no middle ground.

CHAPTER 4

'I *have* missed you, Steve,' Kiran said. It was true. That one summer she'd had to spend away from him had cost her, had damaged their special relationship.

He glanced at her for an instant, then his gaze slid away. Obviously Steve wasn't going to tell her that he'd missed her. Crumpling the hamburger sack with more force than necessary, he looked toward the horizon without acknowledging her sentiment. Something curled tight inside Kiran. He was going to avoid any rebonding between them, and though she'd like to tell him the truth, tell him why she hadn't come back to Cottonwood that summer, she simply couldn't.

It was better that he believe she'd preferred going to an all-girls summer camp rather than spend the summer with him.

'We better get back,' Steve murmured. 'As much as I wish they would, our folks aren't going to vanish into thin air.'

'No, they're not.' Kiran sighed and got to her feet.

'Not until they've extracted their pound of flesh.' She brushed off her jeans and picked at some clinging bits of dried grass. 'So. Should we stop by a phone on the way back?'

'What for?'

She couldn't believe he had honestly forgotten Ginger Foxworth's call. 'Don't you have a call to return? Wasn't that the original excuse behind your escape?'

'Yeah.' He looked puzzled. 'I just realized something. I was so tuned in to the fact that an acquaintance of mine had cracked up his car, I forgot to ask how our team finished. I must be losing it.'

'That's probably a fairly normal occurrence when someone is grieving, Steve,' she said, gently touching his arm. 'A funeral is emotionally draining, not to mention that the only person who truly loved us is gone. Don't be so hard on yourself.'

He stared at her hand on his arm as if it was a hornet. Briskly he pulled away, going to the driver's side of the car. He got in, so she did, too – only to find his stony gaze on her.

'Kiran, I'm getting this thing straightened out tonight with our folks and then I'm leaving. I'm taking a plane out tomorrow, and if you choose to stay behind to deal with whatever junk they decide to dredge up, that's going to be your problem, okay? I don't want you telling me about my grief, or anything else you think you know about me, because you don't.'

He took a deep breath. Kiran tried to rein in the shocked and hurt feelings his words brought her.

'I just want you to know, because I think you're more emotionally involved in this than I am.' He started the car, backing it away from the tree more quickly than necessary. 'Are we square on this?'

They were square, all right. Kiran blinked back a tear she'd told herself she wouldn't shed. She had overstepped a boundary line she hadn't seen by offering comforting words he didn't want. For a few brief moments she'd thought they might re-capture a bit of the affection they'd shared as unwanted children. In telling him she'd missed him she'd thought honesty was something he would welcome.

She'd been very wrong.

'I hope your driver won the race,' she said softly. 'I hope coming out here hasn't cost you anything.'

'It hasn't.' His voice was a growl. 'I won't let it.'

They drove for twenty more minutes in silence before crossing the old slatted bridge that led to the farm. At high noon the sun baked into the land, making it more dismal for any crops trying to outlast the drought. Kiran shook her head. She wasn't experienced when it came to farming, but the wheat looked beaten down.

Tonight, she told herself, it might be worth slipping out to buy a newspaper to check the local forecast. Steve might not be willing to stay and fight, but she certainly wasn't going to let Uncle Caleb's last wishes be forgotten.

He pulled into the driveway and turned off the car. 'Kiran,' he said. 'I'm sorry.'

She looked away from him. 'There's nothing to be sorry for. I understand more than you think I do.'

'It's just that I don't want to mess with them right now, you know? I don't want my old man eating me alive.'

She well remembered how easily his father could make Steve feel as if he was never going to amount to anything. *'Boy, you ain't got the sense God gave a billy-goat. How you ever gonna make it in out of the rain is a mystery.'*

'I do know. I wish they hadn't come.' Kiran looked at the house. A faint movement of the threadbare curtains caught her eye. Her step-mother was spying on them. 'Don't worry about it, Steve. If you can, ignore anything they say. Get on that plane tomorrow and don't look back.'

'What about you?'

'I'm going to stick it out for a while, but, as you said, I'm on summer break. This is going to be a vacation for me, just as soon as our folks figure out their trip was a waste of time.' She touched her hand to his briefly as it rested on the gear-shift. 'I can handle it.'

'I feel like I'm abandoning you.'

He was, actually – again. And the knowledge made him feel bad. Damn, but he couldn't wait to get a state's distance away from his old man and everything to do with him.

'Come on. We just have to tell them that there's no money and they'll leave.' She smiled reassuringly, but Steve didn't feel any better.

They got out of the car and walked inside the house. Over the top of Kiran's shiny blonde hair he could see his old man standing in the kitchen, staring through the doorway at him. Steve resisted the urge to look away, instead forcing himself to meet that uncaring gaze without flinching. Aunt Agnes was in the easy chair, pertly sitting up with a smile on her face, as if she was waiting to hear good news.

'Did you have a nice drive?' she asked.

'It was fine, Agnes,' Kiran replied.

'Did you find the fruit and soda you wanted? I noticed there seemed to be plenty in the refrigerator. You kids must have been hungry.'

He felt rather than saw Kiran's posture stiffen at Agnes's needling tone. Without thinking about it he put a hand in the small of her back. Not where Agnes could see the gesture, but so Kiran would feel his support.

Butch walked into the living room to join the people already engaged in an uneasy tableau. 'Hey, leave'em alone, Ag,' he said. 'They just wanted to have a minute to get to know each other again – right, kids?' His face was round and easy with forced friendliness. 'Say, what we really want to talk to you about is what we're gonna do here with ol' Caleb.'

'Seems to be just fine where he is,' Steve said tightly. Damn his old man for being such a conniving old coot. It would almost be better if he'd just spit out what he was after.

'Well, I didn't really mean that, son,' Butch said

jovially. 'Though Aggie and I do want to talk with you kids about Caleb's final resting place eventually. Right now we figure there's some straightening out to do.'

'Like what?' Steve was going to force his old man to say what was really on his mind.

'Well, like Caleb's will, for example. Surely we should be discussin' that?'

'Not much to discuss.' Steve stepped around Kiran, who still stood in the entryway, as if she were hung up by invisible strings from the ceiling. He could feel the tension radiating from her. 'Truth is, you and Aunt Agnes weren't in the will, so if you came out to discuss that, you've wasted your trip.' He leaned against a dusty windowsill, settling himself in for the explosion he knew would come.

Butch scratched his head, as if he was thinking over what Steve had said. Agnes's eyes shifted from Steve to Kiran, seeking out the weaker prey.

'I can't imagine what he means, Butch,' Agnes said, warily watching her daughter by marriage. 'We were Caleb's closest family, after all. Who could he have left this house and the property to?'

'Uncle Caleb left everything to us.' Kiran's eyes didn't move from the cobra-like intensity of Agnes's dark ones. 'Steve and I, and the local priest, inherited the house and the land to do with as we see fit.'

'Why – why, that's ridiculous,' Butch sputtered. 'You're just a couple of dang – What do you mean, the priest? Caleb didn't have a religious bone in his body. He sure as hell never attended any church.' He paced, highly agitated, before turning to face his son. 'Both of you are lying just to cheat us out of our fair share as Caleb's brother and sister.'

Agnes nodded. 'Brother wouldn't have left us high and dry.'

'I think we deserve to see the will. There's no way Caleb can cut out his own family.'

It took every ounce of self-control Steve possessed not to walk out of the room. 'Let's cut the deck – cut it so that everyone here knows the cards aren't stacked and are being played straight. The two of you didn't have a damn thing to do with Uncle Caleb when he was alive, except to stick him with us whenever you could. There were no holiday phone calls, no birthday cards, nothing. *Nada*. So why do you think he would have left you a single dime?'

'What did you do for him that makes you more deserving, Steve?' Butch asked.

Silence hung in the room. Steve couldn't answer that one. Certainly he hadn't done what he should have by Uncle Caleb.

'He loved him,' Kiran slipped into the silence. Her voice was strong and firm, striking back into Steve the steel that had momentarily slipped under his father's questioning. 'Steve loved Uncle Caleb. I did, too. And he loved us.'

Butch folded his arms across his chest, the beefy fat rolling out from his shirtsleeves. 'Shut up, Kiran. As far as I'm concerned you don't even belong in this room. This is a family discussion, and you ain't family.'

The rage that Steve had hoped wouldn't come began simmering in the pit of his stomach. He was afraid of it, hadn't wanted to have this confrontation for fear of the rage returning. He'd lived too long avoiding it, but now he felt it, like steam rising hotly to the surface. 'How in holy hell do you figure Kiran's not family?'

'She's no blood relation to any of us.' Butch smirked at Agnes. 'We don't really even know where she came from. Kiran's a squatter's child. You could say Kiran's father squatted on Agnes, then left her with someone else's child.'

A bolt of black anger hit Steve so blindingly he felt an incomprehensible urge to murder. Kiran's shocked eyes swam before him. 'Get out,' he said, his tone calm enough to belie the throttle-hold rage had on him. 'The two of you get out. There's a hotel down the road. You'll sleep much more comfortably there.'

'You wouldn't kick us out of our own brother's house, Steve!' Agnes stood, her expression mutinous. 'We have just as much right to stay here as you do.'

'No, you don't. Kiran and I own this house. We did not invite you. You are trespassing. If you're not out in five minutes, I'll call the police and have you removed.'

'Like hell you will,' his father blustered.

Steve pointed a finger in his direction. 'Like hell I

won't. I strongly suggest you don't try me on this. There's nothing here for either of you, and we don't want you around.'

'Now, listen here –'

Steve held up his arm and pointed to the watch. 'Clock's ticking. You have four minutes and forty-five seconds.'

'You son-of-a-bitch. I oughta whip your ass –'

'It never worked before; sure as hell won't now. You're out of shape, Pop, and I'd hate to have to send you out of here looking like something ran over you.'

'You'll be hearing from us,' Butch warned.

'I know.' Steve took that in his stride. This was only a small skirmish in the war.

Butch and Agnes looked at Steve uncertainly one last time before huffing out the front door.

'I suggest you make an appointment if you feel any urge to talk again,' he called after them. 'We don't want to mistake you for petty thieves and accidentally shoot you.'

He let the door slam back in place. Outside, he could hear their car drive away. Round one was over.

He had told Kiran he wouldn't stay past today, which made him rub his eyes tiredly. There was no way she could stand up to Butch and Agnes. They clearly had their minds set on getting their fingers in the pie. Kiran had said she would stick it out, but they were going to make her pay in blood. Steve closed his eyes. Kiran was strong, but he was the only thing standing in the way of her being eaten alive.

'Well, another happy, heartwarming episode from the Brady Bunch,' Kiran said. 'We are such a solid family unit.'

She was trying to make light of it to cover the pain. Instinctively Steve recognized her attempt to wash away the years of being unwanted. He turned, drawing her into his arms before he thought about what he was doing. The gesture was affectionate, yet free of anything but the need to hold her to him and shut out the bitterness. She put her head on his chest and held him tightly in return.

'Are you okay?' he asked.

'I'm fine. You took all the hits. If blood's pouring, it's yours.' She tilted her head to look at him. 'Are *you* all right?'

Steve didn't answer for a moment. He was fine, but the adrenalin was starting to peak in his body. He felt as if he'd just driven a race. 'I feel like I'm going to explode,' he said honestly.

'A perfectly normal reaction in our family.' She paused for a moment. 'Steve, thank you.'

'For what?' he asked brusquely. He tucked her head back under his chin so he wouldn't have to see her eyes. He knew what she was going to say, and he didn't want to be written up as a hero.

'For standing up for me. For standing up against them.' He heard a slight sniffle, as if she wanted to cry but wasn't going to give in. 'You said you weren't as emotionally involved in this as I am and I –'

'Kiran, shh.' He slowly withdrew, taking his arms from around her. 'I wasn't protecting you any more than I was protecting myself. Hell, all you have to do is get that old man and me in the same room and it's bad chemistry. Kaboom!' He pounded his fist into the other hand. 'We can cuss each other over whether it's raining outside or not.'

She shook her head. 'You didn't have to defend my place in Uncle Caleb's will.'

'You're right. I didn't. You're in the will; they're not. So there's no argument. Let's not make this into something it's not.'

Their eyes met and locked. He couldn't help thinking how delicate, how soft Kiran was, with that sweet oval face and the blonde hair gently framing her chin. She was slight, though she carried herself like an Amazon warrior woman. He admired her for not having a nervous breakdown after that touching family scene, though he would have understood if she had.

Kiran watched the changing expressions on Steve's face, knowing she was watching years of emotions burning inside of him. He was a good man, a man of honor and integrity, but he didn't want her thanks. It was clear that the man he'd grown into distrusted letting anyone get more than skin-deep into his emotions. His lips had flattened into a nearly straight line – belligerent. A muscle worked in his cheek as he anticipated her reaction to his words.

'Shall we go pick out the headstones, then?' she

asked. 'I know you'll want to leave this afternoon.'

'That's a good idea. Come on.' He turned to open the door for her.

Kiran stepped past him and walked outside. 'Let's take Uncle Caleb's truck, Steve.'

'Why?'

Kiran shrugged, her eyes roving over the old red truck. He'd replaced it since the one she'd ridden in with him so long ago. 'I would like to.'

Steve considered her request for a moment. 'Let me go find his keys.' He went back inside and Kiran hurried to the truck. This one could have used being replaced, too. It had been banged up plenty, but trucks were meant to be used on a farm. She ran her hand over the passenger-side door handle, wondering if anyone had ever opened this door the entire time Caleb had owned the truck. Had he ever had a passenger, a companion to share the last long hours of his life with?

'I found them.' Steve jogged to the truck. They got in, both pausing in the act of settling into the seats. Their eyes met in amazement.

'It smells like Uncle Caleb,' Steve said wonderingly. 'I mean, it really does.'

Kiran nodded, the tears jumping into her eyes. 'The house kind of smells like him every once in a while, though it's mostly mustiness in the air. But this is just the way I remember him.'

Steve had paused, his hand over the ignition. 'The smell of leather and hard work.'

Kiran closed her eyes. 'He had prickly skin along

his chin. He'd rub it on my face just to hear me squeal. This is just what I'd smell when he did that, and it always made me feel like I was . . . home.' She stopped, realizing she might have shared more memories than Steve would be comfortable with.

He started the truck and it roared to life. 'Why do you think he didn't get along with Butch and Agnes? Those two are close as porcupine quills, but they definitely didn't have any use for their own brother.'

She thought about that as he drove down the gravel lane. 'I never knew. It certainly went past normal brother-sister squabbling, though.'

The relationship had been non-existent. The only time Agnes had ever talked to Caleb had been to arrange Kiran's yearly summertime visit.

'It's strange.'

Kiran didn't reply. They'd often hashed this subject as children. They were no closer to having an answer as adults. She supposed it would be a waste of time to expend too much thought on it now. By Steve's silence she figured he felt the same way.

'There's the market I got the groceries from,' Steve told her.

'Andrews Grocery Mart,' Kiran read. 'That was here when we were kids.'

'I thought it was where Uncle Caleb used to bring us for ice cream. I wasn't sure.'

They passed it by slowly. Kiran craned her neck to see the house that lay up the hill from the market, heavily shrouded by broad-leafed magnolia trees.

'I've always wondered who lives up there.'

'The owner of the market does. Uncle Caleb said it was a huge event when those folks built that place. The design was taken from an old Southern mansion in Georgia.'

'I always thought it looked like a castle,' Kiran said, admiring the round white columns and louvred shutters. 'I used to imagine that a queen lived there, wearing jewels and a crown. And she could jump on the bed whenever she wanted,' she said softly.

'Why would she want to do that?'

Kiran smiled. 'I loved jumping on the bed when I was a child.'

'I can't believe ol' Aggie let you.'

'I did it when she wasn't around,' Kiran confided. And that had been often enough that Kiran had eventually knocked the wooden slats out of the bed with all her jumping. One of Agnes's boyfriends had come in to put the bed back together. She remembered being afraid for some reason, just before she felt searing heat and unbelievable pain –

'Are you going to be okay after I leave, Kiran?' Steve's question cut into her mind's rambling.

'I'm going to be fine,' she murmured. 'I always am.'

She barely noticed when he stopped the truck. They had parked at a shop which had rows of headstones neatly lined up in the front yard for display.

'Oh, this is nice,' she said, hopping out of the car.

'How do you figure?' Steve had followed behind her.

'I had pictured sitting in a gloomy office picking a headstone out of a catalog or something. I like the curb-side appeal of this man's business.'

Steve laughed. 'I'm glad you can see the bright side. I didn't much enjoy myself when I was by here earlier.'

'Yes, but you were alone then.' Kiran squeezed his arm lightly.

She walked to the first row of headstones. There were three rows of different marble shapes, so she wanted to take her time to look them over. Whatever she chose was going to be adorning that land a long time. She wanted it to be something Caleb and Sakina would have liked.

Steve stood back as Kiran strolled through the rows, her concentration as focused as if she were choosing fabric for drapes. His skin prickled uncomfortably at the back of his neck. The sun had risen high in the sky, bringing heat that was nearly sweltering, though some scrubby trees shaded the headstones. He felt entirely out of sorts, but that was probably to be expected. He was still enraged by what his father had said about Kiran. He hadn't expected Butch to pull his punches, but he certainly hadn't counted on the personal attack on Kiran. He couldn't forget the poison in his father's voice.

His gaze flicked to her. It appeared that she had let the incident roll over her. Now she stood carefully choosing a proper dressing for Uncle Caleb's grave rather than stewing over the morning's events. If Butch's snide remark about Kiran being a squatter's child were to be taken for truth, then Kiran of all people should not have to be the one making this tough selection.

He watched her walk, the sun dappling her hair as she stopped first in front of one stone and then another. Something stirred inside him, then lodged squarely in his throat.

She was right. Doing this wasn't so bad. She wanted to be doing this and he was letting her, just so he could watch her. He had stood and looked at these very same stones before, with a heavy feeling of uneasiness inside him. Now the sun shone overhead and a few mocking birds scolded in the trees, and Steve smiled.

It *wasn't* so bad.

Because she was with him.

CHAPTER 5

Kiran decided ordering a pizza for dinner would probably be the best thing to do. Steve had been quiet after they'd ordered headstones. She suspected he had a lot on his mind, but whether it had to do with the race he'd missed or the battle between him and his father she couldn't be certain. There was no way the heated scene could have left him untouched. She had been surprised when he'd tried to shield her from Butch's venom. Steve had told her she was on her own; she had accepted that. She had no need of anyone protecting her.

His defense of her made her feel closer to him than she'd been able to since the funeral. The old Steve was still inside the man with the granite emotions.

She'd been glad to see that Steve again.

Right now he was walking through the dried-out fields. Every once in a while he reappeared in the distance, his tall outline easily visible. She had a funny feeling that Steve was walking through the past he had shared with Uncle Caleb. As soon as night fell she intended to walk to the graves and have her own private talk with Uncle Caleb by the light of the full summer moon. She had a lot she wanted to tell him, thank him for.

For now it seemed best if she got on with cleaning out the house. If they were going to rent it, the old place would need a thorough cleansing from top to bottom. She could buy some new drapes, and do a few other things to make the place look welcoming. Reminding herself to discuss rents and lease forms with Steve, Kiran pulled out a phone book to find the nearest pizza restaurant.

The front door slammed, startling her into snapping the book shut. 'Steve?' she called.

'Yeah.'

He came into the kitchen and Kiran's gaze automatically roved over the dark blue jeans and the masculine broadness under the mesh-weave polo shirt. He was wearing dark sunglasses to protect his eyes from the searing sun, and something inside Kiran tightened reflexively.

'Did you find what you were looking for?' she asked, in the lightest tone she could manage.

Snatching the glasses from his face and tossing them onto the worn Formica kitchen counter, Steve shook his head. 'I wasn't looking for anything.'

Of course he hadn't been. She knew that. He had been wandering through his own memories, just the same as she had been. 'I was going to suggest pizza for dinner,' she told him.

He seemed to appreciate the change in subject.

'Good idea. I'll go out in a bit to pick it up.'

Obviously that was a trip he planned on taking alone. Kiran shut out the reminder that there was still distance between them. 'I've been making some plans I'd like to run past you.' She put the phone book down and he took a seat at the kitchen table across from her.

'Okay.' He pushed a weary hand through his hair, disturbing the whiskey-colored strands in a way that Kiran found more attractive than she would have liked. 'Go ahead.'

'I guess we should discuss whether we're going to lease the house only or lease the land also, and if there needs to be any special provisions for what the land can be used for. We should think about how much we're going to charge, based on those parameters, and then what we need to do to get a lease agreement drawn up.' She spat everything out at once, determined to put a business-like air on the conversation. Hopefully, that would make him feel more comfortable with her, make him feel that their relationship was firmly locked in neutral.

'I'm glad one of us is thinking about the basics,' he told her with a half-attempt at a smile. His expression looked more apologetic than anything.

'Well,' Kiran said brightly, 'I'm having my typical reaction to stress. I tend to think about anything other than what's bothering me. In this case the business angle is keeping me sufficiently occupied.'

'Oh.' He assimilated that for a moment. There

was silence in the kitchen, a quiet that allowed her to hear her own heartbeat. 'I guess I just drive my race car when I'm stressed. Or any car.'

She got up and went to rustle around in a kitchen drawer. After a moment she came up with an old wooden ruler. 'You'll be back to driving tomorrow.'

Without looking at him, Kiran measured the kitchen windowsill, then wrote the figures down on a piece of paper. Sneaking a glance at Steve's broad back, she thought she saw resignation in his posture. Or defeat. Those old ghosts were more than he could exorcize – and she understood. She herself didn't want to spend any time around Agnes.

Taking her supplies into the living room with her, Kiran moved the easy chair over so that she could stand in it. She reached up to measure the window, – stiffening instantly when Steve's strong hands closed firmly around her waist.

'Steady,' he murmured.

It was safer this way, she told herself, leaning to where she could get that last half-inch of the measurements. But, with the warmth of his hands imprinting her waist, Kiran realized instantly she wasn't safer emotionally. She had better measure quickly and get down.

'What are you doing, anyway?'

Repeating the measurements to herself so that she could remember them, Kiran jumped down out of the easy chair. 'I thought I'd pick up some simple drapes for a few of the rooms. Little touches like that can help if we need to look for a renter.'

Though she had no need of his assistance now, Steve hadn't moved back. She was facing him, and way too close.

Uncomfortably she waited for him to move, but he stood there, pinning her with that clear gaze. She could still feel where he'd put his hands to hold her steady.

'Why do you seem to be dealing better with this than I am?' he asked.

'I'm not.' On the pretext of writing the measurements, Kiran reached for the pencil and paper she'd left on the window casement. Her back-to-business attitude caused Steve to move away, just as she'd hoped. He turned to stare out the front window, his gaze scanning the fields.

'I should be thinking about what we're going to do with the crops,' he said, more to himself than her.

'Plow them under, of course.' Kiran sat in the easy chair, aware she had Steve's full attention once more. That made her heartbeat pick up again, uncomfortably so.

'Plow them under?' His expression was considering. After a moment he sighed. 'I suppose there isn't enough of anything to harvest.'

'Well, it would take time to do it, and we're not going to have the luxury of nursing fifteen-hundred acres of land along. We could let a neighbor have whatever is mature enough, in return for him harvesting it, but I don't think there's going to be enough to make it worth anyone's time. It looks pretty grim out there to me.'

Steve nodded. 'I don't have much experience with farming, but the wheat looks pretty cooked.'

'I think it's best if we clear out the land so we can lease it. With the pond down at the end of the property, this would be a great place for grazing cattle.' Kiran leaned her head back on the chair, now allowing her own gaze to wander to the window. 'I just hope we can find someone on short notice.'

Her fingers tightened on the paper where she'd written the measurements. 'Do you think it would be a good idea to hire a property manager? Someone who could deal with any problems that may pop up with the land or the renters, assuming we can find some? I know it would be more out-of-pocket money, but to tell you the truth I think it would cost more in the long run to try to manage the property from out of state.'

'Whoa.' Steve held up his hands. 'You are going way too fast for me.'

'Too fast for the race-car driver?' she teased. 'Too fast for the man who won the Winston Cup a few years back?'

'How do you know that?' Steve narrowed his gaze at her, but his expression seemed pleased.

'Uncle Caleb wrote me. He was bragging about how nobody could beat his nephew on a speedway.'

'Damn it.' Steve crossed his arms and leaned against the wall. 'I should have flown him out to one of the races.' He sighed, long and regretfully. 'He never wrote me.'

'Uncle Caleb wrote me because I wrote to him. I'm sure he felt like he was obligated, otherwise all our communication would have been done on the phone.'

'We did talk on the phone occasionally.' Steve perked up. 'I'm not much of a letter-writer.'

She knew that from her own experience. Every once in a while, when they were kids, something would come in the mail addressed to her, the writing in pencil and fairly straggly. She'd written Steve often, sneaking the letters into the mailbox at the end of the corner where she crossed the street to the schoolyard. How many stamps had she stolen out of Agnes's drawer over the years, just to be able to send a letter to the only true friend she had?

'It's easier to call,' she murmured. 'Uncle Caleb would have preferred that, but I was at school all day teaching and at night I was usually tutoring students.'

She'd struggled to make ends meet. Finally it had all paid off when she'd been offered the job as assistant principal of a local elementary school, and then, at last, principal of a rural high school. She'd been able to buy her own house.

It was small, two bedrooms and one bath, but it had a nicely tended garden and pretty trees. With a few curtains she'd sewn and some careful renovations, the little place had turned into a dream cottage. Her own refuge set at the foot of the serene Tennessee mountains she could see from just about any window in the house.

For a housewarming gift Uncle Caleb had sent

her a check for five hundred dollars to replace the water heater. It had grumbled constantly, and she had written about the odd sounds it made whenever she ran the water. It had worried her into holding her breath until she could save enough money to replace the grouchy old thing. Uncle Caleb had taken that worry right off her mind, though she'd protested.

'*I can't take this much money from you.*'

'*Just get you a good heater and a good plumber to put it in, gal. I cain't sleep for fretting about you coming home one day and finding water all over the floor. It'll make a holy mess if it busts.*'

She'd swallowed her pride and gratefully had the cranky heater carted away. Her letter to Uncle Caleb had detailed the size of the heater she'd purchased, how fast it got the water hot now, and how efficient the plumber who installed it had been. All the details she knew Uncle Caleb would want.

He'd written back that he was glad he could help.

Kiran's eyes watered as she remembered. 'I'm going to miss that crusty old man.' Unwilling to let Steve see her distress, since she'd finally got him onto thinking happier thoughts, Kiran got up abruptly and went back into the kitchen. She put the pencil, paper and ruler back into a drawer. 'I'll call for the pizza now, if you're ready,' she called, snatching up a tissue and making quick work of blowing her nose.

'Better order a large. I think we're going to have company over for dinner.'

Kiran froze. Not Agnes and Butch. It couldn't possibly be. Not now while her defenses were down. Tossing the tissue into the trash, she hurried to the living room. 'Who is it?'

'It's that pretty-boy Father. I guess he didn't think we'd need any warning about his arrival.'

Kiran glanced up at the sour tone in Steve's voice. 'I don't know what bothers you so much about him.'

'I don't know, either.' Steve shrugged after a moment and went to open the front door. 'We weren't expecting you.'

John Lannigan walked inside, shaking Steve's hand at the door. 'I didn't figure I'd catch you at home. I was in the neighborhood and decided to risk it.'

'Hi, John.' Kiran offered him a bright smile she hoped would make up for Steve's coolness. 'We were going to order pizza for dinner. Can we talk you into joining us?'

'That would be great.' He didn't seem to be bothered by Steve's lack of enthusiasm. 'I'll eat almost anything.'

'The old appetite has to accommodate whatever the parishioners are serving, doesn't it?' Steve waved his hand toward the kitchen. 'We can sit in the living room or the kitchen – wherever you'd prefer.'

John held up the papers he had in his hand. 'I suppose the kitchen would be best, since we need to go over these. I wasn't aware of how long you'd be staying, so I figured it would be best if we got this out of the way. I'm sorry, though, that it has to be so fast after the funeral.'

Kiran shook her head. 'We're fine, Steve and I. Come on into the kitchen. Can I get you some water or cola to drink?'

He chuckled as he made himself comfortable at the table. 'Water will be fine, thanks. I don't think I've ever drunk water in this house.'

'It's just the same here as anywhere else, I imagine.'

Kiran jumped at Steve's tone, once again more sarcastic than she thought it should be. What was his problem?

'You're welcome to have a lawyer to go over these documents with you, if you'd like,' John said, completely ignoring Steve's caustic comment. 'Caleb had this will drawn up many years ago, but the handwritten letters, of course, are not legally airtight should you not agree to their contents.'

'So we can contest you being the executor?' Steve asked.

'That, and even the forty acres that were left to me. As you can see, that is not in the original will,' John replied easily.

Kiran put the glass of water on the table in front of him. 'That won't be necessary,' she said quickly. She sent Steve a warning look. Whatever was bugging him about the priest was something he was just going to have to work out himself. She intended to live by every letter of Uncle Caleb's wishes. 'We've inherited far more than we know what to do with. And we're going to need your advice anyway.'

'I'll be glad to help any way I can.' John smiled at her.

Steve sat back and eyed the father. 'What else do we need to discuss?'

John looked startled before he cleared his throat and picked up a document. 'Best as I have been able to research, the land is worth about thirty thousand dollars an acre.'

'What?' Kiran's hand flew to her throat. 'Are you certain?'

'I've called the county tax office and a realtor or two on your behalf. Without mentioning this particular property, I inquired as to the worth of the surrounding land. This area abuts the large homes going up south of here, so a zoning change is even being considered to serve single housing and commercial needs. That runs the value up considerably, especially with the custom-built homes that the builders would like to see planned. Of course that's a conservative figure, since I didn't mention this property. As you may have noticed, this farm backs right up to those new houses, so it's prime acreage.'

'That almost makes me think twice about not selling,' Kiran murmured. She seated herself at the table, trying to take it all in. Uncle Caleb had lived all his life in near poverty when he could have had it so much easier. It was enough to make her want to start crying again. 'Poor Uncle Caleb.'

John reached over to pat her arm. 'I don't think

he was unhappy, Kiran. I think he was living the only way he could see to live.'

'Lonely.' She sniffled. 'Except for you.'

The tops of Father John's ears turned a bit pink as he withdrew his hand. 'I'm afraid I wasn't the companion I should have been for your uncle. Let's just say I needed him more than he needed me.'

'I've been meaning to ask you about that.' Steve speared John with a dark look. 'How, exactly, did the two of you become close enough for you to pick up forty acres of prime land, when I'd be willing to bet that my uncle hadn't set foot in a church in years?'

'Steve!' Kiran protested. 'Will you –?'

'It's okay.' John shook his head at Kiran. 'Really, I would ask the same question if I were in your shoes.' He looked back at Steve, meeting the curious, hard look positioned on him. 'I guess you could say Caleb and I were drinking buddies.'

Steve's face remained immobile. Kiran's jaw dropped. 'Drinking buddies?' she repeated.

'That about sums it up, I'm afraid. We drank together an awful lot. Or you could say that we drank an awful lot together. Either way, that spells out the crux of our friendship.'

'I don't believe this. I don't believe *you*. For a priest, you're a bit strange.' Steve's words were couched in an accusing tone. 'Are you suggesting that our uncle was an alcoholic?'

She could tell by the darkening color in Steve's face that he was going to blow any second. Something about Father John already bothered him; this was going to set him off. Worriedly, she waited for John's answer.

'I don't know if he was a full-blown alcoholic,' John said softly. 'I know Caleb drank a lot. Though I'm not in a position to make a proper diagnosis, I'd say both of us were drinking way too much – especially at the end.'

'Well, then, you're a hell of a priest, aren't you?' Steve growled. 'Why weren't you doing your job? If he was drinking so much, why didn't you –? Never mind. I don't buy a word of this. I never saw my uncle drink a drop of liquor, not even beer. There's nothing in this house to drink it with, except water. There were barely ice cubes in the tray.'

Steve held back the urge to smash Father John in the jaw and rearrange his face. *Probably burn in hell for that*. He was two seconds away from suggesting that the good father had gotten Uncle Caleb soaked enough to sign away those forty acres when John spoke again.

'He drank whiskey straight from the bottle, same as me. It seemed more expedient that way.'

Steve banged the table with a fist. 'I don't like you at all. You're a liar, and I think your superior should be informed.'

'Monsignor,' Kiran and John said automatically.

Steve stared at Kiran. 'You're not buying this jive, are you?'

She shrugged. 'I found a full, unopened whiskey bottle in a kitchen cabinet.'

He only let that stop him for a split second. 'So? It was unopened. The good holy father probably planted it. You did find our uncle, didn't you? Wasn't your story that he'd made his way – staggering, if you're to be believed – to Sakina's grave? What was to stop you from planting a whiskey bottle to make it look like Caleb really was the drunkard you're implying?'

'Steve –' Kiran sounded weary.

'Actually, it was my whiskey.' John nodded at Steve. 'I'd come by to share a drink with Caleb, at the usual hour we liked to meet. After he was through with his morning farm chores.' John stopped and thought for a moment. 'But that day Caleb wasn't sitting on the porch. The door was shut and he didn't answer my call.'

'Probably afraid he was going to end up with a soused priest mooching off of him again,' Steve muttered.

'So I came inside and looked around for him. He wasn't here and the truck was parked, so I went looking for him.' He took a deep breath. 'I haven't touched a drop of liquor since then.'

'You have no need to, obviously.' Steve was untouched by the misery in John's voice. 'You got what you wanted.'

'When someone confesses, you're supposed to listen,' Kiran said softly. 'Will you just listen to him, Steve?'

He stared at her. 'He's feeding us a bunch of garbage, Kiran.'

'Does it matter if he is, for heaven's sake?' she snapped. 'He's suffering, too. He got forty acres. Big deal. Who cares if they just sat on the porch and got smashed once in a while? Uncle Caleb had someone who cared enough to come by.'

Unlike us. The words hung between them. Steve bit the inside of his jaw. Kiran was right. The crucial point was that Caleb had had a friend of some sort. Certainly no one else had stopped by to offer condolences to Steve and Kiran. It was as if Uncle Caleb had existed in a vacuum of endless land and relentless toil – and, quite possibly, liquor.

'Jeez.' He wasn't about to apologize, though he supposed he should. 'Order the pizza, Kiran. I need to drive for a while.'

He would think about everything in the car. Or likely he wouldn't think at all. He would drive fast, down County Road 147, soon to be Bluebonnet Lane, or something suburban-sounding if the city planners had their way about it. Speed was the only way he knew to shut out the demons that were beginning to lift the edges of his mind.

He couldn't let them in.

John shuffled the papers without looking up. Kiran reached for the phone, pausing when a loud booming erupted on the front door.

'Now what?' Steve muttered. 'I'll get it.' Probably the next group of local holy rollers coming to get their hands in the pie, too, he thought in disgust. Flinging open the door, he halted immediately at the sight of his father.

'We've filed a lawsuit against you and Kiran,' Butch said without preamble. 'We're just letting you know so you can be thinking about it. You have no right to shut us out of our brother's property.'

'Look at us standing out here, having to knock on the front door of our own brother's house,' Agnes whined. 'This isn't right, and we've found a lawyer in town who agrees.'

'That's what they're supposed to do, isn't it?' Steve shrugged. He felt Kiran at his back. No doubt the good father's ear was stretched out to hear every word as well. It wouldn't hurt him to know that his forty acres were in jeopardy.

'I never knew a lawyer who didn't agree with someone who was sitting on a pile of money.'

'We want our share,' Butch stated. 'One way or the other, we're going to get it.'

'I should at least get something for all those years I had to care for Kiran.' Agnes's voice was a thin, high-pitched wail that sent Steve's temper back into the red zone.

'Like you did a hell of a lot of caring for her.' He crossed his arms and dared her with his eyes to tell the truth.

'Well, I made sure there was food for her to eat.' Agnes puffed up with her own defense, tight curls quivering above her face with indignation. 'What else was I supposed to do? She wasn't my child. I didn't ask for her. And, by damn, she was the laziest kid I ever saw. All she ever did was read. She could have at least cleaned the house once in a while.'

Steve started to say that it was a damn lucky thing Kiran had been blessed with straight, even teeth or Agnes might have had to put up with a child who had a rabbit face like hers, and that would have been a real hardship, but Kiran pushed him out of the way.

'If the two of you have filed a lawsuit, then you shouldn't be here talking to us. All communication can go through our lawyers,' she stated, her hands on her hips.

Agnes started to protest, but Kiran held up a hand. 'No, don't say another word. You have a right to sue us, but that also means we don't have to talk to you except through counsel. That is *our* right.'

'Kiran, don't try to bluff me,' Butch broke in. 'I know you don't have a lawyer. You don't know what you're talking about.'

'So sorry to have to call *your* bluff, but we do have counsel.' She reached behind her and pulled John forward. 'As a matter of fact we were just going over some documents with him. So, as you can see, you've come at a very bad time. I'm sure you don't want to appear like you have *threatened* us, or engaged in any *ex parte* conversation.'

Steve listened in astonishment to Kiran spouting lies like a teapot. The thing that amazed him the most was that she sounded so sure of herself that even he believed what she was saying. He had a moment to enjoy the dismay on his father's moon-face and Agnes's rabbity one before Kiran firmly closed the door.

She angled an apologetic look at Father John. 'I

hope you can forgive me for dragging you into our family squabble,' she told him. 'You may be able to tell that our family tree isn't an All-American, apple pie variety.'

'I didn't know Caleb had any other family,' John said. 'Who were those people?'

'Our parents, if you can call them that.' Kiran met Steve's gaze for a split second. 'You said the will probably wasn't airtight. Can they get around Uncle Caleb's wishes?'

'I'm not certain.' John scratched his head.

'He doesn't know, Kiran! He's not a lawyer. Jeez, I can't believe you told Butch and Agnes that he was.' Steve paced through the living room, trying to decide if he was more upset by his father popping in again or Kiran's obvious respect for the priest.

'I never said John was a lawyer.' Kiran's tone was brisk and unapologetic. 'I said he was our counsel, which at this moment he is.' She put a hand on John's sleeve, which made Steve quit his pacing so he could keep an eye on what she was doing. 'I hope you can recommend a good lawyer in the parish.'

'I can certainly give you some names of people I trust.' John gazed down warmly at Kiran. Steve felt as if he were being left out of a conversation the two of them understood very well. He was feeling very out of sorts with his cousin.

'I'm going to get the pizza.'

Amazingly Kiran removed her eyes from the pretty-boy priest long enough to look his way. 'I haven't ordered it yet, Steve.'

'Well, order it. It'll be ready by the time I get there.'

He went down the hall to snatch his wallet from the dresser. Glancing up, he caught a look at himself in the mirror. Halting, he forced himself to look longer. His hair was disheveled, as if he'd been wearing a racing helmet. More emotions than he wanted to deal with had his brows pushed together, his eyes bloodshot. He forced himself to take a deep breath. In order, he mentally ticked off the things that were sending him off the track.

Butch and Agnes. They were yanking at his chain, but what was new about that? *I can handle it*.

Losing Uncle Caleb. Harder to cope with. He pushed that aside as a reasonable feeling and something he'd have to handle later.

John's revelation that Uncle Caleb might have been an alcoholic. Painful. Butch drank like nobody's business and was a mean drunk besides. Steve reminded himself for the thousandth time that alcoholism could be a choice, one he didn't have to make. He felt the breath coming easier. Uncle Caleb a drunk, like his brother, Butch? That hit a tender spot and Steve eased back. *Handle that new information later*.

Kiran. Lord, she was grinding him up like tires in a short track race. Was she flirting with that priest or was he . . . was he jealous? He picked at the word again. Jealousy. Lousy, time-consuming emotion. He wouldn't go there, wouldn't let it come in. Not handled very easily if allowed to exist.

He took a deep breath, shoving his wallet into the back pocket of his jeans as he headed down the hall. 'Come on, Kiran, let's go get the pizza.'

She paused in the middle of what she'd been saying to Father John. 'I thought –'

'We both need to get out of here for a while.' He wasn't going to let her protest. He didn't want to have to give any argument for why he didn't want her to stay at the house with a priest who looked like a calendar model. John Lannigan might have been Uncle Caleb's only friend, but he wasn't going to get that close to Kiran – not if Steve could prevent it.

CHAPTER 6

He was losing it. The second he realized he was treating John like a rival, Steve commanded himself to back off.

'Come on, Father,' Steve said. 'Since we've invited you to dinner you might as well show us where the pizza restaurant is. That is, unless we're keeping you from something?' he said hopefully.

'Nope.' John walked to the door. 'I'll be glad to come along.'

'Good. I think the three of us have some more we need to talk about, if Uncle Caleb's estate is going to be sued. I'm not certain, but I believe that may lock up his money and mean we can't rent this place out until the suit is settled,' Kiran said, walking out the front door.

Steve gaped. How in the hell did she do it? Her mind was always going forward. His seemed to be always stuck in warp. The good father followed Kiran out the door, and before Steve could react the two of them had piled into Uncle Caleb's old truck as if there was nothing more natural to do.

Setting his jaw, he went back and got the truck keys. Trying to tell the analytical part of his brain that it didn't matter that there were two perfectly good cars parked in the yard now, his and Father John's, and they certainly would have been more comfortable in one of those, Steve got into the driver's seat. Kiran sat in the middle, which was nice, because her bare arm brushed against his in a warm, sensually close way. Unfortunately John was on the other side, so he was enjoying the feel of Kiran, too.

Kiran. His cousin of sorts. His best female friend, the only friend who had known him since childhood. When she'd pushed him out of the doorway so she could have at Butch and Agnes, Steve had been shocked. He'd wanted to protect her. It seemed she didn't want his protection, or maybe didn't need it. He hadn't recognized the Kiran who had faced down their folks with confidence and daring.

Now he didn't recognize himself.

Steve backed up the truck, banishing the wistful image of Kiran and him in the front seat of a car, with John safely in the back seat. Out of range.

'Now that we're going to the restaurant, we might as well eat there. What do you think, Steve?'

He nodded. What the hell? It was hard feeling like the third wheel on a date. He supposed he should be glad Kiran had remembered he was in the truck, too. 'Fine,' he replied.

Instinctively he pressed the gas pedal hard as he

headed toward the wooden bridge. The truck obeyed, zooming across, roaring with the increased speed. Gravel flew under the tires, crunching loudly as the truck met the country road. Steve reminded himself to slow down, that this was not the time. Wind drifted in from the open passenger window, sending Kiran's hair flying around her face. She didn't seem to notice as she looked around the countryside.

'Do you know what Uncle Caleb's plans were for his crop?' Kiran asked.

'No. He was disappointed, of course, as most of the farmers around here are.' John pointed to some russet-colored cows on a neighboring property. 'That farmer is going to sell off most of his herd. With the drought, there isn't sufficient water for the animals to drink, nor is there enough vegetation for grazing. So many farmers are having to sell off that beef prices are the lowest they've been in a while.'

'Seems like it would be easier to sell to those builders.'

Kiran caught her hair in her hand and held it, which brought her arm within kissing distance of Steve's face. He couldn't believe that thought had popped into his mind. Pushing it away, he concentrated on getting to the end of the long white road.

'I don't think selling was what your uncle wanted to do. Not while he was alive, anyway. The man went with the land. He'd have been lost without it.'

'I can understand that.' Kiran thought about the mountains that encircled her, shielded her from the unpleasant childhood she'd merely waited out. She needed those mountains the same way Uncle Caleb had needed his flat yellow farmland.

'But he certainly hated this year's drought. I know it was sucking the energy out of him.' John pointed to the intersection up ahead. 'Turn right up there, Steve.'

Kiran sensed the unleashed emotions in Steve as he held the truck to a tight turn. He'd been silent the entire way. Seeing Butch had probably gotten him stirred up again, and the threat of a lawsuit hadn't helped. For a minute she'd been afraid Steve and his father might come to blows. She couldn't have borne that. So she'd stepped out to face Butch's and Agnes's venom, hoping that violence could be avoided. It had been easy to do after hearing Agnes brag about how well she'd taken care of her step-daughter.

The only person who had taken care of Kiran had been Kiran. Agnes's bald-faced lie was laughable. Kiran promised herself that, no matter what, she would see that Uncle Caleb and Sakina got to rest in peace.

Steve pulled the truck into a parking space in front of the restaurant and shut it off. Kiran hopped out the passenger side of the truck and Father John helped her down. Steve followed behind, telling himself this was all going to be over soon. He'd be on a plane tomorrow and away from all the agitation roiling through him.

Could he abandon Kiran to a nasty legal battle?

Would he throw out the white flag to Butch that easily? As brave a front as she'd put on, Steve suspected Kiran was vulnerable to Agnes and Butch in a united enemy camp. He warned himself to take everything one step at a time.

There was a booth available, so they headed toward it. Kiran slid in first. Immediately Steve slid in next to her. Hellfire! He didn't care if he did seem rude. It would be hard to eat if he had to look at the good father sitting next to Kiran all night.

'Good evening, Father.' An elderly lady stopped by the table to smile at him.

'Hello, Mrs Burrow. Heard from that niece of yours yet?'

She smiled as if he'd told a private joke. 'The honeymoon lasts for another week, if you can imagine. In my day it seemed like getting to drive to San Antonio for the weekend was enough of a honeymoon.' She winked at the father. 'You know how it is with these young people nowadays.' A benevolent smile was sent in the direction of Kiran and Steve. 'I just wanted to tell you again, Father, how much we appreciate you officiating at the ceremony. It was the nicest wedding I've ever seen.'

'I was glad to do it.' John nodded at her. 'Thanks for stopping by.'

The little old lady beamed. 'Goodbye.' She shuffled off, her happy thanks having pasted polite smiles on their faces. Steve wiped his off as soon as he realized he was smiling. He supposed they were going to have to spend the whole evening having their meal interrupted so people could tell the handsome priest what a good job he was doing.

'You're very popular around here,' Kiran remarked. 'We're lucky you had time to eat with us.' She put her napkin in her lap and smiled at John. 'We're lucky Uncle Caleb had you checking up on him.'

Kiran's words irked Steve. The priest might be handsome, and he might have every old lady in the parish feeling as if he was some kind of Adonis or something, but Steve still thought the man was strange. Kiran laughed at something John said, and suddenly Steve caught a glimpse of what was really bothering him.

He was used to being the star, the center of attention. He was out of the spotlight here. Not only that, but the only eligible woman around was paying attention to another man, when Steve was used to women drooling down his collar when Ginger couldn't beat them off. Suddenly his muscles relaxed in relief and he allowed himself to sit back in the booth and concentrate on the selection of toppings that could be ordered. Now that he knew that he was suffering from star let-down – and not jealousy – he could stop gnashing his teeth about John. He was having a typical reaction to being displaced from the limelight.

It didn't have anything to do with Kiran, nor the fact that she'd just pointed to something on John's menu. Out of the corner of his eye Steve saw their hands brush, though of course he wasn't really looking. Pulling his gaze back to his own menu, Steve told himself again that he wasn't suffering from that lousy, brain-rotting emotion called jealousy.

He just had to let it go and stop vying for Kiran's attention. After all, even if she was the only woman in the world, she wouldn't be the right one for him.

She was like a little sister to him, he told himself. They were family, after all.

That train of thought worked for all of two minutes – until John ordered pizza for Kiran.

Don't go there, don't go there, Steve reminded himself. *Think about Ginger*.

Didn't work. He'd never been possessive of Ginger, not even when he'd found out she was going out with a rival driver. He watched Kiran drink from a glass of water, her lips molding and coming away wet and inviting.

Not being consumed by jealousy was going to require more concentration than winning a four-hundred-lap race.

'I don't know if it's a good thing for me to do what you're asking, Jarvis.'

Bedford Harding, one-time mayor of Cottonwood, shook his head and tamped out his pipe on the porch of Andrews Grocery Mart. 'Maybe it's some old ghosts of guilt, or maybe I've grown a conscience in my old age, but I think you might stir up trouble by trying to buy the Dorn land.'

Jarvis scratched at his neck thoughtfully. 'I've examined every angle, Bedford. I can't think of any way something could come back to haunt us. It's been so long now. Not even a whisper of doubt has surfaced. I believe we scared that black woman so bad that she really did go off and never tell a soul.' He grinned evilly. 'Guess I scared the bejesus outta her by saying it'd be easy to shoot ol' Dorn off his tractor one day.'

'I can't believe she died without telling anyone. It's too easy.' Bedford shook his head. 'I'm probably superstitious, but with Dorn dying his people are going to be going through his things. How do you know that woman didn't leave a diary or something behind that's going to rear its ugly head?'

Jarvis stiffened, staring at his friend. 'You don't really think –? I mean, Dorn would have found it by now, wouldn't he?'

Bedford shrugged. 'I'm just theorizin'. Sides, I don't know that Dorn was in much shape to do much cleaning. Heard from some folks that he was out at the county liquor store pretty regularly.'

'Miserable old drunk.' Privately Jarvis liked a drink or two every now and again. But people like Dorn, who spent every cent they had on liquor, were white trash. Obviously that was where his money had gone, because he sure hadn't spent a penny fixing up the place. What an eyesore. Cottonwood would be better off when those richy big homes went up on that property.

Surely Bedford didn't have a point, though. The specter of his black deed coming back to mess up his plans hadn't occurred to Jarvis. There was no way that Sakina woman had left behind anything that would damn him. Yet it wasn't worth taking any chances, not when so much was at risk. Jarvis thought about the mortgage notes lying in his office drawer that he couldn't pay and slid Bedford an assessing look.

'You could go out to the Dorn place and make an offer in my place,' he pointed out reasonably. 'As a sort of broker, Bedford. Shoot, that would probably help everybody out. Those folks are going to be looking to sell, you could probably use a little pocket change, and I'd like to pick that land up before anybody gets wind of a "For Sale" sign going up.'

Jarvis crossed his fingers mentally. His plan was to make a below-market offer to the Dorn relatives, then turn around and sell it fast to the fancy builders who were anxiously scouting for more prime areas to develop. Cottonwood was in the thick of development fever, and he, Jarvis, could make a killing without ever having to put out a dime if his cards played right. He could get the cash from the builders and pay the Dorns, all by merely being in the right place at the right time.

'I don't know, Jarvis. I'm always looking to make a fast buck, but I want my name to stay clean. I don't have the lust for trouble like I did when we were younger.'

Jarvis didn't like the sound of that. 'Offering to buy land is a little different than wearing a hood over your head and holding a woman down, threatening to shoot her husband.'

Bedford glanced around him. 'You better pipe

down. Maypat's inside the store and she's got ears like antennae. Anybody in this town that wants to know anything, they go to Maypat. Lord knows, my wife practically can't have a headache without visiting Maypat on that rickety wooden stool of hers. Like a shrine with a Formica altar. Maypat says this, Maypat says that,' he mimicked. 'Damn, Jarvis, can't you tell your wife just to ring the groceries up without having to be the high priestess of Andrews Grocery Mart? I sure as hell don't want her telling my wife that we're thinking about cooking a deal on the Dorn land.'

'She'll do what I tell her.'

Jarvis let out a grunt of satisfaction. Maypat hadn't been looking well the past few days. Probably menopause or some other women's function was bugging her. She didn't seem to have the energy to do much of anything besides sit in that stupid room she called her china parlor. All full of knick-knacks and breakables as fragile as she was. Lord knows, if she started acting up, all he'd have to do was wave a crowbar around her pretty little china room and she'd shut up in a flash.

'Don't worry about Maypat. She's an obedient wife.'

'Well . . .' Bedford didn't seem too convinced. 'Let me think on your proposition, Jarvis. I could use some money, that's for sure, but I damn well don't cotton to spending my twilight years in a jail cell.'

Victory spread through Jarvis. Bedford was stalling, probably to get him to up his share, but he'd do what Jarvis asked – primarily because the ex-mayor had never been able to look a dollar bill in the face and say no to anything.

'You think about it, Bedford,' he said mildly. 'But if we're going to act on my little idea we want to do it before someone else gets there.'

Maypat backed away from the screen door without making a sound. Her heart was beating wildly, her mouth dry. Although Jarvis had warned her of his plan to acquire the Dorn land, it still washed panic over her to hear it discussed so casually. Maypat held a trembling hand to her forehead.

Old age, she told herself. *I should go get a physical. It could just be my blood pressure medication needs an adjustment.* She closed her eyes before sitting on the stool. *Jarvis is going to be the death of me, one way or the other.*

Maypat moaned at the errant thought. If he didn't physically harm her, as he'd intimated, the guilt he was stirring up inside her was going to send her into an early grave.

I'd have that in common with Sakina Dorn, she thought wearily. Jarvis would have killed them both, essentially. It was a true irony that Maypat and Sakina had basically nothing in common: one was white, one black. One a wealthy Georgia-reared belle, one a poor farmer's wife. One woman was in a grave while the other was alive, haunted by demons that were slowly, inexorably, sending her toward her own demise.

The only thing that linked them was humiliation at Jarvis Andrews' hands.

Maypat's hands clenched as they lay in her lap.

She wasn't a strong woman, by any stretch. But southern women before her had gone down fighting for their homes, their family. Sakina had bested Jarvis in her own way, whether he knew it or not. With her disappearance she had protected her husband's life. Maypat admired Sakina's strength of character.

She, too, had possessed strength of character – a long time ago. Before she had allowed herself to become cowed by Jarvis's overbearing and threatening personality. Before she had submitted to her role as his possession.

Steely resolve flowed through Maypat's veins. She could best her husband.

And, just maybe, by throwing herself on the pyre of Sakina's life, she could absolve a tiny portion of the shameful knowledge that she should have acted long ago.

CHAPTER 7

Kiran said goodnight to Father John and closed the door, telling herself she had to face being alone with Steve. What she really wanted to do was dump a bucket of ice-cold water over his head. He had been stiff and ungracious much of the evening, though he'd loosened up a little toward the end. John probably thought Steve was just being Steve, and likely hadn't noticed.

She, on the other hand, knew Steve wasn't being Steve – and it made her mad. Though she tried to excuse his behavior as normal for someone who had lost a family member, it was wearing thin. She, too, had lost Uncle Caleb, and still managed to put a smile on her face and go out of her way to be polite to a man who had meant a lot to their uncle.

Turning, she found Steve looking longingly at the telephone in the den. Obviously his whole stay in Cottonwood was getting in the way of his life. That thought made her bitter.

Kiran cleared her throat. 'I'm going for a walk.'

That pulled his attention away from the phone fast enough. 'Where?' Steve asked.

She wasn't going to share her private need with a man who had been acting as if he had as much feeling as an automaton. 'Outside,' she answered, her tone brief. There was no reason to reveal that she was going to have the long moonlit talk with Uncle Caleb she'd promised herself.

'It's dark outside.' He glanced at his watch, obviously concerned. 'Why do you want to go for a walk so late at night? It's after eleven.'

She hadn't realized they had spent that much time in the restaurant with John. It was late, she supposed, but Steve's attitude was making her bristle. 'What difference does it make?' she snapped. 'I haven't asked you to come with me.'

He started walking forward. 'Of course I'm coming with you. If you have a yen to go running around at this time of night, fine. But anything could happen to you out there.'

Kiran put out a hand to stop his forward progress. 'I'll be perfectly safe. I need to be alone for a while, Steve.'

He didn't stop, merely passed her to pick his keys up from the table where he'd laid them. 'I'll follow at fifty paces. You could step in a hole and break an ankle, or –'

He didn't finish his thought, and Kiran's protest died in her throat. She hadn't planned on walking far enough to feel unsafe. In a way it was kind of nice that Steve felt concerned for her well-being.

'I tell you what,' she said, eyeing him in a no-

101

nonsense manner. 'I promise to only stay gone for twenty minutes. If I'm not back by then, you can find me wandering around the family plot. Okay?'

Worry still shadowed Steve's face. She could tell he didn't really like her compromise, but would go along with it.

'I'll be back before you know it,' she said, walking from the room before he could think of another reason to accompany her. Her absence would give him time to make that phone call he was obviously eager to make and allow her to unsnarl some of the many thoughts in her mind that were crying out for organization.

Although it was late, the slight breeze was arid. The night was silent and very black, as if the birds and insects were asleep. Kiran shook off the unsettling feeling that she was very alone as she made her way down to the end of the property. Steve's concern for her safety sent a shiver tickling along her spine. Maybe it *hadn't* been the best idea to venture out. She'd been expecting at least a little moonlight, but the small orb in the far-away sky yielded little illumination. There wasn't a star to be seen. Kiran hurried onward, telling herself she was safe enough on her own land.

She halted, her ears picking up a sudden sound cutting through the unmoving, dense night. The fact that she was only about one hundred feet from Uncle Caleb's grave made the hair on her arms stand straight up for some reason. Straining to see and telling herself not to give into foolish jitters, Kiran moved forward. 'Just a bird rustling some leaves,' she assured herself.

But the sound came again about fifty feet later, easily heard in the grim silence. 'I'm going back to get a flashlight.' she muttered. 'Surely Uncle Caleb had one.'

Steve had been right. She had no business wandering around like this, even if she did need the quiet and solace the night would bring.

A movement in the darkness caught her eye. Kiran's heart began a deafening pounding in her chest. *Someone* was out there. And they were standing by the graves. She had a quick impression of slender height just before she decided she'd better retreat.

The unnerving sound of weeping erased any compulsion she had to run.

Uncle Caleb had another mourner besides Father John – someone who had not come to the funeral. Could not? Or would not?

At this end of the land, so far from the house, there was hardly any light. Still, Kiran crept forward a couple of steps, trying to identify the nocturnal visitor. Obviously a woman, by the sound of her sobs, and suffering heartfelt distress. The woman put her face in her hands and a veil of long dark hair swept forward. Kiran felt her own heart tear a little. Such true emotion for Uncle Caleb kept her from disturbing the trespasser.

That was what the woman was. A trespasser. Though Kiran didn't feel that she would be in any danger if she approached her. Still, the woman was grieving, and that was private. She could hear what Steve would say if he walked down here and found her chatting with a stranger over the graves. Uncertain as to what to do, Kiran turned to go back to the house – and bumped into a hard-packed chest. She sucked in a gasp even as two iron hands grasped her shoulders.

'Easy,' Steve murmured. 'I'm not a bogeyman.'

'Steve!' Kiran's voice was a strident hiss. Ignoring the sudden warmth of his chest, she forced herself to pull away rom his grasp. 'What are you doing?'

'I couldn't wait twenty minutes.' She felt his typical shrug and stepped another inch backward. 'I was worried about you strolling around out here by yourself. Can't be too safe, you know.'

She grabbed his arm as she remembered the woman. 'Look!' Her head whipped around as she pointed toward the graves. 'Do you see her?' she whispered.

'See who?' He craned his neck. 'I don't see anyone.'

'There's a woman over there.' Kiran pointed once more. 'She's standing by Uncle Caleb's grave.'

He hesitated a moment. 'Hello!' he called loudly.

The sound was earsplitting in the close, humid blackness.

'Steve – damn it!'

'What did I do?'

'You probably frightened her out of her wits!'

104

'Kiran, this is our property. If there's someone hanging around, they should be scared. We could have them hauled into jail. It wasn't Agnes, was it?'

'Oh, no. This person was grieving.'

He digested the irony of her answer before starting forward. Kiran stayed put for only a moment before she latched onto the back of his shirt and trailed behind him.

'There's no one here, Kiran. Just the two of us.'

'She was here a moment ago.' She released his shirt and walked past the graves a few feet into the darkness. 'Where could she have gone so quickly?'

A stray twig snapping under her feet made Kiran jump and quickly retreat to the safety of Steve's side. The woman's presence hadn't seemed threatening at the time, but now that she'd disappeared into thin air goose prickles were rising on Kiran's arms. She clutched her arms to her mid-section, and when Steve put his arm around her shoulders she didn't protest.

'If there was someone here, they're gone now.'

'There *was* a woman here, Steve. I didn't imagine this.'

He squeezed her shoulders. 'I'm not saying you did. Are you sure it was a woman, though?'

'Well, yes,' Kiran began uncertainly. Long hair didn't mean it had been a female, of course. But the trespasser had been tall, willowy. She remembered the urgent weeping and reiterated, 'Definitely a female.'

'What was she wearing?'

Kiran looked at the small chunk of marble head-stone at the top of Sakina's grave. Its color was a pale gleam in the night. By contrast, Caleb's grave wasn't marked. She took all this in with a sweep of her gaze as she thought about the figure standing alone, crying. 'I don't know,' she said softly. 'I was so stunned by the fact that someone was here and sobbing her eyes out that I only have a vague impression of her.'

Like a spirit, almost, she thought. *A lonely, mis-placed spirit.*

'I wonder who she was,' she murmured, allowing herself to sag against Steve's protective solidness.

'We'll probably never know.'

His tone was so practical that Kiran sighed. Maybe she was letting herself get too carried away by what she'd seen. 'Do you think Uncle Caleb had a girlfriend?'

The night was empty for a moment. Then Steve said, 'I seriously doubt it.'

'But why would she leave like that?'

'I don't know.' This time she actually did feel his shrug because his arm was around her. After a long moment, he said, 'Kiran.'

It was the tone that caught her attention. She looked up to meet his gaze, wondering if he'd spotted the woman. 'What?' she whispered back.

He hesitated, as if he debated the wisdom of speaking. 'You smell good,' he finally said.

'I . . . smell good?' Kiran didn't take her eyes from his.

'Yeah.'

That was all he said, but what he didn't say told her so much more. His eyes locked on hers in a penetrating stare that mesmerized her. Instinctively his arm tightened around her, and in that split second Kiran felt fire flash from his body to hers. There was a fusing, a melding between them that she recognized as physical. Distinctively hinting at the sexual. Where she might have mourned the loss of their innocent childhood friendship previously, she now felt the stirring of something stronger. Deeper. A connection that two adults might forge – if they chose.

She could not make that choice. Carefully she moved from the shelter of his nearness. 'Maybe we should call the police.'

'The police? For what?'

'To report a suspicious person on the property.' She didn't mean it, but, as she had suspected, her suggestion shattered the strange pulling force holding them.

'I don't want to do that. All you can report is something you thought you saw. That doesn't give them much to go on. Besides, calling the cops would just dump on more trouble that we don't need. I sure as hell don't need it,' he said, reaching out to take her arm. 'Come on. Enough haunting of the dead for tonight.'

He pulled her with him as he walked toward the farm house. She resented his uncharitable words, but suspected he'd said them to keep himself from wondering about the lady and what she'd meant to their uncle. She tended to agree that Caleb hadn't allowed himself to have another love in his life, but, whether Steve wanted to admit it or not, somebody out there had loved Caleb Dorn.

She had not imagined that.

So many thoughts were tearing at Steve that all he wanted to do was get Kiran safely back inside the house and lock the door. He'd known better than to let her go roaming around by herself in the dead of night. Sure enough, she'd managed to locate a specter of some kind hanging out on their property – which wasn't even surprising to him at this point. He didn't think he had a bone left in his body that could be surprised. What bugged him was that Kiran could have been in danger. Not that he was the paranoid type, but all anybody had to do was listen to the evening news to hear any kind of horror story about a woman, a child, or a well-known executive getting picked off – maybe worse.

'Damn it,' he muttered.

'What?' Kiran demanded breathlessly as he pulled her toward the house.

He wasn't going to spook her any more than she already was, but if Kiran really had seen somebody down there she might have been inches away from trouble. The thought made him feel queasy, a sensation he didn't like.

'From now until the moment I go back to California, I'm sticking to you like butter on toast. You don't even go to the store without me. Deal?' He pulled her inside the house, closing the door behind them and locking it. Crossing through the kitchen to the front door, Steve double-checked that door.

'I don't like your attitude.'

Kiran had followed after him. Steve glanced through the front curtains, not certain what he was checking for but needing the reassurance that somebody wasn't making themselves at home on their property. Or availing themselves of the hub-caps on Steve's rental car. 'Sorry,' he said briskly. 'I don't like my attitude either. It doesn't suit my *laissez-faire* approach to life.'

'You're such a smartass.'

Kiran left the room and went down the hall to her bedroom. Steve slumped into the easy chair in the dimly lit den. Tough. He didn't like having to take on a protector role any more than she liked being protected. But Kiran's tale had sent new worries into his mind that were more overwhelming than anything Butch and Agnes had threatened to do. What would he have done if something had happened to Kiran?

Damn it. Why was he attracted to her? Steve groaned to himself and leaned his head back. He had a huge problem now. He was caring *way* too much about her. It wasn't the sexual attraction he usually focused on a woman, that allowed him to distance his emotions. Not this time. He'd gone sneaking along behind her out of a sense of duty, because it was damn stupid for her to go running around in the dark when she could step in a gopher hole.

No. *He'd* stepped in a hell of a gopher hole. The minute he'd realized how close she might have come to . . . well, being kidnapped or worse, a rush of extreme fright had blacked out his brain. He was afraid of what he might have done if anything had happened to Kiran. Of how it would total him emotionally.

He was so afraid. He cared about Kiran and not in any cousinly sense. Right now he wanted to run down that very short hall and pull her into his arms.

She walked out of her bedroom and appeared in the den like a vision he'd just pulled out of his fevered imagination. Though a robe covered her down to her feet, little red-painted toenails winked at him. Her face, washed clean of make-up, was glowing. A refreshingly innocent ponytail held her blonde hair on top of her head. There was no pretense, no come-on from Kiran, and yet Steve heard the sound of a freight train loaded with lust as it rushed through him.

'I'm going to get a glass of water,' she said. 'Do you want anything?'

Steve kept his lips clamped together. He shook his head.

She shrugged. 'Fine.' Pausing to toss a glance at him over her shoulder, she said, 'Are you going to be in a snit all night?'

'Possibly.'

'Suit yourself.'

He heard the sound of a cabinet opening and the sound of water running. It stopped just as abruptly.

Steve braced himself for another barb from Kiran but she sailed from the kitchen down the hall. He heard a cheery 'Goodnight!' before the sound of a door closing. A sigh of relief escaped him. The woman could be a huge irritant, and it seemed she didn't even try that hard to be one.

Leaning his head back once again, Steve closed his eyes and commanded himself to think through the next logical steps. One urgent matter was verification of his flight plans. Snatching the receiver from the cradle, he dialed his crew chief's number. It rang briefly before being picked up.

'Mitch, it's Steve.'

'Steve! I tried to call you earlier. Guess you were out.'

Yeah. He'd been out, having dinner with his specter-raising cousin and Father Goodfellow. 'I was having pizza at what passes for the local restaurant.'

'Sounds like a rousing good time.'

Steve snorted. 'Anything going on out there?'

'Hell, no. It's quiet. Guess you'll make the race this weekend?'

'Yeah. I'm wrapping up here tomorrow and taking a plane out.'

'Are you sure?'

'There's nothing left to do that can't be handled by phone.' He pushed the thought of Kiran out of his mind. He couldn't hang around taking care of her forever. The memory of her panicked face made his stomach clench momentarily. Could she really have seen someone standing at Uncle Caleb's grave? He'd written it off as her imagination, but –.

'The local news station called for an interview today, so I'll set it up for the day before the race if that's all right.'

'Great. Anything else?'

Mitch hesitated for a second. 'I think Ginger's missing you.'

'Don't talk to me about her. Let's take care of business.'

'I'm serious, Steve. She's been calling, wondering when you're going to get back.' There was silence, then he said, 'You're not out there with some woman, are you, Steve? Ginger's got it in her head that you might be letting a lady-friend shift your gears and that's why you haven't returned.'

'I don't care what Ginger thinks, Mitch. She's had her fifteen seconds of fame as a track cutie as far as I'm concerned. Tell her to get off your back.' He pushed away the knowledge that he couldn't deny that some other woman was, in fact, shifting his gears. Kiran had him going at a speedometer-busting pace.

'Hey, I'm with you. I just didn't want to blow her off if you still, you know . . .'

'I don't, Mitch. I don't care who's taking her out.' He paused to get his mind onto more important matters. 'My flight's tomorrow afternoon, and I'm going to call and confirm that as soon as I finish talking to you. Can you pick me up at the airport?'

'Sure. What time?'

'I'm not certain. It's the only afternoon flight.' That would give him maximum time to tie up loose ends and maybe even convince Kiran to take a plane of her own back home.

'I'll check the flight schedule. See you, Steve.'

'Thanks, buddy.' Steve hung up and settled back again, satisfaction rolling over him at business being back to normal. Once he was out of Cottonwood life was going to be a hell of a lot smoother.

In another house in Cottonwood, Lakina was resigned to the full measure of her aunt's loving wrath.

'You've got better sense than that, Lakina Dorn!' The round woman had her arms on her hips and a frown on her face.

Aunt Gracie's rebuke was just what Lakina had expected. She had not expected her to be pleased about what she'd done. 'I have just as much right to grieve as anyone else.'

'Well, I know that, honey. But not out where you nearly got caught.'

Her aunt's lips were stiff with disapproval. Lakina shook her head. 'I thought this late at night was the best time to visit my father's grave. Since daytime hours are off-limits, and I can hardly go knock on the door and ask those people if they mind me tromping through the backyard to visit my mother and father, I thought at the very least a near-midnight visit could be forgiven me.'

'Ain't nobody to forgive you for nothing. It's a

matter of getting caught trespassing, and you oughta know that. They have every right to call the police on you, 'cause they don't know you from Sam.'

It hurt. Lakina hated the words she knew were true. 'They ought to know me.'

'They oughta, but they don't, and that was the way your mother wanted it. Don't go cussin' it now. It ain't gonna change nothing, especially now that your daddy's passed.'

Gracie took hold of her arm. Willingly Lakina allowed her aunt to steer her toward a chair. 'Sit for a minute. Catch your breath, and I'll make you a cup of decaf tea.'

'Something stronger, Aunt, please,' Lakina murmured.

'Oh, I plan on doctorin' it. Lord, I guess I should be thanking you that I'm not having to make a trip to the county jail to bail out my errant niece,' she muttered toward the ceiling. 'I'm grateful, Lord. I certainly am.'

Lakina felt a moment's guilt that she had caused Aunt Gracie concern. She hadn't meant to – had, in fact, intended to leave her out of her plans to visit her parents. Unfortunately, with her near run-in with the woman at the graveside, Lakina had allowed her long legs to make a speedy escape. Gracie hadn't missed the distress she had been unable to erase from her face – and she had pulled the story from her.

'I'm sorry, Aunt Gracie. I suppose I shouldn't have

114

done it. But how could I not?' She sat straighter in the comfortably worn chair that was one of a matched set in the cozy den. 'I shouldn't have to hide. That's my family out there. If I were anyone else, I'd be *expected* to show up at my father's funeral.'

'We went to the funeral, Lakina,' Gracie said mildly. 'We were there, even if we kinda camouflaged ourselves behind some trees. And I know what you're feeling, girl – that you got rights. Everything you say is true.' She set a teacup in front of Lakina. 'But it's just not possible, and that's what you gotta understand.'

'I don't want to. I've got a good mind to go marching up there and tell those people –' She stopped, remembering the woman with the unpretentious blond hair and the unsmiling man beside her.

'What would it change now, Lakina?'

Nothing. She knew that. Revealing herself would only upset people who hadn't done anything to her, who hadn't been the ones that set in motion the events that had taken her parents from her. Still, some righteous indignation inside her wanted to be recognized at last as Caleb Dorn's daughter.

Still, doing so would only bring questions, and grief, to two people who were already mourning. As strange as the late-night encounter had been, it had told her something she could not deny. That blonde woman wouldn't have been braving the darkness if she hadn't cared deeply for the man who was buried under the dry earth.

Lakina let that knowledge comfort her. Her father had not died unloved.

'Promise me you won't do that again, Lakina.' Aunt Gracie took a seat next to her, dark eyes begging for Lakina's word. 'If I could change the past, I would. But I can't, and you can't, either. As sure as the sun will rise in the morning, girl, I would give you back your family. But those same people who hated your mother are still alive, and I don't want them seeing you. I don't want them to know that they didn't succeed.'

She clasped Lakina's hands. 'Honey, listen, I'm old now. If anything happened to you, it would kill me. You know that. I promised your mother I'd keep you safe, and I have. And I will, but you gotta stay away from the past. Are you hearing me?'

'It feels like I'm letting them win, Gracie.' Lakina hated that the most. It wasn't the fifties anymore. There were still some attitudes of the old ways, but by and large the signs around the country that said 'No Coloreds' had been destroyed. Her mother might have been threatened by prejudice, but she, Lakina, had walked catwalks and posed for glamor shots.

She didn't remember everything about her mother that she wanted to. Crystal-clear in her memory, though, was sitting in her mother's lap on a bright spring day, noisy with the sound of children relieved to give up winter's chill. 'You have your father's eyes, Lakina,' her mother had said with a proud smile. 'Green as new spring leaves!' Then she'd hugged her tight, and Lakina had been glad there was a smile on her mother's face, even if it was just because she had green eyes. It was all Lakina could recall of that treasured moment.

The people who had threatened her mother did not deserve to live their lives without facing what they had done. It might have meant nothing to them, but it meant everything to her.

'Sometimes to win the war you gotta first win the battle.' Aunt Gracie released Lakina's hands and got to her feet. 'Maybe it's time I gave you something of yours.'

She went over to an old unvarnished table that was leaned up against a sagging bookcase, keeping it upright. Pulling out an old-style wood and metal post office box that had been converted to a bank and now served as a dusty bookend, Gracie fiddled with the combination.

'That was my piggy bank when I was little.' Lakina couldn't believe Gracie had kept it.

'Yes. And I told you then that if you saved your money you would have something on a day when you needed it most.' She pulled something from inside the bank and held out her hand. On top of the weathered brown palm lay a yellowed envelope with 'Lakina Dorn' written on it in faded ink. 'For over thirty years I've saved this. I don't know what it says, but I figured if anything in life was worth saving, it was your mama's words to her little girl.'

With suddenly shaking fingers, Lakina reached out and took the envelope.

CHAPTER 8

'Damn it, Steve! Wake up!'

He was being rudely shaken awake and he knew instantly he must be late for the race. Jack-knifing to an upright position, Steve rubbed the sleep from his eyes.

'I think someone's outside!' Kiran whispered in a frightened hiss.

Her voice hit him like cold water. He felt as if he'd been fighting to get out of a black cave, and sudden relief washed over him that he was in Texas and hadn't missed the race. His bleary vision darted to the gleaming nightie-thing Kiran was wearing. Though it was long, there was a distinct allure to it. Sleek and pink, the gown encased her from head to ankle in a sinuous curve of sex appeal.

'Steve – my God! Would you please get up? I think someone is outside!'

He shook his head from side to side like a waking bear, making certain he kept his gaze away from Kiran's body as he fought off the cobwebs of drowsiness. It was hard as hell to deny the instant urge to reach out and swipe her tempting body into his lap, but he made a heroic attempt to sound soothing.

'You probably heard a cat. Or a dog rooting around.' Slowly he maneuvered himself to a standing position from the chair.

'No! It didn't sound like an animal. I distinctly heard someone jingling something. Jingling keys, I think.'

'Keys?' He rubbed the sleep from his eyes. 'Why would anybody be jingling keys at this time of night?' He glanced at his watch. 'Excuse me. Morning.' Sleeping hadn't been too wonderful in that chair, but at least he'd been getting some much-needed rest. If he could calm Kiran down quickly enough, maybe he could go get in a bed and snatch that elusive sleep-world back.

'If it was a cat, it could have been wearing a bell on its collar. Or it could have been metal dog tags you heard.' That seemed like a credible answer to him. Satisfied, he scratched his chin and averted his eyes from her wide ones. They were damn blue in contrast to that sweetheart-pink gown.

'Maybe we should go outside and look around. In case . . .'

He didn't like that suggestion one bit. Eyeing the way the satin material smoothed over Kiran's breasts and hips like a second layer of skin he observed, 'I'm dressed more appropriately for scrounging around in the dark. You stay inside.'

'Are you sure?' Obviously catching the meaning

behind his wry tone, Kiran hurried down the hall, reappearing with the terrycloth robe she'd been wearing earlier. 'I never liked those women in old movies who cried, "Help, Help!" and expected the heroes to do all the work.' She slipped into the robe and tied it tightly. 'I'll go with you.'

'Oh, great. Even Humphrey Bogart got to be alone occasionally.'

She couldn't just be a good girl and go get back in her bed. The unwelcome alliance of Kiran's team spirit assaulted him again. He tried to shake it off as he dug around in a drawer for a flashlight. If he hadn't been a loner for so long, maybe he would have appreciated her attempts to help him. As it was, he just wished she'd wait inside while he whacked a few bushes to knock out the bogeys for her. 'No flashlight,' he muttered. 'Must be in the storage shed.'

He glanced at Kiran, who was anxiously looking out the window.

'We don't need a flashlight, I suppose,' she said.

Opening the front door, she went out on the porch. Steve followed quickly behind, not about to let her out of his sight while she was wearing so little.

'Who would have keys besides us?' she mused, apparently not expecting an answer from him.

They had gotten Uncle Caleb's keys to the house, storage shed and truck and put them on a single keyring when they first arrived at the house. It was the only set of keys they'd been able to find, and those had been in Steve's jeans pocket since they'd gone to dinner with John. From what they could tell of Uncle Caleb's lifestyle, he wasn't the type to have kept a spare set at a neighbor's house for emergencies.

'Kiran, you could have heard a car driving down the road. The car could have been dragging something.'

'No, it was more of a metallic noise, a clanking sound. Kind of a clink, maybe.'

'Cars clink.' With unusual superstitiousness, Steve swept that thought to the back of his mind. It was unlucky to invite any talk of cars clanking or clinking a couple of days before one of the biggest races of the season. 'I don't see anything out of the ordinary here.' He walked to the east end of the bushes lining the house, shot a glance toward the rental car, then shrugged. 'Let's walk around back.'

Together they rounded the house. The moon was just as dim as before, but Kiran had turned on some roof floodlights that illuminated the backyard area. 'Nothing here,' she murmured.

He peered past the rose bushes and walked to the opposite corner of the house. Though he didn't see anything, a strange sensation began prickling at his collar. Pausing, Steve scanned the grounds leading down to the graves. Though he told himself he was letting Kiran's late-night adventure get to him, he couldn't push aside the feeling that someone was out there.

Watching.

Of course, Butch and Agnes wouldn't think twice about spying on them, and Steve theorized that was the worst-case scenario. Kiran was nervously looking over the land as well, probably picking up the same foreboding vibes he felt.

She had said she had seen a woman down at the graves – been pretty damn convinced of it. Kiran was not given to flighty moments – the woman was solid as a rock. Warm night air, like a quick exhalation of breath, tickled the hair at the back of his neck. Steve felt his blood run cold. 'Come on,' he said, reaching out to Kiran. 'Let's go inside. Whatever it was is gone now.'

He wanted only to get her back inside the shelter of Uncle Caleb's house, where he could lock the door and keep her safe. Slowly, like a wild animal learning to trust for the first time, Kiran put her hand in his. Steve gave it a gentle squeeze. 'You're letting stuff get to you, Kiran,' he told her as they strolled back to the front. It was getting to him, too. 'Maybe it would be best if you flew back to Tennessee tomorrow.'

'Why? I have too much to do here.'

Even in the blue-black night he could see the determination in her eyes. His heart sank. 'I'm flying out to California on a late afternoon plane. You'll be here alone,' he said, trying to sound reasonable. 'There's really nothing else we can do right now, and I'd feel safer knowing you aren't here by yourself.'

Opening the front door, he waited for her to walk

in front of him. She brushed off the bottom of each bare foot before going inside, showing him a glimpse of slim ankle and a fast peek at the rounded tops of her breasts as she bent over.

'I can't leave.' Resolutely she marched inside. 'Thank you for checking around outside. Obviously my fears were unfounded,' she said crisply. 'I'll be able to go back to sleep now.'

Steve grimaced as he secured the door and made certain the gap in the musty-smelling drapes was closed. She might sleep, but he sure as hell wouldn't. Not now. Not while his imagination was grappling with what was under that sweet pink nightie the robe was hiding. If he could hold her, maybe he could convince himself that leaving her alone in Cottonwood was a good thing to do.

'Are you sure you wouldn't feel better if you had some company?' he suggested, with a devil-may-care smile he didn't mean. 'I can protect you a lot more effectively if we're together.'

'Steve Dorn, that sounds disturbingly like you're making a pass at me.' Her hands went to her hips, making the robe gape a little at the top. 'Are you?'

'Ah, no. Of course not.' Lack of finesse. Put the gear in reverse and try again. 'I'm just suggesting you might feel less frightened if you're not alone.'

A thin smile turned up her lips. 'To be honest, I'd be a lot more frightened if you were sleeping with me. And I'm a loud screamer, anyway. If any more ghosts try to scare me tonight, I'll just give a good, loud scream.' Her smile turned mischievous. 'I'm sure I'm in the best of hands.'

With that, she turned and left him standing there. Steve sighed to himself. Kiran was a hard case for sure. It was tough to believe she wasn't as attracted to him as he was to her, but if she was, she had steel will-power.

'Guess I might as well see what's on the late-night show,' he grumbled. 'What an uncompromising woman.'

If she wasn't frightened anymore, she was braver than he was. He gave up the idea of a bed and settled himself back into the uncomfortably old easy chair, hoping the fuzzy black and white images on the screen would put him to sleep soon. The damn woman had actually managed to give him a case of the willies. There hadn't been anyone outside watching them, except maybe a skunk or a possum. He closed his eyes against the grainy image of a late-night talk show host. With his foot he turned down the volume and told himself to relax.

Problem was, he couldn't stop thinking about Kiran. The worst part was that since she insisted on staying in Cottonwood he didn't think he'd ever be able to stop worrying about her. Definitely not good for a man who needed to be concentrating all his attention on winning this weekend's race.

This was the big one. Qualifying for this race was essential. He needed to prove that he was still king of the road, still capable of being in contention for the big points. At thirty-five, he'd spent a lot of years building a name for himself – a name sponsors could feel excited to link their product with.

Unfortunately he'd had a streak of less than top ten finishes this year. For some reason the younger dogs were beating the hell out of him on the race-track. Newer names were catching the media attention.

There had even been talk of him calling it quits. He had never thought of parking his race-car in the old garage for good, but without the kind of finishes that grabbed the limelight, Steve knew he was falling behind this season. Ginger hadn't been the first person to sense it.

He hadn't raced this week because he'd owed his presence to Uncle Caleb's memory. He'd risked a replacement driver for the team because it had been the right thing to do.

That was the last risk with his career he was going to take.

Kiran closed her bedroom door, allowing the façade of don't need-anyone to crack. Her heart was thundering. Though Steve had only given his suggestion to sleep with her a token feint at best, she couldn't help the rush of wanting that flooded her at the thought. The man was more than passing handsome – what woman wouldn't want to spend the night with a strong, hard-muscled guy like Steve? He could be charming – when he forgot his macho attitude. She could handle all that, because she knew Steve Dorn was a good man inside. What she couldn't bear to think of was being just another Ginger, whom he appeared to have forgotten with the changing of scenery. If she had another relationship with a man, Kiran wanted it to mean more than it would with Steve.

That was almost more terrifying than any monster she might have conjured up tonight. She got into bed, telling her heart to stop racing. Wanting to be more than a fifteen-minute love affair to Steve was just the top layer of what was stopping her, Kiran knew – if she was going to be honest. With herself, at any rate.

It was the shadows that stopped her. Shadows inside her that would be revealed if she allowed Steve to get too close. These shadows could not bear light. She could not abide for them to come out of their well-concealed hiding places. In a relationship of any kind secrets were bound to be discovered, no matter how well hidden they were. Steve was a perceptive man. He would find them, like a conqueror who sets his stake on land he claims.

Tonight there *had* been noise on the wind. She had not fallen victim to mere over-active imaginings. She had heard someone, whether they'd been jingling keys or what, she could not say.

What she could say was that the comfort of Steve's arms was only a hallway away. Though it would be far easier not to have to deal with her fear alone, she would not take those steps out into the hallway. She would not trade comfort tonight for the price that could only be pain tomorrow.

★ ★ ★

The house was still at last. Not silent, because that fool in the chair had left the TV on. From the crack he'd opened in the door, it was easy to tell the man was deeply asleep. His head had fallen back against the chair, his mouth wide open toward the ceiling.

Slipping from his hiding place in a hall closet, he congratulated himself on having the quickness of mind to go inside the house while the two Dorn relatives were outside hunting for intruders. They'd left the front door unlocked and he'd had only to crouch low on the porch and let himself in while they were around back.

'Course, for a minute there, when he'd caught his pants pocket on the thorns in the rosebed and his keys had fallen into the mulch, he'd thought he was doomed. The lights had flipped on, both inside the house and out, and Jarvis had known they were on the alert. The thought of having to flee and abandon his plan hadn't set well with him at all. But a smart man always looked for a way to turn disadvantage to advantage, and, sure enough, he'd been able to do that. So advantageous, in fact, that instead of having to pick a lock and break in he'd been able to slip into the house through an open door.

Noiselessly he padded down the hall. The woman would be asleep in one of these rooms so he had to be careful. He had to be smart if he was going to find what he was looking for. Bedford's idiot suggestion that the black woman might have left behind some diary, something that would damn him, had unnerved him to the point that he was unable to sleep.

Unable to think practically. He couldn't rest until he knew that his secret was safe and buried in her grave.

Some might say he should have waited until the relatives had left to break in. He didn't have the luxury of that kind of time. No doubt tomorrow the kin would go rustling through the pitiful stuff Caleb Dorn had kept over the years.

If they hadn't already. The thought of a jail cell made him break out in a cold sweat. No, they couldn't have done that yet. They'd only put the old geezer in the ground yesterday – on Tuesday. He knew from the local grapevine that they'd ordered headstones and gone out to dinner with Father Lannigan tonight. There was no time for him to wait and see what got dug up tomorrow.

Carefully pushing open a door that was only slightly closed, Jarvis allowed his hand to slowly relax on the doorknob. A closet door had been left open so a little light could shine into the room, and he could see the woman was sleeping like a baby. Obviously she thought the big baboon asleep in the den was capable of protecting her. Jarvis enjoyed a silent chuckle. These two were like helpless children. Anybody could murder the two of them where they were sleeping and there wouldn't be a clue left behind as to who had done it.

Jarvis's eyes narrowed. If he'd been smarter all those years ago he would have murdered that black woman instead of just giving her a good scare. Then he wouldn't be hunting through this smelly old house for anything she might have left behind. He'd be glad to get out of here. The whole place stank, reeked of Caleb and his dirty poverty.

The woman in the bed drew gentle, peaceful breaths. He watched her chest rise and fall, saw the peak of a nipple as it pressed against fabric. Maypat had looked like that once. Young and smooth and sleek – desirable to a man who wanted beautiful things to show the world he'd made it. Made it big.

His tide had turned somehow with the arrival of that black bitch. Into town she'd come, like some African queen to be revered. Regally striding into his market, Sakina Dorn would expect to be waited on. Carefully selecting her grocery items, as if she might find something of a lesser quality than suited her, she would then place her basket on the counter for Maypat to ring up her things. As if Maypat was a servant.

Just the memory of Sakina Dorn's uppity attitude made his blood boil all over again. Maypat had insisted that she didn't mind the farmer's black wife coming into the store. But Jarvis had. And he'd tried subtly to discourage her from coming, through veiled hints.

Of course, back then theirs had been the only place to buy food for a good thirty miles. Dallas was still a forty-five-minute drive away, with nothing but vast grassland in between. Still, she should have known she was unwelcome.

When she'd started phoning in her orders, Jarvis

had nearly come unglued. He'd flat-damn refused to take them. By heaven, Maypat was not going to take her grocery orders for delivery.

It was then that he and Bedford had put their heads together about what to do with the woman. Frankly she had been no different than any other misinformed soul that needed their proper place explained to them. In those days, Mayor Bedford Harding's word was law – and he had tough friends to back it up.

The woman stirred slightly, kicking the sheet lower. Jarvis's eyes darted around the room. A suitcase, a few clothes tossed over a three-legged table. That was all. This room didn't hold what he was looking for. He glanced one more time at the prone, angelic-looking woman. Maypat had laid like that for him, in pretty little gowns, letting her hair, long and blonde back then, flow over the pillow for him.

That was before he'd had his talk with Sakina Dorn. He had boasted of it to Maypat, unable to keep his excitement quiet after he learned the woman had left Cottonwood and gone back to whatever rock she'd crawled out from.

Maypat had never worn a pretty nightie for him after that. In fact she'd never slept in the same room with him again, claiming she would wake him at the early hour she rose to go to the market. He'd protested, to no avail. They both knew the real reason behind Maypat's change of heart. He'd lost her. She only stayed with him because of the southern palace he'd built for her. Or maybe she didn't want to go slinking back home to her Atlanta kin with her tail between her legs – a divorced woman whose marriage had failed.

Jarvis backed out of the room and crossed the hall to another. This had to be where Caleb had slept. It had a double bed and a dresser, no possessions sitting on top. Old-style venetian blinds covered the single window in the room. Quietly he opened the closet, not surprised to see only a couple of shirts hanging there. Two pairs of boots were on the closet floor, one caked with dusty mud, the other pair clean enough to wear to church.

The dress boots appeared to be the only expensive thing Caleb Dorn owned. Jarvis shook his head and shut the door. Well, well. The man *had* parted with a penny once in his life. Distastefully he eyed the bureau and opened a drawer. Underwear and socks. Another drawer was empty. The next one he tried was too. 'Bedford's got me riled for nothing. If she had left anything behind, the old guy would have come forward with it a long time ago,' he muttered to himself. It wasn't as if they had so much stuff that a stray diary might have gotten misplaced. Except for a few falling-apart furnishings, the place lacked even small decoration.

He expected the last drawer to be empty as well. It was the bottom drawer, and harder to get to, but he was surprised to see a dark object lying there. Slowly Jarvis picked up the cheap wood frame and held it to the miserly light coming in through the ratty venetian blind. Even in the dimness he could see the dark eyes and full slanted mouth smiling at him. Raising the blind slightly to let in more light, he looked into the sloe eyes. Her expression was confident. Taunting. Challenging him, even. Resisting the urge to smash the picture of the woman, Jarvis put it back in the drawer.

The bitch was trying to beat him. Trying to best him. He put it back and closed the drawer. Cursing under his breath, Jarvis stole back down the hall, casting one last look at the sleeping man now slumped in the chair, and unlocked the carefully secured door. Moving the door centimeter by centimeter, he went out, closing it behind him. For a second he stood on the porch, trying to get his breath. His heart pounded uncomfortably. That woman was trying to get to him. She was haunting him from the grave for what he'd threatened to do to her husband.

He shook off the thoughts. 'I'm starting to crack up,' he muttered. Heading off down the gravel drive, Jarvis sent a malevolent look back toward the shack. 'Bitch better not try to mess with me.'

Crossing the main road, he got into the car he'd left hidden behind an old deserted house. Not waiting for the car's engine to warm up, he shot it into 'drive'. 'If you're out there, Sakina Dorn, you know those two are like new pups. Easy pickings.'

A black cat or skunk ran across the road in the path of the car's dim headlights. Jarvis cursed. 'I mean it, bitch! You can't beat Jarvis Andrews. You shoulda learned that the first time. I'm gonna buy that land, and when I do, you and your sorry drunk of a husband are moving to the county graveyard.'

Hands flexing on the steering wheel, Jarvis drove on, satisfied that he had set her in her place. For good, this time.

CHAPTER 9

John Lannigan waited for the last parishioner to leave the confessional. He sighed wearily, though it was only ten o'clock in the morning. There was no reason for him to be so weighed down. Last night he'd had an enjoyable dinner with Steve and Kiran – enjoyable after Steve managed to unbend.

He couldn't quite put his finger on what Steve's problem was, but he suspected it might have something to do with John's vocation. Steve wouldn't be the first person to feel uncomfortable around a priest. Of course, priests were supposed to be able to inspire confidence and faith in folks, but occasionally a person didn't have that desirable reaction. As a priest, John wasn't always entirely comfortable with his social duties, either. But dinner with Steve and Kiran had made him feel fortunate to have people he could talk with about Caleb. He missed the old man.

Maybe that was what was making him feel so heavy this morning. He clasped his hands in his lap. Caleb had been of such salt-of-the-earth quality that John had admired him. Caleb hadn't been a happy man, but he had been a good man. He'd called 'em as he'd seen' em, and that was more honesty than some parishioners offered – except in the confessional. There it was up to them whether or not they were being honest. Caleb Dorn had been an honest man every minute of every day.

Liquor had merely kept him alive, John suspected. He'd been honest enough not to try to replace a woman who couldn't be substituted in his heart. Oh, technically perhaps John should have done some counseling on the dangers of too much drink, but Caleb would have only shown him the door. He had not wanted to make himself unwelcome, because Caleb's house had been just about the only place where he'd felt comfortable. A place where he could be just himself, simply a man with no better answers to life's questions than the wild-eyed preacher on the downtown street corner.

And that was the crux of the matter. He no longer felt like a man with a purpose. A man with a meaningful part in life. He'd been trying to force this issue of honesty with himself for a long time, which was why his parishioners had gotten off lightly today. They were being more honest than he was, and he couldn't give them penances when he was the one dodging a serious issue.

It was Caleb Dorn's passing that had made John realize life was short. It could be harsh with its brevity, but if a person didn't find fulfillment, death could be a welcome release.

He didn't want to live out his days like Caleb had. The man had chosen a solitary existence, the same as John, but with one major difference: for Caleb there had been only one woman.

John had his woman – the Church. He should be happy.

He was not.

Not anymore. The truth he'd been pushing away for months came searing into him like heat from hell, but he didn't flinch away from it. He wasn't serving anyone – not himself and not the Church – if his heart was no longer in his work. The strange emptiness inside him had eaten a hole in his feeling of self-worth. Prayer had not healed the wound. This was his life, his chosen love. Being a popular priest was a wonderful existence, but lately he'd had to drag his feet into the confessional to listen to people who were less fallen than he.

The sound of water running in the kitchen awakened Steve. He pushed himself out of the easy chair, rubbed at his eyes and stretched, then went into the kitchen to see what Kiran was up to.

She was already dressed for the day, wearing blue jeans and a lime-green blouse, cheerily dotted with dime-size white spots. Her hair was combed and sleek, shiny even in the dim light. As hot as it was in the house, Kiran looked like a cool dip in a pond, something Steve was beginning to desperately crave.

'You look like you had a good night's sleep,' he said, feeling grumpy about it.

'I did. For some reason I was able to go right back to sleep. I didn't move for the rest of the night.' She turned to smile at him, her lips soft and kissable with a hint of coral lipstick. Steve felt his heart turn over. 'Did you sleep well, too?'

'Uh, good enough.' Truthfully, the only way he could have managed a more restful night would have been sleeping with her. Pressing her close, holding her tightly to his chest would have been better than a sleeping pill. The likelihood of that happening was about the same as a dinosaur appearing in the kitchen. 'What's for breakfast?'

'Grapes. A soda if you want it. There isn't much to eat, but, since you're leaving, I don't see any reason to go shopping.'

She said it without any obvious attempt at trying to make him feel guilty, but he did. 'We could go scout up breakfast.'

'No, thanks,' she said, with a smile over her shoulder. Her hands never stilled at her task of washing out some glasses. 'There's no longer any reason for me to put off going through Uncle Caleb's things. I imagine there'll be some clothes and whatnot that someone in the parish could use.'

She stopped moving briefly, her hands clutching a glass in a dishtowel. Sadness dimmed the cheerfulness in her eyes. 'Well, Father John will know of someone, I'm sure. Plus the house will need a good cleaning before we can rent it.' She put the glass away and reached to pick up another, obviously determined to make herself approach the situation as practically as possible.

He didn't care much for the idea of going through Uncle Caleb's possessions, but it had to be done. Kiran was prepared to do it by herself. Steve scratched his head for a moment, calculating how much time he had before he needed to leave and catch his plane. 'I'll eat some grapes,' he sighed. 'But if we're going to clean out closets, we're eating at a restaurant with substantial food for lunch. That's my best offer.'

'I'll take it.' She shot him a pleased, if surprised, smile.

He spread his hands wide. 'No point in showering if I'm going to do grunt work. Where do you want me to start?'

'In Caleb's room. I'd stack up all the clothes in one area – put things that can't be folded on top of the bed. We can get boxes while we're out and haul them down to the church in the truck.'

'Yes, ma'am.' He made a brief pit-stop in the bathroom to brush his teeth and slick down his hair before going into the last bedroom on the hall. For a moment he stood there, watching the dust particles ride a shaft of light coming through the torn blinds. 'This house is going to need more than a good vacuuming,' he grumbled. 'It's going to need paint. It's going to need a lot of help . . .'

His voice trailed off as he gently tugged the string rope and drew the blinds up. The airy dust particles flew away; a pane of cracked glass met the morning heat of the sun. It was glaringly apparent that the house had not been cared for at all in a long time. 'Why, Uncle Caleb? Why? You could have sold some of this expensive dirt and lived better. You didn't have to have nothing.'

Sudden tears sprang into his eyes. He lightly pounded a fist against the wall. *Why didn't I take a little bit of time out of my schedule to see him? The only person who ever thought talking to me wasn't a waste of breath.*

Caleb had been the only positive father-figure in Steve's life. And he'd died lonely and abjectly poor, a fine repayment for all he'd done for Steve.

'Damn,' he breathed out on a ragged sigh. Slowly he allowed the blinds to fall back into place. Allowing himself to indulge in regret wasn't going to solve anything – nor get the job that he'd been assigned done. Crossing the room, he opened the closet door, his jaw going slack. 'This sure won't take long.'

Gathering up two pairs of boots off the floor, he placed them on the bed. 'If it can't be folded, it goes on the bed,' he repeated Kiran's instructions. 'Those couple shirts and jeans can be left hanging, I guess –' he shut the door again '– and that's that. Someone's whole life practically cleaned up in less than ten seconds. Damn it. *Damn it!*'

He pressed his fingers to his eyes for a minute, before walking over to open the bureau drawers. All five drawers were cleaned out quickly, socks and underwear stacked neatly on top. Bending down, he jerked the sixth drawer open, tentatively reaching

139

inside. 'Holy Christmas!' he muttered to himself.

Lifting out a picture frame, he admired the beautiful woman staring back at him. The image would have been clearer with more recent photography, but there was no mistaking the life in her eyes, the bold confidence in her smile. He felt his mouth move into a silly grin. Jeez. Just looking at the woman pulled a smile out of him.

'Kiran!' he shouted.

'What?' she shouted back.

'C'mere!'

He heard her footsteps on the worn carpeting in the hallway. 'What is it?' she asked, coming to stand beside him. 'Oh, my,' she breathed, 'Is that Aunt Sakina?'

'I doubt he kept any other woman's picture around.' Steve flicked some dust off the cheap frame.

Kiran took the picture from him to examine it closely. 'Why do you suppose he never showed us this picture? I mean, he talked to us about her occasionally. Why not show us this picture? I always assumed he didn't have one. Heck, I remember thinking as a child that they must not have had cameras in the fifties.'

'Not only did he not show us this picture, he didn't even keep it out for himself. It was in the bottom drawer.' Steve nudged it with his toe.

'Well, maybe it hurt too much.' Kiran placed the frame on top of the bureau. 'Father John said that he found Uncle Caleb lying on top of her grave. He was suffering, Steve. Maybe it was just too much to look at this picture and remember what they had.'

She was always bringing up John. Steve hated how it made his heart clench inside his chest. The guy was okay, for a priest, and the mention of his name shouldn't stir up anything resembling jealousy inside him.

For some reason it did. Steve told himself to put a leash on it. They had bigger issues right now than his insecurity. 'What are we going to do with it?'

'Oh.' Kiran looked stunned for a moment. 'I hadn't thought of keeping anything in the house, but obviously that's a keepsake.' She thought for another minute. 'Um, I don't know. We never knew her, you know, so the only reason I'd want it is because of what she meant to Uncle Caleb.'

Sakina watched them from the picture, her dark eyes sloping with amusement.

'But it doesn't feel right to keep it, either,' Kiran finally continued. 'I wish she had some family we could send it to.'

'There wasn't any.' Steve was clear on this. 'If you recall, Uncle Caleb said that when she died he buried her on his land so she could be close to him because he was her only family.'

'Is that the way he said it?' Kiran's voice was soft with remembering. 'Or was it that he buried her here to be close to him because *she* was *his* only family?'

'Whatever.' Steve was tired of talking about it. He couldn't bear to think of Caleb's loneliness. 'Let's decide about the picture later.' He turned to point to the bed. 'As you can see, everything is sorted in here and ready for boxing.'

'Good.' Kiran was back to sounding military-orderly. 'If you don't mind, go find the nearest liquor store and bring back some boxes. We're going to need about ten, I should think.'

'Should I ask Father John where the nearest liquor store is?' He couldn't help the barb, since Kiran seemed to think John was the fount of all knowledge.

'That's right – this is a dry county,' Kiran said thoughtfully, ignoring his sarcastic tone, for which Steve was supremely grateful.

Shut up, he told himself. *Jealousy is for jack-asses and you're working up to jack-ass potential.*

'They probably had to drive into another city for liquor. Your time might be better spent asking at Andrews Grocery Mart in case they have any cardboard boxes they don't want. If that doesn't work, the church is close by. Stop in there and ask John if he's got any ideas. I'm sure he'll be happy to suggest someplace.'

Kiran blithely left the room, unaware that her casual reference to the priest had jabbed at Steve – or rather at the jealousy he was desperately trying to talk himself out of. He rolled his eyes, glancing back at Sakina's portrait. She was still smiling that sultry, knowing smile at him.

142

'I'm in big trouble here,' he told her. 'Big, ugly, better-get-out-of-here-fast trouble.'

She kept smiling.

Steve had gone to Andrews Grocery Mart. Kiran continued cleaning up the kitchen, washing counters and sorting through what could be left behind for renters to use and what should be donated. She appreciated Steve's efforts to help out, since she knew he would rather be having a bad day at the track than doing this. Pausing to look out a back window that desperately needed some soap and a rinsing with the garden hose, Kiran allowed herself a moment's sympathy for Steve. Never in her life had she seen anyone so racked by guilt. He didn't have to say it for her to know that was what was eating him.

That little fake attempt at seducing her last night hadn't fooled her in the least. She sent up a murmured prayer for some peace to soothe Steve's soul. If anyone needed it, he did.

Instantly the tall woman who'd been weeping at the graves flashed into her mind. That person needed peace just as desperately. For the thousandth time she speculated as to who the mysterious visitor might have been. Kiran supposed they'd done the right thing by not reporting the incident, but she couldn't help wishing the woman had stuck around. She would have liked to talk to her. It was an odd piece of the puzzle that simply refused to fit in any reasonable scenario.

After a moment she decided she would go outside and make an attempt to clean the windows lining the back of the house. The rose garden could probably use some watering as well.

Either of those chores would refresh her. Suddenly she needed to be outdoors, soaking up some sunshine and fresh air. It was hot and stale inside the house, and cleaning out cabinets was a dusty chore. She opened the door and walked down the porch steps.

Since it was only mid-morning, the heat hadn't hit its strongest intensity. The back of the house was warm now, with most of the sun hitting the east side, but later in the day this side of the house would be the only shaded spot. She took the dishwater soap and put a little into the bucket at the side of the door. Turning on the water, she filled the bucket with frothy, clean bubbles, then aimed the chill water at the dirtstreaked windows.

Purposefully she set the hose down where it could water the rosebed while she scrubbed a window. It felt good to be outside, hearing the mockingbirds scold and an occasional airplane flying overhead. Kicking her shoes toward the porch, Kiran picked up the hose and rinsed her feet, sighing at the welcome coolness. When her toes started feeling too cold, she pointed the hose toward the window, watching as the dirt and soap melted down in bubbly rivers.

'Hey! I thought you were packing,' Steve said as he opened the door. He came out onto the porch wearing a mock glare on his face that didn't fool her for a second.

'I needed a break.'

He watched as she put the hose down and started on another window. 'This qualifies as a break?'

'Yes. I'm just going to do these windows and then I'll get back to work inside. Did you get the boxes?'

'Not yet. Andrews wasn't open, and I wasn't in the mood to hunt John up yet.'

She sent a tiny spray of water his way. He held up his hands.

'I can see you're going to be little or no help,' she complained in a good-natured tone.

'It's not my fault if no one is minding the till at Andrews. The sign says they open early in the morning.'

'Oh, well. We can drive out at lunch and check around somewhere else. Why don't you go inside and call to put an ad in the paper to sell Uncle Caleb's truck?'

'Sell his truck?'

Steve looked confused, so she sent another little squirt of water his way. 'Wake up, Steve. I know you haven't had a shower yet this morning, but you may get one if you don't start paying attention.'

'Don't you dare, Kiran Whitley. Turnabout would only be fair play, and the idea of wetting you down is mighty appealing.'

She ignored him and focused on smearing the last window with soapy water. It was a little trickier, as

145

it was close to the rose bushes and she wanted as little soap as possible to get near the plants.

'In case you've forgotten, we can't sell anything if Agnes and Butch have filed a proper motion against the estate.'

'Damn it!' she said uncharacteristically. 'I forgot all about that.' Maybe her time in Cottonwood *was* being wasted. Maybe she *should* go on home, since Steve would no longer be around to . . .

To what? Keep an eye on her? Protect her? Nobody had ever done that. She told herself not to let the situation with Butch and Agnes make her retreat into some needy shell.

'We have no reason to doubt them. I'm sure they'll do everything possible to make us miserable.' Kiran picked up the hose again, suddenly thankful that this was the last window. The fun and enjoyment had gone out of it.

'You really ought to go back home to Tennessee –'

A soapy sponge in the face cut off his preaching. 'Hey!' He wiped his face and glared at her. 'Why won't you listen to reason?'

'*Your* reasons,' she interjected. 'You have your reasons and I have mine.' She didn't say she was starting to doubt what she could accomplish if Butch and Agnes were determined to meddle.

'Have it your way,' he said. 'I'm going to take a shower.'

She took a deep breath as he turned to go inside. 'Have it *your* way,' she retorted, turning the hose on his back full-blast.

The satisfaction she got from the square hit lasted only a second. He leaped from the porch, wrested the hose from her grip and spewed water down the back of her shirt.

'Steve!' she shrieked, laughing. 'Stop!'

'No way. We'll shower together, cousin.'

She pushed at his chest, trying to get him away from her, which only served to give him her arms to hold on to. Without mercy, he moved the hose to her head. Cold rivers of water streamed into her eyes.

'You –! Steve Dorn, you're being a pain the butt!' she cried through the hair and water blinding her vision. 'You've made your point! I give up!'

The water ceased. 'Don't you like showering with me?' he asked, his grin mocking.

'No, I *don't*!' she said, heaving all her weight into him and knocking him down on the ground that had turned muddy beneath their feet. Straddling his chest, Kiran tried to point the hose toward his face, but Steve was too quick. Tossing the hose to the side, he grabbed Kiran, rolled over and pinned her.

They paused, each panting a little.

'Your face is dirty,' Steve told her. 'I believe your hair is, too. Let's take another shower together.'

She wanted to wipe the smirk off his face. 'Get off.'

'I'm comfortable where I am, thank you.' He pressed the length of his body against hers for emphasis. 'Are you comfortable?'

'Hardly,' she gritted. 'Of course it's hard to be comfortable with an overgrown jock lying on me.'

He looked offended. 'I never thought of myself as a jock. Are you insulting my intelligence?'

'Not in the least.' She spat the words. 'Only a *smart* man would risk injury to his body parts by lying on a woman who is smarter than he is!' Grabbing the hose from where it lay pooling a small river beside them, she sprayed it full into his face, taking the opportunity to wiggle away from him as he fought her for it. Giving up the hose willingly, she sprinted for the porch. 'I'm going to take this shower alone. Turn the water off, will you?'

She screeched as he ran toward the porch. Letting herself in, she locked the door behind her, knowing full well he had a key but that by the time he fished it out of his soaking jeans, she'd be safe behind the bathroom door.

'What a child!' She listened to him yell at her through the door. 'I mean, of all the childish things to do,' she muttered, completely disregarding the fact that she'd started the water fight.

' "Turn the water off".' Steve mimicked Kiran under his breath. 'No conscience, no sense of fair play.' Besides which, she was going to use up all the hot water getting the mud off her.

Steve turned the water off and rolled up the hose, carefully putting it back next to the rosebed. For one second he allowed himself to enjoy the beauty of the well-tended, colorful roses, before he gently broke off a couple of the more spectacular ones. Hell, the woman didn't deserve a peace-offering, not with that stunt she just pulled, but they'd make the house smell good and what the heck – they would die eventually anyway. They might as well be inside where Kiran could see them if she was so damned set on staying in Cottonwood.

One flower slipped from his hand. 'Ouch!' he exclaimed, feeling a thorn prick his palm as he instinctively clutched the rest of the bouquet. Bending down, he reached for the deep red rose.

Lying next to it in the mulch was a key.

Kiran had said she'd heard keys jingling last night. Denial spread through him, but the key did not disappear.

He had not believed her.

She had been right.

CHAPTER 10

The key made a clinking sound as it slid against the other keys in his jeans pocket. Kiran's fear stirred in Steve's memory. She had said she heard a clinking sound outside her window. Steve went into the house, stopping at the kitchen sink to wash his hands. It was a coincidence finding a key lying in the rosebed. It had to have been Uncle Caleb's.

Steve dried his hands with a paper towel, deep in thought. He could no longer ignore that there were too many strange incidents for his comfort. Most likely the woman Kiran claimed she'd seen and the key were unrelated, but the acute sense of timing he saved for the raceway kicked into high gear. That sixth sense that warned him to ease up at certain times or hit the wall was now on red-alert. Kiran could not stay in this house alone. He could not allow it.

If something happened to her, he would feel . . . responsible.

Steve crumpled the paper towel in his fist and leaned against the kitchen counter. He took a deep breath. *No. I would never forgive myself is more like it. It would hurt worse than anything in my life – as miserable as that's been.*

Of course it would hurt him if anything happened to her. She was his cousin, his childhood friend.

He stared at his running shoes, which were spattered with black dirt. He took another deep breath. Nothing was going to happen to Kiran.

Why take the chance? his conscience asked. He didn't like the ominous meaning behind the question.

'Even if I wanted to take her with me, what reason would I give?' he asked his conscience out loud. 'She's too independent to think she needs protection. She thinks she can handle anything and anybody.'

She had jumped right in to snarl at Butch and Agnes, defending Steve as if he needed it. She had also tried to best him in a water-wrestling match, as if she hadn't known that pitting herself against his greater strength and size was useless.

Kiran doesn't think about what might happen to her.

She didn't like heroines who threw up their hands and waited for someone to save them. She would do the saving herself.

'I've got to get her out of here,' Steve muttered.

Sudden pounding on the front door jolted him. 'Handsome Father John, no doubt,' he said, going to the front door and opening it.

A young man who was trying to look important

stood on the porch. 'I have some papers to deliver to Steve Dorn and Kiran Whitley.'

He was wearing a courier's uniform. Steve eyed him, sensing trouble. 'I'm Steve Dorn. What papers?'

The kid held out a brown envelope. Steve saw a law firm's name printed on the label and shook his head. 'I don't think I want that.'

'Nobody ever wants what I have to deliver,' the kid said morosely.

'Oh, come on,' Steve said. This entire little squatty town was filled with weird characters, right down to the little old cashier at Andrews Grocery Mart who'd stared at him as if he was a ghost. 'If you don't like your job, get one delivering flowers.'

'I wouldn't make as much money,' the kid responded.

'That's a hint if I ever heard one.' Steve dug in his pocket, grabbed out a stray dollar and handed it to him. Without pausing, he swiped the envelope.

'You have to sign for it.'

Steve took the pen he was offered and scrawled a signature.

'Thanks. You've made my day.'

'You're welcome.'

The boy left without thanking him for the tip, so Steve assumed he hadn't gotten as much as he'd hoped for. Going back inside, he tore at the envelope. Nobody ever got as much as they hoped for, it seemed, as these papers clearly stated.

Kiran entered the room, bringing the scent of shampoo and soap with her. 'What's that?'

'A soap opera script.'

She leaned close to peer at the papers. 'I've never liked soap operas myself.'

'Well, you're starring in one now.' He read down a few more lines and cursed violently.

'What's the matter? Isn't your part as big as mine?'

He shot her a black look. 'Our folks want to have Sakina and Caleb moved to a real cemetery. Apparently, their case is that the bodies are buried illegally.'

'Lots of families choose to use their land for burial, especially if it's been in the family for a long time.'

'They don't care. They want everything Uncle Caleb had. Obviously the graves are inconvenient, especially for selling off the land. What a stinko mess.' He sank into the easy chair in the den, still clutching the papers.

'How can they sue us for Uncle Caleb's entire estate if he wanted us to have it?'

'All they have to do is find a lawyer who has time on his hands and who doesn't mind filing the papers and showing up in court. He collects a fee and doesn't give a damn whether his clients win or lose. We, meanwhile, end up fighting for what we were given in the first place. The irony is that we don't want it.'

'Are we going to fight?' Kiran's voice was soft.

Steve glanced at her. 'What the hell does that mean?'

She shrugged. 'You didn't seem that willing to fight in the first place. I remember you saying that I'm more tied up in this than you are.'

He jabbed a finger in her direction. 'You got warmed up faster than I did. But I've never backed down from a challenge before, and it won't be now, Kiran.'

'Even though it's your father?'

'Especially since it's my father!' He was getting mad.

'But you're leaving.'

'Yes, I'm leaving –'

More knocking on the front door stopped what he was about to say. 'Now what?' he demanded, jumping out of the chair to practically rip the door off its hinges.

The elderly man on the porch was so startled that he nearly fell off the top step.

'I'm sorry,' he said, putting up a hand. 'If I've come at a bad time –'

'It's always going to be a bad time. How can we help you?' Steve's voice was too frosty to indicate anything more than impatience.

'My name's Bedford Harding. I know this is awkward, but I've come to inquire as to whether any of the land in this vicinity would be for sale.'

'How the hell would we know? Do we look like realtors?' Steve felt Kiran's hand on his arm, subtly indicating he should take it easy on the old man. He was too irritated right now to pay attention to her.

'I apologize. I *have* come at a bad time.' The old man backed down the steps.

'Wait.' Kiran stepped around Steve. 'Sir, we apologize. We've just lost a member of our family, and aren't quite ourselves just yet.'

She shot a warning look at Steve. He rolled his eyes to the sky. He should have let her open the door to the courier, too, since she was in the mood to socialize with everyone who knocked on it, he thought sourly.

'I'm sorry for your loss, ma'am. In fact, I had heard of your situation, which is the purpose of my visit. As bad as my timing is, I did think to save you from some grief.'

'How?'

The man stepped forward, obviously glad to speak with someone more reasonable than Steve. Steve crossed his arms and glared at the guy, just to let him know that Kiran might be doing the talking but he was still listening – and in charge.

'It has been mentioned to me that with the two of you being from out of town you might be interested in selling some of the land hereabouts. If that were to be the case, it would save you some time and trouble to avoid going through a realtor.'

'I see.' Kiran nodded.

'I do, too. You want to make an offer before a realtor has a chance to overprice the land.' Steve raised an eyebrow.

'You make me sound like an ambulance-chaser,'

the man protested. 'The offer I wish to make is fair and at market value.'

'It's not for sale.' Steve was firm about this, despite the just-a-minute look Kiran shot his way.

'Why don't you just leave us your phone number –?' she began.

'As the lady said, we're not quite ourselves right now.' He reached out and grabbed Kiran by the arm. 'We're not considering selling, now or in the future.' He pulled her into the house and shut the door.

'That was rude!' Kiran was infuriated.

'He was pathetic, trying to take advantage of our ignorance. No doubt he hoped we'd be so confused and grief-stricken we'd sell out at a price guaranteed to have him laughing all the way to the bank.'

She put her hands on her hips. 'I don't like you acting like you've got all the answers. We could have at least taken his number down.'

'Why? We're not selling.'

'I'd rather sell to him than let Agnes and Butch get their hands on Uncle Caleb's land.'

Steve's jaw went slack. 'What are you saying?'

'If they get the land, Caleb and Sakina lose the place they picked to rest in for eternity. I'd do anything to not see that happen.' Her eyes began to glisten with moisture, as if she wanted to cry but was trying not to.

'Oh, Lord. Oh, Lord, don't do that,' he said.

'Why not?' She looked at him, her blue eyes huge as she made an obvious effort not to let the tears fall.

'Crying seems like an entirely appropriate thing to d-d-do right now. So why shouldn't I?'

'Because . . .' He put out his palms helplessly, trying to think of a good answer to a question he hadn't anticipated. 'You just showered. It's hot in here. Crying will just make you all hot and sweaty.'

The tears spilled over. Steve felt like hell.

'I can't help feeling b-b-bad about everything,' Kiran said, crossing her arms in front of her. 'We might not be able to do what Uncle Caleb wanted us to. I'd rather sell to a stranger than break the trust he had in us.'

'I –' Steve was stumped. What he wanted to do was take Kiran in his arms and comfort her, but that seemed like a dangerous thing to do. It might upset her more. The best thing he could do for her was give her a solution.

He was fresh out of them. 'Listen, that man was trying to rip us off, Kiran. He was probably going to buy us out and turn right around and sell to those fancy builders down the way, reaping a healthy profit margin. He sure as hell didn't look like any farmer or rancher I've ever seen. And don't let these papers get you all upset, either. Agnes and Butch can't do anything to us, or Sakina or Uncle Caleb. We're in the driver's seat.'

'You think so?' She looked hopeful.

'Hey, worst-case scenario – we spend a lot of money in legal fees defending what is ours. So what? It was money we didn't have in the first place. We wouldn't have had it without Uncle

Caleb leaving it to us. So why should we let this worry us?' He reached out and gave her shoulder a squeeze. 'Haven't you ever heard that the good guys always win?'

'Not in the courtroom. Lots of good guys finish last.'

He was a little shocked by her statement, and he didn't have a ready rebuttal for it. 'Well, letting all this upset you isn't going to stack the odds in your favor. Why don't you let me do the worrying for a while?'

'I'm not sure you'll do it as effectively as me, that's why.'

A smile tried to seep onto her face but fell miserably flat.

He'd had all he could take. 'Kiran, like you said a minute ago, you don't like it when I act like I've got all the answers. And I don't. But I think you should come to California with me.'

'California?'

'Yes.' He hurried on before she'd could start arguing. 'You won't go home. You can't stay here. You need a vacation. So you have to come with me.' He amended that quickly. 'You should come with me.'

She cocked her head. 'No. I'll just go on home until the fall-out from Agnes and Butch has sub-sided.'

He couldn't believe her quick capitulation. It was too easy. Narrowing his gaze, he said, 'When?'

'I'll see about getting a flight now. Maybe you can

drop me off at the airport, which will save me taxi fare.'

'I can drop you off.' Just to test her sincerity, he said, 'Why don't you start packing your stuff? I can call for some flights for you.'

'I'd appreciate that.' With a wipe at her eyes and a last sniffle, she left the room.

'Just like that,' he muttered, staring after her. 'No argument, no debate.' He would have liked to give himself points for getting her to succumb to his common sense, but he knew better. Dialing a number for one of the few airlines that flew into Tennessee, he managed to get the last seat on a plane. It would leave her waiting at the airport for only an hour after his flight departed.

'Let me think about it,' he told the reservations clerk.

'You don't have long to think about it. The flight leaves at six-fifteen,' she told him.

'I know. I'll call you back.' Hanging up, he jammed a hand through his hair. After a long minute of hard thinking, he walked down the hall into the room where Kiran was.

Her back was to him, a suitcase open before her. She didn't sound as if she was crying anymore, but he couldn't help noticing that her shoulders seemed very slender under the white blouse she was wearing, and possibly slumping a bit. The sassiness that he liked about her had changed to compliance. He hated that. It wasn't her fault that everything about Uncle Caleb's estate was a mess.

I have a feeling it's going to be a difficult thing I'm asking of you, but if ever there was a man up to the challenge, it's you. I'm going to enjoy the fight.

Caleb's words jumped into his mind. So far Kiran had taken the brunt of the fight. He locked his jaw for a moment. It was out of character, and he probably wasn't going to like it very much, but it was time to give Kiran's team spirit thing a try.

'Kiran,' he said.

She turned, her hands clutching the shabby robe. 'Yes?'

'I got you a flight.'

'Thank you.' She turned back around.

'I want you to come to California with me instead.'

She whipped around, her eyes astonished. 'Why?'

'I'd like to show off for you. Hell, maybe you'll even bring me good luck and a top five finish.' He shrugged and tried to act as if he wasn't laying it all on the line when he was. Wherever it took them, right now he wasn't ready to let go of her. 'Come on. Walk on the wild side. Let me take you to California. After the race we can come back here and tie up loose ends.'

'Okay.' She turned back around.

He was so startled by her acquiescence he didn't know what to say for a moment. 'Okay?'

Now she shrugged. 'As you have pointed out before, I'm on summer break. California or Tennessee – right now it's all the same to me. I could use a vacation. But I won't sleep with you.'

She said it so calmly he had to take an extra

second to process the fact that she was referring to sex. 'Sleep . . . with me?' he repeated, just to be certain he'd understood her meaning.

'Yes.' She faced him once more. 'No sex under any circumstances.'

He started laughing. 'I wasn't planning on it, but now that you mention it –'

'No sex.' She was adamant. The laughter died out of him.

'Kiran Whitley, you have an exaggerated opinion of yourself,' he told her, ignoring the sting to his pride.

'Runs in the family.' She snapped her suitcase closed. 'I'm ready if you are.'

Suddenly he wasn't so sure he was ready for a weekend with his too-attractive, suddenly-sassy-again cousin. The key he'd found in the rosebed burned in his pocket. He had to do this whether he was ready or not; he couldn't leave her here alone. 'I invited you, didn't I? I'm ready. But, since you brought it up, does that mean you've thought about having sex with me?'

'Yes. After all, you've mentioned it a time or two. I've heard that the power of suggestion is strong, but it's not strong enough in this case.' She paused, not taking her eyes from his.

'I'll be in a race car most of the time, and exhausted the rest, so you're barking up the wrong tree. But if it makes you feel better I promise not to even mention sex to you this weekend. No power of suggestion from me.'

She cocked an eyebrow at him. 'Don't be so huffy. It's not that you're not attractive, or that I'm not attracted to you. I'm just not at a place in my life where I can handle something like what we'd have.'

He took her suitcase from her. 'I think I heard some distrust injected into that sentence, but I have to shower and we have a plane to catch. Forgive me if I can't debate what we would have, since we're not going to.'

'I'll make sure all the windows and doors are locked while you shower.' She waited for him to leave the room in front of her.

'I'm glad you're coming with me,' he told her softly. 'Even if we won't be sleep-mates, I promise I'll show you a good time.'

Her eyes were big and blue in her suddenly pale face. He sensed she was debating the wisdom of making the trip with him. He could tell her that if he wanted to make love to her, he wouldn't have to rely on the power of suggestion to get her into his bed. They would get there together, both of them willing.

But the purpose of this trip was to keep her safe – and to take care of her for a weekend. It was a small thing to do since she'd just about worn herself out trying to solve the dilemma they were in. To allay her doubts he grinned, reaching out and tousling her hair in a brotherly fashion. 'Don't worry, Little Red Riding Hood. I promise not to eat you, or even take a bite.'

She snorted and pushed him out of the room. 'I've fended off bigger wolves than you.'

He laughed. Maybe she had, but that didn't matter. What counted was that she was feeling comfortable enough again to give him a hard time. As long as she was sassing him she felt in control of what was simmering between them.

He'd keep his hands off her on this trip, if that was what she wanted.

He'd keep his hands off her, but it wouldn't be easy.

CHAPTER 11

'I'm telling you, Jarvis, I don't want any part of this scheme. I went over and did you a favor, but that Dorn boy is plain nuts. He's as crazy as the old man was.' Bedford Harding waved a hand in a circular motion around his head.

Jarvis narrowed his eyes as he speculated on his friend's words. Bedford stood straight as an arrow on the porch of Andrews Grocery Mart, and he hadn't relaxed in the five minutes they'd been hashing this thing. Bedford hadn't been the type to cut and run before, not where profit could be made, but he sure was backing out fast this time. He couldn't figure out what had got Bedford going so bad. Shoot, Jarvis had walked right into the house while the two Dorn kids were sleeping like new babies. The Dorn boy hadn't appeared so menacing with his mouth hanging open while he slept.

Still, Jarvis knew Bedford was caving on him big time, and he sure as hell couldn't tell him he'd walked right into the Dorn house as if he already owned it.

Some placating might be called for. 'Aw, Bedford, don't you think you're letting your imagination run away with you? How tough can a city kid be, anyway?'

'Plenty. He damn near bit my head off.' Bedford paced the length of the wood porch. 'He didn't cotton to me at all, nor what I'd come to say. I say forget about it, Jarvis.'

'You never had skin as thin as a chicken's before, my friend. We done plenty of other things that required more nerve than this.'

'Yeah.' Bedford came back to face him. 'A long time ago. I want to be able to enjoy my grandkids without worrying about them visiting me in jail.'

'How can you go to jail just for making an offer to buy some land?' Jarvis was becoming put out with Bedford's lack of guts.

Bedford shook his head as he stepped off the porch. 'I don't know, but I ain't gonna find out. It's quitting time for me, Jarvis. You'll have to figure out a way to get what you want without including me in the plans.'

He walked to his car, leaving Jarvis to simmer in his own juices. He *was* simmering, too. Bedford wasn't going to be any help – and that he'd never forget. What he had to do now, though, was think up a way to run the Dorn kin off – and soon.

At the airport, Kiran waited beside Steve in the pick-up lane for his crew chief to give them a ride. She could tell Steve was looking forward to getting to his house, and probably back to his life, since he'd become more intense, more engaged on the plane than he had been in Cottonwood. Most likely tension was running high inside him because of the race, too.

She was looking forward to seeing Steve in his natural element. Spending this time with him, watching him race, was something she'd be able to put away in her box of good memories to cherish for ever.

'Where is he?' Steve muttered. 'Come on, Mitch. I've got stuff to do.' He squeezed Kiran's arm gently, as if to reassure her about his edgy mood. 'He should be here any second.'

On cue, a smart white convertible pulled up in front of them. The window rolled down and a gorgeous redhead leaned across the passenger seat to call, 'Hi, Steve!'

'Ginger! What are you doing here?'

Kiran thought Steve's slack jaw and unwelcoming expression would disconcert the redhead who'd obviously expected a different reception from him. She waited quietly, trying not to bring attention to herself, praying that some coincidence was at work and this wasn't their ride.

'I told Mitch I'd pick you up, honey. Get in.'

'Uh . . .' He glanced uneasily at Kiran. 'I . . . ah –'

'It's all right, Steve,' Kiran interrupted. It was clear that he was evaluating her reaction to this turn of events. The feeling inside her was agonizing, and characteristic of acute jealousy, but she told herself to swallow it. Getting through this uncomfortable moment as fast as possible meant it would be over that much sooner. 'But if you don't mind, I'll sit up front. I tend to get car sick if I sit in back,' she murmured.

She didn't know what had possessed her to say such a thing. It was as if her lips had spoken of their own accord and declared a big, fat whopper that the Lord surely would mark on her slate. But she hadn't come to California to sit in the back seat and watch some stunning woman run her hands over Steve.

'Well, okay,' Steve said, obviously trying to figure out if Kiran sitting next to Ginger was a good idea. 'Ginger, this is my cousin, Kiran Whitley. Kiran, this is Ginger Foxworth.'

Steve opened the door and Kiran slid into the front seat, casting a no-nonsense stare at Ginger. 'Yes. I remember talking to you on the phone. It's very kind of you to chauffeur us, Ginger.'

Behind them, Steve tossed the luggage in and squeezed in beside it, his knees poking through the gap in the space between the front seats. Ginger glanced from Kiran to Steve in the back seat, her face an incredulous mask of what's-going-on-here?

'Cousins?' Ginger repeated. She gave Kiran a thorough once-over before looking back toward Steve with a smile that didn't quite contain pleasure. 'Not kissing cousins, I hope.'

Kiran turned, her eyes meeting Steve's. He stared at her, his green eyes hooded. There was a long, tense silence in the car. His expression was wary, but not of her. Wary because he knew. She didn't look away, because suddenly she knew, too. The playing rules had been set up and agreed to before they ever got to California.

They had agreed there would be no sex, but kissing hadn't been declared out of bounds. Ginger's question had inadvertently brought something out into the open that hadn't been decided off–limits. Kiran would be thinking about kissing Steve. He would be thinking about kissing her. They would both be wondering.

All because of Ginger, who from the frozen expression on her face was hoping kissing was the last thing on their minds.

Suddenly Kiran was convinced of something: he might have kissed Ginger many times, but he wasn't thinking about that anymore. He hadn't kissed Kiran yet, but it was definitely on his mind now.

Yet Kiran's lifestyle was totally different from the one Steve and Ginger had in common; it would be a mistake if Kiran allowed anything physical to bubble to the surface where she and Steve were concerned.

'Well, hey,' Ginger said with a fake congenial laugh, 'I didn't mean to upset either of you. I was just making a little joke, like I do all the time. Don't I, Steve?' she asked, adjusting the rearview mirror so she could see his face before she slid the little car out into traffic. He made a noise of some kind, but it wasn't intelligible.

Kiran turned her gaze to the passenger window,

watching cement highway and plants and trees go by that were very different from what she saw in Tennessee. The uneasy silence stretched out longer.

'So, what made you decide to come to California, Kiran? Steve didn't tell me he was bringing anybody back with him.'

She heard the purposeful emphasis on their relationship in Ginger's words and told herself to overlook it. The situation wasn't any more awkward than anything she and Steve had been through in the past couple of days.

'I have some time on my hands.' Kiran was non-committal. 'I've never seen a race, so when Steve invited me it sounded like a good thing to do.'

'Oh. How nice.'

From Ginger's tone Kiran could tell the woman was still searching for the meaning behind her accompanying Steve.

'Did everything go well with the funeral, Steve?'

'It was fine. Thanks for asking.'

Tiny furrows appeared on Ginger's forehead, perhaps from concentrating on traffic, but Kiran suspected they had more to do with Steve's formality. It was clear – maybe even embarrassingly so – that he wished his crew chief had met them at the airport instead of Ginger.

'Well, you didn't miss much here,' she went on brightly, determined not to let Steve's curtness bother her. 'The weather stayed the same, the parties were boringly the same, there wasn't even any new gossip to kick around.'

169

'Really? Mitch told me Dan Crane cracked up his car.'

The tension in the car was electrifying and instant, even to Kiran, though she didn't know who Dan Crane was.

'Oh, Dan.' Ginger gave an airy little laugh and waved a manicured hand in dismissal. 'He made a stupid miscalculation. He'll be all right.'

'Is he racing this weekend?' Steve's voice held more than simple curiosity.

'Why, I wouldn't know, Steve. I haven't talked to him,' she replied, sugar-coated.

'That's not a very nice way to treat someone you're supposed to be going out with.'

'Oh, Steve, that was just . . . that was just – I don't know. Stars in my eyes or something. We only went out a couple of times, and it was never serious.'

Not like it was with you. Kiran heard the underlying message in Ginger's words and felt herself blushing. The woman was very obvious in her pursuit of Steve – so obvious as to perhaps miss the fact that he wasn't interested anymore.

Or was he? Was his bored façade for Kiran's sake? She told herself not to think of that. There had been no mistaking the fire in his eyes at Ginger's mention of kissing cousins. Her hands clasped tightly in her lap, Kiran tried to ignore the tautness in the car and the subtle messages being tossed around in a conversation that didn't include her.

'You should bring Kiran over to swim in my pool,' Ginger invited. 'We could barbecue on the beach.'

Kiran closed her eyes. There was nothing she'd rather do less, except perhaps be forced to eat dinner with Agnes. She hoped Steve wouldn't swallow the bait.

'Thanks, Ginger. But I imagine we're going to be pretty busy.'

'Oh,' she said, pulling up in front of a house with a huge yard. 'Well, here you are.'

Steve got out, taking the bags with him. 'Thanks.'

Kiran was getting out of the car, but she didn't miss the plea in Ginger's words.

'Aren't you going to invite me in, Steve?'

'Thank you for the lift,' Kiran interjected hurriedly, taking her bag from Steve as she walked around the car to stand at his side. 'It was nice meeting you.'

Ginger glanced from Steve to Kiran, then back to Steve again. 'You, too,' she replied, apparently realizing she was unwelcome. 'I hope I see you this weekend, Steve. Good luck in the race.'

'Thanks,' he said again. He took Kiran's arm, turning her to propel her away from the car. 'Bye.'

He didn't let go of Kiran until they were on the porch and Ginger had driven away. Then, taking hold of her chin, he turned her face up so their eyes would meet.

'I didn't know she was coming to the airport.'

'I know that.' Kiran recognized sabotage when she saw it. Ginger had picked Steve up, hoping to have a captive audience and rekindle whatever was missing in their relationship. Kiran's presence had

171

altered Ginger's plans substantially. 'I hope my being here isn't a problem.'

'That's what I want you to understand. I wouldn't have invited you if there was going to be any problems. I invited you because you need a vacation, and this is my way of saying thanks.' He paused for a second, his eyes alight with some emotion deeper than what his words were expressing. 'I wanted you to come with me, Kiran.'

'For protection?' she teased, referring to Ginger. She hoped a humorous approach to their being alone together would break the odd spell that had come over them during the ride.

He laughed and unlocked the door. 'Yeah, cousin. I wanted you here to protect me.'

She walked inside the house in front of him, hearing the door close with a tingle of nerves. Uncertain, she paused in the hallway. Steve set the bags down, reaching out to turn her to face him.

'So who's going to protect you?'

Steve felt like an ass the minute he spoke. The reason he'd had Kiran come to California was so he could keep her out of harm's way. What he'd said, though he'd been trying to respond in the same light-hearted manner she'd used, had sounded ominous. As if she needed protecting.

From him.

He swore to himself that he would not let anything happen between them. Slowly taking his hands from her shoulders, he started to apologize for his remark.

'I can take care of myself, Steve. You know that. So,' she continued brightly, 'this is your place. Very masculine.'

'Kiran, hang on a sec. I think we should get this straight.'

She turned curious eyes on him, but he read the stiffness in her posture. He had made her feel ill at ease.

'Get what straight?'

He blew out a breath. 'I'm sorry. I shouldn't have said that. We set up our terms, and I'm happy with them. What I said – well, I know it sounded bad, but I let my mouth get away from me. You and I can be the best of friends.'

She never took her eyes from his, their light blue gauging him with uncompromising distance. 'I don't want to be best friends,' she said softly. 'I had a man for a best friend once. It didn't turn out well.'

Steve let his mind race while he tried to think of what she was referring to. Him, maybe, and the friendship that had gotten away from them? 'I guess you'll have to let me know what you expect, then. I thought being just friends would appeal to you.'

'It's confusing, isn't it? We have these feelings we're both noticing, and no easy fit for them.' Kiran smiled, but her expression was somewhat sad.

He scratched at his neck. 'Yeah. Maybe you should call the shots and fill me in so I don't mess up this weekend for you.'

She picked up her bag and walked down the hall.

Steve watched her cautiously. 'Which room is mine?'

'The one you're standing in front of.' He hesitated, afraid that she was going to ignore his suggestion. The truth was, he needed her to map out where they were headed – or things might turn more complicated than they already were.

'Thanks. This is nice.' Kiran carried the suitcase inside the room. 'I'm going to change my clothes.'

He bit the inside of his jaw. Apparently she wasn't going to be much help. Walking to the room she'd disappeared into, he stood in the hallway and called, 'So, is this discussion finished?'

'I think so.' Her voice was muffled, as if she was pulling something over her head. Steve told himself not to think about Kiran undressing less than ten feet away from him. 'Nothing's going to happen. You're safe.'

'I –' That wasn't what he'd been worried about. 'Damn it,' he muttered. The woman didn't want to have sex with him, she didn't want to be friends – he snapped his fingers. Kiran was trying to act as if they weren't going to see each other again after a few days. That was what had her tuning him out. He could live with that. He even understood it. 'I'm glad I'm safe, because I sure hate to get hurt,' he told her, reaching for the same tone she'd used in teasing about her protecting him.

'I know.'

What the hell did that mean? Steve decided the conversation was going nowhere. She wasn't going to give up any information and he was going to spend the weekend stepping on emotional mines. Fine. It would keep him sharp for the race.

He started to head down the hall toward his room. A shower was what he needed to clear out the Ginger-Kiran web in his head. Between those two females he could hardly think straight. Unbidden, his curiosity poked at him. He turned back toward Kiran's doorway.

'About the man you were best friends with . . .'

There was no sound for a moment. Then, 'Yes?'

'Why didn't it work out?'

She didn't answer immediately. Steve had just about given up hearing the answer when she said, 'I suppose it didn't work out because we got married.'

Steve's jaw dropped. Kiran came out into the hallway, dressed in a long blue wrap skirt and a long-sleeved white eyelet blouse. Part of him noticed at once how lovely she looked, but it was totally overruled by the ringing in his ears. 'You got married?'

'Yes. To someone I loved dearly – as a friend. And because of that, I lost him.' She reached out and touched Steve's cheek with a feather-light finger. 'Are you all right?'

He felt as if he was in a maze, where everybody could find the exit but him. There was pain from out of nowhere, and from the last person in the world he'd expected to hurt him.

Lakina Dorn stood in front of Andrews Grocery Mart, trying not to let anger and bitterness overtake her. She could not stop it. The emotions washed over her in waves, waves so chilling that she felt as if poison was running through her veins. The little white store, with its country-fresh appeal, was a façade for the evil that lurked inside. She sucked in her breath, feeling her mother's letter crinkle in her hand.

I write this so that one day you will understand how much I love your father. Perhaps when you are grown and have children of your own. I can pass this letter on to you as a way of explaining the past. All of the people you read about will be long dead by the time you hold this letter in your hand, so the names won't mean much to you, not even your own father's, I suppose. Lakina, your father was the kindest, funniest, most lighthearted man I ever knew. He simply had no prejudice in him. But there were others who held hatred firmly to their hearts . . .

Lakina halted the memory, trying not to let herself feel any pain. It was impossible. She had known the sharp taste of envy for too long, and the disquieting beckoning of her father's love that she could not claim. Her mother had believed that she would live to see Lakina grow up, never dreaming that there would be neither mother nor father for her child. She had been robbed of both her parents and part of her past. The people who owned this country market and the impressive house on the hill behind it had robbed her as surely as if they'd stolen into their home and murdered her parents.

I cannot blame Maypat so much, because I think she didn't know the evil her husband and his friends intended. She did not speak to me the last time I went into her store, and I knew then something was wrong because she'd always been as kind to me as any other customer. But I've always wondered about Maypat after the night her husband came and threatened me. Did she know what he was doing? Would she have cared?

Her mother's words lacked the icy anger that was freezing Lakina's heart. Perhaps her mother had written the letter in a calmer state of mind, after the shock had worn off and she'd reconciled herself to the decision she'd had to make.

Lakina knew she would never be reconciled to the past. Even the chance to grieve at her father's burial had been stolen from her. The words on this paper were intended to be a cleansing, soul-searching explanation, meant to heal scars after the people who'd inflicted them were long deceased. The irony was that her mother had handed Lakina the very way to see that these people finally had to face up to the wrong they had done. They should be torn from their comfortably wealthy, élite lifestyle and put in jail to suffer in disgrace.

With one hand clenching the letter in her pocket, Lakina stepped onto the wooden porch of Andrews Grocery Mart and slowly opened the door.

CHAPTER 12

Maypat looked up from her task of putting cans of tomato sauce on the shelf. 'Be right with you!' she called cheerily.

'Take your time,' a female voice replied.

Maypat smiled as she finished up. She was feeling better today than she had in the last week. Finally the dizziness and spells of weakness had passed, leading her to believe that perhaps she had merely been suffering from a virus – and not from the dark guilt stabbing at her conscience as she'd feared.

'Hello! I'm Maypat Andrews. What can I do for you today?' she said, stepping around a display to greet the newcomer.

The woman stood quietly without smiling, as if she was only taking a break from the merciless heat outside, but her moss-green eyes stared at Maypat with something more than simple curiosity. Maypat's heart began beating uncomfortably. The cold, clammy feeling that had plagued her for a week swept her again. She put a hand to her chest, wondering if she was going to faint.

'Are you all right?' the woman asked, but Maypat reached out and felt for the Formica countertop behind her, stumbling around it to her stool.

'I'm fine,' she replied weakly, though it wasn't true. The beautiful woman standing in front of her could have been a ghost. Had Maypat not aged enough in the thirty-some years since Sakina Dorn had died to know that the two of them would probably share wrinkles symptomatic of their age, she would honestly think this woman had come from the past to haunt her.

'I'm fine,' she repeated. 'It's the heat, you know. I should insist my husband install a better cooling system, but he says hot flashes are all that's bothering me.'

She tried to smile reassuringly, but couldn't. The customer didn't smile, either. Maypat swept her hair away from her forehead with a trembling hand. 'Anyway, is there anything I can get for you?'

My father. The words screamed through Lakina's mind. *You can get my mother back. You can get my past back.*

She shook her head. 'I'll just borrow one of these baskets from you.' Picking up a red shopping basket, Lakina carefully watched the old woman. For a moment she'd thought the old woman was going to keel over. She wanted to talk to her, confront her, get some answers for God's sake – but she'd taken one look at her and gone pale as flour. Even now Maypat's terrified stare was pinned on Lakina, as if she expected her to attack her.

This wasn't the way she had planned their confrontation. Lakina blindly looked over packages of noodles and cans of soup, trying desperately to gird herself to get the answers she'd come for. Unfortunately, the friendly old woman had stripped her of some of the righteous cloak she'd armored herself with. After a few moments she realized she would have to leave and return another day. Grabbing a box of rice from a shelf, she hurried over to the counter. Maypat sat fanning herself, but the instant Lakina appeared at the register she straightened.

'Will that be all?' Maypat asked quietly.

'For now,' Lakina replied, just as softly.

Maypat made no move to press the register keys. Instead, she stared at the box of rice. Very slowly, her gaze lifted to meet Lakina's. The two women stared at each other for what seemed for ever.

'That will be a dollar-fifty,' Maypat finally said, never releasing Lakina's gaze from hers.

Lakina held out two dollars. Maypat didn't look at the money. She kept staring as if she were hynoptized. 'I can't take your money,' she murmured.

'Why not?'

The old woman shook her head as if she couldn't clear it. 'You're a first-time customer. It's my way of saying . . . of saying –'

Lakina stared, worried that the woman might be more ill than she was letting on. Still, it wasn't her concern. Why should she feel sorry for her?

'I have to pay you.' Lakina placed the money on

the counter, snatched up the box of rice and turned to leave.

'Come again,' Maypat whispered, using a polite phrase that Lakina knew she must always say by rote.

'I will,' she said as she walked out the door. It was a promise – one she intended to keep.

Maypat's breath left her as the tall, lovely woman went out the screened door. The ricochet of wood against wood sounded like a rifle-crack. Nervously she waited, but the woman did not return. It was deathly silent inside the store, but Maypat felt blood pounding in her ears. Shallow gasps of air were all she could manage. *I'm driving myself crazy. I've been thinking about Sakina all week, and now I've conjured her up.*

The woman's eyes haunted her. They were the soft green of cottonwood leaves. Sakina's eyes had been black as night. Caleb's eyes had been . . . startlingly green in a stone-white face. It was just a coincidence. A mirage.

'I'm acting like a crazy southern belle,' Maypat mumbled to herself. 'Lita!' She went to the back of the store, where the shop girl was bringing boxes inside. 'Lita, come mind the register for me.'

'This load of grapes isn't going to do well in the sun, Miss Maypat. I'd better get them inside –'

'Leave them. I have an urgent errand I must see to.' Without another look back, Maypat exited through the loading door. Hurrying up to the big house on the hill, she quietly went inside, praying she wouldn't run across Jarvis. Grabbing her purse, she took out the car keys and went back out. Winded, she got into the comfortable Cadillac and drove the five minutes to the church. If Father John wasn't in the confessional she'd hunt him down in his office. She just had to let the dark sin of her secret finally see the light of day – before it killed her.

Five minutes later she was in the peaceful solitude of the church. There was no one around to witness her arrival, thank heaven. As her eyes adjusted to the dimness Maypat took a seat in the confessional. There was a stirring from the other side and relief filled Maypat.

'Forgive me, Father, for I have sinned.'

'What is this sin?' John asked. He leaned close, the sound of distress in the woman's voice catching his attention at once.

'I . . . don't know where to start.'

A few seconds passed. He waited patiently until she could get her thoughts sorted.

'I have wronged someone in the community.'

'On purpose?'

'No. Yes,' the woman replied. 'I should have done something. I didn't, and now I'm being punished.'

John frowned. 'Punished how?'

'I'm not sure.' The voice dropped to a frantic whisper. 'I've been thinking about her a lot. And . . . and now I'm imagining things about her.'

He wasn't sure how he could get to the heart of the sin to dispense appropriate counseling and

182

forgiveness. 'These things you're thinking about someone – are they bad?'

'No. Well, I'm not sure. It was a long time ago, but I don't think they were bad. And now I've been thinking about her so much that I think I'm seeing her.'

'I see.' John fumbled around in his thoughts for a moment, trying to decide how to calm the woman. She seemed to be growing more agitated with every word. 'When do you think you saw someone?'

'This morning, in my store. But it couldn't have been her, because her eyes were a different color. They were green, not dark. And she died a long time ago.'

He pinched the bridge of his nose. The poor woman in the confessional was racked by guilt, and maybe a little mad from it. Suddenly he realized she'd mentioned her store. Straightening, he wondered if Maypat Andrews was the stricken woman on the other side of the screen. Good, kind, down-to-earth Maypat didn't have bats in her belfry. And if there was anyone who would never hurt another living soul, it was Maypat. What could she possibly have done to frighten herself into thinking the ghost of a dead woman was hanging out at Andrews Grocery Mart?

Suddenly he realized she was sobbing hysterically. 'Is there anything I can do for you?' he asked. 'Perhaps a glass of water . . .'

'No, no, thank you. Just forgiveness. That's all that can help me now.'

'You are forgiven, of course,' Father John said, still trying to figure out what she could have done that was so heinous. He paused, mulling over a penance to meet the situation.

'I can't stop thinking about that poor man, living out his life without his wife,' Maypat said softly, her voice breaking. 'If only my husband had left her alone, maybe Mr Dorn would be alive today. He had such green eyes. Maybe his wife would be alive,' she added, as if the thought had just occurred to her in the most awful way. 'Maybe . . . maybe she is alive. No. No, that's silly. There are two graves; she couldn't have hidden herself away all these years. There are two graves. There are two graves . . .'

John reared back, his heart thundering. What had Maypat said? Caleb might be alive, and his wife, too, if –

He heard the confessional door open and close. The sobs faded away, as did the shuffling of feet. Nudging the door, he peered out cautiously. Maypat Andrews hurried from the church. The icy water of shock poured over him. What was he supposed to do now, besides pray for relief for Maypat's soul?

The church was quiet as a tomb, but he needed the silence for his own raging thoughts. Someone had done something to Caleb Dorn, something bad enough to make one of the gentlest women he knew break down. Briefly he worried that she shouldn't even be driving, because her state of mind had been tenuous at best. Fortunately she lived close by. How could he help her?

Most likely he couldn't. She was suffering from an agony so deep that she didn't seem able to put a name to it. *Maybe his wife would be alive . . . this morning, in my store . . .*

Impossible, of course. Still, something had shaken Maypat. As the executor of the Dorn will, John owed it to the memory of his friend to check out the situation. There was no way Sakina was still alive, but he could at least make certain of that.

Make certain of what? he asked himself. *I don't believe the hysterical wanderings of an elderly woman, do I?*

What I believe is that I owe it to Steve and Kiran to make sure that Maypat Andrews, who I have always known to be a calm and sane woman – even a bit of a saint to put up with her bullish husband – is not suddenly dreaming ghosts out of the past. I owe it to Caleb, if he is ever going to rest in peace.

'You did *what*? Lakina, you promised!' Aunt Gracie stared at Lakina, anger burning in her eyes.

'I had to. I'm sorry, but I had to do it.'

'I shouldn't have given you that letter. Maybe I should have read it first, then –'

Lakina crossed her arms. 'I had to know what they looked like. Where they lived. I want to know why they hated my mother so much.'

Gracie snorted. 'You can't figure that out yourself?' she demanded, jabbing Lakina's arm with a forefinger.

'The lady in the store didn't seem that concerned

about my skin color.' She'd been upset, but polite at the same time.

'It's not the fifties, hon, or even the sixties! You can shop wherever you like and they can't stop you now! But they stopped your mother, and they did a whole lot more than that.' Gracie paced the room. 'You don't think she suspected who you are, do you? People around here have long memories.'

Maypat had suspected something, Lakina was certain. The expression on her face had been one of . . . recognition. 'No one knew my mother had a child by Caleb Dorn,' she hedged, trying to soothe her agitated aunt.

'Like they couldn't figure it out! You're only her walking image, Lakina.'

She sat up. 'I am?'

Gracie faced her. 'What you got from your white father was eyes, honey, and those eyes make you look exotic. But your mother was beautiful, and she was graceful, and she made people look twice. Yes, you are your mother's very image.'

'I . . . I wonder if she'd be proud of me.' Even now the old wounds were open, gaping.

'Yes, she'd be proud of you. She was, anyway.' Gracie sighed heavily. 'And, yes, he'd have been proud of you, too, Lakina. That's what you're really wondering. Your father thought the moon and the sun shone out of your mother, and he'd have been out of his head with happiness to know he'd had a daughter like you.' Gracie sank into the chair next to Lakina's. 'I sure hope you haven't opened up a box you shoulda left closed, child. Is there any way you can keep yourself from looking back?'

'No.' Lakina shook her head regretfully. 'I don't think there is.'

'Maybe it's time for you to go back to New York,' Gracie suggested hopefully. 'Don't you have a show you can do – maybe fly to Paris and do one of those fancy runway modeling things?'

Lakina caught the underlying fear in Gracie's voice. 'You really think Maypat Andrews could have put two and two together?'

'I don't know. You're going to give me a heart attack, Lakina.'

Gracie was still put out with her. Lakina tried to understand her aunt's feelings. 'Well, let's not get all upset about nothing.'

'Nothing! They threatened to shoot your father off his tractor just because they didn't like the color of your mother's skin! And you go sashaying in there with your mother's features on you like a neon sign and you call that nothing!'

Gracie heaved a deep breath, shooting a disbelieving, unhappy look her way. The doorbell rang, startling them both.

'I'll get it, Aunt Gracie. You just sit there.' Lakina got up and walked to the door. Peering through the peephole, she saw their next-door neighbor. She unlocked the bolts on the door and pulled it open.

'Hello –' Her greeting was torn off by the sight of the man accompanying her neighbor.

'This is Father John Lannigan. He came to my door by mistake, looking for someone by the name of Dorn. Figured he was wanting you.'

No introduction had been necessary. She instantly recognized the dynamically handsome man who had performed the funeral service for her father. Lakina's throat went dry.

John stared at the tall, elegant woman framed in the doorway. His heart beat erratically in his chest; his hands felt as if fire was scorching the palms. He didn't need to second-guess whether he was looking at the woman Maypat had described because the eyes that were watching him with hesitation and fear were as startlingly light an ocean-green as Caleb's had been. Darkly, thickly lashed and unforgettable.

He took a deep breath, everything he had prepared to say gone from his mind.

She was the most beautiful woman he'd ever seen.

'Can I help you?' she asked.

He felt as if he was on the other side of the confessional screen now, and this woman was waiting to hear his awkward confession. 'Might I come in?' he asked. 'I'd like to speak with you on a personal matter.'

'See you later, Lakina,' the neighbor said, stepping off the porch with a curious glance.

Lakina, Sakina blew into John's mind with the strength of dreaded realization.

'Come in,' she said softly.

Hesitantly John stepped past her, unable to take

his gaze from her so that he nearly ran into the elderly woman blocking his path.

'What do you want?' she demanded.

Lakina closed the front door. 'Aunt Gracie, this is Father John Lannigan. By now I guess you've figured out that my name is Lakina Dorn.'

She didn't smile. Neither did he, and the grizzled, older woman looked as if she wanted to thrash him with something.

'We already have a church, and we go every Sunday,' Gracie stated belligerently. 'Ain't gonna be changing churches, either, so you're wasting your time.'

'I don't think that's why you're here, is it?'

He shook his head in answer to Lakina's question. The expression on her face suggested she already knew what he wanted to talk about.

Lakina pointed him toward a dim sitting area. 'Please have a seat.'

'Lakina!'

John didn't miss the unspoken fear in the old woman's voice. Frankly, he was afraid himself. Confronting uncomfortable moments was part of his job, but this time was more scary than anything he'd ever had to do.

'It's okay, Aunt Gracie,' Lakina replied soothingly. 'I think we should hear what he has to say.'

John sat down in a worn chair. Lakina perched on the matching one next to it. Gracie hovered across the room like an upset cat.

He didn't know how to start. On the one hand he

had to be careful to keep Maypat's confession confidential, but on the other hand, if this woman was related in any way to Kiran and Steve, they should know before they disposed of Caleb's estate.

'Recently one of my parishioners died,' he began carefully. 'His name was Caleb Dorn.'

Instantly the two women glanced at each other. Though that felt like confirmation of his suspicions, John acted as if he hadn't seen it and continued. 'With your last name being Dorn, I wonder if you were related to Mr Caleb Dorn. Since he lived not twenty minutes from here, I couldn't help wondering if perhaps you were kin.'

'He didn't leave us nothing, did he?' Gracie demanded.

'No, he didn't.'

'Then why would you come asking if we're related? Seems strange.' Gracie crossed her arms. Lakina remained silent.

'I'm the executor of Mr Dorn's estate. If there are any living blood relations, I think it would make a difference in the decisions concerning that estate.' John hedged for a moment, unwilling to interject the real catalyst for his visit. *Had Lakina even known of Caleb?*

'We have all the money we need,' Gracie stated. 'Don't need any more, so we ain't going to be wanting anything from somebody's estate we never . . . knew.'

Gracie halted, and John saw the stricken expression on Lakina's face.

'Oh, honey, I'm sorry. I shouldn't have said that.' Gracie hurried to hug her niece. 'I didn't mean it that way.'

'I know you didn't.' Lakina's voice broke. 'I know you're trying to protect me. But I need to know. This man doesn't mean any harm to me, Aunt Gracie. Can't I just talk to him – about everything?'

Gracie and Lakina both glanced over at him. He sensed they were waiting for a sign, a nod, to say that they could trust him. They wanted to, expected to, because of the religious position he held.

He ignored the dryness of his throat that plagued him every time Lakina looked at him with those eyes. He told himself that although she was extraordinarily beautiful, and all soft and tear-gentled in a way no other crying woman had ever seemed to him, he wasn't feeling the odd and unwelcome stirring of attraction. That was what he told himself – and he prayed he was telling his conscience the truth.

'I'm willing to listen to anything you want to tell me,' he said. 'I think it would be best for everyone if we get to the bottom of this.'

Lakina sat up, slowly pulling away from her aunt.

'I might as well go get a box of tissues and get us some refreshment. I guess we're gonna need it,' Gracie sighed. 'What would you like, Mr Lannigan?'

'Nothing for me, thanks. And, please, call me John.'

Gracie left the room, taking the heaviness of her doubt with her.

John and Lakina stared at each other uncomfortably for a few seconds. In the confessional he always gave the other person a chance to gather their thoughts. His were as scattered as fallen leaves in autumn; he imagined Lakina's were as unfocused. His throat closed again as he let his gaze travel over her polished-teak complexion, down her swan-graceful neck. She wore her hair long and straight, and it looked right on her. He thought she would look just as stunning with her hair pulled back from her face.

'I think you've already figured out that I'm Caleb's daughter,' she stated. 'But I don't want any part of his estate.'

CHAPTER 13

'In fact, I hope you'll understand that it's best if no one knows of my existence.'

The shock of Lakina's revelation was beginning to set in with John. He had prepared himself to expect whatever happened after hearing Maypat's confession. Certainly he had known something wasn't right, that he had to look further than what the old lady had managed to confess. It had not been terribly difficult to find this house. Several times Caleb had mentioned the neighborhood where he'd met his wife. John had only to drive to this area and start asking questions about Sakina Dorn before helpful people brought him to this address. Apparently the Dorn name meant a lot in this area.

But sitting face-to-face with a daughter that Caleb had never known he'd had was chillingly painful to John. Disbelief still rocked him, and the unfairness of it all was like a kick in the gut. The disquieting emotions Maypat's story had stirred in him were nothing compared to the angst

Lakina Dorn's lovely, totally heartbroken face was making him feel.

'Why?' was all he could ask. 'Please help me understand.'

She lowered her gaze for a moment. 'About what? There's too much to tell a complete stranger.' Drawing an agonized breath, she said, 'The time has passed for anything good to come out of revealing myself now.'

John thought about Maypat's guilt-stricken, panicked confession. 'It was you in Andrews Grocery Mart this morning?'

She nodded.

'Then someone already knows about you.'

'Since you're here, yes. How did she happen to come to you?'

He paused, then shook his head. 'I should say nothing more about that, but just showing up there gave you away.'

'Then I'll leave Cottonwood.' Lakina was firm.

'Why? Your father's niece, Kiran, and nephew, Steve, would be happy to meet you. Your existence, while it might have upset one person, may in fact be a godsend to others.'

'Why?'

'They don't want your father's property. They're not certain what to do about it.'

'I would love to live in my parents' home, but –' She halted, shaking her head slowly. 'Maybe you could suggest they give it to the church, or some other charity.'

'Actually, your father gave me forty acres of land, charity case that he must have considered me.' John laughed, but the sound was humorless. During his friendship with Caleb he had needed the old man far more than Caleb had needed John.

'You were close to my father?' Lakina's voice softened.

'Ah – probably as close as he would allow anyone.' John told himself he would explore Lakina's need to know about her father later. 'Why don't you just meet with Kiran and Steve?'

'I can't.' Lakina brushed a stray lock of hair away from her eyes. 'I mean, I was all for shouting to the world that I am Caleb's daughter. But,' she said on a sigh, 'I've had time to think about it. And now you've shown up and I realize I should go back to New York.' Her voice and her gaze drifted away from John.

'Tell me why,' he pleaded. 'I need to know the best way to help everyone in this matter.'

'Aunt Gracie is afraid I'll be in danger. She says people around here have long memories.'

John heard Maypat's tortured soul again, shrieking through her whispered confession. She had remembered. All it had taken was a few moments of Lakina's presence to send her running to unload her guilt. 'I have to ask you – who are you afraid of in this community?'

She shrugged. 'What does it matter to you?'

'I want to help if I can. Has someone done something they should be punished for?'

'They won't be.'

Lakina pinned him with an expressionless stare. In her words he heard confirmation of the racism her mother had suffered. 'Maybe you should go to the police.'

'And then go back to my life and leave my aunt to deal with whoever decides to take their anger out on her?'

John hadn't thought about that. 'Okay. Let's leave that alone for a minute. What has to concern me the most is your father, because that's where my rightful duty lies. If Kiran and Steve agree not to reveal your presence, will you at least meet with them?' He waited a moment to judge her reaction. 'I think you'd like them. And it could very well help them out of the uncomfortable situation your father's estate is causing them.'

'What discomfort?'

He shifted, wondering how much he could tell without jeopardizing Steve's and Kiran's trust. 'For one thing, even if they're forced into selling Caleb's estate, they don't want the money it would bring. And, most important, Caleb's brother and sister, whom he cared absolutely nothing for, are suing the estate for control. This is burdening Steve and Kiran, because they are determined to do the right thing by your father and he didn't want Agnes and Butch left so much as a penny of his money.'

Suddenly John realized he might be holding a huge stone he could pull out to dislodge the dam of Lakina's unwillingness. 'Your father's brother and sister want to have your parents moved to a local cemetery. Even the resting place they wanted for themselves will be lost to them if Agnes and Butch have their way.'

Lakina's mouth fell open. Fire erupted in her emerald eyes. *Bingo!* John told himself.

'I'll think about it,' she said.

Steve sat across from Kiran, watching as a waiter placed a plate in front of her. After her earlier revelation that she'd previously been married, he'd mumbled a shocked, 'I see,' and stumbled off to the shower to regroup his thoughts.

They hadn't said much to each other during the drive to this posh restaurant, keeping the conversation to awkwardly neutral topics. Some line had been drawn for both of them, and Steve wasn't sure how to cross it.

The damnedest part was how much it hurt that Kiran had considered another man her best friend. In Steve's mind it had always been the two of them against the world. Kiran occupied a place in his soul no one else ever could – it was a place that he didn't need anyone else to inhabit. Even if he'd never seen her again, that place in his soul would still have existed. It was hers, and hers alone.

She had not possessed that same need for him. 'Steve?'

He heard the question in her voice. 'Yes?'

Light blue eyes sparkled at him over the luminous candlelight. 'Ever since earlier back at the house,

I've had the feeling that you're upset about something.' She shook her head as he opened his mouth to deny it. 'I know you too well. You can let down that macho guard a little bit and tell me what's on your mind. I can't stand you looking at me like I've squirted a grapefruit in your eye.'

He managed a brief smile. Perhaps he would feel better if he told her what was bugging him. 'I didn't know you'd gotten married.'

'Well, of course not. I was all of seventeen. You don't think Agnes was going to shout to the world that her stepdaughter was getting married right out of high school? Everyone would have guessed that I was doing it to get out of the house, to escape living with her. People might have suspected she wasn't the good mother to me she claimed. She didn't even want Uncle Caleb to know.'

His eyes locked with hers, sharing commiseration over their unhappy childhoods. 'I wish I'd thought about getting married to escape the old man. Instead I spent most of my time on the streets – until Uncle Caleb gave me the kick in my pants I needed.'

She smiled, her soft pink lips glistening. 'To be honest, getting married wasn't the escape I thought it would be. My husband was planning on joining the military, and moving from place to place seemed like a very romantic thing to do. It didn't work out that way at all.'

He waited to learn the rest, reminding himself that he'd asked to hear more about her marriage, so if he was feeling strange pangs of pain it was his own fault.

'We were kids. We didn't know he'd be gone so much, that we'd be apart so much. Of course, his childhood hadn't been any more sterling than mine, so we'd figured we were the perfect mates for each other. What happened, of course, was no surprise to anyone. I got stuck in a miserable little hut of a house on a base, with no friends and very little communication from my husband, while he got sent off to a foreign country for the first year of our marriage.'

'Sounds tough.'

'It was.' She sighed. 'I was lonely, but it was still better than living with Agnes. Things changed a lot when he wrote to tell me he'd fallen in love with a native girl in the country where he was stationed. He married me so I could be free, and I had to give him a divorce so he could be free. That's what real friends do, isn't it? Look out for each other's needs?'

He didn't know what to say to that. He wanted to meet Kiran's needs while they struggled through this torturous winding up of Uncle Caleb's estate, but how much heartache would it cost him? Old feelings had surfaced in the past few days, combining with new emotions that were distinctly adult in nature, making him see Kiran in a light he'd never expected to. 'So that explains why you and I aren't going to be best friends this time around. You don't want to get hurt again.'

'Well, I guess I realized that there are friends you can share things with and there are friends you send a card to occasionally. I see our friendship being the latter.'

He started at her, wishing she wasn't so beautiful. Wishing he wasn't so attracted to her, much deeper than his usual surface level. It hurt that she seemed to dismiss their relationship so casually while he felt a persistent buzzing of desire every time he looked at her. 'I wish I'd known. I wish I could have been there for you. I know you had it bad with Agnes and everything, but I wish I could have been the shelter you needed.'

Her lips parted slightly with astonishment. 'Steve, your life, what you have carved out for yourself, is so totally different from what I would have dreamed it would become. You never once mentioned your dream was to be a race car driver in all the summers we were together. You couldn't have been what I needed. We couldn't have been what the other needed at all. These few days we've spent together has proved that. You change when you talk about racing, when you're here in California. This life is something you had to have.'

'I didn't know,' he said gruffly. 'Maybe I wouldn't have needed it so much if –'

The waiter brought a giant salad bowl to the table, carefully placing some on each plate. After he left, Steve forced his gaze to meet Kiran's again.

'What were you going to say?'

'I don't know that I would have been so driven if I'd had an anchor.'

'You had Uncle Caleb.'

'Yeah. But you never came back, Kiran. And you were the only real friend I'd ever had. The only person who really knew me. I didn't have to pretend around you.'

'It wouldn't have worked out, Steve. Our friendship wasn't going to stay in its protective, fragile little shell. You were destined to live in California and race. I was destined to live in Tennessee and be a schoolteacher.'

She paused for a moment, sighing. 'As much as it hurt me that my marriage wasn't meant to last, I realized I wasn't in love, and neither was he. We went our separate ways with only the loss of our friendship, which made me sad. But it forced me to fend for myself. I worked during the day and went to school at night, until I finally had a teaching degree. I'm very satisfied with what I do.' She smiled at him. 'Teaching is right for me, and the kids in my school are my substitute for the children I didn't have. It's very rewarding.'

'You don't want kids of your own?' He couldn't imagine that. Soft and delicate Kiran, with her witty and caring personality, would make a great mother. The realization whipped through him like a hurricane. She would be a fabulous mother of some man's children.

'I'm thirty-four, and not checking the singles ads, Steve. I feel good about my life as it is.'

He wondered how much of that statement was a brave front. Wasn't a woman's biological clock supposed to sound an alarm some time in her thirties, making her susceptible to husband-hunting?

'And you?'

Her question made him reach for his glass of wine. 'I haven't given it much thought.' Hadn't until the last five minutes, anyway. Being a year older than Kiran, he still considered himself young, virile, in his female-pleasing prime. Heck, he considered himself more that boy who'd thrown pebbles into the fishing pond with Kiran than the man who was fighting off newcomers for big racing prizes. 'This is a depressing-as-hell conversation. I'm still trying to delude myself that I'm king of the hill, and suddenly it's hit me why all the young dogs are biting at my tail. I *am* getting old.'

She laughed, and he smiled, but it was through pained awareness. 'Jeez. Maybe I *should* start checking the singles ads,' he said gruffly.

'Well, there's Ginger,' Kiran said with a grin.

'As I said, maybe I'll look through the ads this weekend.' Ginger was not a woman he would consider serious commitment with. She was not a mother-to-my-child candidate for him at all. Of course, the reality of his situation was that he wasn't parent material. Neither he nor Kiran had blue ribbon examples of parenting to look to, so the unsettling question of whether Kiran's clock would ever start ticking was actually pointless.

He wondered why such thoughts had to leak into his usually complacent bachelor brain. 'So, after the race this weekend, we fly back to Texas, fend off our parents, and then say *adios*?'

'I guess so.' Kiran's gaze dimmed a bit. 'Let's not think about it right now, though. I want to enjoy this delicious looking salad.'

She picked up her fork and started eating, but Steve took another drink of his wine. Sentiment was robbing him of being able to treat Kiran like any other woman he would ask out for a date. If he could just shake off the memories and the connection of their youth as easily as she seemed to, he could toss aside this lingering wistfulness about having to say goodbye to her again.

'I'm going to go make a call,' he told her, getting up and tossing his napkin to the table. 'If you'll excuse me for a minute.'

She waved him away, smiling at the waiter who'd brought the second course. Steve frowned as he went to the payphone located by the men's washroom. He dialed Mitch's number impatiently.

'Hello?'

'I've been trying to get in touch with you all day.'

'Hey, Steve! You must be in California. The connection is much clearer.'

'It's going to be a lot clearer after I chew your butt for sending Ginger to the airport.'

'Didn't know you were bringing anybody back with you. Sorry.'

Steve snorted. 'Listen, quit trying to be my love consultant, okay? I'm over Ginger.'

'I think I've been informed of that.' Mitch's tone was knowing.

'She come crying to you?'

There was hesitation from the other end. 'Guess she just wanted to know if I knew anything about the woman you'd brought back with you.'

He sighed. 'Look. I need my crew chief to make sure my car's running smooth, not my sex life. Got it?'

'Got it. I was just trying to help.'

'I don't need that kind of help,' he stated firmly. 'What time are we meeting tomorrow?'

'At our usual time, before the sun comes up. Then you've got some interviews set up, so come prepared.'

'Anything else?'

'Not that I can think of.' There was a long pause. 'Hey, Steve, you're not . . . I mean, is she someone important?'

'What the hell difference does it make?'

'Because I've got Ginger on the sofa in my living room, crying her eyes out over you, man,' he hissed into the phone.

'Tell her to dry up and to quit bothering you. If you weren't such a nice guy, you wouldn't let her cry on your shoulder like that.' Steve couldn't believe the woman's act. No doubt she hadn't been mooning over him while she'd been running after Dan Crane. Now she was using Mitch as a crying towel.

'Well, she is kind of nice –'

'Like a barracuda. Listen, the territory's open where she's concerned, if that's what all this concern is about.'

'Are you sure? I mean, I wouldn't want to come between anything the two of you had, man. But I have always, kinda . . . well, you know. She kinda catches the eye.'

Yeah, she kinda catches the eye, Steve thought grimly. *My best friend's eye, unfortunately for him.* 'Mitch, I would pay you to keep Ginger away from me while Kiran is here. I just hope you know what you're getting in to with her.'

'Thanks, buddy. I appreciate the all-clear.'

'You got it. Listen, I gotta go.'

'See you tomorrow.'

Mitch hung up, and Steve did, too, slowly walking back into the main eating area. Kiran sat alone, her blonde hair catching the soft light from the twinkling chandelier overhead. His breath caught in his chest.

'Sorry about that,' he told her, sliding into the chair. 'Is the food okay?'

'I can't believe how good it is. Much better than the hamburgers we ate in the fields.'

He snorted. 'Wonder what Butch and Agnes are up to?'

'I don't care.' She put her fork down and leaned back in the chair, looking very relaxed. 'I'm going to love every minute of this luxurious trip you've bought me. I'm Cinderella for the weekend.'

His stomach hollowed out at her words. Their

gazes caught. 'What if midnight didn't have to be the witching hour?'

'What do you mean?' She was looking at him cautiously, her body no longer relaxed.

'You could stay here.'

'Why would I want to do that?'

He shrugged, trying to act nonchalant. 'I don't know. Maybe you'll suddenly develop a taste for rollerblading in a bikini.'

'I'd be lost in California. My little house by the mountains is the only place I've ever felt completely safe and secure.'

'You could live with me.' Steve threw that out just to get her reaction.

'Oh, that is guaranteed to make me feel safe and secure.' She laughed, punching his ego. 'I don't want to live with you, Steve. I don't want to be anyone's trophy.'

'Trophy? What the heck are you talking about?' Obviously the feisty side of her personality was over its jet lag.

'You know – like Ginger. I'd have to watch women like her hang all over you more than I'd be comfortable with. And I'd have to look a certain way, dress a certain way, so you wouldn't be embarrassed in front of your friends. I'm not exactly a trophy kind of woman.'

He knew what she was getting at – that she didn't have the glamorous looks of a Ginger. Kiran's natural beauty was so much more potent. 'I like you just the way you are.'

'I like you just the way you are, too. At the same time I realize what I like about you makes the two of us completely unsuitable to be housemates. Or anything else.'

The salad wasn't tasting like much, so Steve put his fork down and concentrated on the wine. 'Rejection is the pits.'

She put a hand over his as he clenched the stem of the glass. 'Steve, I know what you're doing. Stop trying to take care of me, please. I don't need it. You're being very chivalrous in a crass sort of way, but, believe me, I'm going to go on being just fine. You don't have to be my guardian.'

'Is that what I'm doing?' He wasn't sure he liked the sound of that. 'Guardian' made him sound old.

'Guardian, or Prince Charming with a sex drive – I'm not sure which.' Kiran grinned. 'All I'm saying is, I don't need a big-brother figure anymore. I found that out with my marriage. So stop trying to think of a way to babysit me.'

'I wasn't,' he said honestly. 'I was trying to think of a way to get you into bed with me.'

She laughed. 'I'm safe on that score. We agreed before we left Cottonwood there'd be no slumber parties.' She slanted him a teasing look. 'Give it a few days. You'll probably find a new sleep-mate at the race this weekend.'

'Kiran, I can't believe you think I'd pick up any old girl hanging around and sleep with her.'

She patted his cheek, which gave him a fleeting sniff of light perfume and a head full of desire. 'Not just any old girl, Steve. If Ginger was an example of the average woman you have chasing you, I'd say you win more than money on an average weekend. But, Steve, if it's any consolation, I think sleeping with you would probably be lots of fun.'

'Fun?' He wasn't sure he liked that description. It wasn't one he'd heard a woman use before.

'Pour me some of that wine, please.' She waited while he filled her glass, then held it up. 'To Steve – may you win this weekend's race and all the others you want. And here's to us – two people who just wanted to be all-American, normal kids. We managed to outrun our childhoods.'

'Are you trying to make me feel guilty? Like, if I'm an average, all-American guy I won't try to sleep with you?'

She laughed. 'Maybe.'

He held his own glass up. 'Then here's to us – two unwanted youths who each found their own way to be wanted. Me with my fans and loose women, and you with your schoolkids. We didn't do half bad.'

They clinked their glasses together and drank.

'So, how about a walk on the beach later?' Kiran asked, her lips wet with wine.

'You're not afraid I'll try to molest you on a sand dune?'

She gave him a winning smile. 'Sex-talk is your big front. I suspect it's all hot air where I'm concerned.'

They finished eating and Steve motioned to the waiter, handing him a credit card. To Kiran, he said, 'I'm glad you understand me. For a minute there I was afraid you might give me permission.'

She laughed out loud, tossing her head back a little as she did. Men stared appreciatively.

'To molest me on a sand dune? Maybe I should,' she said. 'You're going to have an awful lot to live up to, should we ever accidentally fall into the same bed at the same time minus our clothes.'

The waiter brought the bill for Steve to sign and thanked them for their business. Steve nodded absently at him, his eyes focused on Kiran.

'Then again,' she added, 'It's probably best if we don't muddy up the waters. After all, we don't have anything to gain by getting close that way.' She stood, allowing Steve to guide her from the restaurant by her elbow. 'The truth is, it's all fine and good for us to be proud that we could end up as fairly whole, functioning adults. But we may not be out of the woods with this estate thing yet.'

He didn't want to think about the emotional furnace of facing Butch and Agnes in a legal battle. 'So we could have sex as a sort of cementing thing. Something that would hold us tightly together, unite us in case things get really bad.'

'That's the worst excuse I ever heard. We need a better plan than that,' Kiran told him as they walked through the parking lot toward the bluffs.

'Okay. What if we sign the whole damn thing over to a charity, with the amendment that the acre where Sakina and Caleb are buried is left intact?'

Warm night air wafted through Kiran's hair,

bringing the scent of ocean air and night mist to her. She looked up at Steve thoughtfully, feeling excitement racing through her. 'That would solve everything! This whole matter would be over and we could go on with our lives. And I kind of like the idea of being a philanthropist in Uncle Caleb's name.'

'Great. Me, too. Now that we've solved that, what do we do?'

'Go back to your house and call Father John.' Kiran couldn't wait to tell him their idea.

'I was afraid of that,' Steve groaned.

CHAPTER 14

Maypat tossed in her bed, unable to get comfortable. She froze when she heard her bedroom door open, and quickly squeezed her eyes closed. Her door shut a moment later, and she heard Jarvis's heavy tread in the hall.

Glancing at her clock on the nightstand, Maypat saw that it was midnight. Jarvis was certainly up late. The sound of a car starting reached her ears. Shivers danced along her spine. If Jarvis was checking to make sure she was in bed and asleep before going out this late, he was up to no good. This was exactly the way he'd acted over the years when he wanted to keep things from her.

Many times she'd wondered if there was another woman, and maybe there had been at different times. But she had learned, to her regret, that most of the matters that required Jarvis's attention at this time of night had nothing to do with women – and she didn't want to know what he was up to tonight. He was forever cooking up something with Bedford Harding and his other nefarious friends.

Maypat sighed, turning onto her side. As long as his friends were powerful, Jarvis was never going to get his comeuppance. Unloading her conscience at the church today had only served to make her worry more. She had to face the fact that she was the only person who could make sure Jarvis finally got what he had coming to him. Telling the priest had been great for finding forgiveness for her soul, but she knew deep in her heart that she had only stopgapped what she should be doing.

She should be telling the sheriff instead of the priest.

But what if the sheriff turned a blind eye to Jarvis's doings? Could she trust him not to tell Jarvis what she'd done? Her blood chilled and she felt faint and trembly at the thought of what her husband would do to her. Flat on her back, she lay staring toward the ceiling, not seeing it – not seeing anything but haunting emptiness and guilt for the rest of her life.

If Bedford wasn't going to help him out, then Jarvis was determined to do it himself. The first thing he had to do was get those Dorn kids to realize how out of their element they were. Cottonwood was no place for strangers. They need not consider putting down roots here. What they'd told Bedford was that they didn't plan on selling. Jarvis's job was to give them a motive to change their mind.

He was disappointed to see the rental car gone from the Dorn yard. But Caleb Dorn's beat-up

212

truck was in its usual place. The house was dark inside. Jarvis tapped the steering wheel, wondering where they could be at this hour of the night. As much as he hated it, his plan was going to have to wait until another night. But, since the Dorn relatives were gone, he could hide his car and take another look-see around the house – a more thorough inspection to make certain nothing was there that might fall into the wrong hands.

Heading his car down a deserted lane, he made certain the tires were off the concrete and in the tall weeds growing alongside the road. Getting out, he walked beside the barbed-wire fence, his shoes crunching loudly on the white-rock road. Looking around in the humid darkness, Jarvis could spot no one who might be watching, so he hurried down the road to the house. He'd try the door first, but he knew the Dorn kids had probably locked the place up tight as a drum. Most likely he'd have to find another way to get in.

The front door was locked, as was the back door. Jarvis walked back around to the front, trying the windows as he went by them. They were all locked tight. Suddenly, a grin spread over his face. On a front window there was a long crack lining one of the glass panes. The crack had likely been there for years, because the calking around the pane looked original and worn. He could lightly tap the glass out and reach through to unlock the window, and no one would ever blame an intruder's entry into the house. It would look as if the glass had finally fallen in after being neglected for so long.

Satisfied that he'd thought through the situation, Jarvis gave the pane one firm smack with his shoe heel. As he'd planned, the glass fell from the top part of the pane, leaving a nice, smooth-edged piece of glass in the frame. He stretched up, reaching his hand in and carefully unlocking the window from inside. A sudden voice in his head warned him not to leave fingerprints in case the Dorn kids weren't as dumb as they looked. Jarvis pulled his sock off, too, and put it over his hand before pushing up on the window. He grunted, not having expected the wood frame to be so stubbornly stuck. Swiveling his head to check the eerie black rises where trees and bushes stood watch in the yard, Jarvis satisfied himself that he was still alone.

One more good push and the window squeaked loudly as it went up. The hair on the back of his neck tickled. A shudder between his shoulderblades made him reconsider his mission, but it was well worth his time to check the place over carefully. One of the reasons he'd never gotten caught in all the years he had been breaking the law was because he was thorough – not to mention sneaky like a fox.

Hauling himself up, Jarvis kicked a leg over the ledge, pulling himself over. He landed hard on the floor. For a few seconds he lay in the darkness, taking stock of his body parts. Deciding that nothing was broken or cut, he slipped his sock and shoe back on, then stood, reaching out to feel for the wall. 'Shoulda brought the flashlight from the car,' he muttered to himself. But he'd been in here before, so he was confident he could navigate the layout.

Feeling around the wall, he kept going until he felt a closet door. Opening it, he reached inside to jerk on the string hanging inside, grimacing. The frayed string felt like a spider web as his hand brushed past it in the darkness. Dang, but he hated spider webs. This dingy house was likely chock-full of things such as that. Jarvis held off another shudder and tugged on the string. The light came on, blinding him for a moment before he closed the closet door almost all the way, leaving only a thin line of light for him to see by.

Immediately he spotted Caleb's clothes on the bed. Walking forward slowly, he saw that what little the man had owned was folded into neat piles. Obviously the Dorn kids had been busy. He had figured they'd get the sorting out done as quickly as possible, which was why he'd risked the earlier visit to the house. Slivers of worry danced up his spine. What if that big baboon who'd been asleep in front of the TV the other night had found something?

Maybe a little disaster would keep them off-center. Jarvis stared at the workshirts in front of him, mulling through the possible headaches he could cause. A stopper in the kitchen sink with the water turned on would keep them so busy with insurance adjusters they wouldn't have time to deal with anything the old man had left behind. Now that he thought about it, flooding out the house was an excellent idea. Jarvis turned to walk to the kitchen – and saw Sakina staring at him.

'Aa-ah!' He jumped backward, tripping on something and falling to the floor. Throwing out an arm so he could push himself up, his fingers brushed against something soft and thready under the bed. 'Damn spider webs!' he cried, brushing it off on his pant leg as he tried to gain his feet. That grimy old sodbuster had never cleaned his house – Lord only knew there were probably spiders an inch in size under that damn bed.

Sakina smiled, her teeth glowing in her face. 'Bitch!' he screamed, realizing belatedly the image he saw was the same picture he'd pulled from the bottom bureau drawer a few days ago. Some fool had set it out on top. He couldn't stand her watching him like that; she'd been watching him the whole time.

He tried to catch his breath but couldn't. A fiery pain split through his skull. Jarvis reeled, his hands going to his head. She was torturing him! Stumbling to the window, Jarvis threw himself over the ledge, dropping to the ground like a weighted sack. A searing pain in his hand told him he'd been too careless in his haste. Swearing viciously, Jarvis barely remembered to pull the window back down before he crouched and ran toward his car.

Jarvis cursed to himself as he drove back home. He pulled the car into the driveway and shut it off. Getting out, he held his fingers tightly together to stop the bleeding. On the front porch, he examined his keyring under the porch light.

The house key was missing. Jarvis frowned, stiffening when he remembered the rose bush snagging the key ring on his first visit to the Dorn house. It had fallen into the dirt. Surely the key wasn't over there.

Jarvis dismissed that possibility, and he sure as hell wasn't going back. Yet he had to get inside his own house. During the day Maypat left the door unlocked, so she could get in and out, and so could the people who worked for her. He never worried about a house key, but now he was in a jam. He needed a bandage and some iodine for his hand. He'd have to ring the doorbell and awaken Maypat so she could let him in. Unfortunately that wasn't the best idea, either. Not that she would ever question him, but –

Something had been different about Maypat lately. He couldn't put a name to it, but she seemed shakier. More nervous. Surely she hadn't overheard any of his conversations with Bedford? She hadn't liked the way he'd done the Dorn family, not agreeing that running that darky woman off was necessary. The passing of years had finally patched the disagreement between them – rough patching though it was. In the past few days, though, it seemed his wife was avoiding him like the plague.

If he rang the doorbell for her to let him in, she was going to smell guilt on him. He didn't want Maypat to be able to tell anyone he was in the habit of running around late at night. His hand hurt and his back had begun throbbing, but it wasn't worth making Maypat suspicious. Backing away from the porch, Jarvis went down the hill to the store and let himself in the back door. He'd be better off sleeping down here on a burlap sack than giving Maypat any ammunition to use against him.

He was opening a box of bandages when he heard a car pull up outside. Frowning, he went and peered out the store window.

It was a police car.

Maypat turned away from the window upstairs in her dark bedroom. She had heard Jarvis's car and then heard him cursing a blue streak on the porch. When the door hadn't opened, she'd risked a glance outside. The headlights of a squad car should have alarmed her for Jarvis's sake – she'd seen him head down toward the store. If he'd finally gotten caught doing something he shouldn't be doing, well, his just deserts were long overdue. Technically, a good wife would run down there and see what she could do to help her husband. But lately Maypat had realized she wasn't a good wife, and didn't want to be one anymore.

'What did he say?' Steve asked, as Kiran hung up the phone.

'John says to wait a while before we make any decisions,' she replied. 'Not that he doesn't think the charity idea has some merit. He just thinks we should take a little more time to make momentous decisions, as he put it.'

'I see. Good old practical Father John.' Steve sighed.

'Yeah.' Kiran nodded. 'He's so practical that he asked the police to run a few patrols past Uncle Caleb's house while we're not there.'

'That was a good idea,' Steve said begrudgingly. 'Not that anybody would want anything in the old place.'

'It was thoughtful,' Kiran agreed. 'I don't think John's worried about anything being stolen in the house, exactly. Uncle Caleb didn't have enough to entice a robber. What he said to me was that with the obituary being in the paper, and the unexpectedly high value of the land, perhaps people would trespass because of the farm vehicles and whatnot. He was simply being cautious.'

'Well, it isn't like our decision has to be made tonight, anyway.'

'No, it doesn't. But I feel better that we called him. I'll sleep better if we might be coming to some kind of a good decision about the property, and this just may be the way to thwart Agnes and Butch. After all, it's not like we're trying to keep it ourselves.' Kiran shrugged, holding Steve's gaze. It wasn't that late, and she didn't think she'd be able to sleep just yet. 'Are you tired?'

'Nah.' Steve shook his head. 'You?'

'No. Maybe we should take that walk on the beach.' As soon as she said it Kiran realized that wasn't the best of ideas. Moonlit strolls on the beach were romantic. The last thing she and Steve should do was breathe in some romantic night air. 'Then again, maybe we should see what's on TV.'

After a minute of consideration, Steve said, 'I've got a lot to do tomorrow. I was thinking that you probably wouldn't enjoy the practice run, and I'm going to be pretty tied up.'

'Don't worry about me. I'm looking forward to having a quiet day to lie around. Maybe I'll laze around your pool.'

He looked relieved. 'I don't mind taking you with me, but it's not too much fun. If you don't mind making yourself at home during the day, I'll take you to one of the local hangouts for the socially mobile types tomorrow night.'

'You mean do some stargazing?' Kiran smiled. 'I think I'd like that.'

'Great. Listen, I hate to be a party-pooper to-night –'

'It's fine.' Kiran dismissed his excuses, trying not to let herself wonder if he was simply avoiding being alone with her. 'I'm in the mood to get comfortable in a bed myself. I bought a book in the airport, so I'll read a few chapters and unwind.'

'Do you want me to hold the book for you?'

Kiran gave him a slight punch on the arm. 'I don't see you as the bookworm type. Thanks, anyway.' She turned to go down the hall before pausing. 'By the way, thank you for the lovely dinner. I had a good time.'

'It was nothing.'

He didn't say anything else so Kiran nodded,

going to her room. Once she'd closed the door behind her, she breathed a sigh of relief. This felt as if they were roommates, and she could handle it. Steve was at his end of the hall, and she was at hers. They'd gotten through one night of being alone in his home without getting too close, and the first night was probably the hardest. The tone had been set for the rest of the weekend now – and it felt more businesslike than anything. Steve had said he'd be too busy with the race this weekend to pursue a sexual liaison with her, and that was best. After all, she had told Steve being bed partners with him would probably be fun.

What she hadn't said was that she could never make love with him and then walk away as if nothing had ever happened between them. It would break her heart – which wasn't too sturdy to start with.

'Kiran?'

The voice coming through her bedroom door made her jump. 'Yes?'

'Do you want me to tuck you in?'

'Go away!' She was grinning at his teasing, though she wouldn't have admitted it to Steve.

'I don't want to seem like an ungracious host.'

She opened the door. 'You have perfect social graces. I'm impressed. Now go to bed.'

He smiled, slow and sexy. Kiran's heart felt as if it was caught in her chest. They were playing a game, she realized, and she wanted to be the winner.

'I've changed my mind,' he said. 'I don't think

I'm ready to hit the hay yet.'

'I know what's wrong,' she said. 'We used to stay up all night long talking. It doesn't feel the same.'

'We've already agreed that nothing about us is the same.'

'Yes, but sometimes the old ways are best. Reassuring, at least. Give me five minutes to change out of this skirt and heels, and I'll meet you in the den. We'll sit up and talk and watch *I Love Lucy* or whatever reruns are on.'

He didn't hesitate. 'I'll put some popcorn in the microwave.'

Kiran closed the door, her blood racing. She wasn't going to be able to fall asleep for a long time even if she did read – and obviously Steve was as keyed up as she was. There were too many emotions between them to be ignored, and they wouldn't have many more times to talk. Soon it would be all over. They would go back to their separate lives.

In order to win, one had to take chances; she had to take the chance that she wouldn't succumb to the attraction she felt for Steve. Avoiding being alone with him while she was in California was only going to cost her precious time to heal old wounds only he would understand about. She didn't want to be held captive to the past any longer.

In exactly five minutes she was wearing a long nightgown with a robe covering it. Nothing sexy about her attire, she assured herself. She even pulled her hair up into a ponytail and took off her make-up, telling her reflection in the mirror that no woman who planned on seduction did it bare of face. Satisfied, she grabbed up a pillow and a blanket off the bed.

He had already thrown his own blanket into a chair. The smell of popcorn wafted from the kitchen and the TV was turned on to one of the black and white sitcoms she and Steve had loved as kids. Kiran settled onto a sofa, tucking the blanket around her ankles.

Steve's mouth went dry when he spied Kiran in the den. Her hair was brushed and soft in an attractive ponytail. She was wearing some cozy-looking nightgown – he could see the sky-blue cotton collar sticking out despite the thick robe she wore. She turned to smile at him, her face clean and clear-complexioned.

And something struck him from out of nowhere: she was exactly what he'd imagined when he'd bought this house with the big yard and the pool. This woman making herself comfortable in his home wasn't such an impossible dream. Some mischievous demon had told him to eschew the condo lifestyle and opt for a place that might one day tempt a woman – if he ever met the woman of his dreams. He didn't want a Ginger with a gold-plate finish; he wanted a woman who was natural and easy-going, a woman who could make the home he had never had. He wanted an equal.

Kiran was exactly that. The thought was disturbing and abrupt. He put it on hold for now. 'Hope you're hungry. I popped two bags of popcorn,' Steve said.

'Good. This is the show where Lucy misses the cruise ship and the pilot dangles her from a helicopter so she can make the boat. Definitely one bag of popcorn required just for that episode.'

'Yeah.' Steve sat in a chair next to the sofa where she was, a careful distance away. Maybe it wasn't Kiran's biological clock that was ticking. Maybe it was his, in which case it needed monitoring like a bomb he should defuse. Flipping open the TV guide, he said, 'Looks like we have about three hours of oldies to watch. That will use up the other bag.'

'You're not looking at the right week,' Kiran informed him.

'Oh, yeah.' He looked at the cover, realizing he hadn't bought a new TV guide before he went to Texas. 'Oh, well, we'll wing it.' On the TV, Lucy was running around in a slip, trying to convince someone to take her to the boat. He felt himself start smiling before he laughed out loud. Kiran reached out – a hint that he should share the popcorn.

Their eyes met as they passed the bowl. 'This is kind of homey,' he told her.

'We used to do this all summer.'

'I know. I feel like we've time-traveled or something.' The sense of *déjà vu* was familiar, yet unsettling enough that he wouldn't sack out at the opposite end of the sofa where she was sitting as he once had. 'I still think you should move in with me.'

She laughed, shaking her head in a definite no. 'You forget, my ex-husband left me for another woman, and you're a man in constant search of coitus.'

'I resent that!'

She reached over and tapped his knuckles. 'Eat popcorn. It helps digest resentment.'

'Kiran, you make me sound like one of those guys who take advantage of a woman's neediness.'

'Yes, well, I'm very needy emotionally, Steve. I'd want something with guarantees, which would be tough enough to find, but you . . . living with you would scare me to death. Watch Lucy,' she pleaded. 'Let's laugh tonight.'

She was right. Even his career was potentially dangerous. He sighed, giving up trying to fit Kiran into his life. She simply wouldn't. Couldn't.

'You're not emotionally needy. You're emotionally hungry because you were deprived as a child.' Kiran was actually so independent that sometimes he wished she *would* lean on him a little. Obviously she had learned to stop-gap any sort of emotional connection that might hurt her. It was selfish, but he wished they were different people, so that they might fit neatly together. 'I hate to think of not seeing you again,' he said softly. 'Seeing you has been so good.' It *feels* good, he thought, but couldn't tell her.

'Turn the lights out, please, if you're going to be maudlin. If I can't see you, it won't be so hard to turn you down.'

'That's probably a good idea, anyway,' he grumbled, getting up to dim the lights. 'I hate to watch late-night TV with the room all lit up.'

This time he didn't go to the chair he'd been occupying, but took the end of the sofa opposite Kiran. She tucked the blanket around her more securely.

'Don't worry,' he told her. 'You've convinced me. I'm just getting comfortable.'

She acted as if she didn't hear his remark, watching the TV with a too-intent stare. The pilot shoved Lucy out of the helicopter so that she was dangling above the cruise ship, suspended by a cable.

'I could never do that,' Kiran said. 'I don't like anything remotely dangerous. If I missed the boat, it'd just be tough luck.'

'Schoolteachers live such safe lives,' Steve said sarcastically. 'Guns in the classroom, drugs . . .'

'I still feel like I'm in control for some reason. Isn't that why you race? To control something potentially stronger than yourself?'

'Hell, no. I just like to drive fast.'

They looked at each other. He met her smirk with a shrug. 'Watch Lucy,' he told her. 'She makes herself do the unexpected to get what she wants.'

Kiran ate some popcorn thoughtfully. She didn't say anything because she couldn't think of a witty enough rejoinder. It had been hard enough to tell him no when he'd walked into the den wearing a pair of loose-fitting jeans so frayed around the waist that she wondered how the zipper stayed up. He was barefoot, like she was, but he was wearing a T-shirt that spelled sex appeal. His suggestion that she move in with him was ludicrous, of course. A man like him would always be the target for women's advances. She needed stability in her life. She wasn't about to give his smart remark about doing the unexpected to get what she wanted any consideration at all.

She was not a live-life-dangerously type of woman, and she wasn't going to change now.

Kiran had fallen asleep by the time the last Dick Van Dyke episode was over. Steve thought about leaving her where she was. She looked comfortable, so much so that she'd let her arm fall to the floor, her hand open and spilling popcorn onto the carpet. He guessed she'd been awfully tired, and maybe watching TV had helped her relax. He hadn't made one advance toward her, a fact he was very proud of, though his jeans hadn't been fitting right around the crotch for the past hour. Kiran had stretched herself out on the sofa, encroaching upon his space and brushing her bare feet against his. He had told himself to ignore those toenails he remembered were painted a happy, bright red and concentrate on the grayish TV screen.

Though he was completely relaxed, he was never going to sleep this way. He might as well give up and head to his bedroom, or he was liable to end up with a crick in his neck – a very uncomfortable thing when one had to drive several laps around a race-track. Lifting Kiran from the sofa, he cradled her in his arms for a moment, staring down at her face. She looked so sweet, so fresh, that it was hard to believe she'd been raised by a foul witch like Agnes. A rush of protectiveness, followed by warmth, flooded through Steve as he carried Kiran down the hall to her room.

'Goodnight,' he whispered, laying her on the bed and tucking the blanket securely around her. He brushed a light kiss against her lips, freezing instantly as she moved slightly, moaning. What had possessed him to kiss her? He was allowing himself to feel things for Kiran she didn't want him to feel, feelings he was inexperienced with handling, and that was more dangerous than beating off forty other drivers in a big-winnings race.

Still, Kiran had been his best friend as a child. It probably wasn't unlikely that he would respond to her this easily as an adult. Unfortunately they'd both changed over the years, and those changes were the reason they couldn't quite make it work on a deeper level.

You'd have to be awfully good for her, an unwelcome voice chided him. *Are you even good for yourself?*

'Shut up,' he commanded the voice.

Kiran moved on the bed slightly, disturbed by his rough tone in the silent room. Her eyes opened slowly, as if she was still in some hazy dreamland. 'Don't leave me, Steve,' she murmured. She reached out to him. 'Not yet.'

CHAPTER 15

Steve's heart lurched like a stuck gear. Kiran looked too beautiful and way too appealing to ask this of him. 'I can't stay with you,' he said harshly. 'I have to get up early in the morning.'

She didn't let her arms fall back to the bed. She didn't nod acceptance of his refusal. She merely waited, as if she knew he was denying himself rather than her. Her eyes were huge and pleading in a way he couldn't bear to refuse. Slowly he moved toward the bed, and into her arms.

She sighed, as if he was granting her fondest wish. 'Kiran –'

One dainty finger hovered at his lips, stopping his protest. 'I'm having a needy moment,' she told him.

'I don't think you've ever had one of those in your life. You're so independent, I'm taking notes.'

She laughed softly and wound both arms around him. He was astonished by how right they felt lying this way, like two puzzle pieces locking together.

'I need you,' she whispered.

He didn't dare to allow himself to hope. 'How?'

'Kiss me, Steve.'

He tentatively pressed his lips to hers, amazement flooding him at the softness of her mouth. She didn't pull back, though he waited for any sign of hesitation. When there was none, he pulled away enough to look in her eyes. 'Was that all right?'

She smiled, her eyes curving as she gazed up at him. 'For a fast-track man, you're going awfully slow.'

'Well, we had set up our playing rules –'

'Some rules are meant to be broken.' She stroked a finger lightly along the back of his neck, sending tingles down his spine.

'Do you teach your students to break rules?'

'No, but you're not my student. If anything, I expect you're more qualified to teach what we're doing.'

Kiran seemed serious. Steve had tried to get her into bed for days, and now, just when he realized he liked her too much to take advantage of her body, she was hitting his flashpoint. 'What is it that we're doing?'

'We're going to make love,' she whispered, sliding her hand under his T-shirt.

The feel of her fingers stroking and gliding across his back was sweet torture. Steve buried his head in her neck, giving himself up to the moment. 'Will you regret this in the morning?' he asked, pressing kisses along her collarbone.

'Only if you do.'

She was more sure than he would have expected.

He was trying to think of any reason to retreat, while Kiran seemed convinced that being together tonight was right. 'I can't think of any reason I would regret it, but, Kiran, you're not a woman I would treat lightly. I can't offer you anything –'

'Did I ask for anything?' Though the lights were dim, he could see the blaze in her eyes.

'Shh,' he murmured, sliding one hand up under her nightgown. 'I was just making sure.'

'Quit trying to be a noble bachelor and turn the lights out,' Kiran told him. 'Playing twenty conditions isn't going to do anything but make one of us angry.'

'Okay.' She was right. He had been searching for something in her answers, something that would tell him that everything would be all right. That they would be the same two people when they woke up in the morning. They weren't going to be, and Kiran knew that. He stretched and turned out the light. 'I can't see you,' he complained in the sudden darkness.

'It's better that way. A little mysterious,' she said.

He felt her hand slide into the back of his briefs, stroking and kneading his skin as if she was trying to soothe him.

He didn't need to be soothed. He needed Kiran to finally take him over the edge he'd been on since he'd laid eyes on her again. 'My mystery woman,' he murmured into her hair. 'It describes you perfectly.'

There was a robe in his way, and Steve gently

removed it from Kiran, tossing it to the floor. The nightgown he was more careful with as he drew it over Kiran's head before dropping it in the same vicinity as the robe. He caressed the side of Kiran's waist, moving up to pull her closer to him. Their bodies melded together as if recognizing a suddenly remembered harmony, yet they'd never touched like this before.

'You feel good,' Kiran whispered.

'You do, too.'

'It's been a long time for me,' she cautioned.

Steve raised his head. He couldn't see Kiran's expression very well in the darkness, but he wished he could. 'Tell you what. As much as I hate to do this, I'm going to my room to get some protection. I'm going to sprint, but you'll have about thirty seconds to change your mind. Deal?'

He felt her fingertips move to his face in reassurance.

'The stopwatch is ticking,' she said. 'Do some Olympic sprinting, Steve.'

Regretfully, he left the shelter of Kiran's warmth. He forced himself to walk slowly enough to give them both a chance to cool off. One part of him was shouting that he was nuts to give her a chance to back out of letting him make love to her. The other part applauded his restraint.

Restraint, hell. He snatched the condoms from the bedside table in his room and strode back to Kiran's room.

'Knock, knock,' he said, trying for levity in case

she had changed her mind. 'It's your friendly cable man. Do you still require my services?'

'Do come in, sir,' Kiran answered, 'I'm afraid my wiring desperately needs attention.'

Steve shed the rest of his clothes, reaching to find Kiran in the bed before lying alongside her. 'I'll give it a thorough inspection, ma'am, but from the looks of you you're wired just right. You probably just need to be plugged in.'

She giggled softly and ran a hand over his chest. Pulling Kiran into his arms, Steve reveled in her easy compliance. He went softly, slowly, as if she was a windblown flower whose petals he didn't want to bruise. There were things he hadn't known about her before, but that didn't matter now. What he did know was that, though she was delicate, she was determined to flourish in the weedy, hard-baked soil her seed had been cast in. He admired Kiran, his mirror image, who outshone him with her courage.

Moaning with desire he could no longer hold back, Steve took Kiran to him, telling himself to savor this moment because he'd been waiting to feel this way, it seemed, forever.

Destiny had never been on their side. But the way Kiran had made him feel tonight was something Steve could never forget.

Jarvis held his bleeding hand behind his back as he stared down the young police officer standing on the steps of the market. 'Little late to buy groceries, isn't it, son?'

The youngster wasn't cowed. 'I hope you have an alibi for the last thirty minutes, because I believe it was your car I saw parked on County Road 147. If you don't have an alibi, Mr Andrews, I'm going to have to arrest you for breaking and entering.'

'Into my own store?' Jarvis demanded.

'No, sir. Into a farmhouse up the way.'

'Why, I didn't break in anywhere, son. You must have seen a different car. I've been here all night.'

'I don't think so, sir.'

'You calling me a liar? My wife will tell you I haven't left the property.'

'Your wife will verify your alibi?'

Jarvis nodded, furious. How dare this young pup not know who Jarvis Andrews was? Bedford would pull strings to get him out of this – and have this boy bounced to desk duty at the same time.

'Of course she will. You've made a mistake,' he stated haughtily. 'The biggest one you'll ever make.'

'I'll pretend I didn't hear what sounded like a threat, Mr Andrews. If you'll get in my car, I'll let you tell your story down at the courthouse.'

Father John lay in his solitary bed, unable to sleep. He couldn't stop thinking about Maypat. Her voice had been shaking as she'd made her confession. He'd been so shocked by her disclosures he'd forgotten to give her a penance, but as he went back over the conversation he realized penance hadn't been what Maypat wanted. She wanted to erase an overwhelming shadow from her life.

He wondered if she was able to sleep tonight. His mind turned to Kiran and Steve, hoping they were getting some peace at last. Maybe California would put some distance between them and the dilemma they faced.

Of course, it might not be a problem any more if Lakina would reveal herself to them. At the thought of the tall, strikingly beautiful woman, John's heart sped up in a way it had no right to. No wonder people had known whom he was seeking at the mention of Lakina Dorn's name. She was an admired member of her community, someone who had made it to the top. Not only that, but once having met her no one could forget her.

He could not forget her. And therein lay a bigger problem, one he hadn't given any consideration. Lakina's aunt was probably right to fear for her niece's safety. After all, if he couldn't forget her, why would anyone in Cottonwood be able to, either? The catwalks of New York and Paris weren't for the meek of appearance or heart. Here in this little town she would be recognized, her story remembered. The connection of her mother – and Caleb – remembered.

Was he wrong in encouraging her to claim her heritage, the inheritance that should be hers? What was his duty?

John's eyes closed tiredly, weariness overtaking him as his thoughts ran like rats through tunnels. His duty. It was the crucible of his being. Only in this room could he admit that he no longer wanted to claim the priesthood as his life. Listening to Maypat's demons had convinced him further. She had come to him to confess, but he was not worthy to hear her confession.

Monsignor would be dismayed if he knew John's feelings. Counseling would be ordered, as well as soul-searching prayer. Of course, he'd been searching his soul and praying for months, ever since the insidious truth had wended its way out of hiding. How long had he been denying that he no longer felt the work he did counted enough for him do it until the day he died? Maypat and the other parishioners were better than he because they struggled through the ordeal of confession – while he hid from his secret.

A tear seeped out as John opened his eyes, followed by another as he stared out into the impenetrable blackness of his room.

Early sunlight flowed through the window, waking Steve. Abruptly he leapt from the bed, remembering he'd agreed to meet Mitch for breakfast. His gaze lit on Kiran, and he couldn't believe that he'd actually spent the night making love to her. He didn't feel a bit tired. In fact, he was so energized he'd probably make his qualifying run in record time today.

Kiran turned over, the sheet sliding off one leg. Steve stared, his stomach suddenly bottoming out. Puckered, discolored skin starting at her calf led a twisting path up one long, slender limb. His heart was pounding, an inner voice shouting to him to stop. Steve stepped forward, taking the edge of the sheet in his fingers so that he could see her legs to the knees.

Nausea swept him as he stared at the disfigurement of the legs he remembered running through corn fields, bared to the sun as Kiran dove into the fishing hole on Uncle Caleb's property. Since the funeral Steve had noticed Kiran's reluctance to show any skin. She'd worn long skirts and pants, even long nightgowns, the entire time they'd been in Texas, though the temperature had been searing. He had decided her clothing was modest either because of her profession or because one didn't pack halters and mini-skirts when one was attending a funeral.

Kiran had been concealing scars. Somehow, at some time, Kiran had suffered some kind of accident – at least he could only pray it had been an accident. Fear whistled through his mind, haunting him because that wasn't the likely answer. He hadn't known about Kiran's marriage because Agnes had been too ashamed to tell anyone. Was this another one of Agnes's guilty secrets?

He was going to kill the miserable old witch.

Unfortunately, Kiran would not tell him the truth about what had happened. He knew that too well. It wasn't that she was protecting Agnes. She was protecting her right to grow into a sane, functioning woman by outgrowing the shame she'd endured.

She had wanted him to make love to her, but she

had asked him to turn out the lights.

She had been hiding from him.

Steve pulled the sheet back down and covered her with the blanket before snatching up his clothes and leaving the room, closing the door behind him. He hurried to this bedroom, throwing himself into a leather chair as he cursed violently.

Kiran had not risen above her ragged childhood the way she tried to project. She'd had good reason to keep him at arm's length before last night. *My little house by the mountains is the only place I've ever felt completely safe and secure.* She had said his profession was too risky to suit her, and his lifestyle was different from what she would fit in with; he had known all that, too. But he hadn't really wanted to accept it. *I'd want something with guarantees.* She'd admitted that.

Yeah, well. He didn't come with any.

CHAPTER 16

Kiran awakened slowly, allowing herself to enjoy the warm, well-loved feeling of being with Steve last night. Making love with him had been everything she had known it would be. He had made her feel desirable, made passion run through her in rivers of ecstasy. He had asked her if she would regret their loving in the morning. The total contentment of her body testified that there was nothing to regret.

Stretching, Kiran sat up in bed. A shower first, then a lazy day spent around the pool sounded like heaven. She'd be wonderfully relaxed for the star-gazing Steve had promised for tonight.

Somewhere in the house she could hear a phone ringing. Kiran realized Steve hadn't said he might try to call her. Still, the caller could be him. She grabbed her bathrobe and headed to find the phone, deciding that if she listened to the message the caller was leaving, she would know if she should pick up the receiver.

'Steve, it's Ginger. I'll see you and Kiran at the race track. Tell her to take a hairbrush because it's going to be windy. Good luck with the pole race today. Bye.'

Kiran's heart felt as if it was shrinking in her chest. Steve had said there was a practice run today, nothing that would interest her. She had envisioned something like soccer practice, a warm-up session. Ginger had called it a race, one important enough to warrant her presence at the track and a good luck call.

She told herself it wasn't important. Maybe she hadn't been listening carefully to Steve's description. What was a pole race anyway? Racing was foreign to her, except for what Uncle Caleb had written about Steve in his letters over the years – more of a proud uncle's brag than informative discourse. Ginger and Steve shared an understanding of his livelihood. Kiran had told him it was too risky for her. Too unstable, too frightening.

The hairbrush comment bothered her most of all. Ginger's hair was a long, thick wealth of glossy auburn waves. Kiran would hardly need a hairbrush for her bob of straight-edge hair, no matter how windy the day. As unsophisticated as Kiran knew she might be, she recognized two things: one, Ginger was trying very hard to believe that Kiran was simply Steve's cousin and that the relationship was only a family thing, and two, Ginger was trying to draw comparisons in Steve's mind with the brush remark – comparisons that would make him realize how much more attractive she was than Kiran.

Kiran returned to her room, puzzling over the

green-tasting jealousy she felt. Slipping a one-piece swimsuit on, she eyed herself in the mirror. Blonde hair, blue eyes, light eyebrows. Lips that would never need the services of a plastic surgeon to enhance the fullness. Medium-sized breasts that accentuated an hour-glass shape she was proud of.

She turned, forcing herself to finish cataloguing her body. A rear-end that filled out her jeans nicely, legs that . . . Kiran faced the mirror again. Legs that she wished she didn't have to hide all the time. The trail of burns made her wince. They were a part of her, but not a part she wanted anyone to see – especially Steve. Not right now, anyway. Never, actually, since they would soon go their separate ways. He need never learn why she had missed that summer at Uncle Caleb's house.

Steve tore around the track in record time, curiously unaware that he had actually been driving. Mitch ran over to the car, giving him a high five when Steve let down the black latticed window.

'Man, you really had it in the wind! I don't think anybody can beat that time!'

Steve pulled himself out through the window, unfastening his helmet, automatically checking his time. The fastest he'd ever clocked in a pole race.

All because he couldn't get his mind off Kiran. He had teased her about coming to California to be his good luck charm. The charm had worn off when he'd seen her legs. Caustic anger was claiming him, charring his emotions. She was not telling him the

241

truth about her life, and some fine-honed caution he'd developed during his own marred past was warning him that Kiran wasn't going to talk about it because it involved Agnes. Mean-to-the-bone Agnes, who purported to have taken such good care of Kiran. She had never cared about her stepdaughter. Agnes was out to sue Uncle Caleb's estate because she felt she deserved something, wanted a ride on Kiran's back.

Kiran was a fighter. He knew that, had seen her stand up for him and for Uncle Caleb. Would she fight for herself if things got too nasty with Agnes?

He didn't know. Something told him she wouldn't, that this little secret was being covered over. Kiran planned on retreating to her mountain hideaway – her place of refuge – when this was all over. He hated the idea. Briefly he checked whether he hated it because she was willing to walk away from a sexual liaison with him, no commitment required, which was supposed to be the man's role. He, on the other hand, was not keen to think about losing her so soon.

No, he wasn't suffering from machismo. He honestly hated the thought of Kiran having to suffer Agnes's treatment and then return to Tennessee with nothing. He wanted her to come out ahead this time, just this once be the winner in their family round-robin of dysfunction.

'I knew Mark Martin wasn't going to be able to beat your time. You got the number one starting position! Hot-damn!' Mitch was doing high fives with other members of the crew, celebrating the record time and the pole position they'd captured. Steve forced himself to grin, knowing that the position was critical to him. It was always a bonus to be positioned well for starting a race, but for him there had been a long string of top ten finishes and no better for a while. Last time the team had won the pole they'd gone on to win the race the next day – and though it wasn't a guarantee it was certainly something to celebrate.

He wished he felt like it. 'Hey, I've got a helluva crew. And crew chief. This car's running better than it ever has.'

Mitch was grinning as photographers flocked around the car, aiming their cameras at Steve. A few reporters from the sports networks jammed microphones his way, hoping for some sound-bites. He began his stock rambling. 'Yeah, I'm real excited. We weren't sure how things were going to play out . . .'

He stopped when he realized Ginger was standing next to him, smiling at the cameras as if the reporters had come to see her. Or as if she belonged there with him.

'Congratulations, Steve!' she exclaimed, throwing her arms around his neck and planting a victory kiss on his mouth.

Shock cut his response to a short, 'Thanks, Ginger.' She was acting as she always had, he realized, as if she had never left him for Dan Crane – who had captured only a tenth-place starting position today. Steve felt sorry for Mitch, who had seen Ginger kissing him and probably wished she was congratulating him instead. But Ginger would never settle for a crew chief; the guy who was doing the fast driving was the only one she would ever want.

Backing off as fast as he could, Steve nodded to the reporters and hurried to change out of his gear. Far from the cameras, he scrubbed one hand over his mouth. He didn't want to think about Ginger's kiss the next time he kissed Kiran.

Suddenly Steve recognized the error of that thought. Kiran was more badly bruised emotionally than she was letting on. She had said she was emotionally needy. He had disagreed because the front she was putting up had convinced him otherwise. But those burns on her legs told a different story. Kiran was fragile when it came to matters that involved the heart; she maintained a careful distance like he did, though they utilized different methods.

She might be more fragile than he was prepared to handle. Though she had asked him to make love to her, was a few all-nighters enough for a woman who obviously needed more? He didn't have any more to give her – or any woman.

He should not have succumbed to her last night, as wonderful as it had been. If he hurt her, he would blame himself, because he should have been strong enough to say no, to comfort her in a non-sexual manner. She had needed him, and he had tuned into his own craving for her. Tonight he would not make the same mistake, he vowed, and if there was any way to get the truth out of Kiran without cracking her thin, protective façade, he was going to do that, too.

And if he discovered Agnes was the evil villainess in this drama that he suspected she was, then heaven help her. Because he was going to make her pay for hurting Kiran.

Seven o'clock flipped over on the digital clock in her room and Kiran sighed, getting up to walk around. She was dressed and ready for the dinner Steve had promised her tonight. It had been a lovely, relaxing day to indulge herself, but the phone had been silent and she had hoped all day that Steve might call. Of course he had said he would be very busy. She also knew he was taking time out of his schedule to show her around, which she appreciated.

The fact was, she'd taken extra care with her appearance tonight, hoping that Steve would want her as much as she did him. Ginger's message had nagged at her all day, though she had not allowed it to ruin her happiness. She had witnessed Steve's lackluster response to the beautiful redhead, but certainly female instincts were in high gear. It was important to her that she look her best when Steve came home, especially if he'd had Ginger clinging to him all day like a spitball on a chalkboard.

A sudden slam announced his arrival. Kiran could hardly contain her excitement. She raced to meet him.

'Hi! How did it go?' she asked, her heart speeding up. He was wearing aviator-style sunglasses, the lenses so dark she couldn't see his eyes. A shivery feeling of anticipation shot through her as she thought about how sexy, how handsome, this man was who had loved her all night long.

He whipped off the glasses and put them in his pocket as he walked through the hall toward her. She noted at once the strain in his eyes and the lack of the really warm smile he usually gave her. She felt herself blush awkwardly, but consigned it to the fact that she had sounded somewhat like a housewife.

'Fine. Better than I expected.' He halted in front of her, giving her a quick glance. 'You look nice.'

'Thanks. I wanted to dress appropriately for stargazing. I hope I am,' she said shyly, wiggling for an extra bit of confirmation that she looked just right to him.

'Stargazing?'

Her heart sank a little at his obviously perplexed expression. 'You remember – you were going to take me . . .'

She didn't finish her explanation. By the 'I forgot' look on his face, Kiran knew what had happened. 'Oh, well, we can do something else just as well.'

'I'm sorry. It completely slipped my mind.'

'Don't worry about it. You warned me you'd be preoccupied – I had advance warning about racers' amnesia the night before a big race.' She offered him a smile to show that she didn't mind. 'Tomorrow is the big race, isn't it?'

'Of course. Why do you ask?'

'Well, because . . .' Maybe she shouldn't say she'd heard Ginger's message just yet, and that she knew today had obviously been more than just a practice run. 'I was trying to make sure I understood what was going on.'

He took her by the shoulders and led her into the den where they'd watched TV last night. 'Speaking of understanding what's going on, Kiran, I think you and I need to have a serious talk.'

She held her smile in place with an effort. Surely he didn't regret last night? It would hurt like nothing she'd ever felt before if he did. 'Okay.'

'I want to shower first. You think of what you're hungry for, and I'll take you out to dinner. We can talk then.'

He passed her, heading down the hall to his room. Dismay ran cold through her. Steve was not acting like the man who'd held her close last night, whispering sweet sex-talk that had driven her wild with passion as they'd rocked together.

He was acting like a man who'd conquered – and lost interest in his conquest. She shook her head, telling herself that thought was immature. Steve was tired in every cell of his body, and would probably prefer to throw himself between the sheets and sleep, or indulge in some late-night partying with the guys. Instead, he was taking her to dinner to have a serious talk. That shouldn't upset her, because they'd had to have plenty of those since their reunion. It didn't mean something had gone wrong between them.

She had suddenly lost interest in going out. Deciding that he might feel less obligated to entertain her if she called out for dinner, Kiran went to the kitchen to find a phone directory. She could treat him to Mexican food. That was always a safe bet. Picking up the portable phone, she turned it on.

'I forgot I have a dinner engagement tonight. Can we do this tomorrow sometime?' Steve was asking.

A female voice answered, 'Sure. I'll be looking forward to it.'

Kiran clicked the phone off again, closing her eyes on a desperate sigh. She told herself the conversation meant nothing. Waiting five minutes, she walked to Steve's bedroom. Satisfied that the shower water was now running, she called in an order for delivery.

He joined her in the den five minutes later, looking more handsome than was good for her as he scrubbed his hair dry with a red towel. In the dark last night, she hadn't noticed that Steve's chest hair was lightly sprinkled across tanned muscles – a fact that now made her throat close up tight. He'd thrown on the same faded pair of jeans he had worn yesterday, the waistband still dangerously frayed. Finishing with the rubdown, he draped the towel around his neck, leaving sandy strands of hair sticking up in disarray.

'So, did you decide what you want to eat?'

'I have. In fact, I hope you like Mexican because that's what I've ordered for dinner.'

'Ordered?' His deep green eyes were puzzled.

'Well, you looked tired. I wasn't really in the mood to go out. If we're going to talk, we can do it much better here.'

'Oh.' He looked uncertain for a moment. 'Well, okay. If you're sure. I don't mind taking you out, Kiran.'

She was sure he looked relieved. 'It's okay. Go finish dressing. I'll listen for the doorbell.'

He nodded and left the den. Kiran jumped up and went to the kitchen, getting out forks and napkins. She took them into the den, sliding open the glass door leading to the pool. Returning to the kitchen, she found a citronella candle and some other utensils she thought might come in handy. Carrying them outside, Kiran arranged them on the table. Dusk was starting to soothe the skyline and she breathed deeply, enjoying the cooler air and the pool's tiny ripples whenever a breeze blew across the water.

'What are you doing?'

Kiran jumped, her daydreaming mood interrupted. He had changed into khakis and a navy polo shirt that was just as eye-pleasing as the jeans had been. 'We can do a different kind of stargazing eating out here,' she told him.

'Hell, I can't believe I forgot about that, Kiran. I'm sorry.'

She put a hand on his arm, catching his gaze with hers. 'This is going to be even more fun than seeing a couple of movie stars. And much more appetizing.'

Steve didn't want Kiran to act as if he was doing her a favor by letting her hang around with him. He had been a jerk by forgetting the plans she had been looking forward to. His mind had been on the race and a host of other things, but not taking Kiran to hunt up celebrities. It hadn't been so very much she had wanted.

She looked comfortable and enticing in a long flowing skirt that swayed when she walked, and little beige sandals that matched the lighter hues in the material. The sweater top she wore had long sleeves, but it was an open-mesh cotton and looked cool. He couldn't help wondering how much of her body had been burned. Now that he remembered, everything she wore covered her to the wrists.

'Kiran, what did you do today?'

'I swam! I laid out, read a great book, and simply lazed around while you were probably burning up in a race-car.'

He nearly jumped out of his skin when she said burning. 'It was pretty warm,' he said slowly, 'but I had so much on my mind, I don't think I noticed the heat.'

'It isn't as bad as it was in Cottonwood. I think the humidity is different here, or maybe being close to the coastline helps. Don't you think it's not the same kind of heat?'

Steve wasn't sure. He certainly felt as if he was roasting. It had to be his conscience cooking his brain. 'The drought probably had a lot to do with the temperature in Texas. Of course, there have been wildfires in California, so maybe this is just a good location.' Pausing, he watched the breeze blow the skirt daintily around Kiran's ankles. 'So, you swam. Did you bring a bathing suit?'

'Of course! It's summer. I had actually planned on a nostalgic swim in the fishing hole at Uncle Caleb's.' She wrinkled her straight little nose. 'Your pool is nicer, Steve. You've come a long way.'

'I'm glad you had fun. Tomorrow you can test your sun exposure around the race track.'

'Ginger left a message that I should bring a hairbrush because it's so windy.'

'Jeez.' He rubbed the back of his neck. 'Listen, don't pay any attention to anything Ginger says or does. She's got beautiful hair, and she obsesses over it. Wear whatever you've got that's comfortable, put your hair up in one of those ponytail hairdos that looks great on you, and cheer me to first place.'

'A ponytail? I thought I should try to look glamorous.'

Steve shook his head, rolling his eyes. What he liked about Kiran was that she was beautiful without having to work at it. He definitely did not want Ginger rubbing off on her. 'When you wear your hair in a ponytail, you look beautiful, Kiran. You're sophisticated in a carefree way, which . . .' He stopped short of saying *which drives me out of my mind*. 'Which is fine.'

She looked startled and pleased. Steve groaned inwardly. Tomorrow was going to be a nightmare if Ginger decided to take Kiran under her wing.

'Hey, listen, you guys,' a voice called over the fence. 'I've been standing on the porch ringing the doorbell for five minutes. If you want this food, you gotta answer the door.'

Steve grinned. 'I'll be right there,' he said loudly. Aside to Kiran, he said, 'Tenacious fellow, isn't he?'

'Gosh! That got here fast.' Kiran hurried inside. 'Let me get my purse.'

'Cool it,' he said, reaching for her wrist to slow her down. 'You're not buying my meal. I was supposed to take you out. I'm at least buying your dinner.' He released her, grabbing his wallet and opening the front door.

'It's sixty bucks without the tip,' the delivery man said ungraciously.

'Sixty bucks! What's in there? Imported enchiladas? No wonder you wouldn't leave without delivering the food.'

'Listen, buddy, ask your woman. She ordered.'

'Well, I thought you'd be hungry,' Kiran explained sheepishly. 'And I wasn't sure how much food sixty dollars bought in California. I thought maybe this was just expensive.'

Steve tipped the delivery man generously and closed the door, carrying the two huge sacks into the kitchen. 'Maybe you should have ordered a waiter to serve us, too. Heck, we'll have Mexican food for three days.'

'A sopapilla for breakfast would be essentially the same thing as a doughnut.' Kiran began pulling the food out of the containers and putting it onto the plates.

'You thought of everything, didn't you?' Actually the food looked mouthwatering. 'I'm going to sleep like a baby tonight. Mexican food always makes me feel like I need to lie down and nap.'

'I don't think you'll be able to blame it on the cuisine. Didn't you tell me you're always tired after a race?'

'The night before I'm way too keyed up to be tired.' Actually, he was keyed up, but it was from all the stuff he was trying to process about Kiran. He wanted to be stiff and unapproachable around her, now that he knew that he shouldn't have made love with her. Yet he couldn't help wanting to touch her again. When she bent to place the plates on the patio table, her loose sweater rose a little, exposing the smooth flesh of her waist.

Steve wanted to reach out and grab her, wanted to put his arms around her and feel what was under that sweater. She sat down and looked at him expectantly, so Steve joined her, as if there was nothing more on his mind than patio dining.

'Maybe a brisk swim after the meal will chase away the nap feeling,' she told him.

Maybe a brisk swim would also chase away the sudden rush of sexual desire threatening him. 'Maybe. Join me?' he asked, wondering if she would wear the swimsuit for him.

'I don't know. Is it safe to?'

He sat up, his fork suspended. 'Is there a hidden meaning in that question?'

'You know – "just when you thought it was safe to go back into the water",' she quoted from the *Jaws* movie. 'This is California, you know.'

'I haven't noticed any triangular dorsal fins rising out of the water. So, short of dunking you if you keep referring to me as some kind of voracious creature, I think you're safe.'

'This from the same man who couldn't get enough last night,' she murmured. 'Voracious, indeed.'

He couldn't get to what he wanted to know if she continued teasing him. What she didn't know was that she was running the serious risk of being tossed into the pool for an attack of a different kind. 'Either you eat your share of the sixty dollars' worth of food you ordered, or I throw you into the pool and do my best shark imitation, up to and including making love to you until we're both wrinkled like California raisins.'

'And then?'

'Then I renege on my earlier promise not to eat you.' His expression made it clear his hunger was for her. 'Man cannot live on Mexican food alone, you know.'

'Save the sopapillas for breakfast after all?'

He laid down his fork. 'They're the same as a doughnut, essentially,' he mimicked. 'And you'd be surprised how long I can hold my breath under water.'

'Surprised, or pleased?' She gave him an arch look. 'And are you able to back up your boasting?'

'I never boast,' he stated, his gaze serious. 'Would you care to find out?'

She considered him for a moment. The sun shone gently on the water in the pool beside them, the sparkles of light reminding her uncomfortably of her vulnerability. 'Maybe later.' Her gaze tore from his and fastened on the plate in front of her.

'Too much sun exposure today?' He knew better than that, of course.

'Yes.'

'I promise I'll keep you covered.'

She laughed, but it was an uncertain sound. 'If I get any more sun, I'll be miserable at the track tomorrow. When the sun goes down, I'll do my mermaid routine while you're impersonating *Jaws*. I was on the swim team in high school, you know. I bet I can swim circles around you.'

He sat back, surprised. 'Swim team in high school?' he repeated. Was he wrong? Was she not hiding anything from him? Certainly she wouldn't have exposed her legs to teenage friends – kids could be cruel with their taunts.

'Well, I quit after my junior year,' she confessed. 'Why?'

Her gaze slid away from his again, traveling to the side of the house and then the hedges, as if she could look at anything but him. 'Oh, I don't know. It was my senior year, and I was tired of getting up so early in the morning to practise. I had to study –'

'Kiran,' he interrupted. 'You might as well tell me the truth, because I'm going to ask.'

'The truth?' Her eyes were pained blue circles in her face.

'You quit swim team, which you obviously enjoyed. You got married right out of high school to get away from Agnes.'

'Interesting personal history, isn't it?'

'Kiran,' he said softly, not deterred by her flip remark, 'how did your legs get burned?'

CHAPTER 17

Kiran wouldn't look at him. Steve softened his tone. 'Tell me, Kiran.'

'It's none of your business.'

That was true. 'It may not be, but I'd still like to know. You told me about your marriage. Why not this?'

She shrugged, slowly lifting her gaze to meet his. 'I was hoping you wouldn't ask.'

'Maybe I shouldn't.' He reached across the table and took her hand in his. 'Last night, I assumed we pretty much knew each other – enough to . . . share our bodies. Apparently you feel that how you got burned needs to be kept from me. I just wish you wouldn't set up your defense mechanisms again.'

Kiran stared him down. 'Like you don't have any.'

'I drive when I'm upset,' he admitted. 'But I haven't hidden anything from you.'

'What difference does it make, Steve?' Her eyes pleaded with him. 'It was an accident. It happened, and I've moved past it.'

'Was it Agnes?' he asked softly.

'Indirectly.'

He cursed under his breath. It was always Agnes, indirectly or otherwise.

Kiran stiffened. 'Agnes was lousy, but Butch used you for a punching bag. Why does my life have to be the one under the microscope?'

He withdrew his hand from hers. 'How do you know that?'

'I would have had to be blind not to notice the tables turning the night you threatened to beat Butch if he didn't leave me alone. That was a first, if the expression on his face was any indication.'

This was something he didn't intend to discuss. 'Maybe.'

'So you told me he only abused you verbally.'

'That was what hurt the most! But I'll tell you something else: it also hurts that you can't confide in me.' *Especially after last night*, his heart reminded him. 'Jeez! How much closer do we have to get before you give up some of yourself, Kiran?'

'Why should I tell you? We really don't know each other anymore. Do you want days of confessions?' Her eyes locked angrily with his.

'No. But what I'm hearing is you don't want me to know any more about you than a few days' worth of your body in the dark.'

'Am I supposed to take this complaint seriously – from a man who uses his penis as a means of communication?' Kiran crossed her arms, daring

258

him to deny it. 'You'd rather sex be casual so that you don't have to feel anything other than physical attraction for a woman.'

'Not with you,' he growled. 'And any woman I've touched has wanted me to.' *Same as you.* But he refused to point it out.

'Of course. Notching up satisfied groupies goes along with winning trophies. Your ego won't let you lose at anything, because you're too afraid of failing. Yet you want to tell me that I'm crippled emotionally? What woman wants a man to see her flaws?'

'What happened to you is not a flaw, Kiran. It's a serious incident that you're keeping from me.'

She shook her head. 'Look, I told you I was needy. That's a confession most men would run from. I gave you a chance to back out, but you didn't want to take it. Don't try to use my burns as justification. If I wasn't good enough in bed, say so. But stop throwing all this junk at me. I feel like I'm being raped emotionally.'

He went pale as sand.

Kiran sighed. 'Face the fact that we're too different for each other, Steve, and probably too damaged.'

His heart was thundering in his chest. 'I know what you're doing,' he said, his voice dangerously low, 'and fortunately for you my egocentric personality won't allow you to get away with that pathetic excuse. Come on.'

He reached across the table, grabbed her hand and pulled her from the chair.

'What are you doing?'

'You wanted to go out. We're going out.'

'We can't leave all this food lying here!' Kiran pulled back on his hand.

'You're right. I'll carry it into the kitchen.' He began stacking the plates on top of each other.

'I'm not going anywhere with you. You're in a strange mood.'

He paused, staring at her curiously. 'You're not afraid of me, are you, Kiran?'

'Well, I . . .' She wrapped her arms around herself. 'I think we've said some unkind things to each other and –'

Steve cursed fluently, going back to carelessly stacking everything on the plates so he could take it in all at once. 'Kiran, I have never hit anyone in my life, if that's what you're implying. Once I got into a bar room brawl that some of my buddies started and finished, but I don't count that because I'm not sure if I got in any decent punches or not.' He jerked his head in the direction of the sliding glass door, indicating that she should precede him inside. 'If I learned anything in my quest not to turn out like the old man, it was to take my frustrations out another way. Which is racing. So don't try to dissuade me from taking you out by putting up a little fake fear front. I'm on to you, Kiran Whitley. You know I wouldn't hurt you.'

He stopped and thought for a moment before setting the food in the refrigerator. 'I may beat Agnes within an inch of her life, however.'

'I said she was indirectly involved in the accident!' Kiran glared at him.

'Why are you protecting the old witch? That's something I'd really like to know.'

'I survived growing up with her, Steve, and I've gone on with my life. Besides, she's her own worst enemy, and that's punishment enough.'

'I am still strangely possessed to set fire to the old woman and see how she likes it.'

Kiran gasped. 'That's horrible! Why would you say something like that?'

He rubbed his face. 'Because somehow she was responsible for the harm that came to you. She wasn't doing her job as a parent.'

'Yes, but she wasn't my parent.' Kiran's eyes shot blue sparks. 'She ended up with me, a little present she never wanted but kept, always hoping the man she loved – my father – would return to claim us. He didn't, and she got stuck with the booby prize, Steve. So why blame her?'

'Booby prize? You don't really see yourself that way, do you?' It twisted his heart to hear her say it.

'I think it's a pretty fair assessment of what happened. Lord knows, she's no princess of light, but don't say such a horrible thing, Steve.' She slumped a little, her gaze lowering to the floor. 'I know you didn't mean it. I know you're angry. But you're angry with me because you can't manipulate me into telling you what you want to know.' She met his gaze reluctantly. 'Besides, you wouldn't want to see Agnes suffer that way.'

He slowly drew her into his arms, holding her tightly. 'You're a better person than me, Kiran.'

'I know.' She gave his arm a squeeze. 'I'm sorry you saw my legs. You won't be able to forget it now.'

He took a deep, ragged breath. 'She's suing us, Kiran. How am I supposed to feel, knowing that she . . . that you won't defend yourself against her? Won't let me defend you?'

'That's where you're wrong.' She looked up into his eyes, making him crazy with urges no other woman had ever made him feel. 'She's contesting her deceased brother's will. You and I happen to be in the way. She honestly believes she deserves something because they were family, never mind that she didn't like Caleb and he didn't like her.'

'That's so screwed up.'

'Yes, well, that is a part of our family tree, Steve.' Kiran nudged his leg with hers. 'But we'll foil her plans because Caleb specifically asked us to make sure his siblings didn't get their hands on what was his.'

'Will you ever tell me?'

She thought for a minute. He tightened his hold on her, trying to show her that he wouldn't let her go, ever if she needed all night to talk.

'I don't like to remember,' she said softly.

'All right. Then don't.' He tipped her chin so that he could bring his lips down on hers over and over again. She sagged against him, sighing her surrender.

'I can't get enough of you,' he murmured.

'In spite of the fact that I'm a little over-cooked?'

'Jeez, Kiran!' He pulled back to stare at her, too shocked to pursue the sexual thoughts he'd been having.

She nestled up against him, despite the sudden tenseness of his body. 'I was trying to joke about it. I'm sorry, Steve. I just don't want you to feel sorry for me. The real truth is, I'm afraid of fire now, to the point where I won't even light one in a fire-place.'

'You wouldn't need one in California, Kiran.'

Her lips parted in surprise. He defied her stare with a quirk of his brows, letting his remark sink in. 'Are you ready to go out?'

'Where is it that you're taking me?'

He grabbed her hand and headed for the front door. 'Driving. You seriously must learn to drive while you're a guest in my home.'

'I already know how to drive,' she protested.

'Yes, but learning to appreciate the seduction of speed is something you should experience before the race tomorrow.'

'I thought this morning was only a practice run.' Kiran allowed Steve to pull her with him to his car. 'Why didn't you want me with you today?'

'It was kind of a practice run. But I didn't take you with me because I wanted you to relax and do something for yourself for a change. And also because you shouldn't have to sit through two days of watching me go around a race track.'

He opened the car door and helped her in. 'Ginger is,' Kiran complained.

'Ginger is one of those groupies you so kindly accused me of pleasuring for the sake of my ego. She is addicted to men who drive fast and dangerously.'

'Like you.'

'Yeah.' Steve gunned the engine. 'Tonight, you're going to do the fast driving.'

'Are you sure we can do this?' Kiran asked, peering at the first speedway she'd ever been to. 'Somebody won't come ask us to leave?'

'Nah.'

Steve got out of the car and walked around to the passenger side, opening the door and extending his hand to help Kiran out. She let him help her, not releasing him until she was standing eye-to-eye with him.

'The track is open so the drivers can check it out, try out their cars if they need to. There's usually more people than this around, but maybe they all went to dinner.' He waited for her to take the driver's seat.

'Are you sure this is a good idea?'

'It's safer than letting you drive on an open road, where someone could get hurt. Go ahead, get in.' He gave her a cocky grin. 'If you think we might need helmets, I can get some.'

'No, thank you, smart aleck. I'm only going to drive about fifty miles an hour, so that your purpose in bringing me out here will be spoiled.'

'Are you deliberately trying to sabotage my efforts?'

'No. I just understand you too well. If I top out at sixty, that will be sufficient to prove that there is no such thing as the seduction of speed.' She gave him a thorough, silent eyeing in the same way she would do one of her pupils. 'You're trying to make the point that I'm too thin-skinned to deal with anything out of my element. I will handle Agnes when the time comes, and I will retain the emotional weapons that you seem to find so paltry.'

'Jeez, Kiran.' Steve rubbed his hair back from his brow and scratched his head. 'You're nervous as hell, aren't you?'

'Yes,' she said simply. 'I think I am.'

'I'm going to need earplugs to get through this, I can tell,' he grumbled. 'There are some in the trunk with my helmet.'

'I'll be fine,' she snapped. 'I really want to do this. I'm just not used to . . .'

'Cutting loose. Letting yourself go. I know.' He grinned. 'Get in.'

She slid behind the wheel. 'I keep reminding myself that this cute little sports car of yours is not a race car. It has limits.'

Steve was buckling his seat belt and not really paying attention to her. 'Comparable engine, though. This baby runs like a bad girl runs from confession. Mitch and the guys work on this car from time to time for fun. We thought about –' He looked up and saw her face. 'What's wrong?'

'Nothing. Just shut up, okay?'

He looked her over for a moment. 'Kiran, you don't have to do this if you really don't want to.'

'Yes, I do. The gauntlet has been thrown down; the test of courage awaits.'

'What did you say you used to teach in high school?' He was starting to think Shakespeare had possessed her body.

'British Lit, among other things.' She twisted the key in the ignition and the engine started without hesitation. 'See? Nothing to it.' Buckling the seat belt, she adjusted the rear-view mirror to her satisfaction. 'Ready?'

'Ready.' Steve was starting to wonder if this was a good idea. Kiran was literally shaking in her little sandals. 'Just pretend you're following a pace car. The green flag is waving. Go!'

She started off at a sedate five miles an hour, her hands clenching on the steering wheel as she cruised up to twenty-five. They made a quarter-mile pass with Kiran obviously getting the feel of the car, the feel of the track itself. She tested the brakes, and Steve leaned his head back against the seat and closed his eyes, completely relaxing at her cautious approach to driving.

'You'd like driving a real race car,' he told her.

'A car's a car,' she said blithely, pushing down on the accelerator.

Steve opened his eyes. The speedometer needle hovered at sixty miles an hour as they passed the initial starting point. Kiran made another lap at this speed, which was obviously comfortable for her.

A few seconds later, Steve realized the pit area had gone by very fast. He glanced back at the speedometer. Kiran had the car up to ninety miles an hour.

That didn't warn him so much as the intent expression on her face did. So much for restraining herself. Over the road noise, Steve called, 'Are you having fun yet?'

'I think so!' Her concentration was pin-point as she loosened her grip slightly on the wheel, feeling the turns in the oval-shaped track without the death-grip she'd had.

Steve wondered if Kiran realized she was taking the turns awfully fast, testing centrifugal force more than she might be aware of. The mesmerized expression on her face told him that she was in no mind to be cautioned. He glanced over at the speedometer again, edging his hands down to hold the sides of the seat. She had the car up to one-hundred-twenty – and appeared to be in her element.

The wonderfully naïve and adorable woman he'd held in his arms last night was driving as if demons from hell were on her tail. His jaw clenched as he watched the stands flashing by. The top qualifying speed for this track was just over one-hundred-thirty. She might break the record.

His life was held in Kiran's slim, delicate hands, and he was going to die. Nausea crept up Steve's throat, making him feel cold despite the sweat he felt running down the side of his face. Much more of Kiran taking turns as if they didn't exist and he would need a motion-sickness bag.

'I think you've got the idea!' he called. 'Why don't you park her?'

'I'm just getting the hang of it!' she shouted over the din.

He wasn't going to have crucial parts of his car left to drive home with. 'Kiran! Slow down and head back to the gate!'

Reluctantly she leaned back, slightly lifting her foot from the pedal. The car began a gradual reduction of speed. Steve felt his heart rate begin to subside minutely. 'For crying out loud, Kiran! Did your foot get stuck on the accelerator?'

She grinned at him. 'That was fun!'

'I'm so glad,' he said sarcastically, his stomach still in knots. 'Did you disprove the seduction of speed theory, Einstein-on-wheels?'

Kiran examined the controls on the panel as if she was infinitely interested in the car. 'It's amazing, but I think you might be right. I feel a lessening of tension in my body.'

Steve groaned. He wished the tension in *his* body would decrease so he could take a deep breath. As crazy as it sounded, for an instant Kiran had actually made him believe in the expression 'my life flashed before my eyes.'

Outside the window, he could see someone waving his arms at the car. Kiran rolled down the window.

'Damn, Steve! After all the work I've put in on this car, you're treating it like a junkyard heap! It's probably going to need new tires after that stunt, and –'

Steve opened his door and got out of the passenger side. 'Hey, Mitch.'

His crew chief's mouth dropped. He walked to the driver side window and peered in.

'Hi,' Kiran said.

He popped back up to glare at Steve. 'Do you have any idea how dangerous that was? How could you put her in that position? Not only was it hard on the car but she could have injured you the day before the race.'

'It's okay, Mitch. Frankly, I didn't have a whole helluva lot of say in the matter.' Steve couldn't wipe the smile off his face. Kiran must have neared sonic levels to have Mitch so upset. 'She was just taking us for a little spin.'

Mitch cursed and kicked a tire. 'These little city-driving tires are going to have to . . . oh, hell,' he said, giving up on his lecture. 'You must be the cousin.' He reached his hand in to shake Kiran's. 'My name's Mitch. I'm the crew chief for this maniac's team. What the hell did you think you were doing?'

'It's nice to meet you,' Kiran replied, smiling sweetly. 'My name's Kiran, and I was trying to teach the maniac a lesson.'

'I hope you did,' he grumbled, helping Kiran out of the car. 'Maybe you should be our relief driver from now on. Heck, maybe you ought to be our team driver instead of Steve.' He shot another glare at Steve, which made Kiran laugh.

'No, thank you. I just learned I'm too good a teacher to give up my job.'

'So did you learn anything, hot-shot?' Mitch demanded of Steve.

'I learned I have to be in the driver's seat at that speed or I get carsick. Come on, let's go have a drink.' He went around to get in the car.

'I can't. I've gotta finish up a few things.' Mitch shrugged at Steve.

'Where's Ginger?'

His crew chief's eyes slid back to the car as if inspecting it. 'I don't know. I heard she was going out with someone tonight.'

Steve shook his head. It was always going to be that way with Ginger. Mitch didn't know it, but he was too nice a guy for her. She was only going to go with the men who could bring her the light of TV cameras. 'Tough luck, man. Sure you don't want that drink?'

'No, thanks. I'll see you first thing in the morning. Nice to meet you, Kiran.'

Mitch walked away, his shoulders a little slumped. Kiran got in on the passenger side after waving goodbye to Mitch. Steve slid behind the wheel with a sigh. 'I knew she was going to do that to him.'

Kiran looked at him. 'Are all the women you meet like her?'

'No way. Most of these guys are married to great women and have great kids.'

'I suppose she'll find a way to sit next to me tomorrow and remind me to brush my hair.'

Steve laughed. 'I think you can put her in her place.'

'I'll do my best.'

He put his hand on her leg. 'It'll all be over after tomorrow.'

'I know.' Kiran watched the scenery outside the window with great concentration. 'In a way, that's kind of sad.'

'Why?' Steve had figured Kiran would be ready to get back to Texas, finish up their ordeal and get back to Tennessee.

'I'm not really sure. I'm enjoying myself, for one thing. For another, I think I'm having some mental realignments.'

'Oh? I heard California can do that to people. Are you feeling free and easy?'

'No. Well, maybe a little.' Kiran looked thought-ful as Steve glanced over at her. 'I think the sensation can best be described as "unburdened." Yes. I feel unburdened.'

'Even with all the sordid drama in Texas waiting on us?'

'That's a different kind of burden. I'll tell you later,' she promised.

An hour later, Steve and Kiran had finished eating the warmed-over Mexican food that had been relegated to the fridge. 'That was good,' he said.

'Yes. Now all I need is a swim.'

Gentle night air wafted across the pool, teasing the hem of Kiran's skirt. Steve stretched his feet out in front of him. 'You go ahead. I'll watch.'

'I think I will. Close your eyes.'

'Gladly.' He was feeling comfortably weighted from the combination of adrenalin letdown after the brisk ride Kiran had taken him on and the stomach he'd just filled with delicious food. He needed to start getting mentally prepared for the race tomorrow, but his eyes begged for sleep. A sudden splash in the pool jerked his eyes back open.

Kiran's clothes lay in a heap at the edge of the pool. Nightfall darkened the water around her so that he couldn't see the silhouette of her body underneath. She popped up from under the water, slicked back her hair and grinned at him.

'Are you naked in my pool?' he demanded. He knew she was, and her behavior had his complete, shocked attention.

'I have on *something*,' she told him, laughing.

He nudged her clothes with his foot. The flowing skirt covered a pair of silky panties, a bra, and the sweater she'd been wearing.

'You have on *nothing*.' He got to his feet, stripping off his shirt and pants. 'I'm coming in.'

Kiran ducked under the water, swimming to the deep end of the pool. He dove in, his body cutting through the water toward her. She tried to get away, but he reached out and grabbed her, hearing her

272

squeal even underneath the water. Nipping her on the rear end, Steve was rewarded by the delightful feel of Kiran's slick body trying to escape him. He let her get to the middle of the pool before he caught her foot, pulling her close to him.

'Oh, no, you don't.' He wouldn't release her. 'As I recall, you bragged that you could swim circles around me.'

'I can, if you let me go.'

'I warned you about my shark imitation,' he murmured, nipping her ear as he kissed his way down her neck. He slid his hands up to lightly squeeze her breasts. 'I believe I also said you'd be impressed by how long I could hold my breath under water.'

He pressed her close to him. She could feel his erection, could feel his heartbeat pulsing where his arms were tight around her. Slowly she turned in his arms to face him, holding her lips up for him to kiss. 'You win,' she said, draping her arms around his neck. 'But I let you.'

'You did not.' He took her lips with his, massaging her nicely rounded bottom with his hands. The tight, cold peaks of her breasts brushed tantalizingly against his chest. Steve cupped her bottom, lifting her up to settle her around his waist. She wrapped her legs around him, clinging like sea foam. He felt her warmth despite the coolness of the water. 'But you wanted me to catch you.'

'Yes, I did.' Kiran leaned her head back to catch her breath, gazing up at the stars. 'I'm having so much fun.'

The smooth, sleek line of her neck demanded his attention. Steve pressed her close to kiss her there, all the way back up to her mouth again. She parted her lips, so he went there, too, caressing her with his tongue. At his waist, he felt her heating up again. His hands under her arms, he slid her up until he could taste her breasts, then her bellybutton. Turning her over in the water, he licked where he'd nipped her earlier.

'I didn't hurt you, did I?'

'If you did, it feels much better now.'

His tongue slid along the curves of her bottom, up to her spine. Kiran moaned and he turned her over so that he could kiss her thighs. 'You have beautiful legs,' he whispered.

'Thank you,' she said, pulling herself up to him. Water streamed from her hair down his chest as she leaned into him. 'Make love to me, Steve. I've never done it in a pool before, and I don't think I should leave California until I do.'

'The west coast does seem to be bringing out something different in you,' he told her, helping her lock her legs around him again. 'I'm enjoying it.'

She laughed, the sound floating off on the breeze. 'I'm enjoying it, too.'

Steve laid with Kiran in her bed, having toweled her off until her body was pink with buffing. She covered herself with the sheet, snuggling up against him. He closed his eyes, content as he never remembered being before.

'I liked driving on the race track.'

'You liked scaring the pants off of me,' he corrected sleepily.

'That's one way of putting it, I suppose.' She laughed softly, but he could hear the triumph in her voice. A moment passed before she spoke again. 'I'm ready to concede that driving fast is a wonderful way of unwinding.'

'I'm glad to hear it.' Actually, he was barely listening. He no longer cared who had won their skirmish of wits.

'I think . . . I think I outran something.' She was quiet for a while, during which time Steve nearly fell asleep, and then her voice startled him into wakefulness. 'The fire happened when one of Agnes's boyfriends came into my bedroom to put the slats back in my bed. I don't remember it exactly, but I do know that for some reason I wanted to stay away from him. I moved too fast and tripped over the heater in my room. Unfortunately I was wearing a long nightgown and it caught fire.'

Steve's eyes were wide open. He'd gone totally stiff. 'What happened?'

'I was running around screaming, and Agnes's boyfriend caught me and tossed a blanket over me. I thought he was trying to kill me, he was pounding on me so hard. Later, I realized he was scared to death and was only trying to put the flames out, but I was as frightened of being smothered and beaten as being on fire.'

'What did Agnes do?'

275

Kiran was silent for a moment. 'Took me to the hospital for one thing.' She hesitated, before saying, 'And she never saw that man again.'

Rage erupted in Steve. He looked hard into Kiran's eyes.

'Please don't look at me that way. She did her best to protect me, she really did. But it was probably inevitable. I was young, and she had a lot of boyfriends –'

'And she let them –?'

'No, she didn't.' Kiran pressed her finger against his lips. 'I spent some time recuperating in a burn clinic.' Her lashes lowered before she met his gaze again. 'That's why I couldn't come that summer. I'm sorry. I wanted to tell you the truth. But Agnes was afraid of what Uncle Caleb might think if he found out what had happened. So she made up the story about the all-girls' camp.' She laid her head on Steve's chest, feeling tears coming to her eyes. 'Believe me, I wish it hadn't happened. I would much rather have been with you, doing the things we were happy doing.'

He stroked her hair, trying to cool the boiling anger rising inside of him. Holding her, Steve wished he could have saved her from the fire, from the perverts, from Agnes – from everything she'd had to endure.

'We were so innocent,' she whispered. 'You were my best friend.'

He didn't know what to say so he just held her tighter. They couldn't be the friends they'd been before. The childish innocence they'd enjoyed in each other's company could never be recaptured after that lost summer. He wanted to say that they couldn't go back in time, but that they could go forward.

Unfortunately that was a dead end.

CHAPTER 18

'Getting up at this hour is a challenge even for a schoolteacher,' Kiran complained, though she had a smile on her face. She was trying very hard to be interested in the sopapilla Steve had handed her for breakfast, probably as a joke, but she wasn't going to let him know he'd scored a point. The only thing she might be able to eat at five o'clock in the morning was her fingernails, nervous as she was about watching him race.

'Getting up this early is a challenge for anyone. If you want to come later, you could take a taxi to the race track. Or if you think you can find your way, you can borrow –'

'I wouldn't miss out on any of this for the world.' Steve looked wonderfully handsome, never mind that it was still dark outside and even the crickets weren't awake. He looked focused, ready.

'Good. I'm excited about you coming along.' He reached across to tap her finger as she picked at the food in front of her. 'You brought me good luck yesterday in qualifying. You're going to bring me luck today.'

'I hope so.' She managed a tight smile. While she had merely gloated for Steve's benefit on their ride yesterday, she had glossed over her true feelings. Her underarms had been wet, and if she'd had to drive any faster before Steve had called 'chicken,' she probably would have wet her pants. She suspected the only reason he hadn't noticed her nervousness was related to the green tint of his own face – and Mitch appearing in such a timely manner to chew them out for being reckless.

Now that she'd sat in Steve's seat, albeit a modified, safer version, Kiran knew for a fact racing wasn't a sport for her. The steering wheel had felt like concrete in her hands, immovable and unyielding at the speed she'd been driving. 'I hope good luck's what I bring you.'

'How could it be bad? You're the best thing I've had on my side in a long time.' He grinned and took his plate to the sink. A second later he was licking the sugar from her fingertips, left by the sopapilla she'd been picking at. 'And you taste good, too.'

'Come on, Steve.' Kiran actually felt ill from nerves. She pulled her hand away from him, never mind how wonderful what he was doing felt. 'You're in way too good a mood for my comfort.'

'What's the matter?' He looked at her closely. 'You do want to go today, don't you?'

'Nothing's the matter. I do want to see you race. I . . . I guess I'm not a morning person, is all.'

'Could have fooled me,' he said cheerfully, grating on her tightly wound emotions even more. 'You were up before me every morning in Texas. Maybe you stayed up too late last night?' He grinned at her with a suggestive glint in his eye.

'Steve,' Kiran began, her stomach queasy, 'how fast will you be driving today? I mean, what's a typical speed?'

He gave her a big, smacking kiss on the cheek, pulled her up from the chair and into his arms. 'I'm not going to be close to typical today, babe. I'm going to break the speedometer needle right off its spring.'

Her heart slipped down somewhere toward her stomach. 'Is there anything I can say to deflate your mood a little? I don't hear any caution in your voice.'

He laughed and blew a raspberry against her neck. 'I need a great finish today. Heck, I need a win. There are fans to please, an owner to please, a crew team who could use a lift. A few good races, and we might have a real chance at the Winston Cup championship this year.'

'That's important?' Kiran couldn't help feeling she wasn't the good luck charm Steve seemed to think she was.

'It's important if I want to keep driving for this team. It's important if I want to have a big-name sponsor.' He put her down, smoothing her hair affectionately. 'As a teacher, wasn't it important for you to do well every day in the classroom? Wasn't it important that your students learned, and that the principal was happy with your performance?'

'Well, yes.' Kiran realized she was going to have to deal with what Steve did for a living and forget the fear that had slipped into her yesterday with her own daredevil driving. After all, he was good at his chosen profession, and very experienced, while she had been merely proving a point.

'Kiran, if it makes you feel any better, I've been feeling very protective of you lately.' He eyed her. 'Does that put a name to what's on your mind?'

She digested that for a moment. 'Is that all I'm feeling? Protective toward you?'

He kissed her full on the mouth, making her heart-rate soar. 'Yes. And if you think about it for a minute, you'll realize that feeling protective toward each other is scarier than driving too fast on an enclosed track.'

Tilting her head forward, she stole one more kiss from his lips before bravely meeting his gaze. 'Well, come on, then. I'm ready to be your talisman for the day.'

'Do I wear you, rub you, or hang you from the mirror in my car?'

She turned to leave the house with a provocative smile. 'After the victory celebration tonight, maybe I'll let you choose.'

Kiran was not prepared for the noise of the race-track. It had gradually built all day, until the sound felt like furious bees inside her head. Steve had taken her with him to the garage, where she'd sat quietly out of sight until the gates opened. She watched him give a fast interview to a cute young reporter, whom Kiran realized was the same woman she'd heard talking to Steve on the phone last night. Relief had washed over her, but at the same time she was warning herself that this was part of the package deal with a race car driver.

After that, Steve had a driver/crew chief's meeting and then a chapel service to go to, so she wandered around the track, looking at the haulers and the trailers with license plates from practically everywhere in the United States. When it started getting more crowded, she went and got herself a quick bite to eat, then found her seat.

Ginger joined her in the stands, which Kiran fortunately had expected.

'Are you excited?' Ginger asked.

The red leather mini-skirt Ginger was wearing headed north on extremely long and shapely legs as she sat. Kiran couldn't help wishing, however briefly, that she could wear something other than the long, flowing skirt she had on. It was the same outfit she'd been wearing last night, since she had limited clothes packed for the trip. Certainly Steve had seemed to approve of the way Kiran looked, but Ginger looked like a model in the fashionable skirt.

'I am excited,' Kiran admitted, 'but I think I'll be glad when it's over.'

Ginger laughed, pushing her glossy hair behind an ear. 'First-time queasies.'

'Really? You mean I wouldn't feel like this if I watched Steve race again?'

'I shouldn't think so.' Ginger shot her a curious look. 'Are you not expecting to?'

'Well . . .' Kiran hesitated, realizing what was really being asked. 'I don't see how, actually. My home is in Tennessee. I don't imagine I'll be flying back out to California anytime soon.'

'I see.'

Kiran knew what Ginger saw: an opening for herself in Steve's life if Kiran wasn't in the picture. Apparently Ginger believed Kiran had qualified the 'just cousins' theory. It seemed to make the woman happy, if the smile on her face was any indication.

A tightening sensation twisted Kiran's heart. Somehow it mattered that Ginger was scoping an opportunity for herself. A week from now, when she was back in her safe little bungalow, it wouldn't matter who Steve was taking out. Today she didn't want to think about it.

'There are actually many race-tracks on the east coast,' Ginger said casually. 'Several of the Winston Cup races are run in Virginia and North Carolina, some even in Tennessee. I've been to several of those events.'

Kiran listened for the poison dart in Ginger's words but found nothing. What she did wonder was why Steve had never mentioned that fact to her. He had suggested more than once, and seemingly quite seriously, that she move to California to be with him. Why had he never mentioned that perhaps they could see each other on the occasions he happened to be in the east?

'Do you want some popcorn, Ginger?' she offered, hoping to take her mind off the sudden unsettling thoughts in her mind. She told herself there were good reasons why Steve hadn't suggested this alternative to never seeing each other again.

'No, thanks.' She held beautifully manicured hands out in front of her. Red fingernails winked in the sunlight. 'I don't want to get salt under my nails.'

Kiran paused in the act of putting a piece of popcorn in her mouth. Resolutely, she ate it anyway. 'I didn't have any breakfast, so I'll have to survive on concession food.'

'Didn't you have time to eat?'

She shook her head. 'We went swimming late last night, so we didn't eat much of the dinner we'd ordered in. This morning we nearly overslept the alarm, so we didn't have a lot of time to linger over breakfast.' Blithely she smiled at Ginger. 'So now I'm hungry.'

The smile flickered on Ginger's face. Kiran had translated the context of her relationship with Steve so that there could be no mistaking what she was to him while she was in California.

After that, it seemed, Steve had no plans for her, if what Ginger had said was true. It aroused the fear she'd had about getting involved with Steve sexually: she didn't want to be a Ginger. She wanted her loving with Steve to mean more to him than a weekend, coastal convenience. Still, by her own admission, she wasn't cut out to handle his career.

The announcer began introducing the drivers, and Kiran's heart clenched all over again.

'I don't think I believe you about having first-timer's nerves,' she told Ginger. 'I think I'd worry every time I had to watch Steve do this.'

Ginger shook her head. 'I don't feel a thing any more. Oh, I get excited when my friends win, and I'm sad when something happens and they can't finish a race. But I never feel uptight any-more.'

Kiran had heard Steve hint about Ginger not being very sympathetic toward someone named Dan Crane. She wondered if she could ever feel that uninvolved about Steve.

No way. 'He's feeling pretty confident today.' She wished she knew how it would turn out, if she'd bring good luck – or bad.

'I've not seen him this up in a long time,' Ginger confided. Her sudden shriek brought Kiran to her feet alongside Ginger. The green flag signaled the start of the race.

'I thought you said you didn't get worked up about this!' she called. If she had thought it was loud before the race started, the noise level was fairly deafening now.

'I said I didn't worry about the drivers! Most of them know what they're doing! But I love the sport!' she screamed in Kiran's ear. She pulled out a pair of binoculars and seated herself again.

Kiran sat, too, feeling rather breathless. Steve's car was heading around the track at a good clip, much faster than it seemed she'd been going last night. Her insides tightened.

'See, he's leading this lap. That's good!' Ginger yelled. 'The more laps he leads, the more points he gets!'

'I thought coming in first place was the point of leading laps?'

Ginger gave her an exasperated look. 'Didn't Steve explain it all to you?'

Kiran shook her head, feeling even more out of her element. Ginger shrugged, turning her attention to watching the drivers through her binoculars. Kiran wished Steve had explained more. Perhaps she should have asked more questions. Maybe he thought all she needed was a surface knowledge of the sport, just enough to get her through this day. After all, he'd invited her on a holiday, not to make a racing enthusiast out of her. Still, she couldn't help feeling envious of Ginger knowing so much about what was important to Steve.

Her throat tightened, as if popcorn had gotten stuck going down. Steve had said their feeling protective of each other was scary. She wondered what he'd say if she told him protective of him wasn't all she was.

She was in love with him.

Steve banked another turn, coming out into a long stretch as if the road was satin ribbon under the tires. He liked the way the race was going, liked the feel of the car. He'd led several laps, and only lost nineteen seconds when he'd gone into the pit. Mitch had been roaring with excitement, pushing the car back out of the lane and onto the track. Though his insides were tense with adrenalin, Steve couldn't help thinking everything was going his way this time. Winning would give a boost to his point standing, his career, to his team.

What would it mean in terms of Kiran? Nothing. Steve pushed that thought away as he headed into a curve. The speedometer read one-twenty as he straightened out of the turn, shooting down the black length of track. Cars jockeyed for position behind him, but Steve wasn't giving up an inch of his lead. It wasn't the money; it wasn't the points he was after. It was proving he still had the stuff. Forget about the young kids coming up with their sleek looks and bright-colored gear. This was a sport for the hardiest dog, a survival of the fittest. And he was still fit enough to win.

He cursed as the car next to him moved dangerously close, trying to nip off his lead and speed around him. Kiran's clenched fingers on the steering wheel snapped into his mind as he pressed the accelerator down, nudging the needle toward one-twenty-five.

She'd been a good sport this morning, not wanting to confess her worry about the race to him. He understood. His emotions had been tightly strung where she was concerned ever since his father had tried getting nasty with her. Kiran had stayed in Butch's face, but Steve had known then that nothing and nobody was going to treat her like that while he was around. He wanted her safe. She wanted him safe. After she'd unburdened herself last night, Steve had wanted nothing so much as to shelter her for the rest of her life.

He surged forward, keeping the encroaching racer from taking the lead. Mitch shouted instructions into his headset, which Steve obeyed immediately. He trusted his crew chief; they were a winning team. Needed to stay a winning team. He trusted Kiran. He needed her.

Racing and Kiran didn't fit together.

Kiran. Unholy in the sack. Brave as hell. Might get used to his need to drive fast in time.

He might not need to drive fast if he had Kiran. Together they might be safe. There might not be anything to outrun anymore, if he had Kiran.

Out of the corner of his eye, he saw the car making another attempt to pass him. Steve recognized the colors now, knew his challenger was one of the fast-rising stars in the venue. Mitch screamed a command, and Steve jerked the wheel to the left, hugging the inside of the track. The car melted from his vision, and a moment later cars scattered around the track behind him like spilled jellybeans. Steve grimaced. The kid had poured it on too much, too fast. Inexperienced, and too hungry.

Steve was hungry, too. Hungry for his career to stay alive. Kiran was going back to Tennessee. He knew she wasn't going to stay with him. His life as it was didn't match her needs. She was needy, she'd told him. He needed more than she did. With her, the need had been cut to a mere craving.

Realization swept him. He craved this win today, wanted it so bad he would bleed for it. He wanted Kiran in a different way. Like two high-speed cars, his mind dueled, knowing he might have to make a choice. He was comfortable living on the edge. Kiran was not. If he could convince Kiran to stay with him, would he sink into her security and lose his edge?

Lose your edge, lose your edge, a voice taunted. Competing was what he did, what he loved. *You're losing your edge,* the voice jibed. Mitch's scream in the headset jerked Steve's focus to hairline-accurate attention. An out of control car was careening, twisting his way. He jerked the wheel, jamming the accelerator hard to get out of the way. The banked curve of the road wouldn't allow him to make the maneuver. In a split-second flash the car was upon him, turning him end over end until the rolling sensation tore a scream from his throat.

Kiran leapt to her feet, her astonished gaze refusing to believe what she was seeing. Steve's car flipped crazily, while drivers desperately tried to dodge him and the runaway car. Her breath stopped in her chest as both cars finally stopped their sickening roll. Flames shot from the back of Steve's car. Kiran heard screaming, frantic and terrified, like a mad echo in the stands. Someone needed help. She felt

Ginger grip her arms, shaking her hard, but Kiran couldn't hang on.

Several curious faces peered at Kiran. She realized they were looking down at her, and she was lying flat on her back.

'Damn it, Kiran!' Ginger exclaimed. 'Are you all right?'

'I'm fine.' Kiran tried to sit up, but someone gently pushed her back down. She was irritated as hell by that. Didn't they know she was going to get popcorn and who knew what else in her hair, and her skirt was getting dirty besides? She would have to rinse it in the sink tonight to get the dirt out, and if these people didn't quit pawing her, the raw silk would be snagged on the rough cement.

'Man! You're going to have to chill out if you're going to hang around Steve much. Let me help you.' Ginger took Kiran's hand to pull her to a sitting position.

'Did he win?' Kiran hoped so. She must have fainted from the heat of the sun, and hated to think she'd missed the end of the race. She'd been sitting there for a long time with her heart in her throat.

Ginger looked at her strangely. A man in a uniform put his hand on Kiran's wrist, feeling for something. She slapped it away. 'How dare you?' she demanded.

'I think she's fine,' Ginger told the guy. 'Give her a moment to gather her wits.' To Kiran, she said, 'Don't you remember anything?'

'Of course I do,' Kiran snapped. She inched toward the seat. 'Steve was making points. He was winning. Is the race over?'

'Well, it is for Steve.' Ginger's tone was dry as she helped Kiran sit. The man in the uniform tried to get near her again, but she glared him away.

'What do you want?' she demanded.

'He wants to feel your pulse, Kiran. Take a deep breath and relax so he can.'

'He's not going to feel anything of mine,' she stated. 'What do you mean the race is over for Steve?'

'He didn't finish,' Ginger said slowly. 'He had an accident.'

Kiran straightened. 'Is he all right?'

'He's fine. But you fainted.' Ginger dusted off Kiran's skirt briskly. 'I think you'll want to change later, but it's nothing that can't be fixed.'

'Where is he?'

'I imagine he's with his crew. Someone's probably checking him over too, though he looked all right to me.' Ginger hesitated, seating herself next to Kiran. 'Why don't we get out of the sun? Maybe we should go try to find Steve, if you think you're all right.'

'Maybe.' Kiran was uncertain. Suddenly she didn't want to see him. Something was making her dizzy. 'He's not all right, is he?' She turned to watch Ginger's expression. 'Is he?'

'I think he's fine. But when his car caught fire, you went out like a lightbulb.' Ginger looked sympathetic. 'It's understandable, Kiran. It looked horrible. But Mitch and a couple of crew guys jumped the wall and pulled him out through the window. Actually, I think he would have made it out on his own, but they got to him fast.'

Kiran jumped to her feet, scanning the track.

'They've already towed it away. The caution flag came out and nobody else was hurt.' Ginger rose and smoothed her leather skirt down. 'Come on. You'll feel better when you see him.'

Kiran hesitated. 'Maybe I should wait here.' They hadn't made any contingency plans for him being in a wreck. She had bought into the good luck syndrome to the point where she'd half expected Steve to make it to the end of the race with a big finish. 'You go on. I'll finish watching the race.' Actually, she felt dazed. She wasn't sure what to say to Steve. *Guess you needed more than good luck – you almost needed an angel.*

'Suit yourself.' Ginger shrugged. 'I'll go see if I can find him.'

Kiran supposed she was taking the coward's way out. She *was* a coward. Her stomach was tight to the point that she felt actual pain. Memory came rushing back, nauseatingly swift. She remembered the back end of the car bursting into flame. *I can't do this. I'll never be as casual about this as Ginger. Steve's safety will always matter to me.*

'Kiran.'

She looked into the sunlight to see Steve holding out his hand to her.

'Let me get you out of here.'

She was almost afraid to take his hand, the urge to throw her arms around him was so great. People were watching, and she knew she'd already created enough drama with her fainting attack. 'Don't you have something you need to do?'

'Yeah, but we can watch the rest of the race somewhere else. I don't want you baking in the sun for no reason.'

Getting up from the seat, she said, 'Did Ginger find you?'

'No. I must have missed her.'

Kiran ignored his hand and shook her head, indicating that she would follow him. 'She left to find you.'

They left the stands and headed down a wide, paved area. 'It'll be all right. Ginger knows her way around here.'

I don't! Kiran wanted to cry out. She wanted to bury her head against Steve's chest and ask him if he hurt anywhere. She wanted to curse him for the near miss he'd had. Instead, she stiffened her spine and tried to concentrate on the crowd noise. 'I know you've got some things to finish up here. Why don't I take a taxi back to your house so you don't have to babysit me?'

'I'm hardly babysitting you.' He glanced at her as she tried to keep up with his stride. 'You haven't been any trouble, Kiran.'

She halted, setting her feet. 'I appreciate you saying that. But it's been a long day, longer than

I'm used to. If you don't mind, I would really rather get out of the way.' *Are you all right*? she wanted to ask. Her eyes searched every inch of his body, but he looked as good as ever to her, if a bit more tousled from the wind. In her mind's eye, the car rolled over again with sickening intensity.

'Kiran, I'm fine. I'm angry, but that's all that's wrong with me.' He had stopped in front of her, and now he tipped her chin up to meet his gaze. 'I know what you're thinking –'

'Steve, please. Let me go back and take a warm bath. I'll be fine, I promise.' She wrapped her arms around herself, her teeth almost chattering despite the heat. 'We can warm over the Mexican food tonight.'

He studied her with acute attention. 'If you're sure.' Dropping his hand to his pocket, he fished around. 'I don't have my wallet on me.'

Of course he didn't. He was still dressed for the race. Kiran managed a smile and tugged at her purse. 'All I need is a house-key.'

Steve smiled, devastating her heart. 'It's in the cactus pot on the back porch by the pool. Let yourself in the gate.'

'The cactus pot?'

'Yeah. Mitch comes by occasionally.'

And Ginger, too. Kiran forced that out of her mind.

'While I was in Texas he needed to get in the garage for a few things, and he was picking up my mail and stuff –'

'Steve.' Kiran shook her head. 'Don't explain any more. A cactus is the last place a thief would look for a house-key, unless he wanted his fingers stuck by cactus needles. I'll see you tonight.' She started walking toward the exit.

'Kiran?' Steve called after her.

'Yes?' She could hardly look at him. The tension was so unbearable, all she wanted was to get away from him and indulge in an insane crying jag.

Gently he brushed some popcorn from her hair. 'There's wine in the fridge, brandy and whiskey in the bar. Help yourself. The shock will probably wear off in about an hour.'

It would take much longer than that. She barely managed a smile. 'Thanks,' she replied, hurrying off to find a cab.

Steve watched Kiran go with a worried expression on his face. She had practically been quivering with fear, but he had expected her to be spooked. He'd gone to get her out of the stands because he'd known she would be absolutely miserable sitting there, pretending to watch the race. His first thought when he'd seen the charred back end of his car was that Kiran would be freaking out.

He watched her long skirt fluttering about her ankles as she made her escape. He hadn't been far wrong about her mood. Fortunately, she could go unwind at his house. Later, they'd talk. He would tell her that accidents like that rarely happened, and that they almost always looked worse than they were. Hell, he still hadn't been able to spit out any of the dust in his mouth because it was so dry from fear. Kiran brought him more than just luck; she brought him happiness. The accident had not impacted his feelings for her. He would tell her all this when they were alone tonight.

'Where's Kiran?' Ginger asked, catching up with him. 'I couldn't find her in the stands.'

'She went home.' He headed back to the garage. Ginger fell into step with him. 'I don't think she felt like staying any longer,' he said, trying to save face for Kiran. He didn't think she'd like Ginger knowing she was upset over what had happened.

'I've never seen anybody that wigged out in my life.'

He thought Kiran had maintained pretty well. She was a helluva sport. 'She seemed a little shook, but she was cool about it.'

Ginger snorted. 'Cool! She went out *cold* the second your car lit up.'

'Kiran fainted?' Steve stopped walking and jerked to face Ginger. 'She didn't tell me that.'

'Yes, she fainted. I had a paramedic come look at her. Frankly, I didn't think she was going to snap out of it.'

Terrifying awareness slimed its way through Steve's blood. In the stands, Kiran had not allowed him to take her hand, had not touched him. Suddenly he knew he'd lost more than the race today.

He had lost Kiran.

CHAPTER 19

Steve was quiet as he entered the house. It was nine p.m., and with any luck Kiran was relaxing in front of the television. He had tried calling her, but she hadn't answered the phone. Knowing she likely wouldn't pick up unless she knew it was him, he'd tried talking over the recorder to her, but that hadn't gotten him a response, either.

She wasn't reclining on the sofa watching TV as he'd hoped. 'Kiran!' he called softly, heading toward her bedroom. It was dark, so he turned on the hall light to peer in. Not surprisingly, she was sound asleep in bed, the covers pulled up to her chin. She'd made herself such a nice cocoon Steve felt he shouldn't disturb her. Hopefully, morning's light would lessen some of the shock he knew she'd suffered.

Most likely she would never look at a race car again without getting the willies. He'd been damn lucky and she wouldn't hesitate to tell him so. Morning was soon enough to hear it.

Flipping off the hall light, Steve headed to his

room for a shower. He would have liked to treat Kiran to dinner and a relaxing swim – an encore of last night would have been nice – but nothing had worked out the way he'd hoped.

Nor had Kiran gotten the safe, worry-free vacation he had convinced her to take. 'Oh, hell,' he muttered.

Mitch hadn't spared any curses on the driver who'd hit Steve's car. He supposed he'd get to watch the crash in all its flaming glory tonight and tomorrow on the sports channel, so he could view it the way Kiran had seen it.

The shower sent warmth running through his muscles, relaxing his neck enough so that he could flex it. Steve took a deep breath, trying not to let himself worry tonight about what he was going to do about his car, about his career, about Kiran. He'd return to Texas with her tomorrow, go fix the matter with Butch and Agnes so that the whole damn mess concerning Uncle Caleb's estate could be finished, and then try to gently talk around the issue of his relationship with Kiran.

His confidence ebbed mightily on that subject matter. He stepped out of the shower, toweling himself off before stretching out on the bed. The phone rang annoyingly, and he jerked it from the set.

'Hello?'

'Steve? It's John Lannigan.'

Ah, Father Goodfellow when he least wanted him. 'Hey, John.'

'Listen, I hate to bother you –'

'You're not. What's on your mind?'

There was a slight pause. 'This is nothing to get upset about, but I thought you'd want to know that someone tried to break into your uncle's house the night before last. I'm sorry I couldn't reach you before.'

Steve was surprised. All the farm equipment was in an outbuilding and the truck was parked outside where any petty thief could get to it. No need to break into that sagging-roofed house. 'What for?'

'The police aren't sure. Nothing seems to be missing. I went over and looked through the house, but I couldn't tell anything had been taken.'

'There was nothing to take.' Steve rolled his eyes sarcastically. 'Do they know who it was?'

'They thought they had a suspect, but apparently his wife can vouch for the fact that he was home all night.' John cleared his throat. 'Actually, there's something I think you should know, Steve.'

'And I'm not going to like it?' He could feel the tension knotting up his neck muscles again. He'd knocked his body out of alignment today with the rollercoaster roll he'd been treated to – bad news wasn't going to help the tightness. 'Don't tell me. Agnes and Butch sank to a new low and decided to help themselves to whatever Uncle Caleb had. His black and white TV and a full bottle of liquor.'

'Actually, no. I wish it were that simple. Your folks have holed up in a hotel not far from here and were in the process of filing papers, last I heard.'

'How did you hear?'

'I'm the executor,' John reminded him. 'I guess copies of the paperwork must be sent to me. Maybe it was at their request, but I don't know.'

What a pain. Steve was certain the good father hadn't known what he was being honored with by being named executor. 'Sorry you have to be in the middle. We'll pay your legal fees.'

John was quiet for a minute. 'Never mind that. The problem is that apparently your uncle had an enemy in town, who may have been the culprit in the break-in. I have a bad feeling about the man the police suspected.'

'I thought he had an alibi?'

'He does.' The line was silent for a moment. 'I'm not sure I would believe his wife if she claimed he was at home. The cop who was on patrol was absolutely certain he followed the same car that left your uncle's property to its destination.'

'You believe the cop over the wife? Wouldn't she know if her husband was in bed with her?'

The priest coughed delicately. Steve's jaw dropped. 'Oh, sweet Lord. You're not piped into someone's confession, are you?'

John said nothing. Steve squinted his eyes. 'You *heard* who did it in a confession!'

'I can't talk about that,' the priest answered sternly. 'All I can say is that I'm not willing to bet that the wife would be telling the truth if she verifies her husband's alibi.'

'So who didn't like my uncle?' Uncle Caleb

hadn't had any friends, but Steve would have guessed he didn't have enemies, either.

'I can't say. Unfortunately, even in my position as executor, I cannot divulge confessions, nor any suspicions I might have over what little the police have hinted at to me. If the wife won't give her husband an alibi, then we'll know who did it because he'll be locked up. However, I do think you should come back to Texas as soon as possible. I'm worried, Steve. Really worried.'

'Tell me this, then, John. What was in Uncle Caleb's house that anybody would care to steal? I could easily suspect Butch and Agnes, because all their fuses don't connect anyway. But some guy with a grudge? I'd be very surprised if Uncle Caleb owed anybody any money.'

'This doesn't have anything to do with money. Your uncle didn't owe anybody anything. To my mind this has to do with what someone else owed your uncle. My best advice is, come back before something else happens. We were lucky that a policeman was cruising by that night.'

'I'll be back tomorrow.'

'Kiran, too?'

'Of course.' Steve frowned. 'Why wouldn't she come back with me?'

'I was just asking,' the priest answered. 'I'll drop by the house tomorrow night to talk further with you. Goodnight.'

'Bye,' Steve said, hanging up irritably. He wondered what the hell John had meant by that.

Snorting, he figured maybe the priest was simply curious. Kiran wouldn't dream of not returning to Texas. She was more than ready to see this whole matter to its sorry end – Steve had been the one who hadn't wanted to get embroiled in it.

Briefly, he wondered how Kiran would take this latest piece of news. It was getting uglier and more complicated by the hour. He could, of course, not tell her about the break-in. He could even say that everything appeared to be going so well back in Texas that she might as well fly back to Tennessee, that he would let her know how everything was proceeding.

She wouldn't buy his story. It might be turning from bad to worse, but Kiran was a fighter. She might not care to defend herself from Agnes, but she sure as hell would protect Uncle Caleb's final wishes.

Steve closed his eyes, wondering when he should reveal this new twist.

Sudden screaming from Kiran's room shot him off the bed and down the hall.

Kiran was in agony. She ran and ran but couldn't stop the pain. She screamed, frenziedly slapping in her desperation to put out the flames. Someone grabbed her, shaking her, but she couldn't escape. Couldn't get away from the searing torment gripping her.

'Kiran, damn it! Wake up!' Steve pressed her down, trying to keep her fingernails from gouging him, trying to keep her from hurting herself. She beat at her body as if bugs were infesting her, and he couldn't stop her thrashing long enough to get a good hold on her. 'Wake up! It's okay! I'm here with you.'

He pulled her close, taking a clip on the jaw in the process, but he clenched her to him so that she couldn't damage herself. She fought like mad for the space of a second, then her body relaxed. Unwilling to trust this unexpected surrender, Steve didn't release her.

'Kiran? Are you all right?'

Her heart-rate thrummed like a hummingbird's; he could feel it pounding in her temples. Shallow gasps of breath were his only answer. Whatever she had been dreaming about, it had terrified her.

'Kiran?' He barely let her go enough to lean back and see her eyes. They were wide open, the pupils dark. 'Can I get you anything?'

'Just hold me,' she whispered, her voice broken. 'Just for a minute.'

'Oh, baby, I'm not going to let you go.' He cradled her up against him as he leaned against the headboard. 'I'll stay as long as you want.'

He felt her shaking in his arms, was ready for the hysterical sobs that followed. 'Shh,' he told her, gently rocking her against him. 'Don't cry. Shh. It's going to be okay.'

Of course he didn't know if whatever was tormenting her was going to be okay, and whether his presence might make it any better was open for debate. But he kept murmuring soothing nonsensical words to her, in case the sound of a voice in the twisting black void she'd been writhing in was comforting.

'Steve!' She moved against him, her head upon his chest, arms wrapped around him. 'I . . . I –'

'Shh,' he told her again. 'Let me hold you right now. You can tell me everything tomorrow.'

After a moment, she nodded. Deeper, more even breathing told him she was unwinding. She seemed to feel safe now, but he didn't dare pull away. He closed his eyes. They had this night to hold each other, and he would stay until she told him to leave.

Early-morning sunshine tore at Kiran's serene web of sleep. Opening her eyes, she realized two things: she felt very well rested, and she had made a pillow out of Steve's chest. And a very nice pillow it was, she thought, enjoying the view of tanned skin over taut muscles.

Last night's terror flashed into her mind like a nightmare she couldn't flee. She'd been on fire. No, Steve had been on fire. They had both been trapped by fire, in a burning hell all their own.

She should never have made love with him. Steve was not the man to save her. From the start she had known he would be too much for her. He was a risk-taker. She was not, and never would be. Nor could she be happy with someone who was. Security was what she craved.

Gently drawing away from Steve so she could

leave the bed, Kiran let her eyes move from his sandy mussed hair to the stubborn set of his chin. Why did he have to be so heartbreakingly handsome? Why did he have to be the kind of man who thrived on danger – and why did she have to be so drawn to him because of it?

She was looking at her downfall. As if she hadn't had enough of people in her life who weren't good for her, she had allowed herself to cross the line from companions who had been thrown together, to lovers who could not stay together.

How foolish of her. Like an alcoholic who couldn't stay away from 'just one drink' she had told herself 'just this weekend' would be enough.

Seeing the smoke-edged fire seething over the back end of Steve's car had been the hemlock in the wistful fairytale she had begun to believe in.

Edging from the bed, Kiran got up to dress. Steve didn't move, so she pulled the white sheet up to his chest and grabbed her clothes from the closet. The flight they were booked on left in two hours. She couldn't wait to get back to Texas. The circumstances there would put distance in their relationship again – and she had to have it.

Kiran slept on the flight. Steve knew she needed the rest, but he couldn't help feeling that she was sleeping to avoid talking to him. She hadn't said more than one sentence at a time while they'd been getting ready to leave – and he suspected she'd let him sleep until the last minute so he'd be so rushed they wouldn't have time to talk.

On the plane she'd ordered a Bloody Mary, which she'd taken a sip of and then promptly fallen asleep. He'd had a glass of cola, but since the vodka in her glass was in danger of being watered into nothing, he decided to drink it himself. Then he crunched the ice cubes in frustration, with nothing to do but stare out at the wispy clouds linking the sky. Kiran was apparently going to stay in dreamland the entire journey, and as much as he wanted to join her he was tense. Edgy. Wanted some answers.

Mainly he wanted to talk to her. To keep her from constructing the emotional shield he sensed her putting into place. A flight attendant announced their arrival, so Steve took the opportunity to put a hand on Kiran's under the guise of awakening her.

'Kiran, we're almost there.'

Sleepily, she opened her eyes, looking out the window before snatching her hand away from his. She wouldn't look at him as she made herself very busy putting her seat belt on. Steve sighed to himself. The signal he was getting from Kiran was that California had never happened.

Maybe that was for the best. Why let it hurt him when even he couldn't figure out the whys and wherefores of a long-term thing between them?

'I forgot to mention that Father John called last night,' he said, deciding that business-as-usual between them was the only way to get Kiran to talk to him. 'He said Uncle Caleb's house had been broken into.'

306

Her attention was firmly riveted on him now. 'Would Agnes and Butch be so stupid?'

'I don't think so. I don't know what they could possibly want in that house. Anything of value to the estate is tied up in the land, and I'm sure they know that.'

'Did they catch the burglar?'

'No. Well, maybe. John was pretty damn cagey about the whole thing. I had the suspicion he knew more than he felt comfortable telling.'

'That doesn't sound like him.'

Steve crooked his mouth. John could do no wrong where Kiran was concerned. He wished she felt that way about him. Maybe she had – until he'd had the misfortune of someone's car landing on his.

'He fell back on some confession excuse.'

'One of his parishioners broke into the house?' The amazement on Kiran's face made Steve grimace again.

'Even Catholics sin, Kiran.'

'Yes, but why Uncle Caleb's house? This isn't making any sense.'

He shrugged. 'Guess they thought something was in there they could use.'

'I wonder if the house would have been broken into if we'd been there.'

'What do you mean?'

Kiran felt the landing gears lock into place as the plane started to descend. Instinctively she straightened her back to prepare for the landing. Steve watched her curiously. It was part of her nature to prepare for any event; he should know that by now.

'It's okay, Kiran,' he said, putting his hand over hers.

'I know it!' she snapped, moving her hand to her lap. 'I'm not afraid to fly, for heaven's sake!'

He looked so hurt that she pulled her gaze from his and looked out the window for a moment. 'I think someone's been hanging around the house since day one,' she stated softly. 'I don't think it matters that we weren't there when whoever it was finally worked up the courage to get inside.'

'What are you getting at?'

'Something's in there that someone wants. This is not your garden-variety obituary-chasing break-in. Why else would I have heard keys jingling outside the window that night?' Kiran met his gaze, her mouth set in determined lines. 'And don't tell me that it was a car clinking as it passed in front of the house!'

Steve winced at the reminder. 'It was keys, because I found one.'

'What?' Her mouth dropped open. 'You never told me that!'

'I know.' He sighed, knowing Kiran was going to let him have it. 'I forgot, to be honest. I wasn't sure what it meant, but finding the key aroused my suspicions – which is why I wanted you to go to California with me. I wanted to keep you safe.'

They stared at each other for a long moment. The plane landed, jarring them both.

He was relieved when she didn't comment on the

irony in his statement. 'I think it's that woman who was crying at Uncle Caleb's grave,' she told him, unbuckling her seat belt.

'Please leave it on.' He reached over to stop her. 'The light hasn't been turned off yet.'

'Steve Dorn, don't you dare –' Kiran stopped, took a deep breath, and shoved the buckle back into the clasp. 'While I appreciate your concern for my safety, I would just like to mention that my concern for *your* safety didn't seem to be of much interest to you. So, if you don't mind, I prefer that we just leave this relationship as it is. Was,' she hastily added.

'No can do, I'm afraid. But I've gotten the message: hands off.' Steve held up his own hands in mock surrender. 'So, why do you think the late-night lady would break in?'

'Why was she standing out there crying like that? I don't know.' Kiran unbuckled herself again and stood as the other passengers jumped to their feet to start grabbing flight bags. 'She's the only person who seems to give a damn about Uncle dying.'

'John hinted that the police are questioning a man, a married man whose wife would vouch for his whereabouts. Apparently a cop followed the guy home, so they're just waiting to see if the wife confirms his story.'

Kiran stepped in the aisle in front of Steve as he held up the line of passengers behind him. 'Well, we should let the police handle this matter. It really has nothing to do with us. We could have left the front door open to make it easy, because there's nothing in there of any value. I still say it's the woman. She plays a part in this somehow.'

'I'm really going to be shocked when we find out Uncle Caleb was keeping a woman on the side.'

Kiran halted and Steve bumped into her. 'It's the picture we found.'

Steve pushed her forward gently. 'I've already thought of that. It's not the picture of Sakina. Nobody knew about it but Uncle. It's just a piece of paper in a cheap wooden frame.'

She turned to face him as they walked out into the tunnel. 'Why would she break in if she had a key to the house?'

'The key I found didn't fit any of the doors, nor the truck.'

'You know, this is very simply solved. All we have to do is go away again, or pretend to, and leave the doors unlocked. Whoever it is might make a second attempt.'

'I liked your idea about letting the law deal with this better. After all, it doesn't really matter.' They walked to baggage check-in. 'We'll tell Father John we're in agreement to sign the house and land over to a charity in Uncle Caleb's name, then you're off to Tennessee and I'm off to California.'

'And what about Agnes and Butch?'

'Screw them. I'm going to have a word with our mentally dysfunctional parents. And when I'm done, I assure you, they won't contest our plans at all.'

'What is this word you've decided to have with them?' Her expression was startled.

'Never mind. You let me handle this.'

'I've tried to tell you before that I can –'

'I know. Fight your own battles. Believe me, Kiran, this is one I don't think you want in on.'

'What do you mean you won't tell the police I was at home all night?' Jarvis couldn't remember ever wanting to hit his wife more. She was being stubbornly stupid, and it was making him crazy to look at her vacant eyes. They looked like little raisins in pie dough that had too much air in it. 'You know I was home.'

'I don't know anything of the sort.'

Maypat's hands were shaking as she sat in her precious little parlor. He knew she was afraid of him, but he also sensed she meant what she was saying.

'Of course I was here,' he told her impatiently, in a tone that was supposed to remind her that she should think whatever he told her to. Bedford had pulled strings for him, emphatically stating this was the last time he would dig him out of his dirty messes. Eventually the police would come to Maypat. He had to get her to cover him. 'Where the hell else would I be?'

'I couldn't say. All I know for certain is that I was asleep in my own bed, and that is what I intend to tell anyone who asks me.'

'You don't have to tell half the county that we

don't sleep in the same bed, Maypat. It sounds . . . fishy. Like you're trying to hint that I wasn't around. Or like you want everyone to know we keep separate bedrooms.'

She sighed. 'One police officer is not half the county, Jarvis. And I'm not trying to point any finger of mistrust at you. All I can say is what is true. I last saw you in the evening. Then I went to bed.'

'I suppose that's good enough.' He tried to think of a way to convince her pea-sized brain that he had been on the premises.

'How did you cut your hand?'

Jarvis jumped, sticking it into his pocket. 'Trying to get into the store. I cut my hand on the lock,' he lied with ease. 'Now, listen, Maypat, don't you go yapping to the cops about anything they don't ask ya about, hear? They try to act all friendly, but they're just waiting for you to say something they can use against me.'

'Why would they want to do that?' she asked. 'If you have nothing to be afraid of, Jarvis, why are you so worried?'

'I'm not, damn it. And don't start getting lippy with me. Cause if you do, I'm gonna . . . gonna smack the daylights out of you.' He stood straighter and puffed out his chest. 'You just pull those feathers in your little brain together for something other than pillow stuffing, Maypat, if you don't want me making your life miserable.'

He stomped out of the kitchen. Maypat watched

her husband go without comment. After she heard his heavy clomping on the porch steps outside, she reached to take the phone receiver from the cradle. She dialed a number in Atlanta from memory.

'Sister? Please have my old rooms aired out. I've decided to come home.' She hesitated for a moment, listening to her sister's excited questions. 'No, this isn't a vacation. I'm coming home for good.'

She said goodbye and replaced the receiver. After a moment, she picked it up again and dialed another number.

'Father Lannigan? If you could make the time to see me, I would greatly appreciate it. This afternoon, if possible.'

John glanced from Kiran to Steve and then back. Neither of them looked as rested as he'd hoped. If anything, they both seemed to be at the edge of emotion, almost uncomfortable to be around each other. He couldn't fathom what had ruined the carefree camaraderie they'd shared before, almost as if they'd been a team of sorts, united against their parents. Instead of strengthening, the bond between them appeared to have eroded into a glass-fragile uneasiness.

'I have an appointment in a little while, but I wanted to stop by and check on the two of you. Everything is in order in the house, as far as you can tell?' he asked.

Kiran and Steve nodded simultaneously. 'You know, Kiran and I have overlooked a simple explanation for the break-in,' Steve said. 'It could have been a vagrant, or a young kid accepting some kind of dare.'

John nodded, thinking about his upcoming meeting with Maypat Andrews. 'Tell you what. You both look beat. Why don't I come back by this evening, and we'll finish sorting out some details? Will that be convenient for you?'

'We'll be here,' Kiran replied. 'We're going to drive around some of the fields and try to see if they're worth having harvested. From what I can tell, the answer is no, but if you don't find us when you return, you know where we are. I don't imagine it will take us too long. Then we're planning on finishing boxing up the household items.'

'You be careful,' John said, getting up to leave. 'At no time do I want you to leave Kiran alone, Steve. Even just to run down to Andrews Grocery Mart to get boxes. I'd like to be over-cautious, if you don't mind.'

'Excellent idea.' John saw the narrow look Steve sent Kiran's way. 'I'll stick to her like a shadow.'

'I thought you had an appointment,' Kiran interrupted. 'One that you didn't want me in on.'

'You can sit in the car. That appointment won't take long, either.'

'I will not sit in the car!'

Kiran was working up a full head of steam. John wondered if it would be prudent to defuse whatever was brewing between these two before it exploded.

She stood, poking a finger in Steve's direction.

'Whatever you have to say to Butch and Agnes can be said in front of me.'

'You won't like it.'

'You don't know me as well as you think you do,' she snapped.

'Fine,' he retorted. 'Family relations, for the ten thousand-dollar bonus question: how in the hell does Agnes figure you owe her anything when the scars on your legs say you don't owe her a damn thing?'

'Family relations, for the game,' she spat back. 'When in hell did you appoint yourself my avenger?'

He stepped close to Kiran, and John rose, concerned. The conversation had gone beyond him, but he could tell they were locked in the middle of a fierce battle of wills.

Steve touched his finger to Kiran's chin. 'I appointed myself your avenger when I found out you fainted in the stands. You didn't tell me that little piece of information. You're so afraid of being consumed by Agnes that you won't tell the old witch to get off your back. And let me tell you something else, Kiran Whitley, you're never going to get over what happened until you quit letting her run you scared.'

'You're wrong!' Kiran had gone deathly white. 'And crazy besides!'

'I'm right,' he said, 'and either you stand up to Agnes and tell her where to get off tonight, or I do. Once she knows that I know the truth about what happened, she won't be so interested in pursuing

Uncle Caleb's estate. And Butch's spine is Agnes, so if we break her, we break him. They can be out of the picture, but it's going to hurt.' He folded his arms, waiting.

'Anytime you're involved it seems to hurt,' she bit off, tears starting to pour from her eyes. 'You're cruel, Steve, and mighty black-hearted. I don't want to do this, but I will, just to prove you wrong.'

'I don't care why you do it, but I think you should.' Triumph colored his eyes moss-green. 'I'll be with you every step of the way.'

'I don't need you.' She turned to walk from the room. 'Uncle Caleb knew what he was doing by appointing an impartial third party to be the executor of his estate. He must have known we would never agree on what needed to be done. We're too different.' Her shoulders set, her chin held high, she said, 'I'm returning to Tennessee tomorrow, and it's not a moment too soon.'

CHAPTER 20

Kiran was quitting. Steve couldn't begin to put a name to the feeling that gave him, but it was a combination of shock – and fear. The shock came from her giving in when he knew her to be a valiant fighter. The fear was that she was throwing him out like old dishwater – though he'd known their relationship was lost the day of the race. He just couldn't imagine never seeing her again for the rest of his life.

'I'd better go,' John murmured. 'I'll be by later.'

He left as speedily as Kiran had left the room before him. Steve ran a hand tiredly through his hair, sighing. Was he wrong to push Kiran this way? If she wasn't ready to face her emotional demons, that was her choice.

Slowly he went to her room, not bothering to do more than cursorily tap on her door since he knew she wouldn't agree to let him in if he asked. She sat cross-legged on the floor, staring into the closet as if she didn't know he'd come in.

'I'm sorry,' he told her. 'I was wrong. You don't have to confront Agnes, but I hope you understand

I have to tear a chunk out of both of them.' He thought over his next words carefully. 'But I don't want to lose the connection you and I have just because I'm too heavy-handed.'

She turned her face to him. Her nose and eyelids were red, and she had splotches in her cheeks. He had never wanted to put his arms around her and protect her so badly in his life.

'I wish you'd never seen my legs.' She sniffled, running a palm under her nose. 'You're such a conqueror, you think you can just take over any-thing. But it's my life, Steve. I don't have to get into a skirmish with Agnes to be a happy, sane person. Her destiny and mine are no longer connected.'

'You prefer we go to court over Uncle Caleb's estate rather than assure the two of them that if they don't lay off with the he-was-our-brother routine, we'll be forced to expose why Caleb didn't want his siblings to have anything of his?'

'Caleb didn't know about Agnes,' she protested.

'The hell he didn't. Don't you think he knew she was trying to get rid of you every summer by sending you here?'

'Steve, don't!' Kiran's eyes teared up again. 'As sorry as she is, she's the only mother I ever knew. Yes, I'd rather let the law decide to uphold Uncle's wishes than have to hurt her.'

'Have you ever considered that the courts might not? His will isn't exactly airtight.'

She shook her head and reached for a tissue from the nightstand. 'Everything will work out.'

'Kiran, you can't just close your eyes and hope that everything will work out! We have to have some chips on our side of the table!'

'I don't like you electing me to be the chip!'

He crouched on the floor to bring himself to eye-level with her. 'Oh, no, I'm not leaving myself out of this. Me and the old man are going to have a serious discussion of physical abuse.'

'I do not want you beating up on him. He's an old man. An extremely pathetic old man.'

'No, Kiran.' Steve might have chuckled at her misunderstanding if it wasn't so important that she understand he wasn't trying to make her the sacrificial lamb. 'I meant that I'm going to make it perfectly clear that if he tries to do this we're-such-a-loving-family act, I'm recounting from day one every side-armed smack, every backhand I ever took from him.'

Kiran's eyes rounded. 'You will?'

He snorted. 'I would rather not. But I'm not allowing Butch to take what was his brother's. If it hadn't mattered to Uncle, I wouldn't give a damn. But Uncle Caleb asked me to fight, and as much as I hope that's the last weapon in my arsenal I have to use, by God I will use it.'

She was quiet after his admission. Her gaze slid to the soles of her shoes, which she was picking at thoughtfully. The last fingers of light reached into the dusty old room, sending lengthening shadows to counteract the dim wattage in the light fixture overhead.

319

'Did you ever realize how much it meant to have someone who supported you in every way until he was gone?' she asked quietly.

'I don't think I did. I wish I had appreciated him more.'

Kiran nodded, still not looking at him. 'Have you seen what is in this closet?'

He glanced in that direction, but all he could see was Kiran's shoes and her suitcase. 'No. Haven't had time.'

'I just did. I was reaching for my suitcase and I found this.' She pulled out a liquor-store box marked 'Beringer White Zinfandel Wine'.

'John said Uncle Caleb only drank whiskey.'

'I know. This was used for storage.'

Kiran gave him a look filled with some silent message he couldn't read. 'Here.' She reached into the box and tossed a magazine his way.

It was a racing magazine, with a picture of his car on the front cover. Something curled up tight inside of him, threatening to burst.

'This box is full of racing magazines. There are three more boxes in the closet.'

'Oh, Jeez.' It was all he could manage.

'He didn't have cable TV.'

Steve hadn't thought about that. Pained realization swept through him, pulling tight bands around his chest. *Uncle Caleb wouldn't spend money to fix a cracked window, but he bought these fan mags to follow my career because he didn't have cable TV*. He sighed, heavy and hard.

'Do you need to drive?' Kiran asked.

'No.' He wiped at one eye. 'No, I need to cry.'

She didn't comment, and Steve could only be glad the room was getting darker.

After a moment, she said, 'I'm sorry I said I never wanted to see you again. I'm angry that you're making me delve into the past, but it doesn't mean you're not right. I just really need to blame you right now.'

'It's okay. I understand.' Steve had already figured out what Kiran was doing and it hadn't bothered him – except it hurt desperately that she would consider never speaking to or seeing him again. He couldn't figure out how to replace the hole not seeing her would leave in him.

'I'm going to miss having him. He was the one person who supported me.'

He straightened. 'Kiran, you have me. We can always have each other. I have to be on the east coast frequently during the racing season, so I could arrange to see you. I don't think I can go another twenty years without laying eyes on you.' She was listening, he noticed, and maybe that was a good sign. 'I'd support you.' He held his breath, hoping she'd at least agree to this small concession.

She shook her head. 'I can't, Steve. An occasional call will be about all I think I can handle.' She gave him a sad smile. 'I know myself well enough to say that if I tried to return the favor by supporting what you love the most, I'd only be pretending.'

Letting out his breath, Steve realized he had

already known what Kiran's answer would be. A starker knowledge tore the veil of irrational hope from him: it was unfair to both of them, but particularly Kiran, to continue being together as much as they were. They were both bruised enough in matters of love. It was best to finish off the last problem holding them together so they could each walk away with almost whole hearts.

'Come on, then,' he said heavily. 'It's time we pay that call on our parents. I'll do the butt-gnawing, but I need you with me for moral support.'

John tried to appear soothing as Maypat Andrews fidgeted in his office. 'I take it there was something in particular you wanted to see me about today, Maypat?'

She nodded, her gaze unwavering, though he sensed the errand that had brought her into his office was a difficult one.

'I'm returning to my home in Atlanta, Father Lannigan. Tomorrow, as a matter of fact. I wanted to let you know so you wouldn't think I was missing Mass.'

Maypat was one of his first-row pew-warmers. John smiled at her comfortingly. 'I would have noticed your cheery face missing immediately. You'll be missed in the church, in Cottonwood, and no doubt at the market.'

'You don't seem that surprised at my news,' Maypat commented.

'Well, perhaps not. Saddened, of course, but

322

change is inevitable. Is there anything I can do to help you?'

'Yes.' Maypat looked determined. 'I need you to advise me on applying for an annulment.'

'An annulment?' Shock creased his brow. 'I – let's start at the top, because I must have missed something. You're going to Atlanta, and I take it you're going alone?' At her nod, he said, 'You want to end your marriage to Jarvis?'

'I do.' She seemed resolute on this point.

He wasn't sure how to proceed now. 'If I can offer some marital counseling –'

'No. No, thank you.'

'All right.' He sighed heavily. 'You may want to apply for the annulment in your new home parish, but I can certainly help you with the particulars.' He paused, reaching across the desk to put his hand over hers. 'I'm sorry, Maypat. Have I, or the Church, let you down?'

'No. I let myself down, I fear.' Her fingers trembled under his. 'Now it's time for me to right matters, and the only way I can do that is to divorce my husband.'

'I see. And a new location will be healing to you?'

'Actually, I don't want to go through a property battle with my husband. He can have the market, the house – everything. As long as I get a fair financial settlement, I'll be better off with my family. It would be . . . destructive to stay here.'

'Destructive?'

'I'm a bit afraid of Jarvis's moods, Father.'

'Ah.' John could see that point without a guiding spotlight. 'So. You've decided on a course of action. How else can I help you?'

She smiled rather sadly. 'I fear you'll be sorry you asked that question. But here's my greater dilemma: I have a letter I want you to give to the police department.'

'A letter?' John realized the real moment of crisis, the dissection of the triangle, was at hand.

'Yes. Unfortunately, someone's house was broken into the other night. My husband wants me to say he was at home with me. He was not. I don't know if the law allows me to testify against my husband, but needless to say I don't want to. So I've written a letter to the police, which I'm hoping you'll hand-deliver for me.'

'May I see the letter?'

'Of course.' She handed it over. It was unsealed, as if she had anticipated his request.

Out loud, he read: '|"I don't know if Jarvis was on the Dorn property that night, but I will tell you why he might have been. He is determined to buy that land for its resale value. On a more menacing level, I overheard one of his friends suggest to him that perhaps Sakina Dorn had left a letter or a diary behind, which would damn him for what he did to her. In the year of –" '

John broke off, staring at Maypat. 'Why are you choosing to come forward with this now?'

'Because I do think Jarvis broke into the Dorn house. His hand was cut, and he wasn't telling me the truth about how it happened, I know.' She paused, searching John's face. 'He can't go on terrorizing that family, but I'm greatly afraid he will. I want so much to right what I should have righted many years ago.' Maypat looked down at her hands. 'Will you help me?'

'I don't see how I'm helping you.' John glanced to the rest of the letter, which repeated everything Maypat had confessed to him in the confessional. He placed the letter in the envelope, licking it closed before placing it on the desk and sealing it with a thump of his fist. It lay on the dark wood between them, white and clean and minus an address of any kind. 'Maypat, all I know to say is that I wish things could have been different for you.'

'I don't see any use in looking back now. You will deliver this for me, won't you?' she asked anxiously.

'I will.' He thought about the act of cleansing involved in Maypat's decision, and knew that she was more honest than he. She was determined to live her life in truth from now on. At that moment John knew he could no longer keep up the pretense of his life, either. Giving up the Church would cause a scandal, but it was better to do that than live with the travesty of the bigger, more important sin in his heart.

'How did you find out where they are?' Kiran asked Steve as they pulled into the hotel parking lot.

'Their lawyer told the good Father.' Steve slammed the car into 'park'.

'Are you ever going to stop being snide about John?' Kiran asked. 'He's really gone out of his way to help us.'

He threw an arm casually around her, pulling her close for a bear hug she tried not to enjoy. 'I'm jealous, babe. I'm coping as best I can.'

'Jealous? Of a Catholic priest?'

'Can't figure it out myself. I've struggled with it, but the answer's not quite coming to me. I think he's too damn good-looking to be hanging around you. And you look up at him with those big, mushy eyes –'

'I do not!' Kiran wanted to laugh, but she got out of the car instead, closing the door as she eyed Steve over the roof.

'You do. I imagine he has that effect on a lot of women. It's all that black-haired, sexy appeal, combined with that sweet, gentle approachability women just eat up.'

She started laughing in spite of herself. 'You *are* jealous!'

'It's hard to admit.' He grabbed her hand, pulling her close. 'Just think, if we weren't coming here to rout our folks, we could check out a room for the two of us.'

'You're doing it again.' She stopped, the smile sliding from her face. 'Fortunately, I understand.'

'Doing what?'

'Trying to make sex the focus of what's happening.' She narrowed her eyes. 'And you're talking a-mile-a-minute. In spite of all your bluster, you're dreading this, aren't you?'

His face was impassive, except for the lines of pain around his eyes. 'I'm okay.'

She raised her brows.

'All right. My deodorant lost any positive effect it might have been having the minute we pulled into the parking lot.'

'Oh, God,' Kiran sighed, feeling her own pulse-rate accelerate nervously. 'Maybe this isn't a good idea. Maybe we should do this tomorrow. Maybe –'

'Maybe we should get the dog-fight over with and limp back to our own homes to replace the finger-nails and hair we're going to lose.'

'We could have asked them to meet us at Uncle Caleb's house.'

'Nah. I prefer the element of surprise. Come on.' He strode toward the entrance without taking her hand again. All his playfulness had disappeared.

She couldn't help thinking it was all going very badly so far. When Steve bribed the girl working the desk with a twenty-dollar bill and an overload of his smooth personality to give them the room number, Kiran closed her eyes for an instant.

'We don't have to approach this like it's some tactical maneuver!' she hissed at him on the elevator. 'We could have asked them to come down to the lobby instead of ambushing them.'

'Come on – it's our parents, Kiran. We have the right to visit them in their rooms.'

She decided at that point it was best to grit her teeth and prepare herself for whatever lay ahead. Obviously Steve was in no mood to take suggestions from her. Her conscience reminded her that she still wanted to take the easy way out. Giving their parents the opportunity to choose a time and a location for this confrontation would have put the ball in the other court. At least Steve's way the whole thing would be over in a matter of minutes.

'I hope the hotel doesn't call the police out on us,' she muttered as the elevator doors slid open.

'I figure that's guaranteed,' he said over his shoulder. Stopping in front of a door, Steve rapped loudly.

'Who is it?' a masculine voice demanded.

'Room Service,' Steve called back.

'He knows your voice, Steve!' Kiran stated unnecessarily.

'Yeah, but I bet he opens the door anyway.'

'You're on, although I hope you're not expecting him to tip you.'

The door jerked open. 'I didn't order no damn Room – Hey, you ain't Room Service.'

'You owe me,' Steve said to Kiran. He looked his father over, examining the stained, once-white T-shirt and the dirty jeans he wore. 'Leaving for California tomorrow, Butch. Thought we better clear some air before I go.'

'Who is it, Butch?' Agnes asked, coming to stand beside him. Smoke from her cigarette blew from her nostrils as she stared at Kiran. 'Well, well. If we don't have unwelcome visitors.'

Kiran waited for Steve's cue. He cleared his throat, saying loudly. 'If you have time, we should

328

go over the contents of Uncle Caleb's will with you.'

' 'Bout time you came around,' Butch grunted. He stepped back to allow them to enter.

'Why? You running out of money?' Steve walked in and Kiran followed, holding her breath. 'Pretty expensive to stay at a hotel for nearly a week.'

'Shut up/ you son-of-a –'

'Butch,' Agnes said, her voice a coiled warning. Her gray eyes glittered like dirty ice as she looked Kiran over. 'It's nice to know we're not going to have to go to court to get what's ours.'

'Well, not exactly.' Steve grimaced, acting as if he regretted what he was going to have to tell them.

Kiran wished he'd hurry up. His cat-and-mouse game was stringing her nerves like guitar wire.

'What we've come to tell you is that we believe it to be in your best interests not to pursue this matter further. Uncle Caleb stated clearly that you weren't getting one copper penny of his, and that'll probably be good enough for the courts. We're going to donate the whole estate to a charity in Uncle Caleb's name.' He put his arm around Kiran. 'Cousin and me decided he'd like being a philanthropist of sorts –'

'He ain't gonna be a pist of nothin' Butch broke in. 'He's dead, that's what he is. Giving away his money is the most damn-fool thing I ever heard of.'

'I don't hear what's in this for us,' Agnes stated, ignoring her brother.

'Why, nothing, of course. I thought I just made that clear.' Steve held Kiran to his side tighter. 'You wasted your money coming out here. It was a gamble, of course, and gambling rarely pays off, but you took your chances and you lost.' He shrugged. 'End of family mourning act, I guess.'

'Well, I'm afraid our lawyer doesn't see it quite as cut and dried as you do, Steve.'

The brains of the operation was surfacing, Kiran realized, as Agnes stepped closer to Steve in a menacing manner. Steve had been right about Agnes being Butch's backbone.

No. Agnes wasn't coming closer to Steve, but to *her*. Kiran began to take an involuntary step back, but Steve held her to him in a vise-grip.

'Kiran, I hope you're prepared for the excruciating openness of a court battle. It's not unusual for the mental state of one or all of the parties to be questioned –'

'Stop it, Agnes,' Kiran commanded.

'I dare say it would be uncomfortable for you, to say the least, if the court were to discover that after your marriage dissolved you spent some time in an –' She glanced at Steve and blew a stream of cigarette smoke into the air. '– Well, politely termed, a mental hospital. Otherwise known as a loony bin.'

'Shut up!' Kiran screamed. 'Shut up, shut up, shut up!'

Steve clamped her until she couldn't feel her shoulder any more. Fear began a suffocating ascent into her throat.

'Agnes, save your showboating for someone who enjoys C-grade drama, okay?'

Kiran's breath came a little more normally at Steve's matter-of-fact tone.

'Here's the deal. Back off now, and our little family secret stays right here in this hotel room.'

'I don't think you know all our family secrets, Steve,' Agnes suggested in an intimate tone.

'Ugh, Agnes, you gross me out.'

Kiran fought an urge to giggle at Steve's statement.

'You two get the hell out of Dodge,' Steve commanded. 'I don't want to hear anything else about any lawsuit against Uncle's estate or we let our lawyers know, the judge know, the executor of the will know, and anybody else who will listen know, that you two are seriously dysfunctional. Get out now and we don't mention small details like mental abuse, verbal abuse, physical abuse, and –' Steve relaxed his hold on Kiran just enough to pull her up against him more firmly '– sexual abuse.'

'Sexual abuse, my eye! She was never sexually abused! Kiran, I'm amazed you would stoop that low.'

Kiran shook her head, but Steve didn't give her a chance to speak. 'Okay, she never got sexually abused in your home, Agnes, but that was only because the angels were watching over her. If she hadn't tried to get away from one of your merry band of lovers one night, she might not have these lovely beauty marks.' Steve lifted the hem of Kiran's dress just enough to show the beginning of the trail of scarred skin.

331

Butch gaped at her legs. 'What the hell are those?'

'I'll let Agnes tell you all about it. We can't stay to fill you in.' He released Kiran slightly to turn toward the door and open it. 'I believe that when you've had time to think over our little talk, Agnes, you'll realize it's best to take yourself back off to the rock you crawled out from under.' He propelled Kiran into the hall before slowly turning to face Agnes and Butch one last time. 'We don't want this to get nasty, after all.'

He pulled Kiran to the elevator and she let him. She couldn't have been happier when he fairly dragged her to the car. He couldn't get away from there fast enough to suit her.

Neither of them spoke as he pulled onto the highway. The terror that had been gripping Kiran was subsiding, though she still felt dangerously close to having a fit of screaming. She closed her eyes and rested her head on the seat, trying to let the motion of the car relax her.

She felt the car leave the road and opened her eyes. Steve pulled into the white lane reserved for stopped motor vehicles, muttering, 'Just a minute,' as he got out of the car.

A second later he threw up in the grass. Kiran reached over and turned the hazard lights on, before closing her eyes again.

Five minutes later he returned to the car. 'Sorry about that.'

'Don't be. I'm feeling better just watching you be ill.'

He switched the engine on. 'Glad to be of service. I guess we're going back to the house?'

'I'm not in any condition to go anywhere else. Besides, I've got to finish boxing up stuff.' She shot him a curious look. 'Are you really going back to California tomorrow?'

'I really am.' Steve didn't look at her. His face was withdrawn, his expression hidden behind the aviator sunglasses he wore. 'I don't think we'll be hearing any more out of our folks. You've booked your flight, and there's no reason for me to hang around, either.'

'Did you come back to Texas just to have that warm-fuzzy moment with Agnes and Butch?' Kiran's heart ached to hear the answer.

'I said I'd stay to the end, and I have.' He shrugged. 'It's the end, so I'm outta here.'

It was the end of more than laying Uncle Caleb to rest. They both knew that, and they both knew it had to be that way.

CHAPTER 21

Kiran walked inside Uncle Caleb's house with Steve following her into the tiny entryway. 'Are you hungry?' he asked.

Kiran knew she couldn't eat a bite, and, since he'd just lost the contents of his stomach, she doubted he felt much like eating, either. 'No, thanks. I think I'll sit in my room for a while.'

'Sounds good. I'm going to shower.' He walked down the hall and went into his own room.

Five minutes later she heard the shower running. Kiran decided to change into comfortable lounging pajamas before finishing her packing. As much as she had not wanted to face Agnes tonight, the meeting had gone much better than she could have hoped. Steve had been right to go on the offensive.

She pulled her hair up into a ponytail, staring at herself in the mirror. It was over. The bitter struggle she had been dreading was over – courtesy of Steve, basically. Agnes had backed off, with only one emotional stiletto hitting its mark.

Loony bin ran through her mind with poisonous intent.

What had Steve thought when Agnes revealed Kiran had spent time in a mental hospital? He hadn't said anything, nor had he appeared surprised. She squirmed with embarrassment and backed away from the mirror. Down the hall, the water stopped. Steve's satisfied humming reached her. What did it matter, anyway? The last shadow of her life had been painfully dragged into the light and Steve seemed barely affected by it. He had not recoiled from her in disgust.

She glanced down at her feet, noticing that her toenail polish was beginning to chip. She could take off the old and put on a fresh, shiny color tomorrow, when she was back home. Tomorrow she could start over from scratch, with no shadows hanging over her.

'Hey, Kiran!'

She nearly jumped out of her skin at Steve's yell. 'What?' she called back.

'*I Love Lucy's* on. We oughta order some food in and veg in front of the TV.'

'I guess.' She peered down the hall. Steve was fiddling with the single haphazard aerial on the small television. Unfortunately he was wearing jeans and no shirt, which reminded her of how wonderful his body felt next to hers.

It's almost like we fit each other, she thought painfully.

With one hand he adjusted a knob on the set. With the other hand he was scrubbing at his wet hair with a towel, making the muscles in his shoulders and back flex. She swallowed, stepping back into her room.

'You know, I think I might just read a book tonight,' she called.

'Suit yourself.'

She heard the hall door close as he returned to his room. Sitting on the bed, Kiran looked at the single suitcase lying open on the floor and told herself she was happy to be going home.

Rapid knocking on the front door made Kiran slam closed the book she'd barely been concentrating on. She'd forgotten that Father John had said he would return tonight to wrap things up with them. Kiran threw on her thick robe and went to open the door.

Steve beat her to it. He was wearing a shirt now, she noted with relief.

'It's John,' he said unnecessarily, opening the door. 'Come on in.'

'I was hoping you were still awake.' The tall priest walked inside, smiling pleasantly. 'From the sidewalk it looked like the lights were all out. I was afraid you'd gone to bed.'

Kiran's face flamed with guilt. Not that he had insinuated Kiran and Steve were sleeping together, but it had sounded that way to her ears. 'Have a seat, John. I was reading a book and Steve was watching TV.' She indicated the den for him to walk into, hoping her explanation more than conveyed that the two of them had not been cozied up in a bed together.

As wonderful as that might be. 'Can I get you anything to drink?'

'Maybe later, thanks.' John brought a kitchen chair in and placed it next to the sagging recliner. 'So. Where do we stand?'

Steve sighed as he sank into the recliner. Kiran sat opposite. 'We just had a heart-to-heart with our folks,' Steve said.

'Oh?' Clearly John was interested in the outcome.

'I think they've lost interest in pursuing the lawsuit.'

'Really?' John's brows elevated.

'I think it's safe to say that Sakina and Uncle Caleb will remain right where they are.' Steve picked at his jeans, clearly unwilling to go into any more detail.

'Well, I am surprised.' John leaned back, very relaxed in the informal den. 'But extremely pleased. So, what next?'

'Kiran and I both have flights for tomorrow. We're leaning toward renting this place out, or at least leasing the land, until we've come to a decision about the property. It'll take us some time to choose a charity, but that's the direction we're heading in for now.'

'A charity?' John repeated.

'Yes. As Kiran mentioned on the phone, something we could feel good about Uncle Caleb's money being used for. We think he would like that.'

'No doubt,' the priest murmured.

Kiran wondered why he didn't seem enthusiastic.

John had already told them that he had his forty acres and didn't need more. Selling to land developers hadn't appealed to her or Steve.

'Is something wrong, John?' she asked.

He hesitated just a moment too long. 'Not really. I'm just concerned about the property being vacant for very long in light of the break-in the other night.'

'Do the police have any more information about that?'

John looked at Steve. 'I believe they've received a valuable tip,' he said off-handedly. 'Well, surely it's all for the best. You're being wise to take some extra time to mull over your decision.'

'I know I'll be able to think more clearly when I've had some sleep and some time away from here.' Kiran barely glanced at Steve before looking back to John. 'We can't tell you how much we appreciate your help.'

'It's been a pleasure.'

'Yeah, right.' Steve laughed, but the sound wasn't amused. 'I'd be willing to bet you've had to spend more time dealing with Uncle Caleb's will than any of your parishioners this week.'

The priest seemed vaguely uncomfortable. 'Your uncle gave me more support during our friendship than I can repay him for by handling small difficulties with his estate.'

Steve eyed John with avid interest. 'If you're always this easygoing, no wonder your parishioners like you so much. If I'd had someone like you to talk to when I was a kid, maybe I would have gone to Church more often.'

John cleared his throat. Kiran could tell he was somehow distressed by Steve's words. She remembered the old lady in the restaurant beaming at John and complimenting him on the wedding service he'd performed. He was obviously popular, and the fact that he was so humble and generous was probably part of that charm. Steve and she both responded to his warmth, as Uncle Caleb obviously must have.

'Well,' she broke in to ease the awkward moment, 'we'll be in touch with you soon, I hope. Let us know if you come up with any suggestions for suitable charities we could donate to in Uncle Caleb and Sakina's name.'

'I will. And I'll keep an eye on this place.'

'Do you have a key?' Steve asked.

'Actually, no.' John seemed puzzled for a moment. 'I usually sat on the front porch with your uncle. I've spent more time in this house with you two than I did when he was alive. In fact the only time I ever entered it without Caleb opening the door for me was the day I found him.'

'Did we ever find more than one key?' Steve glanced at Kiran.

'No. But we shouldn't be needing ours. We can drop it by the church on our way out tomorrow.'

John thought about that. 'It would be easier if you left it here where I could pick it up. I don't know when I'll be at the church tomorrow, since I've got some people I need to see.'

'That's fine with me. Where should we leave it?'

Steve waited for Kiran's suggestion. She didn't want to think about keys, or locking up, or saying goodbye. All she wanted was to have the whole thing behind her.

'Well, we ought to leave the truck keys, too, so it needs to be somewhere where a couple of keys aren't easily visible,' Kiran said out loud. 'I don't know that I feel right just leaving –'

Soft knocking at the door stopped her train of thought. 'Did you order pizza?' she asked Steve.

'No, but I hope it's a pizza man and not the dastardly duo. Our parents,' he said apologetically to John. 'I'll get it.'

But Kiran had already stepped to the door and opened it, half expecting the old man who'd offered to buy the land to be on the porch.

'Hello,' the tall, astonishingly beautiful woman who was standing outside said. She had skin the color of a polished acorn and eyes the color of deep jade from the Orient. Straight black hair was brushed back from her forehead in a satiny fall.

Kiran's jaw dropped. The woman looked startlingly like the portrait of Sakina. 'You're the weeping woman,' she said slowly. 'The midnight lady at Uncle Caleb's grave.'

Steve was staring at the woman. John came to stand beside them.

'Lakina,' he said, his voice conveying great relief, 'thank heaven!'

He smiled at her, Kiran noticed, as if he was witnessing a miracle.

'Let me introduce you to your cousins, Lakina.'

'Cousins!' Kiran felt Steve take hold of her upper arm, gently reminding her that he was by her side. 'How are we cousins?'

The woman John had called Lakina looked uncertainly from him, to Kiran, and then to Steve. Kiran couldn't help thinking irrationally how similar Lakina's eyes were to Steve's.

'Caleb Dorn was my father,' she said, just a second before her eyes clouded up with tears.

'Oh, my –' Kiran was totally shocked. 'Well, do come in. I mean, don't stand out there like, like, you're not . . . family.' Even as she said it, despite the strangeness of the words, Kiran thought how perfect it was that Lakina was her cousin of sorts. 'You *are* family,' she repeated, making way for Lakina to come into the hall. 'Wait a minute!' She whirled to face Father John. 'You knew about her!'

John was staring at Lakina as if she was an endangered and precious animal that might take flight at any second. His gaze was fastened on her like a starving man's. 'I did know,' he said slowly, without looking away from her, 'but I couldn't tell you.'

'Caleb had a daughter? You couldn't tell us that?' Steve was outraged. 'He had an heir to the house and property, an heir to all of this, and you didn't tell us? For the love of God, Kiran and I have been through a hellacious battle with our sorry-ass folks because of the will – and *you couldn't tell us*?'

Kiran thought Steve was doing a great job of controlling himself. A vein had popped to the surface in his neck; one had surfaced near his eye. He looked as if he wanted to explode, but was doing his best to rein it in.

'I couldn't. I'm sorry.'

'Well, if that isn't . . . I mean, for crying out loud!' Steve stared at Lakina incredulously, before pacing the length of the dining room. 'You put us through hell, John, pardon the expression and no pun intended. But Jesu –'

'Steve!' Kiran gave him a stern look.

'Damn it!'

'She technically wasn't the heir,' John inserted reasonably, 'at least not at the time of the funeral. I didn't know about her.'

'Lakina, please sit down.' Kiran offered her one of the hard kitchen chairs. Amazed, she watched as the woman glided toward it and sat, looking as if she might be posing for a glamor shot. 'Let's take a deep breath, everyone, and try not to overreact. Lakina, my name is Kiran. This is Steve. We're not really cousins to each other. You are Steve's cousin, I guess, by blood. I'm not related to the Dorns by anything more than coincidence, I'm afraid.' She peered at Lakina without wanting to appear rude. 'I don't suppose I'm the only one in the room who notices you and Steve both have Caleb's eyes.'

No one said anything for a moment.

'Where the hell have you been, is what I want to know,' Steve demanded. 'You could have saved us a lot of grief.'

'I couldn't come to the funeral,' Lakina stated.

'Of course not. No one else could either,' he said grumpily. 'Your father didn't have a helluva funeral procession.'

'Actually, I was there. I was watching from behind a tree –'

'Oh, that's a good one. I'll have to use that the next time I want to get out of going to a funeral.'

Kiran shot to her feet. 'Steve Dorn! You are being so rude I can't stand to be in the same room with you! You haven't let her get one word out of her mouth!'

'Well, excuse the hell out of me, but if she'd showed up – what? Five hours sooner? – she could have saved us that unique, down-home-flavored family scene at the hotel.'

'So what?' Kiran demanded. 'You're the one who was all hot and bothered to give our parents the royal shove-off.' She sat next to him, leaning close. 'If you think about it, she did us a favor, Steve. It's over – all of it. It's like a race you've won, checkered flag and all. Like you told me, we needed to get over the past. Now we have.' She gently tweaked his arm. 'Quit jumping on this poor lady. I'm so happy she's here, I think I'm going to treat myself to some of Uncle Caleb's whiskey.'

'That's a great idea.' Steve perked up immediately. 'Would you care for something to drink, John? Lakina?'

The priest shook his head. 'I have to tell you I used to love whiskey, especially the smell of it. But after your father died,' he said, his smile soft for Lakina, 'I haven't been able to touch a drop.' To Steve, he said, 'Can I talk you into a glass of cola, though?'

'Lakina?' Kiran looked at her questioningly.

'Nothing for me. Thank you.'

Though she held Kiran's gaze for a second, she quickly released it to look at John. Kiran realized that Lakina coming to the house to meet them had taken astonishing bravery. 'Please, Lakina, all this is yours now. Don't feel like a stranger when actually you belong here more than we do.' She held up a clean glass, her expression questioning.

Lakina slowly met her gaze. 'I'd like a cola, too, please.'

Kiran was relieved. 'Thank you. Now . . .' she sighed. 'Steve, don't be too stingy on the whiskey for me, please.' She pushed the glasses over for him to top off with cola. 'I'm going to sleep a lot better tonight.'

'I think I am, too, though I'm not exactly sure why.' He looked over his shoulder at Lakina and John, who were shyly eyeing each other. 'I feel like I did when that kid slammed his race car into mine. Kind of like, is this really happening?'

'I don't want to talk about that,' Kiran snapped. '*That* was not a good thing. Lakina is a wonderful thing. You cannot compare the two at all.'

'I'm just saying that the feeling –'

'Is not the same at all! Tonight I feel extreme relief, like a crushing weight has been lifted from us.' Kiran rewarded him with the frostiest glare she could manage before she set the drinks on the kitchen table. She sat, and Steve did likewise. 'A toast is in order, John. You do it.'

'To a happy ending,' he said immediately. They all clinked their glasses and drank.

Lakina shook her head. 'You're both taking this very well.'

'You caught us on the right day.' Steve set his glass down. 'We've had a trying afternoon, so we're too shell-shocked to be completely overwhelmed by the appearance of a secret cousin.' He straightened and looked at Kiran. 'It *is* a good thing, isn't it?'

'Yes. We lost a little family; we gained some better family . . .' She smiled at Lakina reassuringly. 'It's all working out.'

John placed a hand over Lakina's, which was resting on the table. Kiran suspected he'd wanted to do that ever since Lakina had walked in the door.

'I told you they would be glad to meet you.'

'You were right.' Lakina's smile for the priest was beatific.

'Why didn't Uncle Caleb leave you anything in his will?' Steve demanded suddenly.

'He didn't know about me.' Lakina looked miserable. 'My mom and he . . . separated before I was born.'

'Oh, that . . . surprises me.' Kiran frowned. 'I

345

mean, it's pretty clear there was never any other woman for him but her. He even had her buried here because she was all he had.'

'Well, that's the hardest part,' Lakina confided. 'Until tonight I've never been able to claim him as my father. He didn't have to be alone. He could have raised me.' She sniffled once, looking down at her hands. 'When someone loses a spouse, they're often happy to have children to remind them of that person. My father didn't even have that comfort.'

All these overwhelming sentiments were what had made Lakina's eyes well up with tears when she'd first arrived. Kiran nodded in understanding.

'Unfortunately, I didn't want to claim anything that was his, which is why I didn't come to you sooner. The truth is, I still don't want to.'

'Why not?' Kiran asked.

'Well, it's a long story –'

'We've got all night,' Steve interrupted. 'This land is worth a fortune. At the very least you'll come out ahead money-wise. So you might as well tell us what could possibly keep you from wanting to be financially secure for the rest of your life.'

'Oh, no! I would never dream of selling it.' Lakina's eyes widened. 'I mean, it's my home. Or it's my father's home – my mother's home. I couldn't sell it. Besides, I don't need money. I need a place to belong.' Lakina's eyes were soft and luminous with regret. 'I'd hate for all this to be sold to outsiders.'

'What will you do? It is hers by right, isn't it,

346

John?' Steve didn't seem any clearer on the law than Kiran was.

'Technically, Caleb left it to you –'

'Yeah, but we abdicate.' Steve's tone was definite.

Kiran laughed. 'I don't think that's what we're doing, but we don't want it, John. You're the executor, named to make certain we both agree on what happens to the property. Steve and I agree, and we'd rather tear up the wills and say they never existed than have some legal entanglement.'

'I can't live here,' Lakina murmured.

'Well, why should you? It has its limitations,' Steve said generously. 'Shoot, you can build down the way, near the fish pond – something with more than one bathroom in it. Get out a piece of paper, Kiran. If Uncle Caleb wrote his will on old paper, we can amend our rights on the same and be out of here tomorrow without another look back.'

'Wait!' Lakina said, holding up her hand. 'You're family. I wouldn't mind you living on the land –'

'I'm not living in Cottonwood, Texas,' Steve said emphatically. 'It's almost the same as roasting in hell.'

'Steve! You loved this place when we were kids.' Kiran gave him a light slap on the wrist.

'I've become accustomed to air-conditioning since then,' he complained. 'The only time I'm this hot is when I'm in a race-car.'

'Yes, well, let's not talk about that right now,' Kiran said hastily. 'Lakina, neither one of us is in a position to live here indefinitely. You can probably find a tenant, though.'

Lakina didn't nod. Kiran cocked her head thoughtfully. 'Wouldn't that work?'

'I don't think so. It wouldn't seem right.'

John took her hand. 'Lakina, it's none of my business, but, as Kiran and Steve can tell you, as painful as letting go of the past might be, you may experience some great freedom if you do. After all, you could live here, near your parents' graves. It's not a replacement for what you might have had if things had been different, but I don't think you should jeopardize your future because of what happened.'

'What did happen?' Kiran couldn't help asking. 'Forgive me for asking, I'm being very nosy. But what could possibly keep you from living here if you want to?'

'The same thing that kept my mother from living here,' Lakina answered simply. 'People here didn't like her.'

'On this many acres of land, do you care who likes you?' Steve asked curiously. 'It's not like you have any close neighbors.

'Remember the break-in?' John asked.

Lakina gasped. 'What break-in?'

'The house was broken into the other night. Someone was trying to steal something, I guess.' John had put her hand down, but now he patted it soothingly.

'So what does the break-in have to do with Lakina?'

'It's my mother,' she said sadly. 'There were some people here who threatened her into leaving because she was black. The same people are still alive.'

'Unfortunately they seem to want to get possession of Caleb's property,' John added.

'Well, they can't,' Steve said stubbornly. 'It's hers.'

'But they might threaten Lakina, too.' Kiran stared across the table. 'If you know who it is, can't you turn them in?'

'I live in New York,' Lakina said cautiously. 'I travel extensively. My aunt lives in this town, though. I'm worried that whatever I stir up I'll leave her behind to deal with it.' Her green eyes were haunted. 'It all happened so long ago. It seems wrong to make the golden years of Aunt Grace's life miserable just because I want to see justice done.'

Steve scratched at his head and blew out a long sigh. 'I'm going to have to think about this one for a while. It's pretty complicated.'

'Yes.' Lakina smiled her relief. 'Thank you for understanding.'

'I wish there was something we could do,' Kiran said. She felt exhausted by all the emotions she felt for Lakina's sake.

'I don't think there is. But thank you.'

'Well . . .' John pushed back his chair and stood. 'I'd better let you two get some sleep, since you've got flights to catch tomorrow. I'll stop by to get the key in the morning, I suppose, if you still want me to handle this.'

'For now, John. If you wouldn't mind.' Lakina's eyes were filled with gratitude.

'Not at all.'

'That's fine,' Steve said, getting to his feet as Lakina did.

'I have to go, too,' she said. 'My aunt was worried that I . . . I was coming to meet you.'

'She was right to worry,' Kiran said with a grin.

'I didn't mean that,' Lakina said hurriedly.

'I'm teasing. It's been wonderful to meet you. You've taken a load off our minds.' Kiran hugged Lakina briefly. 'I'm sorry we can't take some of your burden from you, though.'

'It's been there all my life. If it doesn't go away in the next few days, I don't think it'll make much difference,' she returned with a deprecating smile.

'Well, if we think of a solution, we'll mention it to John tomorrow.' Steve shook John's hand in the first really warm gesture of friendship Kiran had ever seen him make to the priest.

'Oh, wait!' she cried. 'There's something I think you'll want.' She dashed down the hall, coming back a second later to place the picture of Sakina into her daughter's hands.

Quick tears jumped into Lakina's eyes. 'I do look like her,' she murmured. 'Just like Aunt Grace said I did.'

'Didn't you know?' Kiran couldn't believe that.

'No. I don't have a good photograph of her.'

Kiran fought off the sadness with some wry humor. 'That makes the three of us true cousins, then. Neither one of us knew what our mothers looked like. I don't even know who mine was.'

'To find mine I'd have to put a "wanted" picture in the post office,' Steve agreed.

'Oh, I'm sorry,' Lakina said, glancing from Steve to Kiran.

'Don't be,' Steve said. 'We've just pitched all our regrets into a trash can today – didn't we, Kiran?'

'It was hard,' she said, smiling at Steve, 'in fact, it was the worst, but it doesn't matter anymore.'

'It doesn't?' Steve asked.

'It doesn't,' Kiran assured him, 'and it never will again.'

CHAPTER 22

'I just figured something out,' Steve said, closing
the front door as John and Lakina left.

'What?'

He walked to stand in front her. 'In my letter,
Uncle Caleb said you have his eyes. I thought
maybe he'd gotten senile, because yours are blue.'
He touched her face lightly. 'He was right, though.
You see the world the way he did.'

'I don't understand.'

Steve smiled. 'You take people at face value.
John, for example. You liked him from the start,
where I was suspicious. And with Lakina showing
up here. You reached out to her. I wasn't sure what
the deal was with her at first.'

'I'm not sure what the deal is with *you*.'

He tapped her lightly on the lips. 'From the
beginning you tried to pull me into this situation,
though I resisted like hell. I stay withdrawn from
anything that might . . . might get me involved.'

'Emotionally?'

'Yeah. But you had this approach that sucked me

in. All I could call it was your team spirit. It irritated me so bad, because I could feel you slowly closing in on me.'

She stepped away from him. 'You should have gotten away while you could.'

He shook his head. 'I'm glad I didn't. You saw the best in me. Maybe you see good in everybody, like Uncle Caleb did. I thank God he saw the best in me.'

'I do, too.' Kiran sighed, retreating to a separate corner of the room. 'I wish Uncle Caleb could have held his daughter. He would have been so happy.'

Steve didn't reply. He couldn't for the knot in his throat. An image of a baby daughter never knowing the touch of her father's loving hands brought tears to his eyes.

'Maybe I should have suspected something like this when I saw her crying that night,' Kiran said thoughtfully. 'It happened so fast, I wasn't sure what to think. I wasn't even sure what I saw.'

'Well, a long-lost cousin sure makes this easy on us.' Steve sank back into the recliner, taking a long sip of his drink. 'After I got over the shock and the suspicion, I started thinking about how great this is. Agnes and Butch could contest the will to their heart's content, and all they'd be doing is wasting their money.' He laughed, his mood improving a notch.

Kiran offered him a hesitant smile. 'I hope Lakina will be all right. She certainly has a lot to think about. But I agree, she made everything much easier for us.'

He turned to say something else to Kiran, wanting her to stay with him longer, but the wary look in her eyes stopped him.

'I'll see you in the morning, Steve. I'm going to bed. All this excitement has made me tired.' She waited for him to say goodnight.

'Just the trip to the hotel should have worn you out.' Steve leaned back in the chair, not content to spend an evening alone staring at the TV. He slid his gaze to Kiran, thinking how much he was going to miss her now that they definitely wouldn't have Uncle Caleb's property to bind them together. He couldn't even think of a decent excuse to call her on the telephone once they were back in their respective states. There was nothing left to discuss.

Except for one thing. 'Kiran,' he said slowly, 'there's something I have to tell you.'

She hovered in the doorway. Steve saw the reluctant look in her eyes and realized the time wasn't right. She looked as if she might scream if one more heavy-duty moment got laid on her. 'Nothing,' he murmured. 'We can talk about it tomorrow.'

'Are you sure?'

He appreciated her attempt to please him, but the pink rim around her eyes confirmed she'd had enough. 'I was just wondering if you think Lakina will mind if I ship those boxes of racing magazines to my house. I'd like to keep them as a reminder of Uncle Caleb.' He hoped she bought his diversionary tactic.

Kiran smiled with relief. 'I doubt she wants them, Steve. I think she'll be glad there's something here you can take back with you.'

'I'll ask her tomorrow.' Steve forced his gaze from Kiran's face and pretended to examine the TV again. 'Well, see you in the morning.'

'Goodnight,' Kiran murmured, before walking down the hall and closing her bedroom door.

Steve sighed heavily, leaning back in the chair. The TV with its black and white reruns couldn't capture his attention. All he could think about was Kiran – and, despite the fact that he'd desperately wanted this trip to be behind him, how he dreaded tomorrow. He dreaded having to say goodbye to her.

An insistent pattering against the bedroom window jarred Steve awake. He heard water trickling down the glass and running through the pipes in the house. Kiran apparently wasn't going to miss a last chance to oversee the rosebed before she left. Sunlight streamed into the room, making him realize how well he must have slept. Glancing at his watch, he saw that it was nine o'clock in the morning. Another spray of water hit the panes and Steve jerked up the dusty venetian blind.

'Good morning!' Kiran called.

He raised the window. 'Heck of an alarm clock you are,' he grumbled, trying to sound as if he wasn't glad to see her. 'What are you doing?'

'Watering the plants before we leave. They're

355

going to fry in this heat if the beds aren't wet enough, and I don't want Lakina to find the roses all wilted.' She smiled happily at Steve. 'You should see them! They're in full, magnificent bloom.'

'I'll be right out there.' He pushed the window down and let the blind fall before jumping out of bed. He'd fallen asleep in the easy chair last night, and sometime later he'd stumbled down the hall and fallen into bed without taking off his jeans. Pulling a fresh shirt out of the suitcase, he went into the bathroom for a quick swipe at his hair before heading outside. He wasn't so much interested in seeing the roses as in seeing Kiran – she had looked pretty and rosy herself.

'Look!' she exclaimed, indicating the rosebed with the hose as he joined her. 'Aren't they beautiful?'

It did appear that the roses had received a major infusion of loving care. They spiraled toward heaven with fat, bright blossoms of color. He could smell their sweet fragrance from where he was standing. 'They don't look like the same flowers,' he said. 'You didn't bless them with some cow manure out of a neighboring field, did you?'

Kiran laughed, turning the hose off and rolling it up. 'No. It just must be their season to flourish.'

He had just about run out of admiration for the roses, turning his attention to Kiran instead. She was wearing jeans and a white blouse, and her hair was pulled up in a ponytail the way he liked it. She looked simple and fresh, kind of exotic in her own way.

'We should make one last trip down to the graves before we go,' he suddenly suggested.

'I agree.' Kiran rewarded him with a smile as bright as the sun. 'Let's take some of these roses with us. I can pretend that Sakina can see how well all her hard work has turned out.'

'Maybe it's not pretending.' Steve reached to pick a couple of the blossoms. 'I'd like to think that Uncle Caleb knows I did as he asked, that I gave it the good fight. I'm sure Sakina knows you're taking care of her flowers, and that you welcomed her daughter with open arms.'

'I like happy endings, don't you?' Kiran asked, putting her hand around his upper arm as they walked down the field. 'I feel like I'm living in a dream.'

He refused to say that the happiest ending he could imagine would be having her by his side for ever. There was no point in spoiling Kiran's effervescent mood. 'Me, too,' was all he said, and then, 'Look, the headstones were delivered while we were gone.'

Kiran stopped in front of the graves, admiring the stonework and the lettering. 'It seems like so long ago that we picked these out. I'd forgotten all about it.'

'I had, too. I didn't have any experience picking out stuff like that, but I think we did a good job.'

'Me, too. I hope Lakina will be pleased.'

'I'm sure she'll be grateful that someone cared about her parents enough to honor them properly.'

Kiran slowly turned to meet his eyes. 'Thank you, Steve,' she whispered. 'Thank you for thinking of them.'

'Hey.' He saw tears gathering in her eyes and wanted her buoyant mood to return. 'I might've thought of it, but I sure wasn't going to get through picking them out without you.'

'Well . . .' Kiran sniffled and wiped her nose with her hand. 'It was a family affair.'

'Yeah.' He reached out to lay one rose on Sakina's grave, then walked to lay the other on Uncle Caleb's. Kiran did the same. They both stood looking at the graves, and Steve felt tears in his own eyes. 'For once, a family affair I'm proud of.'

'Speaking of family matters I'm not proud of, I don't think I can say goodbye without mentioning what Agnes told you.' She looked miserable and ashamed. 'About the mental hospital.'

He didn't look at her as he crouched to dust off Uncle Caleb's headstone. 'Damn, Kiran. You don't think I care about that, do you? Jeez, I started to tell the old witch that whatever time you spent in there had to be good because you weren't spending it under her roof, so you were better off.' Glancing at Kiran, he saw the surprise in her eyes. 'Did you think it bothered me?'

'Well, it didn't sound very good the way she blurted it out. The truth is –'

He waved her silent, shaking his head. 'Kiran, babe, you're my anchor. Okay? I don't need to hear any truths. I don't want to hear about your ex-husband and how it crushed you when your marriage broke up. I mean, if you want to talk about it, I'll listen, but you've had to do enough soul-baring. It's past history, you know?'

She pressed her palms together. 'You're right. I really don't want to talk about it.'

'Cool. Hey, so don't let me be the one you feel like you have to explain it to. Besides, we're both lucky we didn't end up as permanent kook-house residents. I just drive around in a metal box with lots of padding like I'm nuts anyway.'

Kiran didn't reply for a moment. Steve went back to inspecting the work on the headstones.

'Steve?'

'Yeah?' He barely glanced her way.

'What did you mean about me being your anchor?'

He let out a long sigh. 'Kiran, you are. You always were, from the time we were kids. I needed you because you were all I had that made me feel normal.' He got up, smacked the dirt off his jeans, and went to stare into her eyes. 'Why do you think I was hanging onto you like a lifeline when we went to the hotel to see the lunatic limbs of the family tree? Didn't you notice?'

'I thought you were trying to keep me from escaping. I thought you were afraid I'd run out of the room and desert you instead of facing up to Agnes.' She averted her eyes for a second.

'No, babe.' He tipped her chin up. 'You were grounding me like a lightning rod. I could take anything the old man dished out as long as I had you next to me. I couldn't let you go.' He wanted to kiss her, but he knew she was too vulnerable right now. Vulnerable wasn't the way he wanted her. He wanted her full of spunk and fire and sass, like the Kiran he knew best. 'I figure Lakina said it right,' he murmured, 'when she said she needed a place to belong.'

'Oh, Steve,' Kiran whispered. 'I'm so sorry.' she leaned her head forward, so that her forehead rested against his chin.

He knew exactly what she was apologizing for. Wrapping his arms around her, he said, 'Don't be. I'm grateful we did this thing together. I'm not happy about the fact that there can't be anymore between us, but that doesn't mean I regret a moment of what we did have.'

Her shoulders started shaking, so he held her tighter.

'I love you, Steve, as much as I can,' she said, her voice breaking. 'I hope you understand.'

'I know. I love you, Kiran Whitley, and if anything ever changes –' He started to say, *I'll marry you in a flash*, but he knew by the dark shadows in her blue eyes that wasn't what she wanted to hear. So he fell back on what he knew best. 'If anything ever changes, I'd be honored to get into your pants.'

Kiran giggled, giving him a light kiss on the chin. 'I'll always remember you for just that reason,' she told him. 'Come on. We don't want to miss our planes.'

* * *

Father John was waiting for them back at the house. 'Hello!' he called, waving as they walked toward him. 'I saw you down there and thought I'd give you a moment alone.'

'We just went to put some of these spectacular roses on the graves,' Kiran said. 'They've been blooming like mad.'

John looked sympathetic as he nodded. 'You've been watering, I see.'

'Yes.'

Steve glanced at Kiran, remembering the time she'd wrestled him for the water hose. He wondered how he was going to get through the next few hours without cracking up.

'I thought I'd get the keys before you two left. It might be better than leaving them out somewhere.'

'Great.' Steve fished around in his pocket. 'You'll let us know what Lakina decides to do? I know everything will go just fine for her, but I still want to hear what happens.' He pulled out several keys, his wallet, and some coins. 'You know, I looked at the window pane that was broken out, John. I noticed the crack in it last week. If somebody hadn't seen the house being broken into, I would have just thought the glass had finally fallen out of the window.' He handed three keys to John. 'I can't imagine what anyone would want in this old place. There's nothing here that means anything except to Lakina, Kiran and me.'

'I think what the burglar was seeking was some-place else,' John murmured.

Steve shot him a suspicious stare. 'You know more about this than you can tell us, too, don't you?'

John sighed. 'I'm sorry. I'll tell you as soon as I can.' He looked over the keys, holding one up. 'This you've marked house-key, this is the truck-key, but what does this one go to?'

'I don't know,' Steve said honestly. 'I found it in the rosebed.'

'The rosebed?'

'Yeah.' Steve glanced at Kiran apologetically. 'Kiran heard a noise outside her window one night that she said sounded like keys jingling. I thought she just had the willies, you know, from stress or something, but later I found this outside. She also thought she'd seen a woman wandering around the graves, so when I found the key I decided it was best to take Kiran to California with me.'

'You didn't tell anybody?'

'What was to tell? The police would have said it could have been lying in the rosebed for ever. Kiran had watered, so any prints on it would have been erased. There didn't seem to be much to go on, except my gut feeling that something wasn't quite square.' He hesitated for a moment. 'It's not Lakina's key, is it?'

'I doubt it. I have a pretty fair idea of who it might belong to, and if it does it will place the suspect on this property. In light of a certain letter I've recently turned over to the police, that new revelation would be damaging indeed.'

'Damaging enough for Lakina to live here if she

wanted to? Safe enough for the Aunt Grace she mentioned?' Steve still hated the thought that his cousin was being chased off her own land. 'I'd like to know that when I leave I'm leaving Uncle Caleb's daughter in good hands.'

He couldn't be certain, but he did think he detected a faint flush creeping along John's neck, just above his shirt-collar.

'Right now I have a good feeling everything will work out for the Dorn family. Something tells me a long, unhappy chapter is about to end.'

'All right, John. I expect to hear from you.'

Kiran had been silent during this entire exchange, though now she came forward to give John a brief hug Steve tried not to envy. He wished she felt as comfortable with him as she was with John.

'Thank you so much for everything,' she told John. 'We would never have muddled through this without you.'

'I was happy to do it. And I suppose I'm ready to tell you one thing I haven't told anyone but a few people at the Church.' John swallowed, his countenance grim. 'I've decided the priesthood isn't for me.'

His gaze darted from Kiran to Steve, and then away. Steve could tell John was monumentally embarrassed about his revelation. Frankly, he wasn't sure what the proper response was to a statement like that. 'Hey, everybody's entitled to a change of profession.' Steve hoped that was the right thing to say. He glanced at Kiran. Her eyes were huge in her face as she stared at John.

'I know you've thought this out carefully,' she said, 'and I know I should be congratulating you, but I'm just terribly relieved you *were* a priest and could perform the service for Uncle Caleb.'

'Thank you. But if you're going to need me for anything else, you'd better hurry.'

Steve knew John regretted the accidental insinuation about marriage behind his words immediately. By the wary expression in Kiran's eyes as she glanced at him she was waiting for Steve's smart-aleck remark. Steve decided to please her.

'Can't think of anything right now, John,' Steve said easily. 'I'm fresh out of confessions and I haven't found anyone to marry me. How about you, Kiran?'

'Just say thank you, Steve,' she said crossly. 'John doesn't want to perform another funeral service on Dorn land.'

'Ah, well.' Steve shrugged. 'Can't blame a guy for trying, can you? So, you're off the hook where we're concerned, John. Thanks for the offer.'

John cleared his throat. 'I'll be in touch soon – when I know more about everything.'

Steve reached out to shake his hand. 'Take care of yourself.'

'I will. You take care of yourselves.'

The priest turned and walked toward his car. Steve faced Kiran. 'Well, that's that. Last one out the door has to lock it.' He fell back on a competitive challenge to hurry her, so he wouldn't have to drag out saying goodbye to Uncle Caleb – and to her.

'Let me get my suitcase.'

He followed her to the bedroom to take the suitcase from her. Silently he got his, too, and met her at the front door. Without speaking, they each took a long look around the dusty, dim living room.

'I'm going to miss him,' Kiran whispered.

'Me, too.' Tears blinded him as he remembered his uncle the last time he'd seen him, waving goodbye as he put Steve on a plane after summer vacation. 'Come on.' Steve swallowed an enormous lump in his throat and pushed the lock in on the doorknob, closing the door for the last time.

Maypat watched silently as the police officer handcuffed Jarvis.

'You could tell them,' he pleaded with her one last time. 'You could tell them I was here all that night.'

She shook her head and turned away. A thousand emotions were running through her, but none of them was the desire to lie for her husband. He cursed her in a string of words designed to offend her, but she let them filter away without actually feeling their effect. A moment later she heard the door close. She hurried to the window, watching as Jarvis was escorted to the police car.

Relief swept through her that now justice might finally be served. If nothing else, Jarvis was finally going to get the punishment he should have gotten many years ago. She said a silent prayer for Sakina Dorn's soul, then retrieved her suitcase from her bedroom. The clothes in the suitcase were all she planned on taking from this house.

With one last look around the living room full of Victorian antiques and fragile china and figurines, Maypat said goodbye to everything she had collected. All breakable, all beautiful, but she didn't need their comfort anymore.

She put on her hat, picked up her suitcase, and closed the door behind her. She was going home to Atlanta – a survivor at last.

'You can't put me in this dinky cell!' Jarvis shrieked. His heart was racing wildly as he felt the concrete of the hall beneath his feet, felt the interested silence of the other prisoners. 'I'm an upstanding member of this community!'

'You're charged with breaking into someone's house, Jarvis. That reduces your rank in Cottonwood.'

'Listen to me.' Jarvis was pleading now. 'I can't stay in here. I'd be happy to do community service. I didn't take anything, for crying out loud!'

The policewoman cracked her gum. 'Your lawyer'll have to work out the details. Last I heard, someone else has entered charges, so you may be here for a couple nights – at least until someone posts bail for you.'

Maypat was the only person who might have, Jarvis realized. As scared as Bedford was of ending up in a jail cell at his age, he sure wasn't going to soil his hands by bailing Jarvis out. The police might start looking at him suspiciously, too.

His breath came in short wheezes as he averted his eyes from the jail cell. 'Please. Don't you understand? I'll go crazy in there! I'm used to living in a big house, to having my freedom. Can't you release me on my own recognizance?'

'Not for this. Maybe after you're arraigned the judge might offer some leniency, if he's in the mood. Sorry, but in you go.' She removed his handcuffs and gently pushed him inside.

'Please!' he cried, desperately frightened as the cell door clanged shut behind him. 'I can't be in here!'

But the police officer had gone down the hall. Jarvis turned slowly, dreading his eyes getting accustomed to the dimness.

And then he saw it, up in the corner of the cell. A large, cottony-looking spider web. It stretched across an entire upper corner of one wall, testament to the fact that it had existed a long time. There were probably spiders the size of his fist just waiting to crawl on him every time he went to sleep.

Frantically he whirled, to clamp his hands around the bars. 'Come back!' he screamed. ''Come back!''

No one heard him, or they didn't care. Jarvis sank to his haunches, glancing fearfully over his shoulder at the web, then checking around his feet for eight-legged creatures.

Somewhere, somehow, he heard the sound of a woman's laughter mocking him. That black Dorn woman was going to haunt him with an army of enormous spiders. 'No, no!' he cried. 'I confess!' No, that wasn't right. He didn't want to do that. They'd keep him in here for ever if he told the truth about what he'd done. 'I repent! I repent!'

He screamed when he felt the web hanging from his mouth – before he realized it was his own spit.

The next morning, when the guard went to shove breakfast through the cell door, she found Jarvis keeled over on the floor, his hands wrapped around his ankles.

'What'd he die of?' someone asked her.

'They think it was a heart attack,' she said, her tone professional and unconcerned. ' 'Course, he didn't seem quite right to me when they brought him in. Kind of loco, you know?' She sighed heavily. 'The way he was laying this morning when I found him sure looked like crazy. Maybe he went completely around the bend. Anyway, we'll find out soon enough.'

After the autopsy, the medical examiner reported his conclusion of death by cardiac arrest. No one ever noticed the harmless house spider Jarvis had stomped to death, its remains barely visible on the tread of his shoe.

CHAPTER 23

In her cozy bungalow in Tennessee, Kiran told herself that the slow, comfortable pace of her life suited her. It was still summer break and there was a lot she needed to do to prepare for the coming school year. She didn't miss the volatility – or had it been exhilaration? – she had experienced with Steve.

He hadn't called, and she had known that he would not. Yet a small part of her wondered what he was doing, how he was. She told that same aching part of her that this feeling would pass, and so would the longing to hear his voice.

She had cable TV hooked up in her house, despite her misgivings. Reruns and old movies were what she planned to watch, she told the service man. As soon as he left she nonchalantly thumbed through the cable guide until she found which channel showed the Winston Cup races. Glancing at her watch, she realized a race was in progress. Deciding she'd just briefly see if she could recognize Steve's car, maybe even watch him race a lap or so, Kiran

369

turned to the channel. Pulse quickening, she allowed herself to settle back and watch a little more.

Before she knew it the race was almost over. A chain broke on the lead car just as it was going into the final lap. Kiran had no idea what the sportscasters were going crazy about, nor did she know about car chains. She did understand that the driver had been a certain winner until the misfortune. Steve sailed in second and Kiran jumped from the sofa, spilling popcorn and her drink as she shrieked with excitement.

The next week she not only watched the race, she taped it on her VCR. This time Steve took the checkered flag, and Kiran watched as reporters swarmed around him and his crew, all wanting pictures and a few words on how he felt about winning the race. Ginger was glued to Steve's side, smiling like a movie star. Kiran's heart stopped for an instant, her delight dimming, until she realized that Steve never looked at Ginger, nor did she ever really look at him. Ginger's total concentration was on the crowd surrounding Steve.

A little sheepishly Kiran went and bought a couple of racing magazines – just to see what she could learn about the sport. To her amazement, she discovered that there was even a NASCAR site on the Internet, and she could read all of Steve's racing statistics, about his car and crew, and his life.

The Internet proclaimed his single status, and Kiran's eyes burned. How long would that statistic be true? Ginger wouldn't be a buffer from Steve getting married for long; one day he would find a woman who wasn't terrified of losing him in a fiery car crash. Kiran closed her eyes, trying to imagine herself worrying every race whether this time he went out he might not finish again, might not finish in one piece.

It happened to a driver one time – his car being wrecked so badly that he sustained injuries. Kiran sucked in her breath as she watched his car rolling. She wondered about the driver's wife and kids. Were they frightened out of their wits? A couple of weeks later, he was back out racing, and Kiran followed his progress, wondering how his wife felt. Did she suffer teeth-grinding fear every time her husband got behind the wheel of his race car?

Steve took third the next race, and Kiran began to study the points system. If he continued to hold this pace, it looked as if the Winston Cup would come down to a tight point race between him and one other driver. But when something so small as a car chain could put a man out of a race, or another driver hitting a car . . .

Kiran couldn't stand it any longer. She vowed not to purchase another racing magazine, not to watch another race on TV, not to get on the Internet another night to vicariously live in Steve's world. It was safe, certainly, keeping up with him without any contact, but it was also driving her mad. Throwing herself into preparing for the first six weeks of the school year, she forced herself to focus on other things.

After returning from the grocery store one day in

August, there was a message on her recorder. She froze at the sound of Steve's voice.

'Hey, Kiran. Just wanted to let you know that John called. Lakina has decided to move into Uncle Caleb's house, along with her Aunt Grace, while she builds a new house down close to the fish pond. John says she's decided to give up the modeling circuit for a while. Apparently she's decided to give the life of a farmer a go. I think they're dating each other, though he never directly came out and said it. I . . . can't help thinking Uncle Caleb would be happy his best friend is seeing his daughter.

'Anyway, I'll be in Bristol, Tennessee this weekend. Hope everything's going all right with you.' There was a hesitation on the tape for a moment before he said, 'I miss you. If you have time, drop me a line and let me know how you're doing.'

She flew to grab a map. Bristol wasn't that far from where she lived. A few hours, but it was mostly highway, and if Steve was going to be this close . . .

'I could do it,' she told herself. 'I just have to buy a ticket at the gate. I don't have to tell him I'm going. That way there isn't any pressure involved. I can just go and see if I can watch the whole race without . . . fainting again.'

Telling herself to ignore the sudden stomach cramps of apprehension she had (and which lasted over the next couple of days) Kiran got into her car and headed to Bristol. She bought a ticket – one of the last ones available. She ended up sitting where she could barely see the cars flying around the track.

Steve's was only easy to pick out because she had his colors memorized.

'Next time I'll know to bring binoculars,' she told the man next to her, who didn't seem to mind her jumping up occasionally to get a better glimpse of Steve's car.

Suddenly his tire blew, just as he was going in to the pit. The car fishtailed, but he managed to make it to where he could get some help. Crew members on another team changed the tire in very good time. Though Kiran was warmed by the camaraderie, the stomach cramps she'd been having all week intensified painfully.

'Excuse me,' she said to the man next to her. He stood so she could scoot by and she hurried to her car. She sat with the windows down, listening to the crowd noise, and when the race was over, Kiran was relieved by the announcement that Steve had placed in the top five.

It seemed his life was going forward. Though his profession wasn't something her weak stomach could endure, she was glad that he was succeeding at what he loved. Racing was so much a part of Steve that she couldn't imagine him sitting behind a desk, or languishing in an office. Taking a deep breath, she wished him good luck in her heart and headed back to her little space in the mountains.

'I'm pretty sure it was Kiran,' Ginger insisted. 'Even in this crowd, I thought I caught a good glimpse of her.'

'No.' Steve pulled off his helmet, not even bothering to glance toward the stands. 'One time at the track was enough for her.'

Ginger handed him a cap with a sponsor's name on it. 'She might have gotten brave in the past couple of months.'

Steve glanced at her sharply. 'Kiran is the bravest woman I know. She doesn't have to like what I do to prove it to me.'

'Whoa. Sorry, Steve.' Ginger held up a hand. 'I put that badly. I meant she might have come to see you race despite the unpleasant experience she had last time.'

He knew Ginger so well it was clear to him she really regretted her choice of words. 'What do you care?'

Ginger shrugged. 'Maybe I don't. But she was nice. She could have gotten herself all worked up about me, about what me and you've been to each other before. I probably wouldn't have liked her if she'd thrown a jealous fit, but she seemed to understand the situation.' She paused, glancing over the crowd. 'Anyway, it's none of my business. I just thought you'd want to know I thought I'd seen her.'

'Thanks for the bulletin.' Steve gathered up his gear, ignoring how his heart expanded with hope that Kiran might have actually come to the track. He'd mentioned it, of course, with a thin prayer that she might get in touch with him. But he had never heard a word from her, and, though that hurt, he understood.

'Come on,' he said to Ginger, 'let's go get some grub.'

It was October in the mountains, with the air crisp and leaves falling to the ground to make bright blankets under the trees. Kiran breathed in, loving everything about the new school year. She was back in her element, her safety zone.

She went inside her house, turning on the television set to watch the evening news. Steve's face popped onto the screen and Kiran gasped, reaching to turn up the volume.

'Finally winning the Winston Cup is something I've wanted for a long time,' he said to the reporter. 'It means a lot to me.'

'What are you going to do to celebrate?'

'I haven't decided yet.'

The reporter thanked him for his time, then other people crowded around him. Kiran felt as if she was having a panic attack of some kind. For a second the camera focused on Steve. Kiran held her breath, watching him, wanting him. He seemed vaguely aware of people congratulating him, but his eyes kept searching the crowd for something – or someone. He looked and looked, then turned to accept something an important-looking man was handing him.

Kiran's heart stilled in her chest. For that one moment she had felt something was wrong. She had seen the remoteness of his expression, knew he wasn't responding to the crowd.

And then she knew. Steve was alone. He had his big win, his big comeback, his fans. Yet he was holding himself apart from everything. Detached.

Just like Uncle Caleb.

Rapid pounding on her door at three o'clock in the morning startled Kiran out of a sound sleep. 'For crying out loud!' she whispered, half-afraid. Throwing on her old robe, and with her portable phone in hand to call the police, she crept to the door. Not for anything was she going to answer.

'Kiran! It's Steve!' a voice called.

She flung the door open. 'Steve Dorn! You scared me out of my wits!' But she flung her arms around his neck, reveling in the tight squeezing he gave her. He smelled like cold air, and the skin of his face and neck was chilled. 'What have you been doing? You're frozen! Come in and get warm.'

Ushering him inside, she took his leather jacket and laid it over the back of the sofa.

'I've been sitting in the car for thirty minutes, telling myself it wasn't a good idea to wake you up at this hour, that I'd get a better reception if I showed up at a decent time.'

'Sit down and I'll get you a cup of something hot to drink.'

He caught her hand. 'I don't want anything. I'm fine. Thanks.'

She realized she was devouring him with her eyes. Instantly she gestured to the sofa. 'Sit down.

376

I want to hear all about your win. Congratulations, by the way.'

Pleasure stole across his face as they both sat at opposite ends of the couch. 'How did you know?'

'Oh, I . . . it was on the evening news.'

'Was it?'

He stared at her, and her heartbeat hitched. 'Well, just briefly.'

'What are these?' He leaned forward, taking one of the racing magazines from the coffee table.

Kiran's face flamed. 'Oh, I was . . . trying to . . .' Her voice trailed off as he glanced back at her. He leafed past the page she had marked with a yellow marker – the page with all his recent stats on it. She lowered her gaze. 'I've been trying to keep up with how you were doing. I was pulling for you.'

'You were?'

'Of course! Just because racing's not for me doesn't mean I don't want you to win.' Her gaze met his defiantly. 'I just can't watch you do any more daredevil stunts, that's all.'

'I'm glad you were rooting for me.' He reached out to twist a lock of her hair around his finger. Kiran's breath caught in her throat.

'I had to,' she whispered. 'I want you to be happy.'

'I'm glad to know I've got a new fan,' he replied softly.

'I'm your biggest, if most faint-hearted fan.'

He loosed his hold on her hair to caress her cheek. Kiran leaned into his now-warmed palm. 'I found myself becoming a devotee – up to and including downloading your stats from the Internet. I even e-mailed your website under a false name one night.'

'Did I reply?'

'Yes. You thanked me for my support.'

They were silent for a moment.

'I guess I should tell you that I even tried to brave watching you race in person,' she confided.

'You were in Bristol.'

'Yes.' She nodded, her gaze sliding away apologetically. 'I found it was too intense, being there rather than covertly keeping up with you in magazines or on TV. When your tire blew out, I sat in the parking lot until the race was over.'

He looked sad. 'Ginger told me she thought she'd seen you. I wish you had let me know you were going to be there.'

'I couldn't,' 'Kiran confessed. 'I didn't know if I could go through with it.'

Silence fell over them. The moment stretched awkward and long between them.

Steve picked up the remote for the television. 'So, you've been watching the races on TV? I feel flattered.'

She took the remote from him and placed it between them on the sofa. 'Yes. And, though it's taken me all summer and a couple months of fall, I've come to a conclusion.'

'I have, too.'

'My conclusion first.' She offered him a hesitant look, knowing it was time to tell him the truth. 'I don't want to live with any more regrets.'

'I don't either.'

She took his hand from her face and clasped it in hers. 'I'll be thirty-five next birthday, and though my biological clock should be ticking, it's not. I don't think it's ever going to.'

He remained silent during her admission, and Kiran was grateful. She needed to say everything in her heart. 'I've gotten a lot of pleasure out of watching my students grow from kids into adults, but . . . as far as raising children of my own goes, I don't really have an urge to do it. I haven't had good role-models, and I don't want to find out I'm a lousy mother. It's an avenue I just don't want to explore.'

'Kiran, are you trying to tell me you're pregnant?' Steve's eyes were piercing.

'No! I just want you to know I'm not motherly. Ginger probably has more maternal instincts than me.'

Steve laughed and pulled her to him. 'I doubt that. He looked into her eyes, seeing her serious expression. 'Kiran, I haven't exactly seen myself in a paternal role. I don't have to have children . . .'

His voice trailed off, but Kiran knew the train of his thoughts. 'To have a happy ending?'

'That's right.'

She took a deep breath. 'I haven't seen very much of the United States, Steve, and my life here is fairly quiet, somewhat uneventful. So, after I saw you on TV tonight, I thought I might consider doing the racing circuit like Ginger does.'

'Ah, no. That wouldn't be my happy ending,' Steve told her, brushing his lips against her hair. 'I'd be more than happy to have you everywhere I go, but it has to be as my wife.'

Kiran nodded, her heart nearly bursting with happiness. 'I can agree to that,' she said carefully. 'I think.' She wanted to say yes, she wanted to be with him, that it hurt too much to think of him spending his life as lonely as Uncle Caleb had, but –

'Now let me tell you my conclusion.' He rubbed her fingertips against his lips for a moment. 'I love you for being willing to do this for me, and don't think I don't know what you'd be going through every week. But I won't do that to you,' he said, his eyes alight with mischievousness. 'Mitch and I have decided to go into ownership.'

'Ownership?'

'Yeah. I'm ready to turn the wheel over to some-one else. It's been a dream of mine for a long time to own my own car, be the guy in charge. It's time to do it.'

'Oh, Steve! Are you sure?' Kiran searched his expression for any sign of regret. 'You're not doing this just because of me?'

He shook his head. 'Not at all. With you or without you, I'm not racing anymore. I love the sport too much to leave it all the way, but I'm ready to move on. Tell you the truth, everything that happened this summer took some of the burn out of me.'

'Didn't look like you'd lost any of your competitive nature to me.' She watched him closely.

'Sure, I wanted to win. I like going out on top. But, Kiran, I don't need it the way I did before – and maybe losing that edge isn't fair to my crew, to my sponsors, to the fans.' He leaned close, brushing his lips against hers for a second. She stilled, and he kissed her more deeply. 'I need you,' he murmured a moment later, as they caught their breath. 'I'll need you for ever. As an owner, I'll still travel, but you can get a teaching position in whatever state we choose to live in, if you want to. I want you to be happy.'

'Actually, I see myself sitting next to you in the passenger seat as we travel around the US. I have to admit that looks like a happy scenario to me. I'm ready to hit the road – live life a little less cloistered.'

'My metal loony bin with wheels is going to turn into a coach. Man!' He grinned with delight. 'I promise to treat you like a princess.'

Fireworks of happiness shot dizzying stars inside her. She looked into Steve's eyes, seeing true love there. 'A long time ago I wished I had a fairy godmother who would whisk me away from everything,' she reminded him. 'I love you, Steve. Don't treat me like a princess. Treat me like you always have, and that will be more than I ever hoped for.'

'I love you, Kiran,' Steve whispered, awed by the love in her eyes.

He leaned close for another kiss, not noticing the

television remote slide to the floor. The TV flickered on, the credits to the *I Love Lucy* show appearing in black letters on the screen.

But Kiran and Steve didn't notice. They were discovering a magical world of their own.

EPILOGUE

The Cottonwood Chronicle
News About Town

As everybody in Cottonwood, Texas, knew, the drought and the heatwave eventually had to end. There's no end to other news in this little town, though, if you're partial for details.

First off, there's a new priest at the Catholic Church. Now, that might not be newsworthy, except it means that much-beloved Father John Lannigan packed up his collar. Though he says he'll always be active in the Church, he's decided to open up a school for children – most particularly troubled teenagers who need a place to live and go to school. Cottonwood should be glad to have John Lannigan at the helm of this project, which, in case you're wondering, will be called the Dorn School, in memory of the farmer who used to own the land.

Some of you might have known Caleb Dorn, who lived at the far end of town on the land backing up to the new homes that are being built. Sadly, he passed

383

away last summer, but it turned out he had a daughter, Lakina Dorn, who has decided to try her hand at farming. That will please you conservationists, who didn't want to see Cottonwood grow into a overdeveloped offshoot of Dallas. Miss Dorn is a world-famous fashion model who will enhance Cottonwood with her presence, no doubt pleasing those citizens on the other side of the fence who are always wishing Cottonwood was a little more cosmopolitan.

Speaking of personalities, a lot of you will be surprised and saddened to learn that the redoubtable Maypat Andrews has returned to her family home in Atlanta. As those of us who have sought Maypat's wise counsel on anything from cold remedies to matters of the heart know, Maypat was a good listener and a wonderful lady. She will be greatly missed.

There is a delightful twist to this story, however. The old Andrews mansion and Andrews Grocery Mart have been bought by Kiran and Steve Dorn. Yes, there's that name again. Apparently they've been attracted to this area by the new race track recently built in Dallas. Steve Dorn is part-owner of a racing team, so they chose Texas, due to it being right smack in the middle of anyplace they need to travel in the continental US. When they're not traveling, Ms Dorn plans on working in the market. She would like to expand her wares to local arts and crafts, and she also intends to open up the bottom floor of the Andrews house to the public, to showcase the wonderful collection of antiques and fine *objets d'art* Maypat Andrews rounded up over the years. Needless to say, this enterprise will be eagerly anticipated by folks around here.

That's all the news for now, but keep your eye on this column, which expects to have a breaking piece of gossip any day now. Seems there could be a wedding soon, and though that's news enough for this area, it's the folks who are making quiet inquiries about the cost of bridal bouquets and wedding cakes that will get your attention. All best wishes to a certain former priest and a certain model who have already been named in the aforementioned paragraphs – we're pleased to report that, even if the crops didn't flourish during this summer's drought, at least love was blooming in Cottonwood, Texas!

THE EXCITING NEW NAME IN WOMEN'S FICTION!

PLEASE HELP ME TO HELP YOU!

Dear *Scarlet* Reader,

As Editor of *Scarlet* Books I want to make sure that the books I offer you every month are up to the high standards *Scarlet* readers expect. And to do that I need to know a little more about you and your reading likes and dislikes. So please spare a few minutes to fill in the short questionnaire on the following pages and send it to me.

Looking forward to hearing from you,

Sally Cooper

Editor-in-Chief, *Scarlet*

QUESTIONNAIRE

Please tick the appropriate boxes to indicate your answers

1 Where did you get this Scarlet title?
Bought in supermarket ☐
Bought at my local bookstore ☐ Bought at chain bookstore ☐
Bought at book exchange or used bookstore ☐
Borrowed from a friend ☐
Other (please indicate) _____

2 Did you enjoy reading it?
A lot ☐   A little ☐   Not at all ☐

3 What did you particularly like about this book?
Believable characters ☐   Easy to read ☐
Good value for money ☐   Enjoyable locations ☐
Interesting story ☐   Modern setting ☐
Other _____

4 What did you particularly dislike about this book?
_____

5 Would you buy another Scarlet book?
Yes ☐   No ☐

6 What other kinds of book do you enjoy reading?
Horror ☐   Puzzle books ☐   Historical fiction ☐
General fiction ☐   Crime/Detective ☐   Cookery ☐
Other (please indicate) _____

7 Which magazines do you enjoy reading?
  1. _____
  2. _____
  3. _____

And now a little about you –
8 How old are you?
   Under 25 ☐   25–34 ☐   35–44 ☐
   45–54 ☐   55–64 ☐   over 65 ☐

cont.

9 What is your marital status?
Single ☐   Married/living with partner ☐
Widowed ☐   Separated/divorced ☐

10 What is your current occupation?
Employed full-time ☐   Employed part-time ☐
Student ☐   Housewife full-time ☐
Unemployed ☐   Retired ☐

11 Do you have children? If so, how many and how old are they?
_____

_____

12 What is your annual household income?

under $15,000	☐	or	£10,000	☐
$15–25,000	☐	or	£10–20,000	☐
$25–35,000	☐	or	£20–30,000	☐
$35–50,000	☐	or	£30–40,000	☐
over $50,000	☐	or	£40,000	☐

Miss/Mrs/Ms _____

Address _____

_____

_____

Thank you for completing this questionnaire. Now tear it out – put it in an envelope and send it, before 28 February 1998, to:

Sally Cooper, Editor-in-Chief

USA/Can. address
SCARLET c/o London Bridge
85 River Rock Drive
Suite 202
Buffalo
NY 14207
USA

UK address/No stamp required
SCARLET
FREEPOST LON 3335
LONDON W8 4BR
Please use block capitals for address

SESIN/8/97

Scarlet titles coming next month:

DEADLY ALLURE Laura Bradley

After her sister's murder Britt Reeve refuses to let detective Grant Collins write the death off as an accident. Britt suspects that the murderer could be someone with family ties, and soon she and Grant find themselves passionate allies in a race against time . . .

WILD FIRE Liz Fielding

Don't miss Part Three of **The Beaumont Brides** trilogy! Melanie Beaumont's tired of her dizzy blonde image. She's determined to show everyone that she can hold down a proper job. And if that means bringing arrogant Jack Wolfe to his knees . . . so much the better!

FORGOTTEN Jill Sheldon

What will happen if Clayton Slater remembers who he is and that he's never seen Hope Broderick before in his life? And Hope has another problem . . . she's fallen in love with this stranger she's claimed as her lover!

GIRLS ON THE RUN Talia Lyon

Three girls, three guys . . . three romances?
Take three girls: Cathy, Lisa and Elaine. Match them with three very different guys: Greg, Philip and Marcus. When the girls stop running, will their holiday romances last forever?